POSTER BOY

N.J. CROSSKEY

Legend Press Ltd, 107-111 Fleet Street, London, EC4A 2AB
info@legend-paperbooks.co.uk | www.legendpress.co.uk

 British Library Cataloguing in Publication Data available.

Print ISBN 978-1-78955-014-6
Ebook ISBN 978-1-78955-013-9
Set in Times. Printing managed by Jellyfish Solutions Ltd.
Cover design by Kari Brownlie | www.karibrownlie.co.uk

N.J. Crosskey lives with her husband and two children in the seaside town of Worthing, West Sussex. She has worked in the care sector for almost twenty years, but has always yearned to be an author. In 2014 she finally found the courage to chase her dream, and began by writing short fiction which has since been published in various ezines and online literary magazines.

In 2015, disturbed by a rise in racism and nationalism, she was inspired to write *Poster Boy*. Since she began, events both in the UK and abroad have made its concept and themes more relevant than she could ever have imagined.

Follow N.J. Crosskey
@NJCrosskey

For Kev, who always believed.

PART 1

ROSA

1

When I was a child, I used to count my footsteps. Whenever the journey seemed overwhelming, or the surroundings intimidating, I would keep the drumbeat of numbers pounding in my head.

The walk home from school was broken down into small numerical accomplishments. *One, two, three*. I watched my shiny black shoes patter on the cracked paving stones, ignoring the uniformed hordes around me. *Four, five, six*. I listened to the predictable, ordered pattern in my head, not the chaos of laughter and gossip. Ten steps and I passed the boys spitting and swearing on the corner, shouting the numbers in my mind, drowning them out. Twenty and I reached the post box.

It's funny how these childhood mantras come to mind right before you die.

Now I need to make these adult feet move. Just a few more steps. I need to take this one last journey through the heaving crowd. I inhale deeply and try to focus. Human life simmers beneath the August sun; its aromas teased out. The scent of fresh sweat in the air is almost sweet.

I fix my gaze on the wooden stage ahead. About fifty steps, surely? No more than from the battered wheelie bin at the end of my road to number thirty-seven's broken gate. Maybe less? My stride was shorter then. If I count loudly in my mind, I can block out the crowd. If I watch my brown boots on the gravel path, I can ignore their faces.

I don't want to see their faces.

The policeman on my right touches my shoulder. "Miss Lincoln? Are you okay to do this?"

I nod. But I realise I'm trembling.

"You'll be fine," he says. "You'll do him proud."

I chance a glimpse of his face. His greying brows are furrowed with concern. He's about forty, maybe more. Strong jaw, bright eyes. He looks like one of those self-assured types. I wonder if he holds anyone's hand. If there's a little girl who will have to count her footsteps when her guardian is gone. My eyes dart away, back to the ground. I shouldn't have looked. Shouldn't have put a face, a life, to the man beside me. Because now I worry what they'll think of him. I feel sorry for his family, for what they'll have to deal with. He'll be vilified. Shredded. He had his hand upon me, saw my own hands shaking. Christ, he can probably hear my heart racing; it's loud enough. But he didn't realise.

Incompetent, they'll say. Maybe he volunteers at the local shelter on his days off. Maybe he's saved hundreds of lives in his career. It won't matter. All he'll be remembered for is today's fuck-up. Perhaps, he'll even come out of this with a posthumous reputation worse than mine. I'm unstable, after all. Understandable, they'll say, after all I've been through. With the twenty-twenty clarity of hindsight, they'll all be aghast at the catalogue of oversights that led to this. To me being escorted to my final destination by the very authorities that ought to have stopped me.

All these people, gathered to pay their respects, were frisked before they entered Hyde Park. Waiting in line like cattle for the pleasure of the indignity, then herded into their positions. The officers stride among them with suspicious eyes, evaluating, profiling. But me, I'm being taken care of, protected from the rabble.

They should have considered this a possibility, troubled as I must be.

He probably thinks I'm scared I'll be attacked again. There's no reason to suspect anything untoward. Who wouldn't be a little flustered, just at the prospect of standing up in front of all these people, let alone everything else? It'd be more suspicious if I were calm and confident. Having strange, male hands on my body is the very last thing that ought to happen to a young woman who has endured what I have. If it were necessary, surely it would be done by the female officer who escorted me here. He's not incompetent, just mistaken.

He'll be crucified just the same. But it comforts me to think he might not be alive to know about it.

It takes forty-five to reach the wooden steps. I leave tomorrow's pariah at the bottom and climb. *One, two, three, four.* I reach the top step. My seat, beside the Archbishop, is the next target. One boot on the shiny platform; two. I don't look right at the crowd, or left towards the other speakers already seated. I keep my eyes on the gaping expanse of blue chair waiting for me to fill it.

One. In my periphery, I can see the white robes of my soon-to-be chair-neighbour. *Two*. The microphone stand comes into view. *Three*. A small beetle spins in frantic circles on its back under the empty chair. *Four.* I reach it, turn with my eyes still on my boots, and sit.

The Archbishop says something to me. I don't quite catch it. Something to do with being sorry for my loss, or my ordeal. It's safe to assume, anyway. So I lift my cheeks. That's as close to smiling as I can manage, relying on my cheek muscles to lift the edges of my lips a little. I mutter a thank-you. But now I've got a problem. There are no more steps. Without the drum beat of numbers in my head I hear the crowd. They're clapping. For me.

"We love you, Rosa!" a woman cries. "Be strong."

They clap louder. They chatter among themselves. I look up at the front row. Expectant faces full of doe-eyed sympathy.

Frowning faces, trying to plaster concern over curiosity. Here I am, Ladies and Gentlemen, in the flesh. Their eyes move over my body. They're thinking about what they've read in the newspapers. What Gridless did to me. They're wondering if I'm wearing long sleeves on a hot day because I've still got rope burns round my wrists. I wonder what they'd think if they knew it was really because of the track marks. And the bomb, of course.

Against my better judgement, I lift my gaze further, scanning the whole crowd. My brother's face stares back at me from a dozen different angles. His picture held aloft on home-made placards. Enlarged, embossed, underscored by handwritten messages.

R.I.P. brave soldier.

Thank You, Jimmy.

London's Angel.

The same photo on every one. *That* photo. The one they chose from the hundreds available. The one that captures the essence of who they wanted him to be but nothing of the truth. Or rather, nothing that *was* truth. Now I know even truth can be changed. Manipulated. It happens all the time. Our perceptions are changed for us so rapidly, it's a wonder we're not constantly dizzy and disorientated. Perhaps we are.

Some of the crowd begin to clap and cheer, others fall silent. A glance to my left tells me why. It's not appropriate to boo and jeer at a memorial service, whatever your political leanings. Cole approaches the stage, in his customary black suit and wacky tie (the black suit says, 'I mean business', the irreverent tie says 'I'm a man of the people'). Today, it's less garish, out of feigned respect I assume. A muted sky blue with an embroidered cartoon dog on it: Dusty, Jimmy's media-approved favourite.

The applause continues, Cole's supporters unmasking themselves with clapped hands. I have a fleeting fantasy that all English Reclamation Party voters are asked to move to the front. I wish I could request it, but I know I can't. Shame.

I find myself counting his footsteps as he approaches the microphone. I have an awful feeling he'll try to catch my eye, shoot me a condescending look of pity. Or worse, mouth a pithy condolence. So I keep my eyes on his shoes and let the numbers sweep my mind away. He stops at twelve and my distraction is gone. I don't want to hear a single word that comes out of his mouth, much less any that concern my twin.

So I think about footsteps. All the millions of footsteps we've taken that we can't undo. The paths we've walked that we can't retrace. I think about Cole's steps. I think about mine. But mostly, I think about Jimmy's.

2

The first steps I remember taking were through the blue doors of our small nursery school, my red-mittened hand firmly gripping my mother's. I was used to a certain amount of raucous noise, I lived with Jimmy after all, but when the doors opened the collective voices of the other children made me step backwards.

Jimmy wrenched his naked hand from our mother's. (He would never wear gloves or hats. It was all Mum could do to get him to put a coat on. He wanted to feel the world around him. Feel the cold, feel the wind, marvel at how red and sore his hands got in the snow.) He ran into the heaving mass of children without looking back. Within seconds he was sporting a plastic Viking hat, brandishing a sword and running around with other boys as though they were his blood brothers.

I clung even tighter to my mother. A woman with a tight perm, enormous smile, and huge saucer-eyes cooed at me in high-pitched tones. She tried to take my hand. I wouldn't let her.

But then a little beacon of light appeared, emerging from behind her own mother's floral skirt. A girl with sparkling ebony eyes, and long black hair tied with a scarlet ribbon. She was the prettiest thing I had ever seen. Or ever would.

"Ah, Soheila," Miss Jenkins, the woman with the

saucer-eyes, said, "this is Rosa, would you like to show her what we have to play with?"

Soheila nodded, beaming. "You want to be my friend, Rosa?" she asked.

And I did. Oh, I did. Such a delicate, dainty hand took mine from my mother's. Such a quiet, peaceful soul. So unlike the charging bull I lived with. She spoke in little tinkles, not great big booms. She told me that her name meant 'star', and to me she was. She was the North Star, guiding me in uncharted waters.

While Jimmy thundered round the room, followed already by the crowd, Soheila and I poured sand in and out of cups, giggling and grinning at one another. At some point Mum left and I didn't even notice.

At the same time that Jimmy and I were taking our first steps into the education system, a young businessman named Jeremy Cole was taking some important steps of his own. Well, it was in the same month at least. In the movie of my life it would all happen simultaneously. Exact truths are less important than a good story, after all.

I often picture Cole, walking through the streets of London towards that bar. But in my fantasies, he never reaches it. A black cab careens out of control as he steps off the kerb, just yards from his destination. Knocks him flat. I'm shaky on the details. Head trauma, organ damage, doesn't matter. The point is there's a lot of blood and a dead body. The point is he never makes it to the heavy oak door. Never orders his favourite, iconic, lime and bitters. Never shakes hands with Jon Heath, the up-and-coming media mogul. Never sets the next decades in motion.

Then he wouldn't be standing in front of me now, spewing bile to the masses at Jimmy's memorial.

Of course, there were plenty of times during those early years of my life when fate could have intervened. Many journeys that could have been cut short. Millions of steps.

Hundreds of people whose actions led us here. All through our infancy the wheels were in motion. Like all children, though, I lived in a bubble that extended no further than my parents allowed. I had no notion of the events of the wider world, until they burst it.

Soheila and I became inseparable, much to the delight of our mothers. Both had worried about their shy, timid daughters making friends. Now they had found one, they did everything they could to kindle the relationship. Mrs Afzal became a regular fixture at our house and I loved her, almost as much as I adored her daughter. She had a broad, warm smile and always wore such beautiful bright skirts and headscarves. I used to tie jumpers around my head and pretend I was her. Mum turned crimson the first time I did it in front of her new friend.

"Rosa, what on earth do you think you're doing?" she chided. "I'm so sorry, she doesn't mean any offence."

But Mrs Afzal just roared with laughter. "Imitation is the sincerest form of flattery," she said. I didn't know what that meant, but she ruffled my hair and gave me a lollipop, so I figured she was pleased.

It didn't take long for them to discover that both their husbands were in accountancy. Our mums already firm friends, our dads soon followed suit and the two families became an intrinsic part of each other's lives.

Soheila and I held hands, and shared dreams, all through infant school. Jimmy had a new best friend every hour; I had only her. But that was the way we both liked it.

One evening, during our first year of junior school, Dad and Kadeem (Mr Afzal) gathered us all together, over dinner, to make an announcement.

"We have decided," Dad said, "that enough is enough. No more London commutes, no more slaving for faceless corporations."

"No more working weekends and never seeing our

beautiful families," Kadeem chipped in, squeezing his wife's shoulder. "We are done with being wage slaves."

Mum frowned and poured a glass of wine. Mrs Afzal beamed. "That's great news, my love. What are you planning?"

"Afzal and Lincoln Accounting," Dad declared with gusto. "It's got a great ring to it, don't you think?"

"It certainly has," Mrs Afzal smiled.

"The loan has been approved, and we've just agreed a lease on a small office. Less than ten minutes' drive away," Kadeem explained. "Oh, this is the start of a new life for all of us. Working for ourselves, spending more time with our families."

"Oh, this is wonderful news," Mrs Afzal clapped her hands. "Oh, Janey," she nudged my mother, "isn't it wonderful?"

"Absolutely," Mum replied, topping up her glass, "and how unusual to surprise us, instead of consulting us."

Dad ignored the thinly veiled criticism and raised his glass. "To Afzal and Lincoln Accounting," he said.

After dinner we meandered into the lounge to rest our full bellies. All except Jimmy, who tore around the garden in his usual style. Soheila and I played My Little Pony on the soft, fluffy rug in front of the television while our parents talked on the sofas. I don't know which one of us first noticed they had fallen silent. But when the chatter stopped we looked up from our game.

Mum grabbed the controller and turned off the TV as soon as she realised we were paying attention, but we'd already seen it. Aarif Ishak (a wild-eyed man with scruffy black hair and olive skin) emerging from an alleyway in Birmingham, holding the lifeless body of a beautiful, blonde little girl in his arms.

None of us had any idea at the time what this would mean for our little bubble.

I saw the little blonde girl again the next morning, on the front page of Dad's newspaper. But this time she wasn't limp and dripping with blood. Suddenly, her rosy-cheeks and baby blue eyes were everywhere. On posters taped to lampposts, on hand-held placards all over the news. 'Justice for Lily' was the phrase on everyone's lips. I didn't understand. But I was fascinated by her image. I would gaze at her porcelain skin, the sincerity of her gap-toothed smile, the blue uniform so similar to my own. I would concentrate hard, and try to comprehend that the girl in the photo was no more. That those eyes no longer saw. That no 'big teeth' would ever grow to fill that gap. That life can end, even before it has properly begun.

But when Lily disappeared from the news, I soon forgot about my inner struggle to understand mortality. The following months passed uneventfully. For Jimmy and me, at least. I imagine that behind the parental curtain things were far more complex, what with my father and Soheila's starting their new venture. But our lives were unaffected, so we didn't give it a thought.

Our days were predictable. Soheila and I worked hard at our lessons, both excelling in almost every subject. Jimmy spent more time out of the classroom, sitting on the small plastic chair in the corridor than he did in lessons. Mrs Henderson tried calling Mum over after school, to tell her about Jimmy's disruptive behaviour, but she was having none of it.

"He acts out because he's too clever," Mum said, determined to see anything Jimmy did as proof of how wonderful he was. "He's not like it at home. But of course, *we* make sure we keep him stimulated."

Even then, I knew she was talking shit. But I was far too polite to say so. It's true, he wasn't the same at home. He was much, much worse. Nothing was sacred. There were holes in the walls, broken fences, flooded bathrooms. He wasn't wantonly destructive, or intentionally violent, he just had to *try* everything, most notably our parents' patience. You could tell Jimmy a hundred times that hopping on the bannister rail was a bad idea, but he wouldn't believe you until he fell. Even then, instead of a lesson in caution, he took it as a challenge.

"I'll make it *next* time," he would say, grinning despite the limp.

Jimmy thought boundaries were for other, less awesome, people. Given the lack of consequences he received for breaking them, I have to concede he was probably right.

And so the bubble continued to float. One small, well-to-do village. Two nice, respectable families joined together in business and pleasure. Four painfully middle-class adults enjoying new cars, dinner parties and sparkling conversation. Two nice, quiet, well-behaved little best friends growing, and dreaming, together. One loud, adventurous little whirlwind of a boy racing through his early years with gusto. Calm waters, smooth sailing, compasses in hand.

But nine months after Lily's corpse invaded my psyche, the news encroached on our daily lives again. By this time, Dad's business had really taken off. He was happier than I had ever seen him, and home every night by six. We were having dinner with the Afzals, Mum having cooked up a storm in our newly redesigned kitchen, when the riots broke out.

The evening started out like so many others. Jimmy kicked the table and rocked in his chair, Soheila and I ate quickly and quietly, and Kadeem regaled us with tales of their efficient but 'hippy-dippy' secretary while we ate.

"I don't dare mention my sciatica," he said. "Can you imagine? She'd probably have a hundred different magic oils to clear it up. She must think we're the healthiest men in Britain. We never complain about anything in case we're forced to listen to passages from one of those self-help books she leaves all over the place."

"Actually," Dad replied, "I have to disagree. I do find those books useful. In fact, there's one about connecting with your inner spirit animal I just couldn't do without."

Kadeem looked confused. "How so? Don't tell me you've got in touch with your spiritual side, Dave."

"No. It's under the back leg of my desk. Sorted the wobble out a treat."

The adults erupted into laughter. Jimmy blew bubbles into his juice with enough force to cause the blackcurrant liquid to froth over onto the cream tablecloth.

"Jimmy," Mum snapped at him. "Where are your manners? Why can't you eat nicely like Rosa or Soheila?"

He shrugged, and proceeded to make farting noises in time with Soheila's chewing motions. Mum had had enough. He was sent into the lounge, plate in hand, to eat in front of the telly, away from civilised company.

A few minutes later he began to shout.

"Muuum, look at this! There's fighting on the telly!" Mum rolled her eyes, dabbed at the corner of her mouth with a serviette and excused herself, presumably to go tell him to keep it down. But seconds after she left the room she too was yelling.

"Oh my God! Come and look at this!"

I don't think the call was intended for us, but Soheila and I followed the grown-ups into the lounge anyway. This time no one rushed to switch off the TV and protect innocent eyes; they were all too busy staring in horror.

On cold, wet concrete streets, where the buildings were decorated with ugly scrawls, huge, raging men wielded planks of wood and iron pipes. Their faces were granite and grimaces, not the silk and smiles I knew. They overturned cars, broke down shop doors, threw bottles with flaming rags poking from their necks, all to the soundtrack of sirens and breaking glass.

Men whose skin was like mine tackled men whose skin was like Soheila's to the ground. Moving pixels appeared in the middle of the scrums, the occasional elbow poking out from the sides of the mysterious blur and launching back in.

"What's happening?" I asked Dad, desperate for him to make some sense of the chaos I was witnessing.

"It's a riot," Dad said soberly. "Birmingham?"

"I expect so," Kadeem replied, putting his arm around Soheila who, like me, looked to her strong, self-assured guardian with terror in her eyes. "It's not here, sweetie," he said, "it's nowhere near here."

"For God's sake, turn it off," Mum snapped. I'm not sure if she was more concerned by the look of fear on my face, or the look of wonder on Jimmy's.

The images on the screen changed. The shaky, claustrophobic footage of street-level insurgency was replaced by a panoramic view of the city. It zoomed in on a building, surrounded by smoke. In between the rising flames, I could just make out the beautiful domes on its roof.

My parents looked at the Afzals. Kadeem took his wife's hand, and tightened his grip on Soheila's shoulder. Dad shook his head and muttered, "Idiots. Ignorant idiots."

I shuddered, though I didn't know why.

"Why are they doing that, Daddy?" Soheila asked.

"Because they're fools, my love." Kadeem stroked her hair.

"It's that Lily girl," Mum said. "The case got thrown out today. Some tampering with the evidence or something."

Kadeem nodded. "I heard something about it on the radio. Those nationalist splinter groups are all over it. That Ishak guy was an illegal immigrant. So they're ranting on about Them and Us and how the system is corrupt. Doesn't matter what the courts say, they think he murdered her. And got away with it."

"So this is their moronic idea of justice?" Dad sighed. "Heaven help us all."

The riots spread like cancer over the next few weeks. A swift and relentless surge where each evening, more towns added their name to the list of shame. Dad watched the news reports avidly, huffing his disgust. Mum tutted at him as she busied herself picking up after Jimmy.

"Must you, Dave?" It wasn't really a question, more her small protest at his filling the screen with such ugly images in front of the children.

"It's an important social issue," he replied. "You can't keep them in cotton wool forever. I only hope their generation has more sense."

Jimmy paid very little attention; he'd just got his first Shades. He'd been nagging our parents for a pair of the new hi-tech glasses, that had all but replaced both mobile phones and smart watches as the 'must have' communication device. Eventually, they gave in and bought him some. An early model, from back when the augmented reality was (by today's standards) almost unwatchable in its resolution. He spent his evenings careening up and down the pavement on his bike, avoiding the undead as they leapt from bushes (courtesy of his new Apocalypse Reality Track) without a care.

But I was fascinated. Every day, after dinner, I would curl up beside Dad when he watched the news. It wasn't just about educating myself, it was about being with him. For half an hour each evening he sat still. A precious opportunity for a little girl to show affection to the most important man in her life. It was on one such evening that I first saw Cole. Or, rather, that I first remember seeing Cole.

Dad's reaction when the aspiring politician appeared on the TV made me jump. In his indignation, he must have forgotten his small daughter was beside him.

"Insufferable, jumped-up little twat," he exclaimed. I felt the muscles in his arm tense under my cheek. I wondered what had made my dad so mad he had sworn (I'd never heard him do so before). It was the tie I noticed first. Bright purple with yellow flowers. The man himself looked younger than my father, with bushy black hair and an almost comically large mouth. His lips flapped as he spoke and reminded me of the floppy, fleshy strips of liver Mum had once (unsuccessfully) tried to get us to eat. Behind the lips, bright white tombstones of teeth were housed. I nodded to myself, thinking I had discovered a great truth. He needed huge lips to cover those enormous teeth. It made perfect sense.

Dad pointed at the screen. "That man there," he said, "is more dangerous than all those idiotic thugs put together."

I studied Cole intently, and tried to follow what he said, but I couldn't understand what Dad meant. He wasn't doing anything wrong; he was only talking. He was saying the riots had to stop. Fighting wasn't the answer. People ought to unify. Surely that was good? But after every sentence he spoke, Dad huffed, or let out an exaggerated sarcastic laugh. I decided if Dad thought he was a bad man, then I did too. Even if I didn't know why. It was almost fun, to hate someone together. Like being at a panto. I snuggled in closer, feeding off our shared hatred. Booing and hissing in my mind.

But then Cole said, "I swear to you, people of England, your voice will not remain unheard. The battle that has started on our streets will be won at the polls." The camera panned out to the crowd he addressed. They cheered, clapped, whooped. Dad had heard enough. He switched off the TV, slamming the remote down onto the coffee table, and left the room. I sat alone, an empty expanse of sofa beside me, a draft on my right side instead of the firm, warm body of my father.

Cole had cut my evening cuddles short, and I despised him for it.

3

After the riots, the world outside my bubble seemed frightening. But at least I had Soheila. When the time came to leave the cocoon of the village and take the bus to our new (enormous) high school, we did so side by side.

Jimmy ran straight to the back, slinging his new school bag down, as though it were a sack of flour, and putting his feet up on the seat in front. There was no misreading his intentions. He was making it clear, from the start, he had no need or desire to sit with us, or anyone else from the village for that matter. That suited us just fine. I knew Jimmy would be looking for a new crowd, a better crowd. I also knew it would be a crowd I would have no place in.

It didn't take him long. Before the bus had pulled up outside the concrete monstrosity that was our school, he had already ingratiated himself with a new gang. Rough-looking boys who slung casual arms around overly made-up, gum-chewing girls. The blue air coming from the back of the bus suggested entry into this rather unsavoury-looking clique was determined by one's ability to replace every other syllable with a curse. Some of them are lawyers and doctors now. Go figure.

By virtue of our academic record, Soheila and I were in the same (top) class for every subject, much to our relief. We settled in well, mostly ignoring our peers and continuing on together as we had always done. Both of us received a pair of Shades from our parents as a reward for our outstanding reports after the first half-term. Which just goes to show how little my parents really knew me: I'd have been happier with one of the old-style wrist devices. Back then I thought people wearing the garish glasses looked ridiculous. It took me a while to get the hang of the rapid, decisive eye moments needed to navigate the menus. The Ocular Motion Recognition back then was archaic. Nowadays any toddler can easily use Shades, but they were buggy and frustrating when I was a kid. Once I mastered it, though, I found I couldn't live without them.

Despite my initial resistance, I was hooked. I downloaded several Reality Tracks, but my favourite was always the garden fairies. It was subtler than the others, you had to look for them closely, but it always made me smile when I spotted a shimmering little fairy hiding behind a dustbin, or skipping along a wall. Soheila used to play one that replaced ugly-looking tarmac with beautiful meadows. She said she found it therapeutic, but it never appealed to me. I guess it seemed like too big a deception. The world is ugly after all. To pretend any different seemed foolish, even then.

Although I had a whole world of information literally before my eyes, my new interest in tech meant the news once again disappeared from my everyday life. That's the irony of Shades. They're supposed to expand the world for you. The whole back catalogue of human knowledge, real-time news updates, the ability to connect with anyone, anywhere. It's all right there just a few centimetres away from your frontal lobe. But you can't use every one of the thousands of features. You can't take in all that information at once. So you have to make your selections. Choose what appears on your menus, give yourself shortcuts to the things that matter to you. You think you're adding, but really you're subtracting. With each option you choose the world gets smaller, not bigger.

Thanks to Shades we've all customised our own realities. The problem with that is they're no longer real. My bubble had become even smaller. Outside of school I viewed the world exactly as I wanted to. The only news that came to my retinas was about the latest films and books (and even then, the Shades had learned not to show me anything other than my preferred genres). I no longer snuggled with Dad; I thought I was too grown up for that, though I'll admit there were times when I still longed for him to call me to the sofa, put his arm around me and discuss the day's events. But he never did, I guess he must have thought I was too old for such things too. So instead I lived life from behind my lenses, which were biased always in my favour. I didn't notice what was going on, didn't even give it a thought, until the ERP caused a bombshell to land on my own front door.

I walked in from school that fateful day to see Dad walking up and down, gesticulating wildly. I knew he was talking to someone, he always paced when he took calls. He didn't see me. He had his own Shades on and hadn't yet got the hang of viewing his screens and the world around him at the same time.

He was angry. I ducked past him as he thundered along the hall and went to make myself a drink.

"And where do you think that leaves me?" he was yelling. "I can't believe you're being so unreasonable."

Mum was chopping vegetables in the kitchen. She looked up and smiled. I pointed in the direction of the hallway, where Dad was raging, and rolled my eyes. Usually, she would make a small laugh and roll hers too. Sometimes even mimic his emphatic gestures, and we'd giggle and shhh each other. But not this time. This time she gave only a weak smile, and looked down at the carrots she was slicing. A little prick of panic hit me, and I knew this was no ordinary phone call.

Dad stormed into the kitchen and slammed his Shades down on the table. "I couldn't talk him out of it," he ranted. "I told him it's only a protest vote, people aren't really that stupid, they'll never do it when it counts. But he won't listen. Stubborn fucking twit."

Mum widened her eyes at him and he realised I was there.

"Oh God." He plonked himself down on a chair. "Rosa, I'm sorry."

He reached out for my hand. I knew it wasn't just the F-bomb he was sorry for. My bubble suddenly seemed very fragile.

"The Afzals are moving, honey."

"Where?" I didn't recognise the squeak that had replaced my voice.

"Australia."

Pop.

I threw down my bag and ran up the stairs. Apparently my Shades' OMR still functioned through tears because I managed to dial Soheila even as the hot sting in my eyes became cold sticky trails on my cheeks. When she answered, my bright shining star looked more like a crashed meteor. Her whole face glistened from the outpouring of saline and snot.

It was true. Kadeem was taking his little family to the other side of the world. As far away from Cole as he could possibly get. The world had been changing, and I had been ignorant, sedated by my own customised version of reality. The ERP had won a huge number of seats in the local elections, including ours.

I guess you never know what lurks behind frills and pomp, what those polite smiles and small talk are really hiding. At least those thugs throwing fire bombs at the Birmingham mosque were honest. They would have glassed Kadeem if they came across him, not shaken his hand at the PTA meeting then stuck their knives in his back from the privacy of the polling booth.

He wouldn't allow his daughter to grow up in such a climate. He said the people of his adopted country had sent him a message, and he heard it loud and clear. I didn't know at the time how it had all been growing, insidious like a silent tumour that makes itself known only when it's too late to remove it. Oh, I'd seen the riots and heard the blistering right-wing rhetoric in the wake of Birmingham. But those things were far away, in my childish perception. I knew there was hatred in the world, but I didn't know it was here. Lurking in the WI, hiding behind the immaculate topiary, coiling through the tiny cobbled high street. Disguising itself behind, "Lovely weather we're having," and, "Oh what a charming sari Mrs Afzal, where DID you get the fabric?"

I didn't know about the whispers. I didn't know that when the little junior school we had attended renamed its annual fun day to 'Winter Fair' the glares fell upon Soheila's mother.

"It's because of *other* religions," the gossiping harpies in the playground had said, shaking their heads and shooting daggers at Mrs Afzal. "*Someone* must have complained."

If I'd known I'd have shaken them, told them how the Afzals had joined us for Christmas dinner, and we them for Ramadan and Eid. But no one told me. I didn't know Mrs Afzal had stopped bringing a bottle of wine to dinner as gift for my parents because the fat, stinking sales assistant in the off-licence had sneered at her and said, "I thought your kind didn't drink?"

I didn't even know some of the kids at school called Soheila 'Muzzie' behind her back. Not until she'd left.

"Has that stinking Muzzie of yours fucked off back to where she came from?" that was the question I was asked in the weeks after her departure. That was when, after the anger and the searing, sickening pain of our separation had subsided, I began to realise Kadeem had done right by my star. However much it hurt us both.

I vowed then and there that I would never be blindsided by the real world again. I deleted all the Reality Tracks from my Shades and subscribed to several news channels. They were heavily filtered due to my age, but Jimmy could circumvent the parental controls. If my parents knew about the snuff films, and later the pornography he watched, they'd have thrown a fit. I'd never told on him for doing his, so he helped me with mine. I wanted to see the world as it really was.

My eyes burned from the daily doses of violence, depravity and wars that seemed to have no discernible cause and no possible resolution. The suffering, starvation and decay that assaulted me at every hourly round up ignited something in my veins. This was the world. Though I had less desire than ever to take part in it, I wouldn't allow myself to ignore it anymore.

But perhaps Dad was right. Maybe, despite the rising tide of racial hatred, the ERP's victories in the local elections had just been a protest vote. Maybe by the time the general election came around the sensible, and traditional, British people would have put their crosses next to one of the three main parties, just like they always did. And maybe they would have. If it hadn't been for Dover.

4

Aarif Ishak and little Lily had got the ball rolling for Cole and his newly formed English Reclamation Party. The riots had given it momentum. But it was the events at Dover that gave it an almighty shove toward its final destination.

In the run up to Armistice Day, during my second year at high school, the whole country had poppy fever. Appearing on television without one after 31st October was practically a hanging offence. All the major parties had clued into the fact patriotism was the drug being peddled by the ERP, and with Cole's bosom buddy Heath now in full control of several major newspapers and networks, the public were lapping it up. The Labour government at the time were no exception. They'd spent millions on ostentatious displays of poppies, lavish televised services and of course the Red Arrow display.

Our school had taken the opportunity to saturate the curriculum with the topic, across all years and in all subjects, including art. We'd spent several lessons creating a huge wreath made out of crepe paper and pipe cleaners to be presented to the mayor at a special service. I was thirteen, and less than impressed at having to travel into town on a Saturday in my school uniform. But, as one of the 'enrichment class' pupils, my attendance was mandatory.

Everyone remembers where they were when they heard the news, or saw the footage, for the first time. Most people were at home, having just watched the two minutes' silence. I was sat on a cold, hard pew listening to the priest ramble on while I waited to be called up to give the crappy PVA glue-stained wreath to the mayor.

We weren't supposed to have our Shades switched on. But Felix, who was sat in the row behind me, had his held between his legs, partially covered with a hymn book. I expect he was watching some awful vlogger or something. The breaking news must have interrupted his stream.

"Holy shit!" His sudden outburst echoed in the stone-walled church. All eyes turned on him. Little old ladies gasped, our head teacher flushed red, the priest stopped talking. All of us school kids giggled.

Mrs Davies marched over to him, hissing her demand that he hand over his Shades.

"But Miss," Felix protested, holding them up so she could see the screens. "Miss, look."

She snatched them, but didn't fold them. Something on the screen caught her attention and her face lost several shades of pink.

"Oh my God," she added to the blasphemy.

By this point the head teacher, Mr Haskin, was watching over her shoulder. He cleared his throat, took the Shades from Mrs Davies and went to speak to the priest.

The adults all began to whisper. I watched the priest's face as Mr Haskin showed him whatever the hell was on those Shades. He held his hand to his chest, before crossing himself. Eventually, he addressed the congregation.

"It appears there has been a terrible accident at Dover," he said. "I think we should all pray for the Red Arrow pilot who has, tragically, crashed."

The man on the other side of aisle had been fiddling with his own Shades. I heard him whisper to the woman beside him, "Didn't look like no accident to me."

The service wrapped up hastily. We never did give our creation to the mayor. But then, all the newspapers would have plenty to keep them occupied. A picture of some snotty kids with a handmade wreath wouldn't be required.

As soon as we got out the door, we hurriedly switched on our Shades. It was there, on the steps of the church, beside the poppy drenched memorial plaque, that I saw the footage for the very first time.

The Spitfires flew over the iconic white cliffs in their famous arrowhead arrangement, leaving short trails of black smoke behind them. As they came about, one of the planes on the right-hand side broke formation, diving diagonally at full speed. When it hit the cliff face the impact caused a huge cloud of dust and debris. I could just hear the screams of the onlookers when, less than a second later, a fireball engulfed what was left of the plane.

We all know what came next. The cliffs seemed to groan and shake. The falling chalk looked like an avalanche as it plummeted into the sea. The dust and debris mixed with the white horses of the English Channel creating an unnatural fog across the waves. As more and more of the cliff face descended the cloud rose up, until it resembled a volcano raining down white ash.

When the collapse finally stopped, the rugged and weathered cliff face, which had become a symbol of our very national identity, was no more. Instead, England was left with a smooth, brilliant white slope at its most famous border. From the air, the cliffs looked like a row of teeth destroyed by cavities.

It was obvious, even to me, this had been no accident. I don't think there was a person in England who believed it was. Maybe when the plane first collided with the cliff, but not after the explosion. And, thanks to having spent the best part of two months studying nothing but the world wars, no one needed to tell me how big a deal this was. I knew all about Vera Lynn and her bluebirds. The symbolism was unmistakable. Someone had used our most iconic fighting plane to attack the very landmark that had symbolised freedom, and home, to our servicemen. This changed everything.

It took only a few hours for them to announce the culprit.

Yousseff Nasir, an RAF serviceman, and by all accounts a blue-blooded patriot. After his death however, his links to jihadists were soon uncovered. He'd somehow smuggled explosives on board, and used his martyrdom to attack the English where it hurt the most. Right in their national pride. The outcry over Aarif's botched trial was nothing compared to this. The government were forced to temporarily ban Muslims from entering the armed services, to prevent more riots. But it wasn't enough. The public were baying for blood. And Cole, with his ridiculous promises to 'send them all home', was the only one who seemed to understand.

So it came as no surprise to me when, six months later, Dad was proven wrong. People *were* that stupid. The following May, in the midst of one of the worst recessions our country has ever seen, and to the backdrop of almost daily terror attacks around the world, Cole and the English Reclamation Party won the general election with a landslide victory.

Dad was shocked. Which made me realise, for the first time, he was not as intelligent as I thought he was. I knew it was coming. I read the headlines. *All* the headlines. Dad read only the publications, and subscribed to only the broadcasters, that upheld his own position: analysis of current events by the liberal-minded intelligentsia; deconstruction of the ERP in witty, satirical columns by people who extolled the virtues of multiculturalism and global cooperation. In the reality he chose to live in there was no way anyone could possibly agree with Cole.

But he didn't see the news I saw. He didn't read the headlines filled with hatred and blame, or listen to the vlogs full of furious rants. He didn't know that British Bulldog (the prolific vlogger whose heyday was in the months leading up to the election) had more than ten times the views for his daily patriotic evangelising than any of the 'wet liberals' he so vehemently despised. And he didn't hear the teens at school spouting the views they heard from their parents. In his (now one-man) office, behind his glowing screen, clutching his grande latte and flapjack, he was as blind to reality as I once had been.

The first major parental row of the new government happened just hours after the election results were announced. While Cole was shaking diplomatic hands, and flashing his tombstones at every camera, Dad was pulling the suitcases down from the loft.

"We're leaving," he announced, heaving the huge brown cases onto his bed.

"Don't be ridiculous." Mum abandoned making breakfast and stormed upstairs. "You always do this. You can't throw a tantrum just because you didn't get your own way."

"Get my own way? Get my *own way*? We're living under a twenty-first-century Hitler, and you think this is about getting my own way?"

"Oh don't be so dramatic. He's just a politician."

"So was Adolf. What are you waiting for Janey? The chimneys to start smoking? I've spoken to Kadeem, he's been nagging me to make the move for ages. He can find us somewhere to rent while we sort out—"

"That's what it's really all about isn't it? You can't make the business work by yourself so you're going to uproot your whole family, disturb the kids' education and tear me away from my friends and family, just so you can go hang off Kadeem's shirt tails. Well, I'm not having it."

Jimmy rolled his eyes, grabbed a slice of toast and picked up his bag. "I'm going," he said. "Gonna meet Ged for a skate before the bus."

"Aren't you bothered?" I asked, still cocking my head, straining to hear the argument that had gotten quieter now one of them had shut the bedroom door. "Dad wants us to move to Australia." I'd long since stopped video-calling Soheila daily, but we still kept in touch. I had made new friends, sure, but nothing close to the bond she and I had shared. I admit, the prospect excited me.

Jimmy just shrugged. "Whatever," he said, and walked out the door.

5

Not all my dreams involve Cole's brutal, painful demise. Some are less altruistic. That I somehow persuaded Mum to change her mind, became the reason the Lincolns were living a million miles away from the ERP, that's my favourite daydream. Oh, I'd feel bad for my former countrymen, left behind to live under liver lips and his cronies, but only slightly. They voted for him after all. In reality, I had no more control over my parents' actions than I did over the voters, or any of the hundreds of cab drivers who hadn't mown Cole down on his walk to the bar.

But I didn't even try.

That's what kills me the most. My own inaction. The row ended when Mum told him, point blank, he could go if it meant that much to him, but it would be without her, or us. It stopped him dead. When he came downstairs he looked defeated, pale and shaken, all the fire gone from his eyes. A man who'd just realised his opponent held the winning cards. No matter what he drew, or how well he bluffed, he'd never beat that flush. There was no point in even playing any more.

But maybe I'd held the ace he needed. If I'd thrown in my hand, maybe I'd have upped the ante. If I'd reasoned, pleaded, cried. Hell, if I could go back now I'd scream, shake her, set fire to the house if that's what it took. I'd do anything. *Anything*. But I did nothing.

It probably wouldn't have made any difference. But I'd give anything to have tried.

Instead of jetting off to sunnier climes, it wasn't long before we found ourselves heading to bleaker, more polluted ones. Dad had remortgaged the house to buy out Kadeem's share of the business when he upped sticks two years before. But when the economic crisis started to bite, he couldn't make the repayments. He had no choice but to pawn his soul again, sell up and go back to his former employers.

More blazing rows ensued. He didn't want to commute, Mum didn't want to move. But this time, he held the winning hand in the battle, though it must have been cold comfort given that the war was already lost.

"You want to move us all just so you don't have to sit on a train for an hour?" Mum raged, slamming her wine glass down on the dinner table.

"For an hour? Come on, Janey, you know what it was like. You can't have killed that many brain cells with Zinfandel that you can't remember. Twelve-hour days, delayed commutes, working weekends and holidays. I'm not going back to paying for a house I never get to spend any time in. That ship has sailed."

"Well, I'm not moving, so you'll just have to suck it up, or think of another way to make it work."

Dad smiled in that leisurely, almost eerie way people do when they know they've won.

"Oh, I have," he said, "I've got the perfect solution." He teased tagliatelle onto his fork in casual, circular movements, "One that would mean I could keep the business *and* we could keep the house." He stabbed a couple of peas with the tip.

"Well, go on then Mr Big Shot, what is it?" Mum asked.

Dad grinned, and raised his fully loaded forkful. "*You* could get a job." He shoved his food into his mouth and clanked his fork back down on the plate (I swear it sounded like 'Ta Da!' as it hit the china). You didn't need to be a telepath to hear the mental checkmate that passed between them.

Mum picked up her glass, downed it and poured another. She scowled as she finished her pasta (and how bitter it must have tasted), but she didn't say another word.

So, at age fifteen, Jimmy and I left the only home we had ever known. Yet the only person who came to wave us off was Kelly Matthews, my brother's on-again, off-again girlfriend. Her acne-ridden face was smeared in mascara, snot and tears as she watched our car pull away and leave our childhood home for ever.

Before we'd even turned the corner, Jimmy had blocked her.

"Christ," he whispered to me, "bit grim. Thank God we're leaving."

I tutted at him and leaned over his shoulder to peek at his Shades screens. He navigated to his contacts menu, where he had her listed as *pigeon tits*, and blinked three times in quick succession to ensure the girl with the unsatisfactory mammary glands could never find him, by any electronic means, ever again.

"You bastard," I whispered back, not that I really cared. I had bigger worries. New house, new school, new city. I was petrified, but Jimmy couldn't wait to start his new life.

"It'll be great sis, you know it will," he said, squeezing my hand. "We're too good for this inbred backwater. We'll fit right in to the city, you'll see."

I suppose he was trying to be kind, but we both knew the truth. I didn't do well with change whereas he thrived on it. If diving into a new environment was a case of sink or swim, then I hit the water gasping, and barely stayed afloat. Jimmy didn't just do lengths; he built his own goddamn pool.

I hated almost everything about our new life in Harringay. Our house was smaller, darker, more oppressive. Dad said he chose the area because of the greenery. But a few manmade parks couldn't compare to the rugged beauty of the hills I used to gaze at from my bedroom window. I felt penned in. I missed the sea air sweeping across the Channel, reminding me that other worlds existed. My snot turned black as my body tried in vain to filter out the pollution before it could poison my lungs. I missed the pure darkness of nights without streetlights. I even missed the relentless squawking of sea gulls every time a storm rolled in.

Jimmy didn't seem to care about any of it. He was enthralled. Intoxicated by our new environment. I was too scared to brave the city streets alone, but he pioneered. We hadn't been there a week before he knew all the shortcuts, all the hang-outs. I was still rearranging my furniture, in a futile attempt to make my new bedroom feel bigger and brighter, when he decided he wanted my company.

"C'mon, Rosa, stop being such a hermit." He grabbed a jacket from my wardrobe and thrust it at me. "Let me show you around."

I didn't want to face the reality of city life, but I knew I couldn't hide forever. And Jimmy's confidence always made me feel safe, so I figured it was best to take my first foray with him beside me. I knew it wouldn't be an offer he'd extend again once he'd made his own friends.

It was on that first jaunt out around the area that I discovered the only thing I truly loved about our new locale: Green Lanes seemed untouched by Cole's influence. A little pocket of the world that had rejected Reclamation. The air was full of exotic aromas, and a symphony of different tongues. Brightly coloured shops, with produce from every corner of the globe, lined the street. A dozen different cultures, all co-existing. All going about their business as if the ERP were nothing but a myth.

"This is what it's really about, Rosa," Jimmy said. "*This* is London."

We wandered through the crowds, eating falafel from a street vendor's cart and listening to the buskers with their steel drums and saxophones. And for a short time I thought he was right. Perhaps this city was where I would find my place. Perhaps it was somewhere where my ideals were still in fashion. Perhaps I could be someone here after all.

But then, there was school. In our own ways we were both big fish in little ponds before. At our old school, I was far and away the highest academic achiever. Jimmy was the biggest presence, the largest character, the main talking point. But when we arrived at our new, far bigger, comprehensive in North London we both had competition.

There were many far smarter pupils than me. I'd been top of the small accelerated-learning group in Sussex, but only just scraped entry into the far larger 'gifted and talented' group at my new school. And I couldn't cling onto my place there for long. I wasn't falling behind, the teachers hastened to explain to me, I was still making 'terrific' progress. But standards here were so much higher… It hurt like a kick to the guts.

So I found myself without a claim. One of the crowd. Nothing special. Nobody but a new girl from the sticks with no friends. Oh, I was still in the top classes, just not the elite ones. I was, by definition, pretty good but not good enough. In the same league as hundreds of other pupils. That was when I realised I was destined to be someone-who-went-to-school-with-someone, not someone myself. I never dreamed that someone would be Jimmy.

At first I thought he too had conceded defeat. Accepted he wasn't top dog anymore. Those on the highest rung of the social ladder were easy to spot. Leo Watts and his 'bloods'. I eyed them when we first walked in, slouching by the lockers, oblivious to everyone rushing past. Perfectly preened girls, with tiny waists and false eyelashes, hung off them like Christmas baubles. Even the teachers stepped around them rather than ask them to move. I figured Jimmy would ingratiate himself with them, do something effortlessly cool in their line of sight, or flirt with one of the unattached bimbos mooning close by. I should have known better. Jimmy didn't want to be one of the elite; he wanted to define what elite was. He'd never have been content to be a hanger-on.

He didn't introduce himself to the top clique, but the next rung down. The ones who were almost there, but not quite cool enough to make it into Leo's gang. Christos, Denny and Kinga. Jimmy found his brothers. I made some friends of my own. The type that clung together like barnacles in the hostile waters of high school but quickly evaporated on the breeze of adulthood. He gathered disciples who, once anointed by his light, would continue to worship at the altar of Jimmy Lincoln long after his death.

Maybe it was providence that caused Jimmy to rise through the ranks, like oil through water, and bring his cohorts with him. Maybe it was luck. I once thought anyone decent would have done what Jimmy did for Christos that day. But now, knowing more about this cesspit we call humanity, I'm not so sure.

6

Christos was my favourite of Jimmy's new musketeers. He had an easy manner and a calm humility. He was cool by virtue of not trying to be cool, and didn't look down his nose at those who weren't. Of course, he didn't *date* those that weren't either. So I existed on his radar only as his mate's sister. My extensive studies of his emerging stubble and slight dimples were all in vain.

I tended to hang around in the foyer before school, hoping to catch a glimpse of him, maybe even say hi if I could find the guts. One morning in summer he sauntered in, with a sticking plaster protruding from the short cotton sleeve of his shirt. There were nudges and whispers. Everyone knew what it meant. He'd got chipped.

In a short time the small mark on a newborn's arm became as normal as the peg on their umbilical cord, and nobody even notices the thin silver scar on your shoulder – it matches theirs after all. But this was the first wave. It was new, it was different. And it wasn't a symbol of patriotism. It was a mark of shame.

Back then, the Citizen Chip implants were only for immigrants, or benefit claimants. The two groups most despised by Reclamationists, the ones the media told us were to blame for everything. That was how the whole scheme started and the only reason you had to have one: if you needed benefits, or if you came from a different shore. They stopped paying people directly into their bank accounts. If you wanted your unearned money you had to stand (or hobble, or be pushed in your wheelchair – this applied to *all* benefits after all) in line each week and have your arm scanned. Just like an immigrant. No chip, no cash. And if you wanted child benefit your offspring had to be scanned too. Thus, only the very poorest continued to claim it. Nobody wanted to degrade their children if they could manage without it.

The kids in the foyer eyed him and sniggered. But a quick raised eyebrow from Denny was enough to stop the whispers. Christos was on the second rung after all; there was no one from the masses who would challenge him. Only Leo had that right.

"Filthy fucking scrounger!" The top dog caused the heaving throng to still and hush. Leo pushed his latest blonde tail away and strode toward Christos, all sneer and spittle. He punched Jimmy's dimpled friend on his smarting shoulder and squared up to him, nose-to-nose.

"Dirty little benefit boy," he jeered. The crowds gathered, forming a wide circle around the two. "Taking what doesn't belong to you, like a stinkin' muzzie!"

Christos wasn't a fighter, but he wasn't a coward either. He didn't flinch, or look away.

"Why don't you fuck off back to your skank whores, Leo?" he said.

"What the fuck did you say to me?" Leo's voice grew louder. He jerked his head from side to side and set his mouth in a sneer. "What the actual fuck did *you* say to *me*? Who the *fuck* do you think you're talking to? You pissy little cunt."

Jimmy had been by the lockers fiddling with some giggling bimbo's long hair. I'd joined the gathered spectators. I didn't normally give a crap about the Neanderthals and their scuffles, but this was Christos. As much as I tried to fight it, he made my teenage stomach turn to liquid. Jimmy heard the commotion and I felt his hand on my shoulder.

"What happened, sis?" he asked.

"Christos got chipped," I replied. Jimmy just nodded, and the crowd parted for him like the Red Sea as he strode toward the confrontation.

"Back off, Leo," he commanded, his voice unwavering.

"Fuck you, Lincoln." Leo didn't even turn round to face Jimmy. He and Christos were still nose-to-nose. "This ain't none of your deal."

"It's alright, Jimmy," Christos called out, standing a little taller now Jimmy was close by. "Leo's just pitchin' like a tampon-bitch."

I didn't see Leo reach into his pocket, I was too far back. But I heard the gasps.

I went up on to tip-toes and saw the light bounce off the metal in his hand. How the hell he got a knife into school I still don't know to this day. Security had been stepped up as part of Cole's 'Social Safety' initiative. There were metal detectors at every entrance, and religious dress was banned under the assertion that it could be used to conceal weapons. What a joke. The Jewish kids couldn't wear Kippahs, but thugs like Leo could swathe themselves in full-length leather jackets, with multiple pockets.

He gripped a small switchblade tight in his right fist. Shoving his left forearm across Christos' throat, he pushed him back against the wall.

"I'm gonna fuck you good, scummer," he said, raising the blade up so the tip touched Christos' right eye. "I'm gonna blind you, you scrounging little cunt."

Jimmy moved quickly. He reached out and grabbed Leo's blade-wielding hand, holding it fast, and kicked him in the back of the knee. We all inhaled, and grimaced, as we heard the sickening crack. Leo fell to the floor, but Jimmy still had hold of his arm. He was shouting, swearing. Jimmy wrenched the blade free from his wilting grip. Leo grasped at his leg, the bulge of his kneecap sticking out in the wrong direction. Jimmy could consider himself the victor. But he didn't stop there.

He squatted down and knelt on Leo's broken knee. Leo hit out at him with his fists. But Jimmy had already given the nod to Denny and Kinga, who both stepped forward and took hold of one arm each. Jimmy stood back and they wrenched him on to his knees. He pulled up the right sleeve of Leo's shirt and sliced a neat line across the top of his arm, in the same spot as Christos' chip wound.

"There's only one scummer here, Leo," Jimmy spat in Leo's face, "and I'm looking at him."

Jimmy stood up and addressed the crowd. "Anyone else got a problem?" he said, waving the blade. The students erupted into cheers and applause. I couldn't stop myself from joining in. Jimmy threw the knife to the floor as the faculty came running.

He got suspended, but only for three days. There was no shortage of witnesses lining up to testify that Jimmy was merely intervening to stop Leo blinding Christos. And Jimmy was no dummy. He told the head teacher she was lucky he wasn't going to sue, his dad was an accountant at a law firm, he had connections. Clearly the school weren't doing enough to prevent weapons being brought in. If he hadn't been there, hadn't put himself in jeopardy, they could have had a murder on their hands. He would take the standard punishment for fighting, but no more. In fact, he demanded the school took decisive action against the perpetrator. Leo was expelled.

After that, no one at our school got stick for being chipped. When Jimmy returned, it was to a hero's welcome. Mum was beside herself at his suspension. Dad gave him a cursory ticking off for brawling, but was glowing with pride. He thought Jimmy was looking out for the less fortunate, being altruistic. Really, he was only looking out for himself. With Leo defeated, the school was his for the taking.

But I won't deny it was a better place for it. For me at least. Suddenly I was not to be messed with. Jimmy became the ultimate arm accessory for the popular girls. Being a bitch to his twin sister wasn't a good way to ingratiate yourself, or win the dubious honour of being his next lay.

Nobody really knew what our relationship was like behind closed doors. That we rarely spoke at school was obvious, but that Jimmy also never said a bad word about me (so his gang have told me, anyway) meant it wasn't worth the risk. For all anyone knew we discussed them all at length over our cornflakes. For all the bimbos knew I had his ear. We didn't, and I didn't, but I confess I did nothing to dispel the idea. Our penultimate year in compulsory education was drawing to a close when Jimmy humiliated Leo. Why shouldn't I coast the last year at school, socially at least, off the back of some perceived twin-connection? Letting them believe that messing with me would get them into grief with Jimmy meant I was left alone.

In reality, we led such different lives that we hardly conversed at all. Apart from who was going to have the first shower or the last piece of cake, we spoke very little. He was always out for one thing. My barnacle buddies were as painfully boring and sensible as I was. Oh, we caught the odd film, went on the odd shopping trip, even snuck the odd high percentage cider, but mostly it was just me, my Shades and my homework of an evening. Jimmy only dashed in to be fed, if he bothered coming home at all. His last full summer on Earth, when we were both seventeen, was full of friends, parties, synthetic highs and sex. I think it was the best time of his short life, and I think it was a better time than I have ever known.

It was also the summer I lost my virginity. Or, perhaps more accurately, threw it away in a fit of heartbreak.

7

I knew they'd started messing with synthetics. Jimmy must've thought I was blind if he didn't realise I'd worked it out. But when you're topped up your judgement is screwed every which way and then some. I should know. He thought he was being discreet. But I noticed how he avoided making eye contact with Mum and Dad, the way he developed that nervous shake in his legs and scratched at his arms as though he'd been bitten by fleas. I looked down my nose at the time; pride comes before a fall I guess. They weren't even illegal back when Jimmy was doing them. That meant they weren't as dangerous as what I was on when Gridless took me. But they were harmful enough.

His synthetic high of choice was G-Star, which is like watered-down hooch compared to Krenom. Guess I'm more hardcore than my twin after all. But for high school kids with limited funds it was readily available, and you could tell yourself it wasn't really a big deal because there were no needles involved. Part amphetamine and part opiate, it gave a rush of endorphins, followed by a mellow high that left you energised and chilled all at the same time. But you'd spend the next two days drinking water by the gallon and pissing like a racehorse.

Christos had already taken some when he turned up one evening looking for Jimmy. It was lucky for him it was me who answered the door. His eyes were like saucers and he was shuffling from foot to foot, giggling at the garden gnomes. It should have been really unattractive. But when he greeted me with a bear hug, and kissed the top of my head, I didn't care that the affection was chemically manufactured.

"Rosa! Hey, how's tricks?"

I stepped outside, pulling the door up behind me. His voice was several decibels louder than usual.

"Christos," I hissed, "shhh! Our parents are just inside…"

"Aww man, Mr and Mrs L! I should say hey, they're so chill!"

"No, they're not. Seriously, Christos. You're topped up, just be quiet."

"Okay, that's good, that's all good. I'm just looking for my bro, where's he at?"

"He's already gone out. Some party or something, I don't know."

"Oh, sure. Sure. Yeah, guess I'm a bit late anyway. Thanks, Rosa."

"No worries, have a good time."

"What about you, baby? What you doing this fine evening?"

I shrugged, "Nothing. Reading, I guess."

"What?" Christos frowned. "Why don't you come with me?"

It was a bad idea. Nuclear bad. And I knew that. But even though I told him so, my will had already started to dissolve. I protested, but when he started to insist I chose to ignore what I knew (*he's topped up, he's not interested. Jimmy will kill you*) and let myself believe he actually wanted me.

"Jimmy wouldn't want me there," by the time I'd made my final excuse I was already halfway down the road in my head.

"Oh, c'mon, babe, that's bollocks and you know it. Jimmy's cool. Anyway, you're coming with me. Ain't none of his business what chick I choose to invite."

I was the chick Christos chose to invite. Hardly a fucking declaration of undying love was it? But somehow my hormones interpreted it as being asked on a date. Hell, in my mind he was practically calling himself my boyfriend. You should never underestimate the stupidity of a clever teenage girl.

So the thumping of my heart (*he chose me, he chose me*) drowned out all reason, and chased any shred of caution away. I yelled to Mum and Dad that I was going out, and got grunts of recognition back. Mum was already halfway through a bottle and Dad was wrestling with his accounts.

We walked the dusky streets and Christos took my hand. So easily, so casually. With so little respect for what that did to my insides. We talked crap. I can't even remember what we said, I was too busy trying to take footage in my mind. I wanted to harness the moment, keep it forever. The buzz of the streetlights as they blinked on, the sound of our shoes as we matched our steps, the summer breeze caressing us both. You wouldn't think a North London street on a Friday night could be romantic, but it's amazing how you can train your perspective to block out swearing yobs and puking drunks when you're sure, so sure, this is going to be the night that changes everything.

Even when we wandered down Green Lanes, past the shops I once loved, I couldn't feel sorrow at the boarded-up windows. Rats darted among the festering waste that had been abandoned on the kerbside when the owners had fled, or been raided on some bogus charge. But I didn't care. For once, just once, this night was going to be about me. I deliberately didn't look at the last remaining Turkish restaurant as we walked past, because I knew the purple graffiti (*Roaches Go Home*) would snap me out of my fantasy. And why shouldn't I have some happiness? The world was going to Hell, sure, but couldn't I have just one night off from dwelling on it?

It turned out Jimmy and his mates played fast and loose with the definition of 'party'. What we were really attending was a small gathering of miscreants sitting around on broken benches, next to the disused community centre on the edge of the park. Nevertheless the girls were dressed up to the nines, in the smallest items of fabric they could find. When Jimmy saw me coming he wasn't impressed.

"Rosa!" He pushed the joint he was holding to the girl next to him and came running over. "What the hell are you doing here?"

"Hey, Jimster!" Christos held out his hand, but Jimmy didn't take it. "S'all good, bro, I told her she should come hang."

He's playing it down, I told myself. *He doesn't want to tell my brother he's dating me. Fair enough.*

"Fuck, man." Jimmy started to raise his voice, but then he clocked Christos' pupils. "Jesus, dude, you're blitzing." He turned his attention on me. "What were you thinking? Can't you see he's topped? Right, I'll have to get you home, Dad'll brick if you walk back by yourself."

I felt the indignation rise in me, my confidence stoked by Christos' hand in mine.

"Why should I go home?" I snapped. "I've got just as much right to be out as you!"

"Rosa, c'mon," he lowered his voice to whisper. "This ain't your kinda party, sis."

He was right. I was already starting to shiver and the prospect of sitting around with toppers wasn't exactly appealing. But... Christos.

"How do you know what my kind of party is?" I asked. "You don't know anything about me."

Jimmy snorted. "Yeah, I hear the milk-and-cookie sleepovers with the stiff gang get *wild*."

"Fuck you," I snapped. Then it dawned on me, the real reason he wanted me gone. "I already know you take SIGHS, Jimmy."

His face fell. He started to protest but I cut him short. "I'm not as naïve as you think. I've known for ages. That's what this is about, isn't it, you think I'll lag? Well, I haven't, and I won't. Not if you treat me with some fucking respect anyway."

"Fuck," he said, "I didn't know you knew. Okay. Fucking

stay if it means that much to you. But I don't want you touching that shit."

"It's good enough for you!"

"Yeah, well that's me, isn't it? I'm a cluster-fuck, Rosa, you know that. And those girls," he gestured to the bimbos on the steps, "they're fuck-ups too. But you're not. I just… I just don't want you to be like them. You're better than that."

I rolled my eyes. "Drop the big brother act, it doesn't suit you. Anyway, you're only three minutes older than me. Doesn't exactly qualify you to give advice."

"That's 180 more seconds of oxygen, sis, don't knock it." He smiled.

"You're worrying about nothing anyway, I'm not interested in any of that shit. I wouldn't mind a drink though."

He turned and whistled. "Kinga," he yelled, "fish out a can for my sis here, will you?"

I took my place on the steps with the vagrants and Kinga threw me a can of strong lager. I guzzled it, to calm the nerves and help me fit in. It wasn't long before they were all so topped they wouldn't have noticed whether I was drinking or not. But after my third can their smoking, swallowing and snorting stopped being uncomfortable, and I was babbling about nothing like the rest of them.

It must have been just before midnight when the van drove past. There was no mistaking it. Loudhailer on the top, Union Jack on the side, blacked-out windows. It slowed down as it drove past the park.

"Raid," Kinga yelled. "There's gonna be a raid, look!"

Everyone watched the van slow to a crawl. The raid was going to be close by.

"C'mon, guys," Denny said, "let's watch."

Everyone stood up. Everyone except me and Jimmy.

Jimmy grabbed Fi, the tall brunette he'd been sucking face with, and pulled her back down into his lap. She giggled, and wiggled her arse on his crotch. "I'm good here," he said. "You good?"

Fi nodded, and brayed like a demented donkey before trying to hoover the contents of Jimmy's stomach out through his mouth. I shifted awkwardly. I was going to be left alone, next to the squelching noises and the fake orgasmic groans the donkey gave every time my brother so much as touched her shoulder.

By now, Christos was jogging across the grass with the others, but he turned and yelled to me.

"Rosa, come on, you can come with us. We'll look after her, Jimmy."

Jimmy came up for air. He was so topped he slurred. "Whatever. I ain't her fucking keeper."

Faced with the choice between being a witness to my twin's sexual exploits, or taking the hand of the guy who had robbed me of my reason and letting him whisk me away I… Well, I think it's fairly obvious what I did. I ran across the wet grass, down the street and past the boarded-up mosque on the corner, towards the now stationary van with the rest of them.

The raids were happening all the time. But I'd never seen one, apart from on my Shades. Any legal immigrant who wanted to work, or claim benefits, had already been chipped. If you were foreign-born you couldn't get a job without first being scanned, well, not a legal one anyway. But there were plenty of immigrants who neither claimed benefits nor worked for legitimate employers. Poor saps who were slogging their guts out for unscrupulous employers who paid them, in cash, below the minimum wage. I say poor saps, but that's not how most people saw them. Parasites, filthy vermin bringing violence and disease into our city, taking jobs that could have been given to patriots. Somehow, in the public eye, the greedy employers exploiting them had been absolved. The way to tackle the problem, the ERP believed, was not to prosecute the business owners, but remove the illegal immigrants, forcing them to employ citizens instead.

The initiative, known as Operation Reclamation, created thousands of new jobs for the unskilled, out-of-work youth, which made it even more appealing in the public eye. Parents encouraged their thick, bullish offspring, who were too uneducated for the regular police force, to sign up as Immigration Enforcers. It was the ultimate career for former school bullies because they got to pick on those weaker than them for a living.

The enforcers had already broken down the door of the shabby mid-terrace by the time we got there. We were all panting. The three other girls smoothed down their hair, and ran index fingers under their eyes to remove any smudged mascara. Christos squeezed my hand and then let go.

He stepped forward to get a better view, and everyone else followed. I hung back by the streetlight, but they lined the route from the front door to the van, and when the officers emerged, dragging young Filipino women in silk nighties by their arms, they did not wave them off. In fact, they smiled at the assembled youths, swaggering as if they were celebrities on red carpets, not bullies manhandling defenceless women.

It was clearly a brothel. A few white British men slipped out of the door amid the fracas, looking red-faced. The officers weren't interested in them. Kinga started the heckling.

"Fucking foreign whores," he shouted. "Who'd pay for your stinking cunts anyway?"

The enforcers laughed. One of the captives, an older woman with a deep scar on her cheek, managed to pull away for a split second. She yelled something in her own language at Kinga and spat at the ground in front of him.

The officer she'd pulled away from raised his baton and struck her on the head. She fell to her knees, wailing with the pain.

"Fuck you, skank," Kinga yelled back. "I don't speak Oooga Booga!"

The officer wound her long black hair round his fist and pulled her to her feet.

"Disrespectful little whore," he sneered, hitting her with his baton again, this time in the stomach. She screamed and clutched her abdomen as he threw her in the van.

They kept coming, twelve of them at least. Everyone was fired up. The boys shouted, sneered and swore. The girls joined in.

I guess everyone has that one moment in their lives. The one you would give anything to erase, because you know you were wrong. Inexcusably, horrifically wrong. The guilt at what I did next still gnaws at me. I'm a despicable person. It's the monkey on my back that I try to hide, that I never speak of, that no one but those who were there that night has ever known.

Sophie, the leggy redhead with a penchant for lycra, went for it. I've never heard anyone spit quite so much vitriol at other human beings. I found out years later her parents had split because her dad was a little too fond of foreign hookers. So I guess it was a kind of catharsis. An outpouring of grief rather than racism. I've excused her actions in my mind long ago. But I still can't excuse mine.

Her tirade was so loud, so relentless, that the others stopped slinging their own insults and listened.

"Fucking buk-buk Fliggers, fucking stinking pineapple monkeys!"

Christos whooped… and put his arm around her waist.

I started to hyperventilate. Everything I thought was so close, had convinced myself was a foregone conclusion, was falling from my reach. If I didn't do something, anything, he'd be putting his lips on hers later, not mine.

It was the worst, most shallow motivation in the world. My fucking hormones. But the panorama of the world disappeared and I was in a tunnel. There was suddenly no past or future. There was only this one pivotal moment, and I had to salvage it somehow.

I picked up a stone. A big fucking jagged stone from the driveway. I pushed between them all and threw it. My aim was off; I was pretty pissed. I meant, honestly and truly meant, for it to land by the door. To look like I was being aggressive but didn't throw well. But it went higher and farther than I intended.

It whizzed past the front step just as a young woman was being pulled out, her toddler following behind, grasping her hand.

It hit the kid on the arm. A little boy with huge brown eyes. Barefoot, pyjamas on and a ragged teddy bear under one arm. He screamed and burst into tears. His mother wrenched her arm free with the primal strength women find in themselves when their cubs are under threat, and cradled him. She looked up at me, tears streaming down her face. Not with anger but with disbelief. A fleeting glance, before the officer marched her and her crying child to the van and shut the doors, but one that haunts me every single day of my life.

The worst part was that the others applauded, clapped me on the back.

"Wow, girl, you got that tailless monkey good!"

"Go, Rosa!"

I felt sick.

When we got back to the park it was obvious what Jimmy had been up to. He quickly zipped up his flies.

"Hey, Jim-bud," Kinga yelled, "your sis is *fierce,* man!"

Jimmy frowned and studied me. "What you on about?"

"Oh, bro, you shoulda seen her!" Denny said. "She got this fucking Flig kid, right on the arm."

"She what?"

"Sweet aim, bud. She clocked him with this fuck-off rock. Jeez, girl, you oughta try out for the cricket team!"

Jimmy grabbed me by the arm and pulled me away from the others. My guts were churning.

"What the fuck is the matter with you?" he snapped.

I was staring at the ground. What could I say? I was trying to impress your mate cos I want to sleep with him?

"Look at me, Rosa!"

I looked up, and that's when I saw them in the corner of my eye. Christos and Sophie melded together in an amorphous lump of limbs and tongues. His hand was down her lycra shorts, hers were on his crotch.

"I don't feel well, Jimmy." I puked on his shoes.

8

That was the last straw for Jimmy, covering his new J-Lanes in luminous orange vomit.

"Fuck!" He wiped his precious footwear on the long grass and grabbed me by the arm. "That's *it*. You're going home. Come on." He started to frogmarch me across the park. Fi pouted.

"Hey, I'll take her, man," Denny piped up. "I was gonna split soon anyway. I've gotta help my old man with some biddy's fence in the morning. Says he'll pay me, and I'm cleaned right now so I need it."

Jimmy stopped, looked me up and down, then let go of my arm and shoved me towards Denny.

"Okay," he said, "but you take her right to the door, got it? No splitting up at Duckett, you watch her go in."

"I swear, man," Denny said. He crossed his heart and turned to me. "C'mon, let's get you home."

I was dizzy. I glanced back at the writhing mass. Christos didn't even look up.

Denny chatted at me as we trod the pavements. My head swam with unwanted images. Like a montage of pain and guilt, devised by some sadistic demon and played on loop. Christos and Sophie, the little boy crying, his mother looking at me with those defeated eyes. Everything started to spin, and merge, like a sickening kaleidoscope. I threw up again, this time in someone's azaleas.

"Whoa, easy tiger!" Denny caught hold of me as I stumbled backwards. "Here." He handed me a bottle of water and I took a long slug, grateful for the cool, refreshing liquid. We sat for a few moments on a low wall, and the world came back into focus.

"Thanks," I said, handing him back the bottle. He grimaced, probably thinking about the backwash.

"You keep it," he said. "Haven't you ever had a drink before?"

"Course I have," I snapped, "I've just never had SIX before."

He laughed. "Well, first time for everything I guess."

"Not for me." I was already thinking about it. Had already decided it was the only solution to my situation, that's how screwed up my judgement was. I fished for it. I took the conversation down the line deliberately. I knew he'd ask what I meant, and I knew I was going to steer us there. I have no one to blame but myself.

"What?"

See? He had no choice but to ask. Now I could take us down that road, the one you can't come back from.

"First times," I said, "they don't happen to me."

Denny frowned and I waited for the penny to drop. I knew he was thick, and topped. In fact, that was what I was counting on. Nobody with any intelligence or sobriety would do what I was angling for, not in his position. But for some reason it seemed so vital. Another pivotal moment, another way to try to salvage something from this evening. If I could just get fucked, by anyone, it would validate me somehow. Make me feel I wasn't disconnected from everything else. I told you, never underestimate the stupidity of a clever teenage girl. That goes double for a clever teenage girl with alcohol in her bloodstream.

"You mean you're a..." he said at last. I nodded. "Oh." He shifted awkwardly. "Well, hey, that's cool y'know."

"No, it isn't," I said. "It's the total fucking opposite of cool."

Denny shrugged. "Horses for courses man, horses for courses. You just gotta do what you gotta do. So what if you're not up for it yet? Don't matter, right?"

"But I am..." I whispered, "I am... up for it."

"Oh. Oh, I see. What's the deal then? Guy you want not into it? Must be a fool if you ask me. You don't gotta worry about some pansy-ass. He's an idiot if he's turning you down."

I swallowed hard. Was I really going to do this? Throw myself at a guy I wasn't even attracted to? Yes. Yes I was, because tonight had to mean *something*. It couldn't just be about me injuring a kid and getting my heart stomped on. I had to reclaim it. I had to do something, a massive something, to eclipse all the shit and take back control. In my idiocy I thought losing my virginity would push the rest of it into obscurity.

Like the whole world does, I overestimated the power of sex.

"I want... you." I heard the words for the first time as they fell from my lips. I felt disassociated.

Turned out he didn't need much convincing. A few minutes ago he'd balked at even sipping from the same bottle as me and my vomit-mouth, but put sex on the table and all that was forgotten. His lips were on mine, cold and slimy and possessive. Somehow my feet were moving, he guided me into an alleyway and I crumpled to the ground. He covered me, like a lion taking down a gazelle, and my limbs folded beneath him.

I closed my eyes, tried to work out what it was I ought to be feeling. I was sure it wasn't the gravel on my now bare arse, or the worry that I might stop breathing from his weight upon my chest. He was breathing heavy, cold sprinkles of spittle pebble-dashing my ear. He was groaning, but I seemed to be missing the point. All I could think about was the zipper sticking into my hip, and whether I could wiggle enough to stop it hurting without causing offence.

And then the sharp pain tore through me and made me gasp. I thought something was happening, changing. I thought now I'd know, now I'd get what it was all about. But the pain flew away leaving nothing but the gravel, the zipper and the feeling of being crushed. He was there, wherever that was. He was in the nirvana you're supposed to reach. I could tell from his grunts and scrunched up eyes. But I was still just on my back, half dressed in an alleyway. Wherever this was supposed to take me, I guess I missed my stop.

After he finished we walked the rest of the journey in silence. He gave me a brief hug at the gate and I ran inside, not looking back. I rushed upstairs and stared at myself in the mirror. Nothing had changed. I didn't feel transformed or clued-in. I felt like the same girl I was half an hour before, but with another regret to add to the pile. I felt tricked. Not by Denny, but by the world. There was no rite of passage, no coming of age. No great and glorious moment when the trappings of maidenhood are shed and a woman is born. There was, in fact, no big deal at all.

I shoved my blood-stained knickers to the bottom of my bedroom bin and lay down. I put on my Shades, played some music to try to take the evening away. But when I closed my eyes all I could see was that little boy's crying face.

9

Sometimes, in the womb, one twin absorbs the other. They call it foetal resorption. It consumes its sibling entirely, leaving no evidence of its existence. I think on that sometimes. Send a futile telepathic message through time and space to the cluster of cells I once was. *Absorb him, eclipse him.* If Jimmy never was, then I could be. If Jimmy hadn't existed to die, then I could live.

But I know it could never have happened. If one of us were to have consumed the other, it would have been him. He was always stronger and smarter. He could have taken the womb for his own if he wished; he always took everything he wished. Anyone who knew Jimmy and thought he wasn't part of their crowd because *they* didn't want him to be was deluded. If he wanted you, he got you. If he didn't, he didn't care what you thought of him. You were always exactly where he wanted you to be, always did exactly what he wanted you to do.

He allowed me to live in utero, only to force me to die on this stage.

Cole finishes his speech at last. Ending on a sound bite.

"Strength, community and hope. Young James Lincoln epitomised these virtues, these virtues that we of the ERP strive to uphold. I thank you, Jimmy, and I will always do my best to honour your convictions with my actions."

The crowd applauds. Cole nods slowly, fakes a sniff and a fast blink to give the impression he's fighting back emotion. He walks to his seat, three down from mine, folding his palms in his lap. His left foot taps the stage, causing his brown laces to jiggle. He surveys the clapping crowd, the smirk of self-satisfaction flickers across his face. I wonder what tune he's playing in his head. Probably something majestic. Something by Beethoven perhaps. Something he feels would be a fitting soundtrack to his magnificence.

Two to go.

Alicia Browne stands up. Slick grey pant suit, coiffured blonde bob. She's got one of those smiles the wearer thinks looks congenial, but it somehow makes her look colder than a blank stare could. Head of anti-terror ops: you don't get there by being gooey on the inside. Pure unadulterated steel. She takes the mic and begins in her usual fashion.

"I am honoured today to pay homage to a true patriot. A young man with passion, conviction and courage."

What a joke. Jimmy didn't have conviction. His only cause was hedonism, his only ambition one of personal gratification. He didn't ponder the nature of existence, or the best way to create a better society. The questions that plagued him were where he could score his next synthetic, or which of the girls would be most likely to drop their knickers. He certainly didn't support the ERP, even though they've made him their poster child. Knowing Jimmy, if he'd been alive to do so, he wouldn't have bothered voting at all.

The only time I heard him have a conversation that came close to political was when he argued with Dad about getting a Citizen Chip. That was back when they weren't compulsory and you needed parental consent. The ERP were moving towards full roll-out, for all citizens, starting with volunteers. Even then, he didn't want the implant because he believed in what Cole was trying to accomplish; it was because of the credit incentive they were offering.

That's who he really was. Someone willing to have an

implanted device, against their own father's moral convictions, simply to get a new Shades update. Dad refused, of course. But as soon as he dragged his hungover body out of bed on our eighteenth birthday, Jimmy went straight to the council building to get his CC, and then straight onto the Shades site to download the latest updates. That he 'volunteered' for the initiative was all the ERP needed to claim he was a 'loyal supporter of English Reclamation'.

That, and the fact that he saved Cole's life, of course.

Predictably, Alicia started ranting about Gridless now. "The greatest threat to liberty that we have ever seen," she proclaims, before insisting they're funded and propped up by our enemies overseas. Bullshit. Trust me, if they had that kind of money you'd already be dead.

But that's how it works; I see that now. People would be behind Gridless if only they knew the truth. People *were* behind them, when they first came on the scene. Even Jimmy had one of their pins on his backpack. That little fact has been covered up of course. They said he didn't live long enough to know what they were really about, else he'd never have supported them. Maybe they're right, I don't know. But he, like most irreverent youths, found them hilarious at the time. Almost everywhere you looked at school the sigil (two shackled hands, one black one white, reaching for each other as their chains break) could be seen on notebooks, bags and coats. Everyone loves a good joke, especially at the establishment's expense, and that's what they appeared to be. Just jokers.

It didn't take long for the new Citizen Database (on which all the information contained in the Citizen Chips was stored) to get the tongue-in-cheek nickname the National Grid, and there were no shortage of people who objected to it. The old parties had tried to introduce something similar, so Dad told me, back before I was born. But that was just cards, and even then the public didn't like the idea. Before Jimmy died, the consensus was that forcing the chips through against public opinion would cost the ERP their majority in the next election.

I guess Gridless, and Jimmy, inadvertently handed them their next term on a plate.

So when the cyber criminals calling themselves Gridless started their hacktivist antics, it was to huge public love. Who doesn't want to see the Prime Minister posting a meme of himself sitting on the toilet? Or listen to hacked phone calls between the Education Secretary and his mistress, in which he calls her Pooky? It was hilarious, it was subversive, it appealed to the lowest common denominator and it hurt no one but the politicians. Even when they leaked the private numbers of the cabinet, or published their as-yet-undoctored budget reports, no one cared they were doing something illegal. No one thought it would go any further, because no one realised how much further the ERP were going to go, or that Gridless knew what their plans were.

We merrily logged on to watch an anonymous guy wearing a suit of armour, and speaking through a voice changer, as he announced their next target. You had to be quick: the powers that be removed the vlogs as swiftly as they could, but by then someone had already copied it and uploaded it elsewhere. It usually took them a few hours to track down and remove every copy. That was the biggest joke of it, they would give 24 hours warning about who was getting hacked next, but even with that, Gridless were so good at what they did their victims were never able to stop them.

Few people actually listened to what he was saying, it was all just a joke as far as they were concerned. But, as Greg explained to me, the funny stuff was never meant to be the point. It was to get attention, to get people talking about them, to garner support for the real cause. They knew the awful truth the ERP were hiding, and they knew where the CCs were going. They had an inside man. They knew what was coming and they wanted to stop it.

They'd have done it, too, if it weren't for Jimmy.

10

I don't know when Jimmy got home that night, but by the time I'd emerged from my bed the next day he was already dressed and on his way out. He glared at me as he put his jacket on. I didn't need to be reminded I had behaved appallingly. It had all come flooding back to me the moment consciousness had elbowed the brief relief of sleep out of the way.

"You going out?" I squeaked. I knew it was a stupid question, but I had to break the silence.

"Yeah," he replied, picking his keys up from the bowl on the shelf. "What are your plans for the day, sis? Gonna go find some more foreign kids to stone? You were right about one thing, Rosa, I don't know you at all."

Tears pricked at the back of my eyes. The sickening tide of shame that ripped through me twisted itself into a tsunami of anger. How *dare* he? How dare he lecture me when he hung round with those idiots in the first place? Why should I be chided when his mates were revered? I wanted to hurt him. I wanted to bring someone else down with me into his disgust, even if it meant lowering myself further too.

"I fucked Denny." As soon as I said it, it became another rotting specimen on my heap of regrets.

He stared at me, shook his head and walked out the door, slamming it behind him. I didn't want to see anyone. I didn't even get dressed. I told Mum I had cramps, and spent the day in my room wallowing in a mire of shame and self-pity behind my Shades. That's where Jimmy found me when he burst in that evening.

I didn't hear him knock, he probably didn't. He threw my door open and chucked a packet at me. I picked it up and stared at it. The morning after pill.

"What the—" I started to protest.

"You think I don't know that fucker rides bareback?" Jimmy snapped. "Just sort your shit out."

He was gone again and I was alone. I took the pill. I hadn't even thought about the potential repercussions. I was grateful, really grateful. But I knew it would forever be the elephant in the room, so I never thanked him. Another one for the pile.

After that, Jimmy's gang never came to the front door again. Not until after Jimmy was dead and they came to pay their respects, and answer my parents' questions. A few days later I happened to look out of the window and saw them, waiting for him across the street. Denny had a black eye and several stitches in his lip. So I guess Jimmy had made peace in his own way. It must be so much easier, being a male. You take your penance in the form of blood and bruise, superficial and fleeting. Once the wounds are gone you never have to pay for your transgression again. But my scars, well, those never heal.

For the rest of Jimmy's life I was considered radioactive by his groupies. Christos no longer even nodded when we passed in the corridors. Denny would get wide-eyed with panic and walk out of his way to avoid being within a ten-metre radius of me. But it suited me fine. As far as I was concerned I'd had my teenage dalliance with drink and sex, and that one night had left me with so much shame and regret I would never go there again. When school came around in September I had resolved to buckle down, get through my final year. There would be time for reinvention when I got to university, away from the shadow of my twin, and away from anyone who had witnessed my most heinous deed.

We shared a womb, shared a home, shared a school. But

for that last year we may as well have been strangers. In all our times together I'd never noticed the glimmer of affection, respect even, in Jimmy's eyes. Not until it was gone.

I can see it now, in those blown up photographs held aloft by the crowd. It bores a hole in my heart because I know it isn't for me. He'd hate me even more now than he did back then. I've done everything he told me not to, and many things he thought too dark for me to ever dance with.

11

The worst thing about losing someone is when you forget they're gone. Those ordinary everyday moments that come after the grief has stopped consuming every second of your consciousness. Maybe you're just making a drink, and your sadistic mind tricks you into grabbing an extra cup for them. Or you're watching something on TV and you think to yourself how much they'd love it. Then it hits you all over again. You're back to that afternoon, when the train of your life got derailed. When the police rang the doorbell and everything changed, forever.

I play the last time I ever saw him over and over in my mind, even now. It's always been that way. Even when I was so fucked on Krenom I didn't know, or care, what day it was, I still saw the front door of our family home closing in more clarity than I saw my current surroundings. It's only poignant in hindsight, of course. Had he come home that day nothing about our breakfast would have stuck in my mind. It's as though your brain takes a snapshot of someone, just in case. The next time you see them it's wiped like chalk from a blackboard. But if they never come back there's nothing to overwrite it.

He was wearing his blue T-shirt with Dusty on it (that's where his apparent love of the cartoon came from. I think he liked the *F**k sobriety* slogan more than the show itself).

The dog held a beer in one hand, a spliff in the other, and his eyes were spirals. To show he was topped, I guess. Mum tutted at the profanity, even though she'd seen it hundreds of times before.

"I do hope you're going to get some decent clothes for when you start your job?" she said, handing him some toast as he sat down opposite me.

"Of course, Mum," he replied. But he rolled his eyes at me when she wasn't looking. I grinned. The distance between us had never closed, not since that night almost a year ago. But when it came to being exasperated with our parents we were usually on the same page.

"Where are you going today anyway?" she was asking Jimmy. I wasn't going anywhere, as usual. Since school had ended, I hadn't made any effort to keep in touch with my former classmates. I was in a sort of limbo, waiting to start a new life at university. Jimmy, on the other hand, was making the most of six weeks of freedom before his apprenticeship was due to begin.

"Out," he said between bites. "Nowhere special, just out with the guys."

"Dinner?"

"Don't know. Probably be back."

"Well, I'm making lasagne."

"Okay, well, then I'll definitely be back." He grinned, wide. His eyes had that sparkle as he got up from the table, still clutching his toast, and gave her a crumb-covered kiss. She had her hands in the washing-up bowl and scrunched up her nose as he put his sticky lips on her cheek, but smiled nonetheless.

"I'm gonna eat this on the go, I'll see you later."

And that was the last thing he ever said to us.

I watched from the kitchen table as he held his toast between his teeth, put on his jacket, grabbed his keys and left the house. In my recollection, the door closes with a telling thump. There's an air of portent, of finality, about the way the letterbox sways as it shuts and his silhouette fades from view. Of course, I felt no such omen at the time. But our brains like to conjure up telltale signs retrospectively. The lack of control over the chaos that is life would drive us all psychotic otherwise.

I don't know how I filled the next few hours. Shades, vlogs, music, books. Nothing out of the ordinary. The day wasted away like so many before it, and I with no notion of the impending meteor.

It was just after three o'clock when the police car pulled up. Every second from that point is etched in my memory. I was making a sandwich. Ham and lettuce. It would remain untouched on the kitchen counter until I threw it away the next day. When they started walking up our path I yelled out to Mum, who was in the middle of watching a mystery she would never learn the conclusion of.

We watched the officers approaching and exchanged looks. We thought perhaps Jimmy had been arrested. Even with Mum's ability to view everything he did through rose-coloured glasses she knew, deep down, he wasn't hanging with a good crowd.

They rang the bell. Mum smoothed down her dress and cleared her throat before answering. I guess she wanted to appear a pillar of the community, even if she was about to be told she was the mother of a criminal. But when she opened the door the policemen didn't look stern, or even authoritative.

"Are you the mother of James Lincoln?" The tone was soft.

"Yes."

They removed their hats.

"Mrs Lincoln, may we come in?"

"Oh my God," Mum gasped, lifting her hand to her mouth as she stepped aside to let the officers in. "Is he alright?"

Once inside, the taller of the two policemen looked Mum in the eye, and put his hand on her shoulder.

"I am sorry to have to tell you that there has been a terrible accident."

"What kind of accident?" Mum's voice was a whisper.

"Your son was involved in a fall, resulting in a collision. His friends called the emergency services, and the paramedics did everything they could. But… there's no easy way to say this, Mrs Lincoln. I'm afraid James was pronounced dead at the scene."

My arms went out instinctively. I caught her as she folded like a concertina, and eased her to the floor. I had never before heard such primal, animal sounds coming from a human being. The sound of grief so acute, so raw, it can never be overcome. A sound every mother prays they will never live to make.

I wasn't in my body. Somehow my legs were moving, my arms raising her to her feet and guiding her inside, but I couldn't feel them. Autopilot had been engaged, taking control of my physical being. The officers came inside, sat down beside her on the sofas. My robot limbs moved me to the kitchen and I began making cups of tea.

I snapped back into my head briefly, and called Dad from my Shades. I told him to come straight home and then hung up. I didn't know what else to say. I was scared to speak, scared to even think, because I knew the pain was coming, the grief. And I didn't know what might trigger it, what might send me hurtling into the abyss. Like when the dentist prods at your cavity with that little metal spike. You know one of those pokes is going to hit the nerve, but you don't know which.

The initial sobs and screams from my mother were soon replaced with frantic questions, as if finding a flaw in the policeman's logic might resurrect her son. I set the cups of tea down on the table, and sat beside her to listen to my twin's fate.

He'd fallen from a bridge onto the A406, into the path of oncoming traffic travelling at 40 mph. They say he died instantly. They say he didn't know about the lorry, whose driver slammed on the brakes but couldn't stop in time. They say he didn't feel its wheels mangle his limbs and spread his remains over a ten-foot stretch of road before it finally halted. I want to believe them.

He'd been topped, of course. The lab reports the next day

confirmed it, but I already knew. I knew the moment they told us his friends had confessed to daring him to walk along the rails. They'd all been topped off their heads on G-Star. They thought they were invincible. The boy who never put a foot wrong, literally or metaphorically, had made his one catastrophic misstep.

Kinga told us the whole story later, in between sobs and with eyes that would continue to see the sight he described for the rest of his life. Especially when they were shut. He'd been doing so well (if anything about taking such a stupid dare in the first place can be considered 'doing well'). Over halfway across, arms outstretched, one sure foot in front of the other. Then he wobbled and recovered. He turned to face them, grinning, and yelled, "That was close!" As last words go they were pretty fucking stupid. Especially considering that the twisting of his torso to utter them caused his centre of gravity to shift.

He fell. Almost in slow motion, Kinga said. As though everything was on pause. But really, before anyone had a chance to react, the sound, the squeal of tyres on tarmac, the crunch of metal hitting metal, it all signified the end of Jimmy Lincoln. And the start of everything else.

They raced towards the road, driven by pure adrenalin and panic. By the time they reached the kerb, there was no Jimmy. Kinga says it was the hand, the hand protruding from the axle of the lorry, that made him throw up.

The lorry driver came to see us too, a few days later. He was wracked with the guilt of a good person who could have done nothing more than they did, but still blames themselves. None of us held him responsible, but I think that just made him feel even worse.

The police were still with us when Dad rushed through the door. No one needed to tell him Jimmy was gone. One look at Mum did that. She wept in my arms as the officers sat opposite, hats in hands. He stood still, staring at the tableau of grief before him. The older of the two officers stood up.

"Sir, I am so sor—"

"How?" Dad's voice sounded cold, hard. So unlike him. They explained the accident again. Mum curled into a foetal position on the couch, and covered her ears with hands that held sodden tissues. As if the first telling had put her in Hell and the second was the Devil tormenting her.

Dad didn't say a word. He nodded and walked through the room, past us all, and out into the garden. I felt the goose bumps rise on my skin and stood up to follow him, with no idea as to what I was going to do, or say. But the younger officer held out his hand and touched my shoulder.

"Leave him, Miss. Give him a minute."

They must be experts, I guess. Must have given this news to so many families. Must have seen the different ways people react when their world collapses. Must have known what he was going to do, for neither of them looked surprised when the sound of breaking glass rang out.

He was smashing up the shed. Overturning his work benches, throwing his tools. An old camping stove hurtled through the last remaining pane, disintegrating it. One policeman gestured to me to sit down beside my weeping mother, which I did. But I watched as he entered the garden, and paused. It seemed like he was waiting, counting. As if these bursts of grief-turned-rage are finite and they knew exactly how long they took to burn out. After a few moments, the crashing and smashing stopped, and he moved forward.

The sight of my dad, my rock, being held in the embrace of a uniformed officer, as he wept on his shoulder and crumpled to his knees among the debris of his own making, was the prod that hit the nerve, and then there was nothing left in my world but pain.

12

There had never been a Rosa without a Jimmy. Even at a time when I had no concept of a world beyond the uterus, I was with him. There were no months of solitude, of growing alone. There had never been any world, any space in my life, without Jimmy in it. Even when we grew distant, we were still always connected.

Now I was alone.

We all were. Although we three, the Bereaved, occupied the same physical space we none of us could feel anything beyond our own pain. We couldn't understand each other's own, personal, loss. An arm around a shoulder, the passing of a tissue, the making of a drink. All physical gestures meant to convey a shared understanding. But inside, deep inside where the grief keens, our roads diverged at that moment, never to rejoin.

My parents lost more than a son that day. Something inside each of them was extinguished. A candle snuffed out. It took me a long time to realise what it was that left their eyes. It was hope. It was the death of aspiration that comes from knowing that the best of your life is over. That for every moment, of every hour, from now until you die, you will have only one burning, all-consuming wish. And it can never come true.

When we were left alone, three damaged hearts in a house that seemed soulless, we none of us knew what to say or how to be. The weeping gave way to anger, and my parents threw missiles of blame at each other, before crumpling again, and sinking into tears. My father wrapped his arms around me, and held my head so tightly to his chest I thought I might suffocate, but I didn't care. Yet as close as we held one another, we couldn't feel each other, not really.

At some point, among the seemingly endless hours of emptiness and pain, I went into Jimmy's room. His duvet was still piled up on his bed from when he had thrown it aside that morning. I pulled it around myself, pushed my face into it and inhaled his scent. The sweet, musky smell of the almost-man he was caused my stomach to twist in longing and regret.

I buried myself deeper in the quilt, pulled it around me until all was dark. I closed my eyes, breathed deeply and regularly. I listened to my own heartbeat and pretended I could hear his echoing around me. I was in the womb, in warmth and darkness, and I imagined him beside me, imagined reaching out and touching him. We were back where it all began. Back together. I stayed so still, concentrating on my fantasy, blocking out the unfathomable reality. Eventually I fell asleep.

I woke to a brief moment of blissful amnesia, before recollection swept in once again. Downstairs, Mum had fallen asleep on the sofa, Jimmy's baby book open on her chest. I covered her with a blanket and crept into the kitchen.

Through the window I saw life: the milkman pulled up outside number twenty-two, whistling as he left their order on the cracked doorstep. A little old lady pulled her shopping bag behind her, heading to the local store as it opened. Cats stalked the gardens trying to catch the early birds, but lacking the hunger that drives true hunters to succeed. Everything was rolling on. Everyone was waking to just another day. Beyond these walls the world continued, ignorant to our devastation.

I might have held on tighter to the purity of our isolated pain if I'd known how fleeting our solitude would be. For just a few more hours, we would be alone with our memories, with our truths. Because, unbeknown to us, the circus was already on the road, and it was heading our way.

13

The morning after Jimmy's death we moved around the house like ghosts, each locked in our own personal torment. Taking steps that led nowhere, doing tasks that meant nothing. Occasionally one of us would howl as the chains of our grief rattled us into despair. But mostly we were silent. Going through motions, attending to our ablutions. Our flesh and our souls disconnected. Sitting for a moment, only to rise and pace again, orbiting one another.

The suited men rang the doorbell at 11:05am, rousing us from our insular reflections. There was no emotion on Mum's face when she answered. She had no reason to worry what tidings a stranger at the door may bring. There was nothing left for anyone to destroy. They held their ID badges up, and asked to come in. She didn't speak, just nodded, and moved aside to allow them to pass.

The first of the two, a large man with grey nostril hair and a noisy exhale, introduced himself to my father with a handshake.

"Hello sir, I am Detective Sergeant Mills, of the Public Information Department, and this is Officer Greyson. We are most sincerely sorry for your loss."

Dad nodded, surveying him with red ringed eyes. "Thank you," he replied, "but why are you... I mean, what can we do for you?"

"We have some further information regarding James Lincoln's death." His words hit me like a thousand cold needles. "Perhaps we could all sit down?"

We took our places on the sofas, and the large detective continued.

"Now, as I'm sure you're aware, James' unfortunate accident caused a traffic collision—"

"Oh God," Dad interrupted, "was someone else hurt?"

"No, no, sir, nothing like that. Few cars written off, I imagine, but nothing that insurance won't cover. No, quite the opposite in fact."

"What do you mean?" Mum squeaked.

"Well, ma'am, one of the cars involved, the first one to collide with the lorry that... well, the lorry involved, was carrying a Mr Daniel Knight, a person wanted by the police in connection with certain cybercrimes."

"So you've come here to tell us you've caught a hacker?" Dad stood up, his voice was rising. "Well, bully for you. Do you think we care? We've lost our..." He sat back down and choked a sob. "We've lost our son."

"No, sir. No, of course that's not what I'm here for. I wouldn't dream of encroaching on your time of grief if it weren't vitally important. You see, Mr Knight is the person we suspect to be at the head of the organisation known as Gridless. I take it you've heard of them?"

"Of course," Dad snapped, "everyone's heard of them. I still don't see why—"

"As well as Mr Knight himself, we found contained within the vehicle some evidence, very strong evidence in fact, of a terrorist plot."

"A terrorist plot? Gridless are just hacktivists."

"Apparently not anymore, sir. My officers have been working through the night, acting on the information recovered from the vehicle – blueprints, names and the like – and we have, after a series of raids, seized several pounds of nitroglycerin and details of a meticulously planned attack on the London Underground."

"Nitroglycerin?" Mum asked. "What are you talking about? What kind of attack?"

"From what we have so far been able to piece together, and I'm certain more details will come to light now that we have several of the suspects in custody, an attack was scheduled for next week. Tuesday, as it goes. The very day Prime Minister Cole intends to be at Victoria, unveiling his latest initiative. At 8:45am, when the whole of the Underground would be filled with innocent commuters, Gridless had intended to bomb several stations on the Circle line simultaneously, using explosives hidden in thermos flasks. Mr and Mrs Lincoln, had they succeeded, the death toll would have been catastrophic."

"What are you saying?"

"I'm saying, sir, that had it not been for young James' accident, we would never have uncovered this evidence, and therefore we have every reason to believe that the attack would have taken place. In short, James' tragic death has saved hundreds, possibly thousands, of lives."

Mum wailed, Dad paced; I sat still, trying to absorb what they were telling us.

"Now I know that this doesn't bring your son back, and doesn't in any way ease your pain, but I hope, in time, you can find some comfort in the fact that his death was not in vain. His sacrifice has saved so many other families from a loss such as yours. In many ways, he was a hero."

I couldn't believe what I was hearing. The smell of bullshit managed to kick my brain into gear and I broke my silence. "He fell off a bridge! He was high on drugs!"

"Shhhh." Mum shot me a dark look, as if the police wouldn't find out from forensics that he had G-Star in his system and my outburst was giving them new, incriminating information.

"Yes," Sergeant Mills shifted in his seat. "We are aware that there seemed to be traces of a synthetic high in his bloodstream. However, in light of all the good he has done, and of course remembering that the substance in question isn't *technically* illegal... well, we feel that information would be best kept private, out of respect for the, uh, deceased."

"Private?" Dad asked. "Private from whom?"

"Well. Now we come to the reason for my coming here so quickly. This is a matter of national security, and national importance. I'm afraid a press statement is unavoidable. We wanted to be sure you were fully up to speed before the media get involved."

"The media?" Mum asked.

"I know this is a lot to take on board. But your James—"

"Jimmy," I said softly, "he was called Jimmy. He hated James."

"I see." Mills nudged Greyson, who hastily put on his Shades, presumably sending the information to someone. "Well, Jimmy has single-handedly prevented possibly the worst terrorist attack England has ever known. Worse than Dover, from a casualty point of view. The public are going to be interested. Very interested. We will of course station an officer outside your property round the clock for the next few days, weeks if needed. To keep the vultures at bay, as it were, until you're ready to speak to them."

"Vultures?" I wasn't sure what he was getting at.

"Ah, sorry, I mean the journalists. They tend to swarm all over things. Not that you've anything to fear from them, they'll be on your side. Everyone will be on your side. Your Jimmy was a hero after all. But they can be a little *persistent*, which may not be what you want at this time. We have a team of experts on hand, to help you deal with them. Prep you for interviews, that sort of thing. But all that can wait until you're ready. For now, though, well, it falls to me to ask you a rather delicate question."

"And what would that be?"

"Well, sir, the head of anti-terror ops, Ms Browne, is due to make a statement in a couple of hours. Detailing the alleged plot, and young Jame— Jimmy's part in preventing it. After that, well, the Prime Minister's advisors are working on his reaction speech now. Obviously, no one's expecting any of you to make a statement yet."

"Yet?" Dad asked.

Mills cleared his throat. "But the public will want to see the face of the brave young man who has saved so many lives. So, with your permission, we would like to use a suitable photo."

"Oh." Mum went to the mantelpiece and picked up the digital frame that circled through all our family photos. "Of course, I'm sure they'll be something on here. I hadn't even thought about anything like that yet."

"Why can't you just use his avatar?" I asked. "That was the picture he chose for himself."

"We have had a look at his social media, yes," Greyson piped up. "But, uh, we felt perhaps you would prefer a different image?"

Jimmy had been proud of his avatar picture. So proud in fact that he hadn't changed it in almost a year. Most people change them more often than their pants, but not Jimmy. He said it was a classic. Three days' stubble, reefer hanging from his lips, bottle of Jack in hand, thumbs up to the camera, T-shirt declaring *Fuck the law* and some skank's cleavage pressed up to his cheek. He was right. Classic Jimmy. But classic Jimmy was about to be redefined.

Mum hated it, of course. "Is that really how you want people to think of you?" she had asked him. "Jimmy, that isn't you at all. You're a clever boy, a decent boy. What would employers think if they googled you?"

Jimmy had just grinned and told her she worried too much.

Now she had the opportunity to choose his brand, she intended to take it.

"Quite right," she said, scouring the pictures in the frame. "I never liked his avatar. So unlike him. Totally posed. One-off."

The officers looked at each other and Mills shuffled

forward in his seat. "Perhaps then, ma'am, you would like us to, uh, take care of his social media?"

"What do you mean?" Dad asked.

"Well. I imagine once his name goes public there'll be a lot of people interested to know more about him. They'll want to send condolence messages, that sort of thing. I just thought, maybe you'd like us to… clean up his profiles? We have experts who can do that sort of thing, you know. Tighten his security settings; change the picture to something more fitting. For the sake of his memory and your privacy."

"I think that's a wonderful idea," Mum said. "Thank you."

"Well, I don't think so," Dad leapt to his feet, the wobble in his voice gone. "He lived online! His profiles are him. They're all we've got left of him."

Greyson stood up. When he sprang into action, I could see his manner was more empathic, more disarming, than his colleague's. He'd waited in the wings until he was needed, then he stole the show.

"I think perhaps Sergeant Mills hasn't made himself entirely clear, sir. No one is suggesting we remove anything, just tweak the settings so that his personal pictures stay just that. Personal. You will still be able to access his profiles, just as he left them, but maybe you would prefer that certain information wasn't publicly available? Perhaps, I could demonstrate?" He pulled a laptop out of his briefcase. "If you would permit me?"

Dad softened. He nodded and sat down beside Greyson as he booted up his machine.

"See now," Greyson said, "if I google Jimmy Lincoln, this is what we get."

He opened up Jimmy's profiles. Photo after photo of debauchery. Jimmy drinking, smoking, open-mouthed and topped. On a bar terrace, bare-chested, giving the finger. Mooning from a car window. One bimbo, two bimbo, three. He scrolled through his status updates:

Gonna get blitzed bitches.
Need me a loose babe tonight, any takers?
Feeling fucked, sweet night topping with y'all.

"All we're suggesting, Mr Lincoln, is that perhaps you would prefer these images and updates not to be seen by Joe Public? Jimmy has his security settings low, which is typical for a lad his age. It's all about socialising, having a presence. Trust me, his profile is in no way a true reflection of who he was. It's all an advert, an image he wanted to project. I know that's not the real Jimmy, and you know it too. But, the public take things at face value. I'd hate for his memory to be sullied by what was, clearly, a normal teenage phase. We want to protect you, and him."

Dad shook his head at the images on the laptop. Though I wondered if there wasn't a little seed of envy behind his disapproval.

"So you're just going to lock it down? Not change anything?"

"Exactly. Our team can hack in, set all these photos and messages to private. Then you'll be given the password to access his account, as it was, anytime you wish."

"So what will people see then? If this is all locked down?"

"Anything you'd like them to," Greyson said. "We'll change the avatar of course, to a photograph of your choosing. We can leave it at that, or we can add pictures you'd like to display. Even messages if you wish. Think of it as an online tribute."

Mum had a wistful smile on her lips; you could almost see the cogs moving in her brain. She could make the world see what she saw through her mother-tinted glasses. Jimmy could be the boy she chose to believe he was. Dad's frown hadn't lifted. He was trying to process truth against an onslaught of new information and spin, but Mum was already caught up in Jimmy-the-hero.

"What a lovely idea," she said. "Thank you so much. It would be such a comfort. It's what Jimmy would have wanted."

You can't accuse a grieving mother of talking bull. It's an

unwritten law. You have to let them say whatever they want, think whatever they want. If they want to wax lyrical about how their child was a genius you can't contradict them. Even if you know full well they were really thick as shit. I knew she was wrong. Jimmy would have wanted to be remembered for who he really was, not for what Mum wished he'd been. But I couldn't call her out on it. I couldn't bring myself to break her further by pissing on her grief parade.

"I've found several good pictures," she said, holding up the frame. "I just can't choose between them."

Greyson gave a warm, congenial smile and placed a hand on her shoulder. "Don't worry, Mrs Lincoln. Why don't I send all your choices to our team, they can pick for you?"

She looked up at him, and matched his smile, her eyes wet. "Oh, thank you, yes. That would be so helpful."

14

The police and their media savvy experts were delighted to be 'helpful'. They promised to take care of everything, and guide us through what was to come. Once permission had been given, the transformation of Jimmy's online presence happened almost instantaneously. Within minutes the unsavoury avatar was gone. *They* had no difficulty in choosing the image that would define Jimmy for the masses.

It's the photo that stares at me now, from all angles. The one that has replaced my own memories of his face. Whenever I look back to a time when we were together, a time before he was distilled into a product, that picture has been cut and pasted over my recollection. I remember him arguing with me over whose turn it is to choose the Sunday movie. He's in his pyjamas, he's only eight or nine, but his face is that post-pubescent grin, even as he yells in my mind. Walking through the park at four years old, choosing filthy pine cones for our 'collection', but now he looks like a tottering puppy with his head too big for his body because that image is spliced on.

It was taken at Dad's annual company barbeque the year before Jimmy died. One of the only occasions when he would comply with parental requests to dress respectably. I guess he knew how important it was to Dad. He'd had to go cap in hand to his old firm, take his old job again, but with worse terms and conditions than before. Being back where he started had to stick in his craw. I think Jimmy got that. We could at least play the perfect kids once a year, to make it easier for him.

The landscape had changed somewhat in the eight years Dad had been absent. It was, for one thing, decidedly more homogenised. There were still some workers from ethnic minorities on the payroll, but they had abandoned any outward show of their own culture. Gone were the saris, the hijabs, the turbans. All for the sake of their careers, of course.

Jimmy had worn a smart cream pullover with a subtle logo: Jingo, the major sports brand. The striped J with the crossed ivy leaves beneath it is visible in the picture, just above his chest. It gives the subtle impression that Jimmy was athletic. He wasn't. Not that he was unfit, he could run damn fast when he wanted to, but he never did anything so contrived, so ostentatiously wholesome and conformist, as play sport. We were sent hundreds of pounds of vouchers for Jingo, and a rugby ball signed by their CEO. Jimmy didn't own a single other item of clothing by them, and that one had been bought by Mum specifically for the event. He never wore it again.

He'd also shaved, something he did only under duress, and his slightly zig-zagged dimples were highlighted by the angle. The grin on his lips caused faint creases round his eyes. They would have deepened over time, to form wrinkles that his loved ones would affectionately call laughter lines. Had he lived. The sparkle in his eyes was for Mum. She had taken the picture on her Shades, after shoving a napkin at him and demanding he wipe the ketchup from his lips. In the original photo you can still see a slight pink tinge under his bottom lip from the offending condiment. But not in the image that appeared on Greyson's screen. They must have cleaned it up.

How *thoughtful*.

The officers in our lounge continued to be just as thoughtful. Mills sat sipping lukewarm tea from a dainty china mug. His fingers were too big for the ornate handle and he cradled the accompanying saucer in the palm of his hand. He made me think of an adult trying to play along with a toddler's tea party.

He listened, and nodded enthusiastically, at Mum's cathartic outpouring of Jimmy anecdotes. She didn't know, or perhaps didn't care, that he was humouring her.

She smiled for the first time since the news as she regaled him with exaggerated tales of Jimmy's bravery and intellect. How loving he was, how extraordinarily sweet a child he had been. Only a mother can brush over the act of breaking a window in one breathless sentence, then languish over his ensuing regret; shifting the focus of the tale to her son's heartfelt contrition and handwritten apology, so that he comes out smelling of roses.

Dad excused himself, said he was going to take a shower. I think it was just all too much. I tried to leave as well, intending to go shut myself in my room, but Greyson called me over to his screen.

"Rosa?" He looked up and smiled. He was younger than Mills, and had an air of ease about him that instantly soothed. "Do you want me to run through this with you?"

It was the first time anyone official had spoken to me directly, other than to prevent me following my father into the garden the day before. Greyson was the only one who seemed to acknowledge *me* in all this. I couldn't say no. I was desperate for the attention, though I didn't realise it at the time.

"Have you got your Shades?" he asked as I sat beside him at the large coffee table. I nodded, and pulled them out of my pocket.

"Okay, good," he said. "So, this is his profile as the public see it." I looked at the screen. As well as the newly uploaded avatar several other changes had been made. Instead of *Jimmy L* his screen name was now *RIP Jimmy Lincoln*, and his bio read *Hero of London*. All his photos were gone, replaced by the images Mum had struggled to choose between. Each one was vivid, flawless. Not a spot or a scratch. Even in the picture of him on his skateboard (in which I knew for a fact he'd had a slight black eye from a previous fight), he looked clean cut and unblemished. And they'd removed the cigarette from his hand.

"But log on from your Shades," he said. "The password is HX34-lZ."

I obeyed and accessed Jimmy's profile. The avatar was still the same, of course, and the new pictures had been added. But all his old ones were there too, along with all his updates and messages from his friends.

"I know this is strange, Rosa," he said, "but it's not gone. You've got the password now. You can look at his real profiles anytime you want."

I nodded, moving my pupils rapidly, scanning through his camera roll. I stopped when I came to one of the two of us on a roof terrace in Malaga, taken a couple of years ago on a family holiday. He had his arm round me, grinning. I was wearing a green dress and a pink flower in my hair. That was the night he and I had gone out for dinner by ourselves. He'd bought me a blue cocktail that tasted like coconut, and asked the waiter to take our picture. The caption read, *Me and my beautiful sis*.

I never even knew he'd uploaded it.

My eyes filled with tears and I took off my Shades. I dug my fingernails into my hands, trying not to lose it in company. But when Greyson put his arm around me I sobbed into his shoulder. Mum was onto Jimmy's chivalry (ha!) and she didn't even notice.

"I'm so sorry, kiddo." Greyson stroked my back gently.

"It's not him," I said, trying to compose myself as I pointed at his new profile. "It's not Jimmy."

Greyson sighed. "I know," he said softly, "but what's coming… I think you'll be glad we did this. And you can still see him how he really was. No one can take away your memories."

"It says he was a hero," I whispered, "but it was just an accident. He didn't do it on purpose."

"I know that too. But it's still true that people would have died if it wasn't for him. Even if it was an accident. Maybe it was fate?"

"I don't believe in fate," I said, wrenching a tissue from my pocket.

"Fair enough. Me neither, as it goes. But people, most people, they don't do well with chaos."

"What do you mean?"

He glanced at Mum and Mills. "Maybe we should make some more tea?" he said, with a deliberate stare. I nodded and followed him into the kitchen.

"Rosa," he said when the kettle began to make noise, "you're a clever girl. I can see that. Can I be honest with you?"

I nodded.

"We missed this. Totally missed it. If it wasn't for what happened to your brother yesterday... well. Can you imagine, Rosa, how scared people would be? If this had gone ahead and the best and brightest minds in anti-terror had no idea? It would be meltdown. People are always looking for an easy answer, they don't see things like you and I do. We know it's not black and white, but that terrifies them. So, if we have villains then we need heroes. It gives a kind of balance."

"No one's going to believe Jimmy did it deliberately!"

"Of course not. I'm not suggesting that. But they will want someone to thank, just as they want someone to blame. And it seems wrong that the police should take the credit. At the end of the day, it *was* Jimmy who prevented it. And doesn't it help, just a little bit, that he didn't die for nothing? That some good came from a tragedy? I think, even if it doesn't help you, it will certainly help your mother."

It sickens me now how naïve I was, how easily played. It was the oldest trick in the book, appeal to my intellect. Make me think I was a cut above. I was being let into the inner circle, trusted with more information. It was just a deeper level of deception, I see that now. But I was young and stupid, and buoyed by thoughts of being special. My mother had been won over by the shameless praise of her son, and the opportunity to rave about him uninterrupted. I had been manipulated for my altruism and delusions of intelligence.

I played right into their hands.

15

Alicia returns to her seat, to the soundtrack of rapturous applause. Her ice-gaze flicks my way briefly and the edges of her mouth twitch. She doesn't know whether she ought to smile or not, doesn't understand the etiquette. Doesn't know how to behave in unscripted interaction. I smile, but not at her. I smile at that one little tell there is, underneath the manufactured frosting, still some part of Alicia that resembles the woman I first saw on the screen the day after Jimmy died.

She'd only been in the post a few months back then, and hadn't yet had cause to make a public statement. She had a lot of personal reasons to thank Jimmy. Her head would have been on a plate if it weren't for him. I suppose the nervousness in her address came not just from stage fright, but also from knowing how close she'd come to fucking up her career.

No wonder they'd moved fast to get Jimmy's profiles doctored. It was less than two hours after Mills and Greyson had arrived when the broadcast interrupted all UK channels. We gathered on the sofas, not realising that what was about to happen would send our lives into even more chaos than our loss already had.

She hasn't changed much aesthetically, I guess. But her demeanour was different when she took those steps from the door of the station toward the cameras and fluffy grey mics. She looked panicked, harassed. The press had been told a statement would be made, but nobody except us and the police knew what it would be about.

"Ms Browne! What's happening?"

"Alicia! Over here, is this a matter of public safety?"

She threw frantic, wide-eyed glances sideways. She was drowning in it. It fell to a large officer with a voice like a foghorn to pull her out of the quicksand.

"Hush down, ladies and gents! Questions after."

The vultures fell silent. The camera zoomed in on her, shuffling papers in her hands. Her pinky was shaking; she gripped the pages tighter. The whole of England stopped what they were doing and listened to the news of how close we came to disaster. At first, she spoke only of the uncovered plot. The spectators gasped as she detailed the planned bombings, and potential death tolls. I wondered for a moment if they'd decided to cut Jimmy out of the picture altogether.

But then, from among her pile of papers, she pulled out a photograph. Mum gasped, recognising her son's image held in the sweaty, trembling fingers of the rookie head of anti-terror.

"This information came to light because of the tragic death of a young man who has been officially named as James Lincoln." She held the photo, *that* photo, aloft. The camera zoomed in even further until our screen, *everyone's* screen, was filled with my twin's grinning ketchup-free face. "Yesterday, at 2:14pm, James fell to his death from a bridge over the A406. Amongst the drivers involved in the ensuing collision was a Mr Knight, who we now believe to be the leader of the notorious criminal gang, Gridless. In his vehicle, the officers on the scene found evidence of the planned terrorist attack. James, known to his friends and family as Jimmy, has, with his death, saved the lives of countless English citizens. Because of his actions, we were able to find and detain the terrorists in our midst before they could carry out their horrific plans."

We sat in silence. Processing. Mills and Greyson studied us, not knowing whether to speak. From the table my Shades broke the stillness with frantic beeping. I realised I was still logged into Jimmy's account.

The notifications went berserk. The hit counter stuttered through the numbers.

110 visitors.

546.

2,678.

The messages flooded in faster than the eye could read, causing the page to be in constant motion.

R.I.P.
You're a hero.
Always in our hearts.
Cheers, dude, you saved my life.
England thanks you, brave soldier.

Mum watched the deluge with an exaggerated squint before grabbing Greyson's laptop and scrolling to the bottom. She wanted to read every word, every tribute. The smile was back on her lips, even as tears fell from her eyes. He'd been right; it *was* helping her. It gave her something to hold onto, took her attention away from the fact that he was gone.

Dad said nothing. He stared at the TV without really seeing it. I used to think Dad's silences came from a sage-like wisdom. I thought he was observing and collating information, mulling things over. He was strong and capable. He let the lesser mortals react and gabble, but saved his words and actions until he knew the answers. But after years of looking to him, waiting for guidance that never came, I realised he was adrift in the world just like the rest of us. He spoke no words, not because he was deep in contemplation, but simply because he had nothing to say.

A police car pulled up outside and Greyson excused himself to go and greet them.

"What's happening now?" I asked Mills.

"That'll be the afternoon shift," he said. "They'll be stationed there until 8pm, then hand over to the graveyard shift. But don't worry, they'll not disturb you. If you felt like making them a cuppa now and again I'm sure they wouldn't object though."

I went into the kitchen and watched through the window. Two uniformed policemen positioned themselves at the gate to our front garden. Greyson clapped them on their shoulders and came back inside.

"Right," he said, "we'll be leaving you in peace now, you'll be well looked after."

They were heading to the front door when two vans pulled up.

"There we are. That didn't take 'em long," Mills said gesturing outside. "I was hoping to get away before they arrived. Never mind."

"Who is it?" Mum asked.

"Journalists," Mills said. He strode to the kitchen window and pulled down the shutters. "They'll be wanting to talk to you, but I'd advise against it for the time being. My officers won't let them bother you. I'll drop by tomorrow, see how you're doing and talk about the next step."

"Next step?" Dad broke his silence.

"Well, you'll be wanting to leave your house sometime," he said, "and they won't quit until they've had an interview, or a statement. Trust me, I can tell you from experience there's no point trying to avoid them, you can't. The best you can do, and the best we can do for you, is to make it on *your* terms. When you're ready, we can prep you, and you can give them what they want, but in your own way. You can give a scheduled statement to all of them at once, like Ms Browne did, or an exclusive to just one. We'll go over your options tomorrow, there's no hurry. But it might be best to get it out of the way before the funeral."

None of us had even thought about a funeral yet. Greyson picked up on the shock on our faces.

"We can help with that too," he said. "If you want it to be private, we can close the roads so the crowds don't interrupt."

Crowds. It seemed insane. There would be crowds at a funeral for a drugged-up teen? But just as we were all trying to get to grips with the idea, a bridge appeared on the TV. Its rails were covered in flowers, and ribbons, and people were lining up to leave their offerings.

"Oh my God!" Mum thumped back down in her chair, as if she'd been kicked. "Is that where it… where he…?"

Greyson looked solemn. "Yes, ma'am," he replied.

She burst into tears again.

If there's one thing the English are good at, it's standing in line, waiting their turn. They queued in single file, all along the pavement and up the steps to the bridge. One at a time they stepped onto it, laid down their tribute and solemnly walked on. Some dabbed at their eyes with tissues, some simply stared at the ground. The reporter approached a young woman in the line who was holding a small bunch of carnations, and a hand-written card that said simply *Thank You*.

"May I ask why you've come here today?" the reporter quizzed.

"I feel I have to," the young woman replied. "I have to say thank you. Jimmy saved my life."

"By that you mean you could have potentially been involved in the blast?"

"Oh, definitely, there's no question in my mind. I'm always on the Circle line at that time in the morning. If it wasn't for Jimmy… well, it doesn't bear thinking about."

The camera panned out, and showed her ripe, enlarged stomach. Mum gasped.

"Can I have a show of hands?" the reporter called out to the crowd. "Who here would have lost their lives next week if it hadn't been for Jimmy?"

Dozens of hands went up. Mum inhaled sharply.

"So there you have it, Hugh," the reporter addressed the camera. "All these people, and hundreds more, are today feeling a huge debt of gratitude, as well as immense sorrow, for the sacrifice of this brave young man. We are getting reports that several major employers, who would have suffered the decimation of their staff, have announced that they will be closing, as a mark of respect, during his funeral, whenever that may be. And of course, we mustn't forget that among the potential victims who are today counting their lucky stars, and giving thanks to Jimmy Lincoln, is the Prime Minister himself. Jeremy Cole was of course scheduled to be at Victoria at the time of the attack, leading police to suspect that he was in fact the main target. He is expected to release a statement. For now, though, London is united in shock, and gratitude. Jonathan Kingsley, BBC news, above the A406."

"All those people," Mum shook her head slowly. "Dear God. He saved all those people."

Dad and I exchanged a look. I don't think we ever really understand another person just from a knowing look. I think we just reaffirm what we ourselves are thinking. But I took it to mean that we both knew the heroic angle had more holes than ten square miles of putting greens, but for Mum's sake we'd not voice our thoughts.

"That's what we've been trying to tell you, ma'am," Greyson said. "Your son was a hero."

She nodded, smiling through the tears. "I always knew. I always knew he was special. I just wish he wasn't gone. But… all those lives… It's what he would have wanted." She cleared her throat, wiped her eyes and stood up suddenly. "It shouldn't be private," she announced.

"Ma'am?"

"The funeral. Any of it. This is what he died for. And people want to thank him. We mustn't be selfish. He wasn't just our Jimmy, he means so much to everyone now. If they want to show their respect they ought to be allowed to."

"Janey," Dad stepped forward, tried to put his hand on her shoulder but she pushed it away, "I don't think—"

"No, Dave. Don't. I won't let you change my mind on this.

He was *my* boy, my baby. I know what he would have wanted. He gave his life. It's only natural people will want to thank him. He deserves that."

Mills shuffled awkwardly. "Well," he said, "there's no need to make any decisions now. We'll come back tomorrow, give you folks time to think things over."

They hastened out of the door, sensing marital discord, I guess. I left my parents arguing downstairs, and watched from my bedroom window as the waiting media swarmed around the two detectives.

I turned on some music, to drown out the sound of my parents' heated exchange. Afternoon turned to evening, but I stayed alone in my room reading the online comments sent to Jimmy. My stomach hurt from a hunger my mouth could not face satisfying, and the goosebumps that rippled down my arms with every message commending his 'sacrifice' filled me with unease.

16

When I awoke the next morning I was shivering, and the closed curtains felt oppressive. I threw them back, bathing my room in the glare of summer morning sunlight, letting the warmth of it thaw me.

They were still there, the news vans and the policemen. A young woman with a blonde bob approached the largest vehicle, a cardboard tray full of Starbucks cups in her hands. She banged on the side of the van and her dishevelled colleagues emerged with half smiles, wiping grit from their eyes and gratefully receiving their morning pick-me-up.

A guy with a dark, bushy beard sat in the open drivers' door, sipping at his coffee. It was only when he glanced up at my window that I realised I was staring. He squinted, then waved.

"Rosa?" he yelled. His voice was muffled by the double-glazing, so it sounded as though he had a mouth full of marshmallow. "Hey, Rosa! Can we talk to you?"

I stepped back quickly so I could no longer see them, or they I. But when I chanced a peek I could see it was too late, the buzz had already started. Mr Bushy Beard had got them all excited. Burly men shouldered huge cameras in haste, twisting at the lenses and pointing them at my window. Huge fluffy grey mics were being extended. The more beautiful of the people smoothed down their fringes, straightened crooked ties, or applied lipstick in wing mirrors, ready to be on screen at a moment's notice.

I rushed out of my room, shutting the door behind me.

Downstairs the light was muted by the drawn shutters. The odd beam breaking through the cracks played host to dust particles locked in their spiral dance. Mum, fully dressed in a cream blouse and pencil skirt, bustled in the kitchen, spraying and wiping the granite counters with yellow-gloved hands.

"Rosa," she looked up, and arched an eyebrow at me, "did you open your curtains?"

"Yes, but… Mum, what are you doing?"

"Well, don't," she said, scrubbing the hob so vigorously her boobs jiggled. "Mills said to keep them closed, for now. And what does it look like I'm doing? They're coming back today, remember? And goodness knows who else. There's so much to do."

She pulled off her yellow Marigolds and hung them over the kitchen tap.

"I've ordered a suit online," she said, pulling her Shades from her pocket. "Would you like to see it? I went for grey. I thought black was a bit… depressing."

"A suit?" My eyes flicked round the kitchen. Everything was sparkling, even the floor tiles. I glanced at the clock. It was only six thirty. "Who for?"

"Jimmy, of course! I know we can't have an open casket, but that's no reason not to do things properly. I've been thinking about hymns."

"Hymns?"

"Yes. I'm leaning toward 'Amazing Grace', what do you think?"

What did I *think*? I thought she'd lost her mind. "Jimmy was an atheist!"

"Oh, don't talk rot. Even if he was he's not now, is he!"

"What do you mean?"

"Well, he's in heaven now. So, yes, you've made up my mind. 'Amazing Grace' it is. Perhaps we ought to have something modern too. What was his favourite song, do you know?"

"'Saturday Morning Pitchers' by Apocalyptic Zombies," I said, without missing a beat.

Mum screwed up her nose. "Oh, that won't do. That won't do at all. What was the one that was Christmas number one last year? You know, it was everywhere... such a pretty, uplifting tune, and she had a marvellous voice. Something about walking in the light?"

I knew exactly the song she was talking about. The one sung by that year's largely prosthetic 'next big thing'. The video featured her wandering around a picturesque snow-covered village, wearing a white fur coat that was open at the front to show the bikini underneath.

"Jimmy hated that song."

"No, he didn't! It was beautiful. Everyone loved it."

"Yes. That's *why* he hated it. He couldn't stand manufactured pap, he even used to rant about it!"

"He downloaded it!"

"Yes, *for you*!"

"Oh come now, Rosa. There's no need to get upset, you'll wake your father. Fine, we'll think of something else. But nothing to do with zombies or drugs. Something fitting."

I couldn't think of anything *more* fitting than zombies or drugs. But I kept my mouth shut. As much as this calm and efficient version of Grieving Mother unnerved me, it was preferable to the terrifying out-of-control howling. I resolved to tread carefully, so as not to wake the primal beast.

Greyson returned later that morning, without Mills. Instead he was accompanied by two other police officers, both female. He made a beeline for my father. The older woman with a double chin and a non-threatening mumsy demeanour struck up conversation with my mother. The younger, thin-as-a-rake officer with a cropped and streaked hairdo that was meant to be 'subversive' in a conformist way, smiled at me and said, "Hiya, Rosa, I'm Officer Jinks, but you can call me Zara."

Zara Jinks? Seriously?

It was like one of those kids' puzzles where you have to draw a line connecting people to the correct tools of their trade. Can you help the farmer find his tractor? What does the milkman drive? They were the workers, and we were the objects. It could have been called 'Link the officer to the Lincoln', and it was as transparent as any game devised for preschoolers.

They brought with them 'exciting' news (or 'hot buzz' as call-me-Zara put it. I don't think that was ever a phrase, even in the noughties). Cole was coming.

"The Prime Minister? Coming *here*?" Mum's eyes darted round the coving, checking for errant cobwebs.

"Yes," Greyson smiled. "He wants to give you his condolences, and his thanks, in person."

"Well, that really is so thoughtful. Isn't it, Dave? Rosa?"

Dad and I exchanged another one of those looks. But this time I couldn't keep the peace.

"You're not actually going to let him come in our house, are you?" I was speaking directly to Dad, and I swear I saw him shrink several inches as my question hit him.

"Rosa, now come on." He was looking at the floor. Dear God, he was going to agree to it. In that instant an unwanted truth hit me. He was a coward. An armchair dissenter, with no courage in his convictions. Just as the well-to-do of my childhood village only showed their bigotry in the privacy of the polling booth, he would only profess his liberalism behind closed doors. My rock wasn't a rock at all. It had been a mirage, a clump of sand that would wash away on a hostile tide.

"You called him Hitler!"

Mum's eyes widened in horror. Dad flushed red. Greyson just gave a disarming smile.

"Rosa, this situation transcends political opinion," he said. "Your brother saved his life, and hundreds of others. He's not coming here as the Prime Minister, he doesn't care how your father voted. He's coming as a man who owes another man his life, and wants to express his thanks. That's all."

"Bullshit!" I wasn't angry at Greyson, or even Cole – not in that moment. I was angry with Dad. The façade I had chosen to see had slipped. He was no longer a strong, wise and righteous guardian. He was a weedy, balding, middle-aged man tossed about like flotsam. I had no ally. I was completely alone.

"Rosa Louise Lincoln!" The cords in Mum's neck bulged as she middle-named me. "Go to your room!"

"With pleasure!" I stormed upstairs. I could tell from the tone of Greyson's voice that he was still wearing a sticking-plaster smile. He harped on to my parents about anger being a natural part of the grieving process. I slammed my door.

I pulled the curtains closed again, although no one was angling for a glimpse of me anymore. They were busy setting up for Cole's arrival. I wasn't important.

I don't know how many minutes passed, cradling my despair, before the knock on the door.

"Rosa?" It was Jinks. "It's Zara, honey, can I come in?"

I didn't answer, but she opened the door anyway, stepping in nonchalantly, surveying the posters on my walls.

"Sweet crib," she said, sitting down beside me on the bed. "Politics is a drag, huh?" Oh fabulous. She was going to try to 'engage me on my level', except of course she had no idea what my level really was. "I mean, none of them really get what's important to our generation, right?"

Our generation? If she'd been a teen pregnancy statistic she could've been my mum. If there's one thing my teenage-self hated more than bullshit, it was condescension.

"Actually I think politics is very important. I care about the world we live in," I said. And I'll confess to the self-righteous tone. I wanted to show her she wasn't dealing with an average teen. I didn't realise, of course, that that's exactly what every average teen does.

"Well, that's great. You're a clever young woman, Rosa.

Really clever." There was a slight sneer to her words that made me feel a little uneasy, and put me on the defensive.

"And I hate the ERP," I snapped.

Zara laughed. I thought, for a second, she was going to continue to pursue the 'I'm your buddy' tactic and agree with me. Say something like, 'Yeah, they're a bunch of twats, but hey they won't be in much longer.'

But I was wrong.

"Well, guess what, honey?" she said, her whole demeanour changing. She crossed the legs that had been slightly open in a casual, relaxed manner, and her smile was half-lipped now. "Thcy don't care."

I was shocked by the change in her tone. I didn't know how to respond. I opened my mouth to speak, but nothing came out.

"That's right, princess," she continued. "They don't give a shit what your adolescent ill-informed opinion is. They're busy running the country. So you can sit here nursing wishy-washy ideals of liberalism and kumba-fucking-ya all you like, but not one single shit will be given in Westminster over your opinion."

I stood up. "How dare you speak to me like that?"

"What's the matter, chickadee? Choking on your entitlement?" She stood up, grabbed my right wrist and dug her fingernails in, hard. She brought her face close to mine and looked me straight in the eye. "You listen to me. I don't care how you feel about Cole. This country doesn't care how you feel. No one cares how you feel, not today. Go exercise your democratic right at the polls. Stage a fucking protest at whatever god-awful uni you end up at for all I care. But right here, right now, you are going to play nice. You will shake his hand, you will smile. You will say nothing political at all, to anyone. This is about your brother, not you. So get the fuck over yourself, or I'll come down on you like a hail of shit."

I wish I could go back, now that I'm older and less easily blind-sided. Slip through some wormhole, and be back in my eighteen-year-old body. I'd slug her across the face for one thing. For another, I'd use any one of the magnificent comebacks I've constructed in hindsight. But my stuttering inaction remains another regret. No adult had ever spoken to me like that before. I was stunned, and intimidated.

"I don't have the time or the inclination to babysit your angst," she continued. "You've made your views clear, now you will accept you are not the one in charge and comply. Do we understand one another?"

I nodded and she let go of my wrist. I pulled my top down to cover the red marks her grip had left.

"Good." She smiled. "You know, Rosa, you don't know as much about life as you think you do. Not yet. But that's okay. When you step out of your privilege and into the big wide world you'll see how naïve you are. And your priorities will change. Everyone's do."

She wasn't wrong, of course. Everyone does change their priorities when they get older. When you're young you don't give much of a shit about the things adults stress over. Matching towels, keeping the lawn tidy to impress the neighbours, special offers on cereal. You see it for what it is. Bullshit. Gilded paint on the bars of a cage. But, at some point, a switch flips in your brain and these things start to matter. Most people would say their angry, self-righteous teenage self was misguided, naïve. But maybe that person was the truest version of themselves they have ever been. Maybe the shift in priorities comes, not from maturity, but from more years of exposure to the status quo. More years of watching their TV, of reading their news. Endless days of paying bills, and being surrounded by the conformity of adult company. Maybe it's socialisation, not discovery. Older doesn't always mean wiser. Sometimes it just means jaded, and indoctrinated.

I wonder how many middle-aged people would survive the judgement of their teenage self?

17

As for *my* teenage self, it had been beaten into submission. Both by the shock of Jinks' aggression, and the feeling I was completely alone in my objections.

Nothing was said when I slunk back downstairs, and Jinks had replastered a smile on her floppy-fringed face. The house was all bustle, and briefing, pushing aside the clouds of grief for a while. Which even I was grateful for, begrudgingly.

The press, it seems, can smell VIPs on the breeze. They began clicking their cameras, and vying for positions, several seconds before the town car turned onto our road. Guards and police gathered around, holding back the reporters. One of them must have gone to the same training school as Officer Foghorn, as his commanding boom silenced them.

"There will be a statement shortly," he bellowed. "Please step back, ladies and gents."

They complied, forming a wide semicircle around the car. Liver Lips stepped out, straightened up and brushed himself down. Today the tie was yellow.

The first thing that struck me was how much shorter he was than I had imagined. In comparison to the officers either side he looked so small, so inoffensive and insignificant. A pussycat trooping with lions. The next thing that surprised me was how charming he was.

If the hypothetical game of join the dots had been in place,

I would have struggled to connect the sincere, humble-looking man with the rhetoric and policy I knew he stood for. As soon as the front door closed behind him, putting walls between us and the cameras, the pomp and officiousness of the Commons was entirely gone. Shed like a skin.

He spoke no words at first, just took my mother's hand and kissed it. Holding it between his palms he looked her straight in the eyes. Then, as if overcome, threw his arms around her in an embrace. When he pulled away his eyes glistened. Turning to my father he reached out for his hand and shook it vigorously. Then his gaze settled on me.

He gave me a half-smile, his brows furrowed. It was the sort of look a passer-by might give a starving puppy by the roadside, in lieu of food. Sympathetic, concerned, but for no more time than it took to turn the corner.

He put his palms, those fat greasy palms, on my shoulders. Then those lips, the ones that have uttered so much damage, the keepers of the tombstone teeth, touched the top of my head.

Finally, he broke the silence.

"Forgive me." There was no authority in his tone. His voice was dull and scratchy. There was no polished, confident air to his words. No rhythm, no punch. He sounded deflated. "I don't know how to express how I feel meeting you all. I am so very sorry, and so very awed."

Mum looked as though she might cry.

"May I get you some tea, Prime Minister?" The English answer to everything.

"Why, yes. Thank you. You are too kind."

Mum rushed off to the kitchen, the rest of us meandered into the lounge. I clocked Jinks checking her reflection in the hallway mirror. She straightened her blouse in such a way that it settled a few centimetres lower than before, and showed the tiniest hint of the crescent of her cleavage. She approached Cole, her face set in a professional smile.

"Is there anything we can do for you, sir?" she asked.

"Ah," he said, smiling and shaking her hand, "the Public Information Department! Backbone of the country. I should have known you would be on the scene taking care of the family. Sterling work. Thank you for your concern, Officer..."

"Jinks."

"Officer Jinks. Beautiful name. But I am here simply to express my sympathies, and thanks, to these marvellous citizens. I don't need anything."

Jinks nodded, smiled and took a seat directly opposite Cole, leaning ever-so-slightly forward with her back straight, affording him the best possible view of her assets.

I wish I could say I sat there seething, full of righteous hatred for the tyrant in our midst. But as we all sat, sipping from the undersized china mugs, and Cole talked, I started to see *why*. Why crowds lapped up his silver-tongued words, why he commanded such loyalty from his followers, and why Jinks was so desperate to impress.

I had only ever watched him on TV, through a filter of preconception. My impressions coloured first by my father's opinions. I'd only ever heard him speak of politics, and my disgust at his stance made the words sound jagged and poisonous before they were even spoken. To me he was always dressed in the villain's garb, speaking words I was predisposed to boo and hiss at. But now we were backstage, the make-up was off and the words unscripted. He was just a man.

He spoke not of scroungers, immigrants, or English Pride, but of loss, grief and understanding. He turned to me and told me of his own brother's death, when he was fifteen. Of seeing the light fade from his eyes when his ailing heart gave out, the feeling of being adrift without his sibling. The passion in his eyes almost moved me to tears. He looked at the carpet, hands clasped together between his knees, as he spoke of his gratitude. Of how he had been pacing all night, thinking about how close he came to being killed. How our loss had saved his life and he couldn't ever begin to repay that. The circles under his eyes seemed to qualify him, and the almost whispered tone added authenticity to his words.

For a short time, as we sat listening to him, I felt the weight of his presence smooth down my objections and I thought that Greyson had been right. This transcended politics. This wasn't about the ERP; this wasn't even about the Prime Minister. He hadn't come here for any nefarious reason. He was just a man. Just a man who owed his life to another man, and knew how lucky he had been. Just a man who understood the sharp ache of loss and was overwhelmed with gratitude. Just a man.

Just an exceptionally clever, manipulative man.

18

"You need spare no expense for the funeral." Cole took a digestive from the plate on the coffee table. "The government will cover all costs, and all of my resources are at your disposal."

"Oh." Mum looked flustered. "Oh that's very kind, but we couldn't possibly—"

He waved a hand, swatting her objections away. "Madam, it is the very least we can do. That's not to say it need be a public affair, you can keep it private if you wish, and our officers will enforce that. Anything you want."

"Well," Mum's eyes darted to Dad, then me, then back to Cole, "I was just saying yesterday, when we saw how many people have been touched by Jimmy's death, it would be selfish not to allow them to pay their respects, if that's what they want to do…"

Cole smiled, tombstones bared. "Say no more, Mrs Lincoln. I am overwhelmed by your generosity and public spirit, even in your time of grief. Of course, I would expect nothing less from the woman who raised Jimmy Lincoln. How about St Paul's?"

"St Paul's?" Mum nearly choked on her garibaldi.

"I think a state funeral is more than fitting for someone who has given so much to their country. We can televise the service, or not, as you wish. People will be content to line the funeral route if you want to keep the actual service private. Anyway, the PIDs will help you decide all of that. As I say, everything is at your disposal. Utilise any resource you wish."

"This really is too much."

"No, Madam. No, it's not nearly enough. But don't worry, I have come up with ways to honour Jimmy properly. Enduring ways."

"What do you mean?" Dad had a tongue in his mouth after all. I'd begun to wonder.

"Well," Cole put down his cup and leaned forward, elbows resting on his knees. It looked jarringly casual. "While I never had the privilege of meeting Jimmy in person, it seems to me that he was the type of morally upstanding young man who always put others before himself, am I right?"

Ha!

Mum nodded emphatically. "Oh yes," she beamed, "absolutely."

"I thought as much," Cole continued. "So, while a proper funeral is most definitely in order, I get the feeling that he would have wanted something more substantial, something that would benefit others. Something that would benefit the country he died saving. Now that would be a far more fitting tribute to an altruistic man. I shall be giving a speech to the press outside in a few minutes, and I'll outline it all then. But let's just say I am determined that his death will not be in vain. I shall be taking decisive action to ensure such terror can never threaten us again, and to get justice for Jimmy."

Justice for Jimmy? What were they going to do? Demolish the bridge? Arrest the tarmac? It was ludicrous. I wanted to laugh, or cry. But Jinks tightened her grip on her cup, and raised an eyebrow at me. I wilted in my chair and kept my sass to myself.

It all wrapped up pretty quickly after that. Cole stood up, and began the slow shuffle to the door that people do when they want to leave without being impolite. Cups chinked back into their saucers, spurious pleasantries were exchanged.

Mum spewed gratitude, Cole gave polite insistences he was the thankful one. A very British goodbye all round.

"Let me accompany you to the officers outside, sir." Jinks held the front door open for him.

"Thank you, Officer Jinks." His eyes flicked over her figure. "Thank you all so much, once again. You might want to close the door after I've gone, I'm afraid the media are a necessary evil in these times. I shall see you all at St Paul's, but in the meantime please feel free to get in touch if you need anything, anything at all."

So apparently he'd just invited himself to my brother's funeral.

19

You don't expect history to be made outside your front door, with the lilac drapes at your bedroom window wonky in the background. But that's exactly what happened. Our facias became iconic, the speech having been broadcast so many times. I think Mum put a few extra thousand on the asking price just because of that. I suppose, in her perceived martyrdom, it was about survival not greed. It's amazing how you can spin your reality to believe owning 'nothing but' a four-bedroom London house makes you virtually destitute.

Cole took up position at a lectern that had been placed in front of our house, and Mum turned on the TV to watch his speech. It was surreal. Even as the crowd were shhhed and he shuffled his papers ready to begin, I could see on the screen the shadows of Greyson and Jinks, who were loitering in our kitchen, watching the spectacle.

"I have come here today, to the home of Jimmy Lincoln, to pay my respects to his family, and to express my deep, enduring gratitude on behalf of the English people." The polish was back. His voice commanding, authoritative. He stood tall (though a little shorter to me now, as I knew him to be no more than 5'6". I wondered if camera crews were instructed always to film him from an angle that gave him greater stature.

He looked straight at the camera, many hours of coaching

by Heath having given him the skill to make such a constant gaze seem natural, not creepy.

"I know you will all join me in offering the Lincolns your thoughts, and prayers, at this most difficult time. We all owe Jimmy Lincoln a huge debt. Not just because of the lives that would have been lost, but because he has afforded us an opportunity. An opportunity to reflect on what could have happened. An opportunity to examine our security without first having had to endure the decimation of our beloved capital. And, most importantly, an opportunity to learn and to change.

"From speaking with his family, I have learned a little more about the man to whom we owe so much. He was a man who was the very best of us. He was a man who believed. Believed in England, believed in reclamation. He was one of the first to volunteer for the Citizen Scheme. He was a man who put his country before himself. So, I feel, and I know you will agree, that it is of the utmost importance that we honour his sacrifice. We cannot, we *will* not, let his death be in vain. Therefore, my ministers and I have devised several new initiatives in response to the lessons we have learned. The lessons that Jimmy has taught us."

A shudder ran through me, but I was transfixed.

"I know you are all as disgusted and angry as I am that the evildoers came so close to carrying out their vile plot. I pledge to you that they will be severely punished. Both as a deterrent to those who would threaten our freedoms, and in the name of justice. Yesterday I was told by my advisors that the law does not allow us to give them the same sentence they would have received had their heinous schemes come to fruition. I replied, in no uncertain terms, that in that case the law needs to change!"

The crowds that had begun to gather whooped. Even the reporters clapped.

"It is wrong, it is unjust. Because let me make this clear to you, ladies and gentlemen, there is no doubt in anyone's mind that these cancerous traitors in our midst would have committed their atrocities had Jimmy not intervened. Therefore, they should be punished as if they had. The streets need to be safe; England needs to be safe! I am immediately implementing a Law of Intent for all cases of terrorism. This means that if you plot to kill or maim English citizens, you will stand trial as if the deed had been done. So rest assured, these filthy architects of destruction will be charged with the murder of three thousand English citizens. If found guilty they will never, ever walk the streets again!"

Three thousand? Was he just plucking numbers out of the air?

"And I am sending the message, loud and clear, that I will not be swayed by terrorists! The planned unveiling of our new initiative, the mobile Citizen Chip vans, will go ahead. This is what Jimmy would have wanted. You will be able to come along, to any one of hundreds of conveniently placed points across the country, and show your support. Both for English Reclamation and for Jimmy Lincoln, by receiving your chip, just as he did.

"Now more than ever it is vital for us to unite, to stand tall, to send a message to those who would destroy what we are building. We are England! We will no more lie down and play dead. We will no more tolerate the destruction of our values and traditions! We are not an easy target for scroungers and terrorists from across the globe! We are a country in which hard work and loyalty is rewarded. A country which *demands* that our streets be once again safe, and our children once again have the opportunities they deserve. If you are not with us, you are against us! We will no longer tolerate freeloaders, or those who wish to cause harm to the people of this fine country.

"Therefore, from April the first next year, our vital services will no longer be available to anyone who does not have a Citizen Chip. We will not spend our resources on giving health care and education to the very people who seek to destroy us!

They cannot expect to come here and be housed, healed, and educated. They cannot take vital funds away from citizens, only to throw our hospitality back in our faces in the form of terror! Our own, home-grown terrorists can no longer stay off the grid if they wish to partake of the fruits of our labours. I have a message for Gridless and all their ilk: you are biting the hand that feeds you, and it will no longer be tolerated. If you are not IN the system you cannot expect to take FROM the system! English taxes for English workers!"

I was so shocked I spoke aloud without meaning to.

"That's suicide," I said. "Political suicide."

I glanced at Jinks, expecting a scowl, but she just smiled. I guess she didn't care if I made a spectacle of myself now that Cole was gone.

"You think?" she asked, sidling up to me.

"Well, yes. Public opinion is against the chips, and he's making them compulsory? He's digging his own grave!" I'd thought him cleverer than that. I couldn't believe that with less than a year to go before the next election he was going to do something so unpopular. Jinks just laughed.

"Jimmy changed the game, honey," she leant down to my ear and whispered, a gravelled edge to her tone, "and Cole just played checkmate."

It didn't take long for me to realise she was right. I'd been too caught up with losing Jimmy, and the chaotic insanity of the media attention and VIP visit, to even consider how the public at large were reacting. The world had been charging forward outside these walls, while we had been frozen in our personal grief. And Jimmy had indeed changed everything.

Before Jimmy died the opinion polls had not been Cole's friend. The last stat I'd seen said that 75% of the country strongly disagreed with the Citizen Chips. But I hadn't been watching anything, other than the mourners lining up on the bridge, since his death. There wasn't just grief and gratitude out there. There was anger, hostility and the ERP's old ally: fear.

It's often said that the enemy of my enemy is my friend, and it seemed the public were embracing that concept. Gridless was formed in objection to the chips, and had planned to stop Cole's new initiative (and despatch him in the process). Now that they were public enemy number one, to criticise the chipping scheme was tantamount to aligning yourself with terrorists.

The street-level reactions were all the same. Women carrying shopping bags were stopped by reporters for their opinions, and all seemed to agree that the most important thing was public safety. They declared they would be getting their chips as soon as possible, all in honour of Jimmy. No one seemed to care they were effectively being forced into it.

"Why would anyone object to something that will make the streets safer?" one woman with a leopard-print top and broken teeth remarked. "Unless they got something to hide."

Thanks to Jimmy, the chips had gone from being Cole's worst PR problem to the jewel in his crown, and the next election was in the bag.

Even the archbishop, taking the (*seven*) steps to the microphone in front of us, has the device. I wonder if he's privy to its extra function. He opens with a prayer, but all I can think about is that he's wearing his long robes in the blistering sun. I wonder if he's as hot as I am. Probably not, I've got the Semtex and shrapnel to contend with after all. Still, he looks out of place. Exposed. No gilded platform high above the rabble, no statues of cherubim blowing trumpets surrounding him. Not like at Jimmy's funeral.

It's not the same man standing in front of me now of course. But it's hard to distinguish. The robes make them amorphous in my mind. I guess there's something unique, individual, under there somewhere, but you'd never know. I guess the same could be said for the funeral itself. We had gathered to remember a real person, a person with many layers and a personality all their own. A person who had flaws... But you'd never know.

There was nothing of Jimmy there that day. My own

countenance was scrutinised by the press. There were lots of theories as to why I didn't cry at my twin's funeral. Too overwhelmed, in shock, keeping it together for the sake of my parents. At least, those were the kind ones. Other gems, mostly from the tabloids, declared I was a cold hard bitch or just a jealous sibling. But none of them were right. None of them realised that nothing, *nothing* about the service reflected the brother I loved in any way. The bishop only spoke his name once for Christ's sake.

The whole thing was surreal. Detached. From the moment we stepped out of our door, and into the waiting hearse, nothing seemed real, and I don't think it ever has since.

PART 2

TERESA

1

Greg hands me a coffee that tastes like dishwater. He lingers behind me, watching my screen. He sips his own latte, but I don't think he actually tastes it. He's fixated on Rosa. Can't take his eyes off her. I give a little snort when I realise I'm exactly the same with Cole. I'm supposed to be taking it all in, watching for problems, but my gaze keeps settling on his face. It occurs to me that Greg and I are both about to watch the people we've been manipulating get blown to smithereens.

I don't know how he feels about it. He plays it cool, but I suspect our little Rosa has gotten under his skin more than he lets on. I can kind of empathise. Not that I care about Cole; I have nothing but contempt for that disgusting limp-dicked bastard. But still, there's a strange unease mixed in with my relief that I'll never have to feel his slimy tongue on my body again. Three years is a long time. It's almost like the end of an era.

My work Shades beep, a message from Greyson.

Hey Jinks, hope you're feeling better?

God, I hate that arrogant bastard.

"Problem, Terri?" Greg looks jumpy. I wish he'd chill out. He's starting to make me nervous.

"No. Just Greyson. Nothing PID related, don't worry."

"Okay." He exhales, and paces the room behind me. "She looks nervous. Do you think she looks nervous?"

I roll my eyes. "Of course she's fucking nervous. What do you expect?"

He's really starting to annoy me now. Not least because everyone's so bloody pleased with him. He's the man of the hour. They don't know how easy it was for him, how fucked up she was anyway.

Me, I'm a pro. It takes a hell of a lot more skill to do what I've done. I should just be pleased, I know. It doesn't matter how we got here, it's the endgame that's important. The bigger picture. The future. History will never speak my name. In a few hours the whole world will have Rosa Lincoln on their lips, but Teresa Clarke will forever be unknown. It doesn't matter.

He's playing Rosa's statement on his Shades. I recognise the little sob, like a hiccoughing seal. The guys in the other room are already hacked into the networks; it's good to go. It'll be broadcast everywhere as soon as the bomb goes off and takes sad little Rosa with it into infamy.

I make a deliberate effort to look away from Cole. I can see a slight bulge just above his chin and I know he's picking his teeth with his tongue. I can almost hear the squelch of saliva. I turn my attention to Rosa. Greg's right, she's looking nervous. But then she always does. Apart from a few extra lines on her face, and a few less freckles, she looks no different from when I first met her. Pathetic and startled. She has a slight air of defiance that she thinks makes her come across as intelligent, but really just makes her seem stand-offish. She's got the same speckled blue eyes as her degenerate brother, but none of his charisma. The camera doesn't love her. She looks washed out in every picture.

Even though we're on the same side, and this couldn't happen without her, I just can't bring myself to sympathise. She talks of the higher cause, but thinks of nothing but her own pathetic self-pity. Daniel would tell me not to judge, that everyone's struggle is important, every person's experience unique. He'd talk about the bigger picture, the goal. I wish I could speak to him, just once. He'd be so proud of all I've achieved, of what I'm about to do.

But I haven't seen him for years. All because of James fucking Lincoln.

2

I was at work when the news came through. Greyson and I had been sent to the television studios to check up on *The Raids*. We had to make sure the producers were playing the game by our rules.

It was the latest in a long line of programmes that demonised people under the guise of 'informative entertainment'. The concept was nothing new, there were plenty of similar tricks used when I was a kid. Back then the enemies they wanted everyone to blame for all the country's ills were benefit claimants. My foster mum used to tune in every week, to indulge in a spot of self-righteous condemnation. These days it was the illegals under the spotlight.

The Raids was the most popular of all the ERP-funded shows. More than seven million patriots tuned in three times a week to watch immigrants being dragged from their hovels, hopefully kicking and spitting.

The show had become one of the best propaganda tools the government had, so it was closely monitored. They were under strict instructions to portray the illegals in a certain way. Under no circumstances were they allowed to broadcast any of them speaking English, unless they were swearing. No subtitles. If you can communicate with someone it makes them seem less different, less threatening. We wanted filth. Degenerates fighting, resisting, cursing. Not too much human interest, we couldn't have them showing any sob stories. These people had to be a drain on our society, a threat to our safety. Or, at the very least, a burden on our moral fibre.

We'd been called in because one of the runners had reported concerns over the new producer. Apparently he was one of those 'artistic integrity' types, trying to make a name for himself rather than doing what he was told. He was good, though, the ratings were up since he took over. They didn't want to lose him if they could help it. So they decided he needed 'guidance' (which was the official way of saying he needed to be reminded who paid his wages and taken down a peg or two).

When we arrived at the studio the problem was obvious. The guy in question, a flamboyant little ginger tosser, was clearly spoiling for a ruck. They were editing footage of a young Ukrainian family being rounded up. The father only had one arm; he'd been subject to torture in his own country. The shots had to be cut so you couldn't see the stump. There were no two ways about it. Public sympathy for the illegals was not to be encouraged, that was fundamental. Let that in and it wouldn't get through the censors. Everyone knew it.

But this twat's ego was bigger than his common sense. He pranced around, waving scripts in Greyson's face.

"It's a perfect shot, it's the money shot. Look!" He tapped at the screen and showed us the footage. The mother was ranting in her own language. Perfect. The broken windows and car tyres in the background. Sublime. Eldest kid kicking the cameraman, youngest covered in dirt. Bingo. But through it all there he was, right beside them. A drained, haggard-looking man, eyes glistening with tears, and that fucking ill-stitched stump. No. If the cameraman had had enough sense to film him from the other angle then maybe. But as it stood there was no way on Cole's scorched earth that was staying in.

Greyson let the guy rant and rave about how the scene was 'quintessentially *Raids*' until he ran out of steam. Then he spoke slowly. "Sir, all we're asking is can you edit him out?"

"What?" The producer looked as though he might have an embolism. "No, I can't edit him out. The kid's leaning on him for Christ's sake."

Greyson shrugged. "Then I'm afraid you'll have to cut it."

"It's the best scene of the week. I don't take orders from jumped-up bobbies who know nothing about cinematography."

Greyson grinned. He turned to me and raised his eyebrow.

My turn, and I was fired up for it. I'd spent the morning having to get heavy with a poor Imam who'd done nothing more than accidentally misspell a name on his accounts. But we'd shut down his mosque, the last remaining one in Islington. Ever since Cole declared it illegal for any institution to promote 'non-British values' we'd spent most of our time scrutinising temples, mosques and synagogues, looking for any slight misstep that could be interpreted as unpatriotic. I charged him with fraud, and forced him to shut the doors for good. The look in his eyes when he pleaded with me to think of his congregation, and all the work they were doing for the homeless, was playing on my mind. Persecuting the innocent was a necessary evil; I had to play the perfect PID to stay hidden. But every now and then, it pricked at my conscience.

This little shit stain in front of me was exactly what I needed to take my mind off it. People like him made my blood boil. Their protests were always egotistical, self-serving. Just like all those god-awful student activists, pretending they're trying to change society by locking themselves in a building, or holding a public rally. Ignorant glory hunters. You don't make real change by jumping on anti-establishment bandwagons and flaunting your discontent for the cameras. Real change has to come from within, hard-won by true soldiers. People who put in decades, people who play the long game with their cards to their chest. People who don't seek recognition. People like me.

I removed my Shades and put them in my back pocket. I held his gaze as I stepped forward, edging closer until I could smell the chorizo he'd had for lunch. He only came up to my chest but he didn't look away, even though he must have been straining his neck. I smiled.

"My colleague has asked you nicely to—"

"I don't give a shit! I'm trying to make *television* here, and—"

"My colleague has *asked* you, now I am *telling* you. You either edit him out, or you cut the whole scene. If you continue to make my life difficult I will not hesitate to charge you with obstructing public information, which carries a maximum sentence of ten years in prison under section twelve of the Public Information Act.'

He scowled and opened his mouth to protest. I didn't give him the chance.

"Moreover, I will personally see to it that your entire family is slandered in the press. We'll throw in some allegations of paedophilia perhaps, and you'll get passed around the shower blocks to be devoured like the milky ginger pudding you are. Because, regardless of whatever self-important delusions of grandeur you are suffering from, the fact remains that this 'jumped-up bobby' has been given direct orders from the government, which grant me the jurisdiction to deprive you of your job, your home and your liberty… and even destroy your name."

He tried to come up with a retort, but settled for storming out. The last ditch protest of someone who knows they're going to have to toe the line, but still feels the need to make a pointless show of not being happy about it.

Greyson stared at me, wondering how I'd react. He knew I didn't tolerate disrespect, or indulge pansy-ass displays of defiance. If I was pissed off (which I was most of the time, working for the enemy will do that to you), I'd usually have them back in front of me issuing a contrite apology, sometimes with their pinky bent backwards in my fist. But I was feeling generous. It was less than a week until Cole would be nothing more than a splattered mess to be scraped up outside Victoria station. I let the little twat have his last stand. It wouldn't matter in the long run. I wouldn't be a PID much longer.

The producer will never know how lucky he was that my Shades didn't ring until we were back in the car. If the news had come ten minutes earlier he'd probably still be sucking dick in prison right now. As it was we were driving through Kensington when I got the call, Greyson sporting a face-splitting grin.

"Hoo man, did you see his *face*?" he started enthusing, and I sighed inwardly. The trouble with Greyson was that he wanted to shag me, which made him act like a cross between a peacock and a puppy. When he wasn't strutting around showing off, he was bouncing around gushing about how brilliant I was. Neither stance impressed me, and both were becoming tiresome. "Oh, that was classic, Jinks. Total classic. Little prick didn't know what hit him."

"Yeah. Well, it wasn't difficult. Guys like him are all front, no nuts," I replied.

"You were amazing. It was all I could do to keep a straight face. We make a great team, eh?"

He was fishing. He wanted me to gush back about how his amicable, professional demeanour was the perfect set-up for my 'take-no-prisoners' approach. I couldn't bring myself to stroke his ego. I was actually relieved when the office called. For a few seconds anyway.

"Get back here now, guys." Leila cut to the chase, as usual. "We've got a major incident. Mills is calling a meeting in thirty minutes. All PIDS on deck."

"What's happened?" Greyson yelled out, before I could answer. Another thing that wound me up. He seemed to be incapable of letting me take calls on my own Shades without butting in.

"Terrorist plot. You won't believe it but the Met have caught him."

"Him who?"

"Public enemy number one. Knight himself."

I felt sick. The whole world started to spin. *Daniel*? They'd caught *Daniel*? It wasn't possible. He was the PIDs' number one target. We were a pain in Cole's arse. Daniel's irreverent broadcasts had managed to garner far more public support than could be tolerated. All PID officers had access to everything we had on him, and it was sweet FA. There were no leads, no informants, absolutely no trace of him at all. He was safe. *We* were safe. And we were so fucking close. I checked the PID records ten times a day. There was nothing, *nothing* to suggest we were anywhere close to finding him. This could not be happening. And if they had Daniel, what about the others? Had they raided HQ? Were any of us safe?

I cleared my throat. "How?" I hoped I didn't sound as shaky as I felt. "The trail was cold."

I'd made damn sure it was.

"You'll never guess, some drugged-up kid fell off a bridge, caused a pile up. His was one of the cars that crashed."

He'd crashed? My stomach churned. "Is he alright?"

"Who, the kid? No, he died at the scene."

"Not the kid, Knight. Is he okay? I mean, will we be able to question him?"

"Broken a few bones, I think. But don't worry, he can still talk."

"Good." I thanked God he was alive. I couldn't have held it together if not. Though maybe he'd have been better off dead. He'd never talk, and they'd never give up. I try not to think about what they must have done to him over the years. I don't even look at the records; I can't bear to imagine. If I were a better person I'd have wished him dead in the crash. My relief that he wasn't was selfish. I don't think I could keep going in this world if he wasn't in it somewhere.

3

At the office everyone was buzzing, flapping around like startled seagulls. Walking into the chaos I felt numb. All I could think about was the night before. The smell of Scotch on Daniel's breath as he hugged me, the sparkle in his eyes. He'd stroked my cheek, staring straight at me as though he were looking past all the superficial crap and into my soul.

"You did good, kid," he told me, his voice like thick silk. "Stay strong, Teresa. I'll see you on the other side."

Just five days. Five little days and it would all have been over. All the years of training, of preparing, of walking through the lion's den. I'd worked so hard for it. We all had. It was so close we could almost taste it. Teresa Clarke's passport and plane tickets were tucked behind the clock on Zara Jinks' mantelpiece. Ready to leave the lies behind. Ready to watch from across the globe as England awoke to a better future. And all because of us.

Now it was over. Pulled out from under me, leaving me giddy. Mills bustled in, and the room fell to a restless hush.

Stay strong, Teresa.

"Right," Mills put his coffee down on the desk and adjusted his trousers over his beer gut, "I know it's knocking-off time for most of you but you're gonna have to forget whatever plans you had for tonight. This is big. We're gonna have to go public much sooner than I'd like, so we need an angle. The situation is this." He pulled down the screen behind him, and brought up Daniel's mugshot. The bile churned in my guts. "We got the bastard."

Everyone cheered.

"But," Mills continued, "it's not all good news. It turns out he was even more of a menace than we thought. Which means we have some explaining to do. Somehow, as well as *not finding* the son of a bitch, we – and I'm including *all* of you in this – managed to miss the fact he's not just a hacktivist pain in the arse, he's a fucking bomb-toting terrorist too. So, right now anti-terror are jumping up and down, demanding our heads on plates. The shit is hitting the proverbial fan and it's about to cover us all. Now you know, and I know, anti-terror couldn't find their own dicks in the dark—" The department roared and clapped. "*But* they're gonna cover their own arses by flaying ours. They're claiming they would have found him themselves if we had done our jobs properly. Seeing as we can't prove otherwise, we need to do some *major* damage control. Cos I'm telling you now, Browne is not prepared to take the rap for this one, ladies and gents. If anyone starts throwing blame at anti-terror, she is gonna point her French manicures firmly in our direction. And frankly, I can't find a good reason why she shouldn't. We need to take the heat off them pronto or they'll drop us in the fire too.

"Fortunately, our chums in anti-terror are a bit busy right now rounding up the rest of Knight's team. So that buys us a few hours to work out what the fuck we're going to do about this mess."

The rest of his team?

I tried not to hyperventilate. How? What information did they have? I was supposed to warn the others if the PIDs were onto us. Was it already too late? I needed to find out exactly how much they knew.

"Sir," I squeaked. "Perhaps if you can tell us exactly what information they have, we can formulate our response?"

"Always running off the block before the pistol, aren't

you, Jinks? I was just getting to that." He perched himself of the edge of the desk, a stance he always employed when he wanted to come across as 'one of us' rather than the big boss. A stance that always made me wary.

"In a nutshell guys, the situation is this: Knight was unconscious in his car, carrying no identification. The only thing the cops on the scene found was a locked briefcase in the boot. Luckily for us, they needed to ID the guy to call his next of kin, so they had just cause to break into it. And that was when they hit pay day. Damn thing was stuffed full of blueprints, diagrams, notes… a fucking treasure trove. Plus, every page had Gridless' logo at the top. The blueprints were for ten stations on the Circle line. From the notes and diagrams it was as easy as doing a toddler's dot-to-dot to work out what they were going to do. If fate hadn't thrown us a bone, ladies and gents, then next Tuesday at 8:45 ten suicide bombers carrying nitroglycerin disguised in thermos flasks would have blown up the London Underground. The death toll would have made it the biggest terrorist attack our country has ever seen. And we had no fucking clue."

Whistles and gasps filled the room. My own shock wasn't feigned.

It was *bullshit*. Total fucking bullshit.

I shoved my hands between my legs to stop them shaking. It was a lie. A huge fucking lie. The only target was Cole. Gridless had never intended to kill innocent people.

I knew the PIDs lied to the public; it was our job. Public MISinformation Department, that's what we called ourselves behind closed doors. I'm not naïve, never have been. I knew there were things even a PID officer wasn't privy to. But I thought we got the truth, mostly. It was our job to take the truth and spin it into lies. For the 'greater good', of course. But I was wrong. We weren't as high up as I thought we were. We ourselves were being fed lies, to twist into insurmountable untruths. A tangle of bullshit so tight the end could never be found.

One bomber had become ten, one deserving target (Cole) had become hundreds of innocent victims, and all before the story even went public. We never wanted to kill people, we wanted to save them, from Cole. Nitro-fucking-glycerin? What were they on? The real plan was far more simple: One guy. One vest. One assassination. Okay, there probably would have been a bystander or two, but Tom wouldn't have pressed the button near innocents if he could help it. But they were trying to paint us as mass-murderers, even within the supposed inner circle. I felt sick.

He was talking again, and I hadn't been listening. Too caught up in righteous fury. I needed to pull myself together. Falling apart wouldn't help anyone, least of all Daniel.

"I'm sorry, sir," I interrupted. "I was taking it all in, about the plot. I missed what you just said."

He glared at me. "Please try to focus, Jinks, we're against the clock here."

I muttered a second apology and he continued.

"Right, for the benefit of Jinks, and anyone else who drifted off, I'll reiterate. Transport police tracked the journey he'd made via CCTV and number plate recognition, and managed to trace it all the way back to an industrial estate in Dagenham. No cameras in operation on the site, so they had to raid every building. But they found it. Gridless HQ. All their tech, all their weapons, even that fucking suit of armour they use in their broadcasts. Not to mention at least half a dozen terrorists happily pissing about hacking and plotting, praising Allah or whatever the fuck they do."

I gritted my teeth. Gridless had nothing to do with religion. But I'd be a fool to think they wouldn't claim every single member was a radical convert. Fuck, any decent PID would suggest it. Exaggerate the threat, blame it on Islam.

I wondered who'd been there when they raided. Who was lost? Schyler for sure, she was practically living there she was so focused. Probably Josh and Stoke too. There was nothing I could do for them now. Mills told us anti-terror were studying the footage from the A-road round the corner from HQ, looking for frequent comings and goings. Painstaking process, they had to eliminate all the legitimate workers from the industrial estate. It would take them a few hours. If the others realised what had happened they might have time to get away before anti-terror tracked them down. But how could they? We weren't going to go public until the morning, and no one was contacting each other. It was Daniel's orders. We were too close to the goal to take any risks.

They all relied on me to tell them if the police were onto anything. My stomach flipped over. I guess *they* all thought I was more in the know than I really was too. I was the lookout, the most protected. It was vital to everyone's safety that I, as the one working undercover with the enemy, was untouchable. None of us were buried deeper than me. I had no links with HQ, never even visited. Different name, different history. Kyle sorted it all out for me, created an identity and a watertight backstory so the real Teresa Clarke would be untraceable. It was essential. If I was going to be our secret weapon in the PIDs, the real me had to be invisible.

All this they did for their own security, as well as mine. An early-warning system, ready to blow my cover and help them get away at a moment's notice. I owed it to them, surely? Even it meant leaving a trail that would eventually uncover me.

"I'm sorry, sir," I stood up. I must have looked pale because Greyson reached out a hand to me. I batted him away. "I feel a little sick."

"No stomach, eh, Jinks?" Mills laughed. I wasn't listening. I dashed out of the room, down the corridor into the ladies.

I locked myself in a cubicle and sank to the floor. It was over. It was done. My friends, my comrades, my everything. Instead of stopping Cole we'd only succeeded in giving him more ammunition. He'd use this, with the help of the PIDs; he'd use it to do more damage. More oppression, more control. And thanks to Heath's press coverage, the public would worship him for doing so.

The only thing left was for me to warn the remote team, the ones who wouldn't have been at HQ during the raid; if they hadn't been tracked down already. I had their numbers memorised, though I'd never called them. It was impossible to cover your tracks over Shades. Even Kyle couldn't work that kind of miracle. Once you were on the radar every call, message and picture you'd ever sent was unearthed. That was the secret beauty of Shades. Everything was stored, for ever, in the Ever Cloud. No one had ever hacked it.

My fingers trembled as I put them on. This was it. The second I made the call, it would all be over. The cyber trail I left behind would lead them to me. I took a deep breath, trying not to think about the methods anti-terror used to extract information. Trying not to think about the nerve stimulators I knew they'd been developing.

It was my role. My sacrifice, for the greater good. It didn't matter if my part came to an end, as long as there were others left to continue the fight.

And what if there weren't? The thought hit me like an electric current. Hadn't I just learned that I wasn't in the loop after all? What if they already suspected there was an inside man? What if Mills was lying? Maybe they had them all already, but were withholding the facts, hoping others would expose themselves? What if I was playing right into their hands? The others could be in custody already; if I added myself to the pile there'd be no one left. No one to rise from the ashes and start again. No hope.

And even if some of the remote team hadn't yet been caught, would they really carry on the mission, or would they run? Leave the rest of us to rot while they fled the country? Joss, Rach, Kit... Were any of them strong enough? And could they achieve anything without an inside man... Without me?

I thought back to when Daniel told me his plan to infiltrate the PIDs. His belief in me. He'd been right. Being a PID meant doing things, awful things, things that went against the very principles we were fighting for. He didn't believe that any of the others had the strength to play the long game like I did. I had no ties, no family or loved ones. I had nothing to hold onto in this fucked-up world. Nothing except the cause. That was why I was the strongest tool we had.

And that was why I was our best hope now. That was why I was Daniel's *only* hope.

I took off my Shades and shoved them back in my pocket. I *couldn't* get caught. Daniel would die in prison, all his work would be for nothing, unless we won this war. To do that we would need our very best. And that was me.

The mission not the man. That was what Daniel always said. The mission came first. Could I do it? Lose everyone, everything, and come back stronger than before? I knew what Daniel would say, what he would want of me. And I knew how to do it.

I picked myself up, wiped the tears from my eyes and strode back to the meeting room, head held high. I threw open the door.

"Ah, Jinks. Nice of you to join—"

"The kid, sir," I said. "The kid is the angle."

4

Mills glared at me. "Little late to the party, Jinks. While you've been busy powdering your nose the rest of us have actually been working. We've decided—"

"You've decided to pretend he crashed because anti-terror were in pursuit," I interrupted. I knew how their minds worked, how unimaginative they were. "Big up Browne's department, keep everybody sweet. Public feel safe, and thankful we have such a skilled force looking out for the country. But, with respect, sir, it won't wash."

He sat back down on the desk and folded his arms. "Alright Jinks, I'll indulge you. Tell me why your colleagues are wrong, why *I'm* wrong and what makes you think you're so clever you've come up with a better solution?"

"Sir," I cleared my throat and addressed the room. Most of them were sneering, looking at me like I was the piece of dirt that made the class stay behind after the bell had sounded. I didn't let them faze me. I knew I was right. "There are too many witnesses," I began, "and that's just on the ground. I bet someone's uploaded footage, am I right?"

"We've already taken it down," Samantha, Internet Enforcement, piped up from the back. "Out of respect for the family."

"We all know that's bullshit," I replied. "There'll be screenshots, it'll resurface. It only takes one witness to point out the crash was caused by a falling kid, not a police chase, and the conspiracy theorists will be all over it."

"We can shut them down, Jinks, we always do." Mills waved his hand and began to stand up, he was going to dismiss me, make me sit back down. I couldn't let him.

"Sir, the best way to hide the truth is in plain sight. If we don't tell any lies, we can't be caught out. This is too damn important to put to chance. I, for one, am not happy for my job and my reputation to be reliant on Samantha and Ken's abilities to track down and silence conspiracy theorists. Especially when they can't even keep incriminating footage off the Dark Web."

There were sharp inhales of breath all around the room. They knew I was referring to the images of Cole with a prostitute that went viral last year. How those two didn't lose their jobs over that I'll never know. It was a major scandal, and a very black day for our department. No one ever mentioned it anymore.

"Let me get this straight, Jinks," Mills ignored the shock in the room. "You're suggesting we tell the truth? Fess up to the fact anti-terror were clueless, and crucify ourselves in the process? Good idea, I'll send the proposal out now. While I'm at it I'll print off all our fucking P45s, shall I?"

"No, sir. I'm not saying tell the truth. I'm saying don't lie. I'm talking about deflection, shifting the focus. Instead of talking about whether or not the authorities did enough, we take them out of the picture completely. Make it all about the kid. Make him a hero. Young patriot saves thousands of lives… The public will love it. Whip it right up, his face on every front page, interviews, memorials, a statement from the Prime Minister. Everyone will be so busy worshipping him they won't even question why anti-terror weren't on the case. The public love a good hero, sir, and they're far more interested if that hero is an ordinary citizen, not some faceless official."

I had them. I could see it in the way their faces had softened.

Sneers turned to frowns, they were thinking it through. Time for the big gun.

"Instead of seeing this as a disaster we need to survive, we should be looking at it as an opportunity to shine. To really bury past mistakes and prove our worth. We could potentially turn this crisis into PR gold for Cole, sir."

Mills was silent. He twisted his lips and clicked his tongue the way he always did when he was thinking.

Greyson spoke up. "I think it's a great idea, sir,"

You would.

"Me too," Dylan chimed in. "I think she's right, we could turn this into a positive. Plus, there's less risk of, er... complications, if we're not hiding anything."

No need to worry your colleagues' incompetence could cost you your job in other words.

"I do see your point, Jinks," Mills conceded, "but there's a grieving family involved here, if they don't play the game it could be a disaster. We'll need pictures, statements, everything. We'll need the kid's whole fucking life if we're going to have enough to feed to the public to keep their eyes off anti-terror."

"Sir, if I may?" Belinda, or 'mother-hen' as we affectionately called her, raised her hand. She rarely spoke in meetings. A middle-aged lady, she had a son who'd died fighting in Afghanistan. She never spoke of him, but we all knew the story. Quite possibly the nicest woman I've ever met, except for the fact she was a PID of course. She always looked out for us all, and was slightly obsessed with ensuring we kept our sugar levels up. There were always some of Belinda's homemade treats on offer by the coffee machine.

"As a mother who has..." she took a moment to compose herself, "*lost* a son, I think knowing they died a hero, and for a greater good, is all that stands between you and madness. If I thought my boy died needlessly, senselessly... I don't think I could live with that. It would be a kindness for this poor woman, to allow her to remember him as a hero, rather than a drugged-up fool. I don't think there'll be any objections."

Mills nodded respectfully. "Okay. Well, Jinks, it seems you have redeemed yourself after all. I shall submit the proposal to Number Ten straight away. We'll see if Cole is as convinced by your idea as your colleagues are, eh?"

"I just have one request, sir, if I may?" I asked.

"What would that be?"

"Can I be named, in the proposal?"

He stared at me. "You sure you want that? You know he might hate the idea?"

Mills usually put his own name to any proposals sent to Downing Street. A show of solidarity, he said. He was prepared to take the rap for his team if their suggestions fell flat. Of course, it also meant he got the credit if they were well received. I wanted my name on this one; I needed to get noticed. Needed to get on Cole's radar. Mills wouldn't hear of it normally, but this one was a gamble. I figured he'd be happy for me to own the risk.

I nodded. "Yes, sir, it was my idea, and I know it's controversial. I appreciate the way you take the responsibility for our actions, but I don't think it's right you take the risk in this instance."

"Alright. If you're sure. I like that, Jinks. Courage of your convictions. Prepared to sink or swim with this one, eh?"

Yes. Yes, I was.

5

The approval came through from Downing Street within minutes. He's a savvy guy, Cole. Not savvy enough to spot a black widow in his midst, but then most guys lose their mind once their trousers take control. Even Alicia was on board. She's a smart cookie too. Why throw accusations around between departments, undermine public confidence, when you can remove blame entirely? Mills clapped me on the back, leaving a sweaty palm print on my blouse as a dubious badge of honour. He asked if I wanted to come along in the morning, tell the family.

I couldn't think of anything worse. I declined, and threw Greyson a bone instead.

"Sir, I'm honoured you'd ask, but I'm not sure my approach is what's needed right now. I'm not so good with the touchy-feely stuff. But I think you should take Greyson, sir. He's much better at being congenial than I am."

"Alright," Mills said. "Greyson, you're up. We'll give them until tomorrow afternoon; let them get over some of the initial shock of the kid's death. The public announcement can be held off until then."

Greyson beamed, practically wagged his tail.

"Actually, sir," I said, "I'm still feeling a little queasy. Would it be alright if I knocked off now, got some rest? I'll be back in early tomorrow raring to go."

"Okay." Mills surveyed the room, everyone was bustling. Most of them would be pulling an all-nighter. But I had somewhere I needed to be. "Seeing as how you've saved our bacon today, Jinks. I'm gonna need my brightest fully operational tomorrow, this lot'll be burnt out by then. Just you make sure you're here at the crack of dawn, eh?"

I nodded. "I will, sir. I just need a few hours' sleep."

"Fine. You go too Greyson. I'll probably be stuck here all night. At least one of us should be on the ball when we go to see the family tomorrow."

Greyson followed me out to the car park and grabbed my arm.

"Hey!" he said, still beaming. "Thanks for that, Jinks, I owe you one."

"No problem." I pulled my car keys out of my pocket, trying to signal I wanted to get going. "You're better at the public relations stuff than me, makes sense you should go."

"Well, I really appreciate it. Actually… would you let me shout you dinner? You know, to say thank you?"

"Sorry, Greyson," I said as I strapped myself in, "I wasn't kidding when I said I wasn't feeling well. I just want to go home."

"Fair enough. Another time then? I know this great little—"

I pulled the door closed and drove away. When I checked the rear-view mirror he was still stood there, staring after me. Looking like an abandoned puppy. I didn't have the time or the inclination to care about his feelings. I needed to work out what the fuck I was going to do next.

It was nearly 10pm. If anyone had managed to get away, there was only one place they'd be heading. Tower Bridge at midnight. That was the meeting place, hidden in plain sight. If the worst ever happened, that was where anyone still free would go. But I was never meant to be in that number. I was supposed to be the one to blow my own cover, to give the rest of them the chance to make that clandestine meeting. Could I show up? If anyone did get away, surely they'd hate me?

I'd hate me if the roles were reversed. I'd push me over the fucking side.

There probably wasn't anyone left anyway. But, what if there was? If I was going to do what I planned some help would be damn useful. Maybe they'd see sense? You have to roll with the punches. Things don't always go according to plan. Under the circumstances, I'd done the best thing for our cause. Surely they'd see that, if they let me explain. I couldn't pass up the chance of help in my mission because I was scared they'd be pissed at me. I couldn't be that weak. The goal had to come first, and the best way of achieving it was to have them by my side, if any of them were still free. I had to know.

I rushed home, changed out of my uniform and tried to scrub the feelings of guilt, and despair, away in the shower. Every time Daniel's face popped into my mind I had to push it away. I couldn't bear to think about what they might be doing to him, how scared he must be.

He'd been the first person in my life who didn't treat me like a puzzle that needed to be solved. And the first person who gave me a reason to stop running. I'd never stayed in one place so long, not since my waster mother had shot her veins up with more shit than they could handle. After that, I'd gone from pillar to post. Always a burden, always an issue.

When I kept my mouth shut, and my head down, they thought I was 'repressing trauma'. When I acted out I was showing 'violent tendencies'. They were always looking for reasons to label me, reasons I might be dangerous. So as soon as I got out of the system I moved. And kept on moving. Trying to outrun my genes, I guess.

But Daniel didn't want to change me, or fix me. He showed me I was never broken to begin with. To him, I was a solution, not a problem.

I turned the shower to cold, letting the icy water snap me out of my pity party. If I allowed myself tears, they might never stop. No one ever changed their lot by crying about it. He taught me that. He taught me how to be strong, how to be courageous. How to walk this world without him, if I had to. It would be an insult to him if I fell apart.

On the Tube I watched the people getting on and off. So routine, so oblivious. Tomorrow when they alighted, it would be with a shiver. Tomorrow, when they stepped onto the platform their heads would be full of explosives and death tolls. The strangers of today, sitting beside one another in silence, trying to pretend they haven't noticed each other's presence, would tomorrow pass comment, strike up conversation. Like twittering birds spreading the news of the dawn.

It's only acceptable for the English to converse with strangers in the case of national disaster, or freak weather. They revel in the opportunity when it comes. And just as a sudden squally shower can become a veritable monsoon in the retelling, the great British public would finish the job we started. Down grocery aisles, in doctors' waiting rooms, on platforms and commutes: Gridless would become the root of all evil. James Lincoln would become legend.

6

I waited on the bridge, watching lights dance on the water. Couples ambled past me arm-in-arm. A drunk asked me for a light. I told him I didn't smoke, and then pulled a Marlboro out of my pocket as soon as he left. Nice of him to remind me of the distraction.

Leaning on the side, looking out across the Thames, I couldn't tell if the churning in my guts was grief that no one had shown up, or relief. I chucked the cigarette into the water and checked my Shades. 00:15. I was the only one left.

I pulled my jacket tight around me, keeping my Shades on to disguise the tears that threatened to fall, and tried to stride purposefully though my legs felt like jelly. As I stepped off the bridge someone grabbed my arm. Without thinking, I clenched my right fist and swung it, hitting an anorak-clad torso with full force.

"Shit!" The guy stumbled backwards, covering himself with his arms. "Teresa, it's me!"

Teresa?

He looked up at me, from beneath his hood. Wire-rimmed glasses, no Shades. Slightly hooked nose, and two days' stubble. It was Kyle.

"Kyle?" I pulled him to the side, into the shadows. "How? I thought you'd been caught?"

Of all the ones who could have escaped, I'd never have

picked Kyle. He was always at HQ. Without an early warning he wouldn't have had a hope.

"Well," he tried not grimace at the pain, "I could say the same about you. Some lookout you turned out to be."

His words stabbed at me, but I couldn't let him see weakness. "I did what I had to. They were already on everyone's trail. If I'd blown my own cover it wouldn't have achieved anything."

"I know," he replied. "It was the same for me."

"What do you mean?" Why wasn't he angry? And why wasn't he in jail?

He sighed. "Terri, I've been hacked into the PID network for months. All the calls, all the emails."

I was shocked. It didn't make sense.

"Why? I was undercover, I was keeping you all up to date, why would you take a risk like that?"

He smiled. "Because of something like this. I'm the same as you, the mission not the man. Just like Daniel taught us, eh? I didn't think relying solely on you for information was… advisable."

"You mean you didn't trust me?"

"Should I have? Would I be here now if I did?"

I scowled. It was a fair point I guess.

"Anyway," he continued, "it wasn't about trust, it was about security. And don't tell me I've hurt your feelings. You're bigger than that. You want me to believe you acted for the mission? You need to accept I did too."

"I couldn't contact anyone without blowing cover. You're telling me you were there, at HQ, and you knew they were coming… and what? Did you just run out on them without saying a word?"

"I couldn't save them, Terri. I knew what they were doing, tracing the cars. Even if they got away from HQ they'd have been picked up later. Everyone has been, you know."

"So why not you?"

"When I heard the call, I left. Said I was going for a piss, slipped out the back and ran. Left my car there. They've already raided my house; Kyle Redwood is a wanted man. But I have other means."

I didn't doubt it. It was Kyle who created Jinks' identity for me, stood to reason he'd have a back-up of his own. Still, I couldn't quite believe what I was hearing. To look them in the eyes, knowing the police were coming, and run out? Like a rat?

"How could you?"

"Ha! You're one to talk. Seems to me like we both strung them out to dry."

"How dare you, I've explained why I did what I did. Some things are—"

"Some things are more important." he interrupted, and pulled a USB stick out of his pocket. "Things like this."

"What is it?"

"All our plans, all our intelligence, all our contacts. Downloaded, erased from our systems, and all on here."

"You can't have had time to erase everything properly!"

"For all the front you're still naïve, aren't you, Terri? This isn't new. Do you think I'd let everything sit there, at HQ, where anyone could find it? Oh, there's plenty there, they think it's payday. Lots of incriminating stuff, no reason to think there's anything left to find. But this… this is how we'll rebuild. Come back stronger."

"I can't believe you! If Daniel knew—"

"Oh, Terri, you really think he didn't?"

I stared at him in disbelief. He was lying. He *had* to be lying.

"You're telling me Daniel was okay with it?"

"No." Kyle reached into his pocket and pulled out a hip flask. He took a swig of whatever he'd filled it with. "I'm telling you it was his idea."

"No." I squared up to him. He was taller than the ginger tosser from *The Raids*, but I still looked down on him. "I don't believe you. He wouldn't have put me in harm's way if he didn't have to. Why would he want me to spend all these years, all the training, all the risk, if you could just hack in and get the same information. More even. It doesn't make sense."

Kyle laughed and offered me a swig. I pushed the flask away and he tutted when some of the dark liquid spilt on the pavement. "It makes perfect sense, if you get over yourself and stop believing you're the fucking chosen one!"

I resisted the urge to punch his lights out. I needed to hear what he had to say, work out if he was lying. The broken nose could wait a few minutes. Kyle, like everyone else, thought there was something going on with me and Daniel. They were wrong, of course. But Daniel said we shouldn't set them straight. "No one should know all your truths, Terri," he would say. But… he did. He did know all my truths. And I thought I knew his.

"I'm going to pretend you didn't just speak to me like that," I said, "because I want you to explain yourself before I decide which of your limbs to break."

"Ooh, big scary Terri, eh?" He was starting to slur. He'd had way more than what was in that little flask. "You're so used to it, aren't you? So used to throwing your weight around, acting like the Queen of fucking Sheba. And no one ever tells you you're not as clever as you think you are, because you're Daniel's little fuck buddy! Well, he's gone now, isn't he? So you're going to have to face up to the truth. You were no different, Terri. I know you thought you were. But you weren't. The same rules applied to you. Why did you think Daniel would tell you everything? He didn't tell anyone everything. Hell," he started waving the USB around in my face, "*this* is supposed to have everything, he told me it did. But do you think I'm stupid enough to believe it really does? Do you think I don't know there's a very good chance one of the others had one too? Secrets and lies, princess, secrets and lies."

This was the second time in one day I'd discovered I wasn't as in the loop as I thought I was, and it ripped through me like a knife to the back. No one wants to learn they're not as important as they thought they were, especially when they've worked so hard and given so much. But as angry as his words made me, I knew he was telling the truth. He was too pickled to spin a coherent lie, and his bitterness was genuine.

"Alright," I said, "it's just you and me now, whether we like it or not. So give it to me straight. Why? What was the plan?"

"What it always is. The mission. At any cost. Protecting our comrades, well, that was supposed to be your job. Didn't work out so well, eh? But it wasn't the main concern. That was always protecting this information. Daniel knew we could carry on, even if we lost people, as long as we had this. You think I deserted? I didn't. I followed my orders to the letter."

"He ordered you to abandon everyone?"

"No. He ordered me to get this data away. And myself, because I'm the only one who can use it. He told me to stay hacked in, always. Listen to every call. If I ever found out they were onto us, I had to get away. Protecting the information was priority number one, and that was my responsibility. Warning the others was yours. We didn't bank on things going down the way they did. Turns out I heard about Daniel a good hour before you did. I knew they'd be coming for us, so I did my part and got away with the USB. I hoped you'd find out in time to warn the others. But here we are, just the two of us. Be angry all you want, but at least my charge is safe." He put the stick in his pocket and patted it.

My head was spinning. I felt betrayed, though I knew it was irrational. Daniel was always upfront about his dishonesty. It's how he evaded the authorities for so long. There wasn't a single person in the world who knew everything about him. It was just that I'd thought I was the closest. But that was my own stupidity. And it didn't change anything. Here we were, a hacker and an undercover PID, with dreams of taking down the government. We had mountains to climb, and we wouldn't get there indulging in self-pity, or holding onto grudges.

"Okay," I said. "I take it you've got a new identity and a safe house?"

He nodded.

"Right. Well, I've got to be at the office in a few hours, so let's not waste time. If we're going to come back from this we need to work out how. And you need to show me what's on that stick. Let's go, take me to where you're staying, and we'll grab some fucking big coffees on the way. No throwing blame around, no sulking. The past is the past."

"The past is the past," he agreed.

7

"The girl could be a pain in the arse." Greyson deposited a muffin next to my laptop and I straightened up abruptly. I couldn't fall asleep at my desk, I was supposed to have had some rest the night before. Instead I'd spent it with Kyle, poring over salvaged data in the scummy little bedsit his new alias occupied.

Mills and Greyson had just returned from the Lincoln house. Everything seemed to be going according to plan. Browne's statement had been broadcast and people were reacting exactly as predicted. But clearly something was troubling Greyson.

"What girl?" I tried to sound alert. I don't think I pulled it off.

"Christ, Jinks, you look dreadful. Still feeling rough?"

"Yeah, a bit. I'll be fine. What girl?"

"The kid's sister. *Twin* sister in fact. She's not buying it. I think I got through a bit by flattering her intelligence, but I'm not sure it's enough."

I snorted. "His twin? So she's what, sixteen?"

"Eighteen, Jinks, the kid was eighteen. Not like you not to know all the details."

"Okay, whatever. Sixteen, eighteen… it doesn't matter. No one's going to pay her any attention."

"The whole family is going to be in the spotlight, especially after tomorrow."

"Tomorrow?" Shit. What had I missed?

Greyson looked confused. "You must have heard?"

I shook my head.

"Cole's doing a PR stunt, visiting the family home ahead of his statement."

Adrenaline coursed through me, banishing my fatigue. Cole was going there? It was perfect. More perfect than I could have hoped. I had to be there. I didn't think the girl was anything to worry about, but if everyone else did she could be my way in. Playing on someone's fears is the best way to manipulate a situation.

"Well, then that *is* a problem," I said. "We can't have this girl sticking her oar in, it's a critical time. One chink and public opinion might not go the way we need it to. Someone needs to make sure she stays in check."

Greyson nodded. "That's what Mills said. He wants me to go back tomorrow, make sure she's on board. But I don't know. I don't know how to relate to teenage girls, never been one. Plus, I think she might need a firmer approach."

I feigned a sigh. "Spit it out, Greyson. You want me to go with you, don't you? Just say it."

"Well," he shuffled awkwardly, "yeah. I just think you'd be better at it. I mean, I know you said you didn't want to do the family stuff, but—"

"Alright. I'll do it. But you owe me."

He beamed. "Thanks, Jinks."

Perfect.

Kyle and I had spent a good chunk of the early hours trying to figure out how I could meet Cole. It needed to be soon, while my name was still fresh in his mind as the PID golden girl who had come up with the hero angle. We'd gone back and forth and drawn a blank at every turn. There just wasn't a way for a lowly PID officer to get an audience with the PM inconspicuously. And now the opportunity had fallen into my lap.

The downside was that I had to endure Greyson bouncing around, gushing about meeting the Prime Minister. He prattled on for half an hour about what tie he should wear, like I gave a shit. If it all went to plan Cole wouldn't give him a second glance, let alone care about his choice of neckwear. To save my own sanity I suggested we take Belinda too. As the mother of a deceased hero she could relate to the parents better than either of us. Mills agreed, and Greyson soon realised Mother Hen would indulge his fashion dilemmas with far more enthusiasm than I would, and left me alone.

I kept telling myself it shouldn't be difficult. Cole was a notorious philanderer (a huge part of the PID's function was to cover up his vices), and he didn't seem too fussy. I'd never had much of a problem attracting a man's attention if I wanted it, there was no reason why I couldn't catch his.

I stared at myself in the mirror. I knew what I had to do.

8

Greyson was right. Rosa was a pain in the arse.

I had the measure of the family as soon as we pulled up outside. Well-presented end of terrace, Audi parked outside, hanging baskets by the front door. Painfully middle-class, probably never felt anything close to hardship. From what Greyson said the dad was left-leaning, but in a purely philosophical way. I figured the girl would be your typical spoilt little rebel. Head full of liberal notions, but bank account full of daddy's generosity. I didn't think she'd pose a problem, didn't think she'd even speak up. But I was wrong.

The mother was all styled hair and pressed clothes. She let us in, and I instantly smelled bleach and acrid air freshener. I smiled. She'd lost her son two days ago, and yet she was still keeping up appearances. She was going to be a piece of cake.

The father was dishevelled, still in his dressing gown. Obviously less concerned with outward appearances, but still no trouble. His eyes were sunken and red-rimmed. He shuffled, rather than walked, towards us. He'd been beaten down. Grief had knocked the stuffing out of him (if he even had much to begin with). He'd comply, simply because he was lost and broken. He'd not have the gumption to object to the treadmill we'd put him on.

Belinda gave the mother her best sympathetic look, and put her arm around her. She opened by telling her she'd seen the photographs of Jimmy and could only imagine how proud she must be of her wonderful son. The mother responded enthusiastically, needing no encouragement to launch into a monologue about her deceased offspring. Greyson strode over to the father and shook his hand warmly as if they were old friends. He was good, I'll give him that. He ignored the scruffy appearance and talked business, regaling him with tales of all the dignitaries who wanted to pass on their respects. By engaging Mr Lincoln as an equal he gave the guy some dignity he sorely needed. People are always more inclined to trust those who flatter them.

Flattery wasn't my style, but I'd try anything to make sure the day went smoothly. It was essential to my plan.

I spotted Rosa for the first time as she emerged from the living room. An entirely unremarkable girl with scruffy brown hair and puffy eyes (from crying, I assumed). I made a beeline for her, with a deliberate half-smile. Teenagers are either angry or nonchalant. Either way, they don't appreciate adults grinning at them like Cheshire cats. It makes them suspicious. Me too, as it goes. At least we had that in common.

"Hey," I said, making a conscious effort to sound informal. "You must be Rosa, right?"

She looked up at me from behind her stringy fringe, without a hint of a smile. She left the slightly-too-long pause teenagers always do before nodding. I guess they're trying to assert their importance, or take control of the conversation, by making you wait on their reply. I guess that's what a psychologist would say anyway. But to me it's just plain irritating.

"I'm Officer Jinks. But you can call me Zara. I'm sorry about your brother." I resisted the urge to add 'kid' on the end; I was supposed to be on her level. I could already tell it wasn't going to wash.

She shrugged. She wasn't going to give me anything to work with. "I know you really don't need us crashing in like this," I continued, "but we've got some hot buzz to tell you."

Fuck. What a stupid thing to say. She visibly recoiled from

my faux pas. *Hot fucking buzz*? I'd have thought me an idiot in her shoes.

Greyson heard my bum note and winced. But, as he has an irritating habit of doing, he swept in and rescued me.

"That's right," he said, "we have some very important news."

Intel, that's what I should have said. All the vloggers are saying intel these days.

The family looked at Greyson.

"The Prime Minister wishes to visit you."

"The Prime Minister?" Mrs Lincoln looked around the room. Checking it was up to her self-imposed standards, I guess. "Coming here?"

"Yes," Greyson smiled. "He wants to give you his condolences, and his thanks, in person."

I thought I heard a little snort come from Rosa's freckled nose. *Yeah*, I thought, *you're not wrong, kid. It's total BS*.

"Well," the mother tried to catch the eyes of her husband and daughter, "that really is thoughtful, don't you think so, Dave? "

I had my eye on Rosa, and I noticed a dark look pass between her and her father. Clearly a subversive undercurrent. But the dad kept quiet. His silence must have enraged Rosa, because she found her voice.

"You're not actually going to let him in our house, are you?"

Oh, hell. She was going to be trouble after all. Greyson raised an eyebrow at me, but I gave a slight shake of my head. Not yet. I wanted to see if the parents would rein her in first.

But her spineless father just looked uncomfortable. He didn't even look her in the eye when he muttered, "Rosa, come on..." Hardly a strong parental presence. I couldn't begrudge her frustration. I could see it, simmering beneath the surface as she eyed him with disbelief. She was going to blow.

"You called him Hitler!"

I don't know whether it was the red flush that bloomed across his face, or the near swoon of mortification from his wife, but I've never struggled to hide a smirk so much. Under normal circumstances, I'd have clapped her on the back for calling them out on their middle-class hypocrisy. But I couldn't have her causing tension. Not here, not today.

"Rosa," Greyson stepped up to the plate again. Clearly her parents couldn't control her, "this isn't about politics. The Prime Minister doesn't care how your father voted. Your brother saved his life, and hundreds of others. He's not coming here as the Prime Minister, he's just coming as a man who owes another man his life, to pay his respects."

Wrong move. The blue touch paper had already been lit, time to stand back and let the fireworks burn themselves out.

"Bullshit."

She wasn't wrong.

"Rosa Louise Lincoln!" Mrs Lincoln turned a shade of maroon that clashed terribly with her peroxide perm. "Go to your room."

"With pleasure!"

Rosa stormed up the stairs. I never had anyone invested enough in me to bother sending me to my room when I was an angry teen, but I knew the drill. The door would slam in three… two… one.

Bang.

Greyson gave the embarrassed parents a spiel about anger being a natural response during the grieving process, but I wasn't listening. I was trying to figure out how I was going to deal with her. For a spoiled little rich girl she had some balls, I give her that. Would she be bold enough to act out in front of the Prime Minister? I didn't think so, but I couldn't leave it to chance.

Seducing a man is different to seducing a woman. It comes down to the same thing – ego – but the scene has to be set differently. Women are more receptive to advances when they're vulnerable. A woman on top of her game, feeling confident and self-assured, is less likely to go home with a chancer. But catch her when she's just been dumped, or fired, or fallen out with her best mate, and a sympathetic ear and a flurry of compliments could be all that's needed to drop her knickers.

Men, on the other hand, are hornier when they feel confident, when things are going their way. Being successful works like a bottle of Viagra. But if they feel undermined their dicks shrivel up like raisins. The meeting needed to go exactly the way Cole wanted it to if I was to be in with a shot.

I touched Mrs Lincoln on the arm gently. "Would you like me to go and see if she's okay?"

"Oh, great idea," Greyson said, as if that wasn't the plan as along. "Jinks is fabulous with teenagers, Mrs Lincoln, she's one of our youth liaisons."

What a load of crap. But the mother nodded and smiled, so I had the green light.

I made my way up the stairs, past family portraits hung at perfect angles on the wall. Snapshots into a past full of wholesome, conformist fun. Twin toddlers holding ice creams, the whole family windswept and ruddy-faced (but not so much as to be uncouth) at Stonehenge, the boy on a climbing wall. (That's what rich kids do. They don't climb trees for free, their parents pay for them to climb artificial indoor constructions.)

Hers was the room down the end of the corridor. I walked past the other closed bedroom doors. It wasn't hard to tell which one had been the boy's. It was covered in stickers of various bands and vlogger logos. I bet Mrs Keeping-Up-with-the-Jones had hated it when he was alive; I bet she thought it ruined the ambience of the pastel curtains and strategically placed yukka plants. I paused for a second, and checked out his choices. Apocalyptic Zombies, Sweeny and the Phatz, Venom Nitrate. I might have liked this kid. Shame we had to turn him into the boy in his mother's gallery of wishful thinking. I felt a sudden, unwanted pang. Maybe that was part of his sister's problem too. We were carving his memory up, scooping out the guts and creating an image. Like cyber-taxidermists.

And it was my idea.

I reached out and touched the door frame with my palm. "Sorry, kid," I whispered. Then I saw it. Poking out from under a poster of some godawful games vlogger. Two shackled hands. It wasn't unusual. Until Daniel was caught (and we became the devil incarnate in the public eye) it was trendy for teens to support Gridless. For the most part they'd all grow out of it, once the thrill of rebellion gave way. But the irony of finding a silent symbol support from the kid who all but destroyed us made me inhale sharply.

I shook it off, and headed to the closed door at the end. I could hear some drab, almost operatic rock coming from inside. I knocked, knowing there would be no reply. I'd start off softly; maybe she'd be easier one-to-one.

"Rosa? It's me, Zara. Can I come in?"

I opened the door without waiting. She was sat crossed-legged on the bed. I looked around. The whole room was non-descript, much like her. Dusky pink walls dotted with small pine shelves that housed gaudy knick-knacks and more pastel curtains. A photo of some Muslim girl on her desk, a violin covered in dust on a stand in the corner. It was painfully boring and tidy. People like her can choose to be anything they want. Yet they always seem to choose mediocrity.

"Sweet crib." I lied. She barely glanced up. I sat down beside her, adopting my best 'open' body language. "Politics sucks, huh? I mean, none of them get what's important to our generation, do they?"

She wasn't going to buy it. I already knew it. I wasn't so out of touch that I couldn't remember how far away thirty seemed when I was eighteen. I looked younger; most people took me for mid-twenties. But even that was an impossible gulf to someone her age. But hell, at least I *tried* to play nice first.

She looked up, those speckled blues burning with self-righteous angst.

"Actually," she said, her voice dripping with sanctimony,

"I think politics is very important, I happen to care about the world we live in."

Oh, you arrogant, jumped-up little piss stain.

I didn't see red. I saw fucking neon. If there's one thing I can't stand it's condescension. Especially from a wet-behind-the-ears little rich bitch who's never lived a day of her own life.

"Well, that's great," I hissed. "You're a clever *girl*, Rosa. Really clever." Gloves off. *No, I am not on your level, sweetheart, I'm fucking way above it.*

She either didn't pick up on my change in tone, or was so self-fucking-satisfied that she didn't care.

"And I hate the ERP," she whinged.

I wondered for a second why she was goading. Then it hit me. Rich kids don't know the real world. They don't get brought up, they get 'parented'. (If you're middle-class the act of raising offspring warrants its own fucking verb.) They don't get sworn at; they get invited to 'discuss their bad choices'. They get 'time-out', not a whack round the head. They never have to face up to the reality that no one cares about their whiny, self-obsessed opinion.

I laughed, because I realised how easy this would be.

"Well, guess what," I said, "they don't care." She opened and closed her mouth like a suffocating fish. "That's right, princess," I was beginning to enjoy myself, "they don't give a shit what your adolescent ill-informed opinion is. They're busy running the country. So you can sit here nursing wishy-washy ideals of liberalism and kumba-fucking-ya if you like, but I tell you now, not one single shit will be given in Westminster over your opinion."

She stood up, still affecting defiance, but the wobble of her chin told me she would crumble if I pushed. "How dare you speak to me like that?"

Someone fucking should have before now, missy.

"What's the matter, chicken? Choking on your entitlement?" I stood up and grabbed her arm. I dug my nails into the freckled, pudgy flesh and bent down so my eyes were level with hers. "Let's get this straight, honey; I don't care how you feel about Cole. This country doesn't care how you feel. No one cares how you feel, not today. If you don't like it, go cast your vote at the polls. Stage a pathetic protest on whatever godawful uni campus you end up at I don't give a fuck. But right here, right now, you are going to play nice. You will shake his hand, you will smile. You will say nothing political at all. This is about your brother, not you. So get the fuck over yourself, or I'll come down on you like a hail of shit."

She was defeated. I let go of her arm and she stared in horror at the red marks my nails had left. It was probably the first time anyone in her closeted little world had hurt her deliberately. She pulled her sleeve down. She was too scared of me to tell anyone. I know how that feels. She'd get over it. And be stronger for it. In fact, I thought I'd done her a fucking favour. But I guess not everybody has the inner strength to overcome the shit in their lives. She certainly doesn't, I know that now. She just gave up and drowned in it. Luckily for us.

9

The mother gushed at me when we got back downstairs. Must have thought I was some kind of miracle worker. I wonder what she'd have thought if I told her I swore at her precious little princess, or if she'd seen the marks. Rosa's done far worse to herself since then, many a filthy fucking needle has pierced that doughy flesh of hers. More than that too, I expect. Not that I'm one to talk.

I felt confident. Rosa had been shocked into submission, the press were gathering, and Greyson had talked Mr Lincoln into getting dressed. The stage was set. I excused myself and went to the bathroom, touched up my make-up and pulled down my top a little.

I watched from the kitchen window as the car pulled up. My heart was pounding. I've never wanted someone to want me so badly. Rosa caught me doing a last-minute preen in the hall mirror and eyed me with disgust, but I didn't care. As long as she behaved.

I held back while the family greeted him at the door, the sound of his voice sending tickles down my spine. When Mrs Lincoln stopped fawning over him long enough to go and get the kettle on, I saw my chance.

I took a deep breath, set my lips into a smile and walked up to him. Greyson shot me a puzzled look, which I ignored.

"Is there anything I can do for you, sir?"

His eyes fell upon me. Not my face, that's not his style, a few inches south of there. Good. After a second too long he raised his gaze to meet mine, a slow smile creeping across his face.

"Ah, the PIDS!"

Right. You were just checking the badge on my lapel, eh? Course you were.

He turned his face toward Mr Lincoln, but his eyes were still on me.

"Ah," he said, smiling and shaking his hand. "Backbone of the country. I should have known you would be on the scene taking care of the family. Sterling work."

Mr Lincoln nodded weakly, and Cole turned back to me.

Ask me my name. Ask me my name.

"I don't need anything, thank you, Officer…?"

Bingo.

I stared directly into those sludgy brown eyes. "Jinks."

The recognition flashed across his eyes, he blinked quickly, searching his memory.

Yes. You've heard my name. Come on. Remember.

The smile grew wider. He had it.

"Officer Jinks?" There was a slight rising intonation; he was surprised. I must have been a shock. He'd probably thought the mastermind behind the James Lincoln legend was some deskbound middle-aged blimp.

That's right, baby. Brilliant and beautiful. And coming straight for you.

He cleared his throat. "Beautiful… name."

I smiled. "Thank you, sir." I touched my neck, deliberately. Watched as his eyes flicked up and down my body. Christ. Daniel was right. Men were easy.

Mrs Lincoln interrupted our moment when she approached with a tray of hot drinks. We moved into the lounge. I practically knocked Greyson out of the way to secure the seat opposite Cole. I had to keep this momentum going. I also needed to be in Rosa's line of sight. Couldn't have her screwing anything up. Men love strong, brilliant women, but only when they're feeling strong and brilliant themselves. They've got to feel superior to you. As fucking pathetic as it is, it's true. I might not be doing much for equality by pandering to his complex, but sometimes you've got to play the game their way if you want to win.

Cole did what he does best. He talked. He held court for a good half hour, blathering on about his empathy, spinning some yarn about his brother. Even Rosa looked as though she might shed a tear. They were all so enraptured by his well-practised display that they didn't notice how often his eyes settled on my breasts.

Poor Greyson. All that time picking out a tie. Should've got implants if you wanted him to notice you.

After he'd got the family to agree to a publicised, over-the-top funeral, he made his way to the door. I tried to sidle through the others, as inconspicuously as possible. I needed to get a moment alone. Otherwise he might take the horn he had for me and stick it in someone else. Men are fickle like that. The path of least resistance, or least effort required, is the one horny scumbags like him usually take. If you want to be more than a mental image for them to wank to, you have to make yourself available.

When the rambling goodbyes were over I made a bold move and touched him on the arm.

"Shall I escort you to the officers outside, sir?"

It was all of ten steps. He didn't need an escort. Greyson glared at me.

Cole smiled wide, those awful teeth showing.

I had my hand in my pocket, my fingers clasped around my business card, intending to slip it in his jacket. But there was no need. As soon as the front door closed behind us he turned to me.

"You're a very impressive young lady, Jinks," he said.

"Thank you, sir." I glanced down, trying to look coy. He

clearly wanted to be the one to instigate things. You've got to let them do it their way.

"I wonder if you'd like to discuss how you came up with such an outstanding strategy. Perhaps tonight?"

I smiled and gave a single nod. Those watching thought nothing had been exchanged but a formality. The gracious PM, taking time out of his busy day to give a courteous thank-you to a humble officer.

He shook my hand, running his thumb in small circles across my palm, and leaned up to whisper to me.

"Plaza. Room 311. 8pm."

10

I went for classic black lace with matching stockings. You never know what these bastards are going to be into, and I had to make sure this was more than just a one-off. Matching undies does the job for a single encounter, but adding the stockings suggests you're more adventurous. Wondering how far you might be willing to go gives them a reason to come back for more.

And he did.

The others think I had it all planned, even then. They think I somehow knew how the future would unfold. That when I spritzed my knees with Dior, when I ordered that cab, when I entered that lobby, I knew where it would all lead. But I didn't.

It's certainly true that when I walked into that hotel room and took the Scotch he offered me, when I lay down on that bed and opened my legs, I had only his destruction on my mind. But I didn't know, back then, how we would get here. I certainly didn't know the part Rosa would play. When I left her house after Cole's speech I thought I'd never see her again.

But I knew we had to keep going. I knew we had to rebuild. One brick at a time, until the foundation was stronger than ever before. I didn't know how, I didn't know when, but I knew we had to try. Learn from our mistakes. My mistakes. I needed to climb higher, know more. If you want to win in this game you don't have any friends, and you keep your enemies close enough to taste their sweat.

It wasn't the first time I'd used a man's libido against him. And it probably won't be the last. I needed to do my part. Kyle was busy on the dark net, bringing our armchair supporters into the fold, burning their minds with the same truth that brought me to Daniel in the first place. The truth we won't let stay buried.

The truth that made Cole's touch even harder to bear. His lips even harder to kiss. That first night I couldn't look him in the face as he grunted and groaned. Even the quadruple scotch hadn't blurred reality enough for me to forget.

After the recruitment drive, a lot of the Gridless newbies asked why I didn't just kill him there and then. Stick him through the heart while his pants were down. Which made Kyle and me despair for the next generation, and lament even more the loss of so many good people. We really were playing the big leagues with only our reserves on the pitch.

You've got to be strategic when you kill a leader. It's too easy for them to become a martyr. Can you imagine what would have happened if I'd sliced his throat that day? With Gridless considered the worst terrorists since ISIS, and opinion polls on his side? I'd have made him a saint. Not one single politician would dare to oppose the strategies he'd outlined in his speech that afternoon. You can't argue with a dead hero. Heath would have had a very easy job in making his legacy untouchable. England would have been condemned to an even longer ERP reign.

No, it has to be the right moment. A moment like now, when the whole world is watching. A moment when you can, even just briefly, show them the man behind the curtain. Once Rosa's statement is broadcast, everyone will know the awful truth, and there will be justice.

When they finally see what they've been sold, I hope the people tear this country down in rage.

PART 3

1
ROSA

I wonder if Soheila's watching. The cameras are focused on the archbishop, but I must be visible in the background. There are millions of people tuned in. But it's strange how, once you get over the shock of being in the public arena, you start to only care about certain eyes. The rest of them become nothing more than background in your mind. I don't care about the faceless masses. I don't care what Mr and Mrs Joe Public think of me. You have to get like that, otherwise it would drive you mad.

It took me a long time, and a lot of mistakes, to learn how to live with it. Jimmy's funeral was watched by eighteen million people around the world. That's more eyes than I can even imagine. Yet it didn't occur to me at first that I would never be anonymous again. I thought if I could just get through that day then it would all be over. That's supposed to be what funerals do. They give you closure. Everyone lives day by day when they're grieving, the counsellor they appointed for me told me that.

"You have to allow yourself time to heal," she would say. "Take it a day at a time, or even an hour, or a minute if you have to. You don't need to think about tomorrow yet. Just keep going, eventually you'll find the way ahead will clear."

I'm sure that's great (if a little pithy) advice for most

bereaved teens, but it didn't work like that for me. Taking things a day at a time and not thinking about tomorrow was part of the reason it got so out of hand. And the PIDs were pretty keen to make sure we didn't think about anything beyond the funeral too. If we had, perhaps Mum would have changed her mind about it.

But she was so focused on giving her son the best send-off, she didn't give a thought to life after Jimmy. I guess to her there simply wasn't one.

But I was eighteen. Intelligent, ambitious, not exactly a supermodel, but not a dog either. I could have had a life of my own. I could have had a career, met a decent guy, had a couple of kids, a dog, and all that jazz. Lots of people lose a sibling. They always grieve, but they move on, become a person in their own right. Cole lost a brother and went on to be Prime Minister, for Christ's sake. But when the world won't let your brother go, you can't either. I became simply 'Jimmy's sister', a whole life utterly defined by my sibling. A whole identity imposed on me, always overshadowed by an image of a boy.

An image that wasn't even true.

Jimmy was all anybody talked about. But the more they talked about him, the further away he seemed. When we returned home from the funeral I was desperate to talk to someone who hadn't joined the herd, someone who saw through all the crap. Someone who knew Jimmy for who he really was. I looked at the photo on my desk. Soheila. We hadn't talked in months, but I knew she'd be the one I could count on. Plus, she was on the other side of the globe. Her news didn't come through Cole-filtered lenses.

I didn't think about the time difference, I was so consumed with my need to speak to someone rational. When she answered she was in her nightclothes, her long thick hair uncovered, tumbling over her shoulders, eyes like pin-holes. I'd woken her up. But she didn't seem to care.

"Rosa!" She was squinting at me, her mouth twitching as

if it were unsure whether to smile or not. "Oh, Rosa, are you okay?"

She was once again a beacon of light in the darkness. Everything around me had become so polished, so preened, so artificial and camera-ready. Here she was, just as she is. Dishevelled, half asleep. But such beauty lay in that open, genuine face. It had been so long since anyone had spoken to me without an agenda, I'd forgotten what true compassion looked like. Oh, my star. The sight of her made my eyes water and my throat close up. I couldn't speak. I just shook my head as the tears fell onto my keyboard.

"I wanted to call you," she said, "last week when we heard. But Dad said we ought to wait. Damn him, I knew I should have called you. Oh, shit, I'm so sorry."

There were so many things I wanted to say. So much to tell her, so much I needed to get off my chest. But the floodgate had been opened, and the tears I hadn't been able to cry at the funeral couldn't be held back. I didn't dare glance at my own image in the top right corner; I knew I was a red-faced snotty mess. I heaved with the sobs that had been hiding inside. Soheila whispered and cooed, not trying to take the situation for herself, just letting me be. Letting me feel.

There was a noise in the background. We must have woken her parents. She called out, "It's Rosa," and the door to her bedroom opened behind her. A fluffy purple dressing grown moved closer, and Mrs Afzal bent down into my line of sight. Her own hair long and loose. I'd never seen it down before.

"Rosa. Oh, my darling." She touched a hand to the screen, as though she were trying to place it on my shoulder. And I wished I could step through the screen, be with these two angels, be in their embrace. Be with people who would rush to find a tissue when I cried, not a microphone.

"Oh, honey, we're all so sorry," Mrs Afzal said. "Kadeem tried to call your father, but he didn't answer. We thought you might all need space. Is there anything we can do?"

I took a deep breath, but my outpouring had given me hiccups. My stomach muscles spasmed as I spoke.

"It's all crazy… Everyone's… gone… crazy… I… just… need… a… friend."

The two Afzal women looked at each other. Soheila widened her eyes, her mother thought for a moment, then nodded.

"Okay," she said. "I'll book the flight in the morning. Rosa, tell your mother not to worry, I'll arrange a hotel for Soheila, she's got enough to deal with without a house guest."

I couldn't believe it. All these people around me, and not one of them gave me what I needed. Yet my star would fly across the world just to be by my side. She was, and always will be, the very best of people.

Oh, God, what have I done? What would she think? I picture Soheila's eyes watching me from behind those cameras. And I feel ashamed.

2
TERESA

Kyle was staying in a run-down townhouse converted into eight squalid bedsits. After the opulence of Cole's hotel suite, the smell of piss in the hallway was a stark reminder of our situation. The funeral had gone well, and Cole had celebrated by taking his success-induced testosterone out on my body. The afternoon had been spent ordering room service, and languishing on silk sheets, in between mercifully short episodes of fucking. I tried to forget his slimy hands, and how his face looked like a constipated toad above me. Sleeping with the enemy hadn't yet become passé. Fortunately, it had already become productive.

I stepped over the discarded beer bottles, my ridiculous diamante heels squelching on the carpet, and let myself in. The room smelled of booze and marijuana. Kyle was lying on the torn sofa, bottle of Jack in his hand. He didn't even look up. I strode past and dumped the small shopping bag I was carrying onto the cracked work surface that served as a kitchen.

"Bread, milk, and pot noodles," I said. He grunted. I pulled a pair of counterfeit Shades out of my pocket and chucked them at him. "I need you to hack the National Grid."

That made him sit up.

"You fucking what?" He was slurring. Jesus.

I sighed. "Seriously, pull yourself together. You heard me.

I need you to hack the National Grid. And I need you to leak the info, badly."

"Oh. Oh, right, yeah. Cos it's that easy."

"There's some stuff on those knock-offs." I pointed to the Shades in his lap. "I got what I could off Cole's while he was having a shit. Should help, I guess."

"What stuff?"

"How the hell should I know? Didn't exactly have time to study it. Anyway, you're the hacker. I'm just the cum bucket, remember?"

He flushed red. So he wasn't so obliterated that he didn't remember screaming insults at me the day before. I had to get this guy sober. Seeing as he relied on me to bring him everything it shouldn't be too hard. I should never have bought him alcohol in the first place, but I felt sorry for him trapped here. He was a doer like me. Control freak some might say. Either way, I could sympathise. Inaction is enough to drive you crazy.

He got up and examined the groceries I bought.

"This it?" He looked disgusted.

"Yes. I am not bringing you any more booze, Kyle. I'm serious. Not until this is done."

"Fucking hell," he muttered. "You know I can't leave this sodding dump, don't you?"

He was the UK's most wanted man. With CCTV and facial recognition everywhere he just couldn't chance it. Coming to Tower Bridge to meet me that night had been a massive risk. But at that point the photos of him hadn't gone public. Now the whole country was looking for him. The fake identity he'd created for himself could get him a bank account and false references, but it couldn't change his face. He couldn't just pop to the corner shop. So he had to hide here, behind a locked door in a house full of illegals and toppers, the kind of people who are so busy hiding themselves they don't notice anyone else.

"Well, you'll fucking well die here, sooner rather than later, if you don't do something."

"What do you mean?"

"The chips, Kyle, the fucking chips."

I sat down on the filthy armchair and wrenched my shoes off. I really hadn't thought things through as well as I should. We knew making the chips compulsory was the grand plan, everyone with half a brain knew it. I also knew that using the Lincoln kid to get Cole out of a PR nightmare would have the nasty side effect of giving him an excuse to rush them through. I'd thought it a necessary evil to get higher up, and in a better position to take him down. But I hadn't fully comprehended all the repercussions. I hadn't counted on Cole's arrogance.

"You're not going to stop him rolling them out just by hacking the system!" Kyle snapped.

"I know that. Don't you think I know that? How fucking stupid do you think I am? But the bastard's less cautious than we thought. He thinks the system's watertight, that it can't be hacked. He's so fucking sure of it that he's including military, and police. *All* police. Think about it. What happens to us when I get chipped? What happens to *you*?"

He turned pale. Yep, that was the fatal flaw all right. If I got chipped I could be traced. Anywhere, anytime. That was the extra function the public didn't know about. GPS as standard. The government could already see the location of every benefit claimant and legal working immigrant in the country. Soon everyone who didn't want to die from lack of health care would be on the grid too. Their data tracked constantly. Everywhere they went, everyone they knew, anything they bought. Analysed and scrutinised, all in the name of public security. And, as a nice little sideline, sold to advertisers. Cole and his cronies all had shares in DatStats, the market leader in consumer data farming. Not that anyone knew, the PIDs covered those tracks for them.

But that wasn't the worst of it. As well as your personal information and your immigration and employment status, the chips also contained details about your tax contributions. That's what you call forward thinking. Once all the illegals had died or been forced out by their inability to access services, Cole would claim the evil-doers were still among us, hiding like rats, living off our scraps. Security had to be stepped up. We had to weed them out. And so a chip would be needed even to purchase goods. Every shop would be required to scan its customers, with fines or imprisonment for business owners who sold to the unchipped. Then frontline services would start to give priority to those with the highest tax contributions. Better schools, better healthcare. All that was coming, down the line. Most of it's already upon us now. Daniel's predictions have come true one by one. But that day, the problem we faced was more immediate.

If I got chipped, the game would be up. And Kyle wouldn't have anyone to feed his sorry arse. We had to act. He had to pull himself out of this funk.

It seemed I was right; it was the lack of anything to do that was crippling him. Partly my fault, I'd urged him to pull back a little from the recruitment drive. The Dark Web was under constant scrutiny from the PIDS. That was a pain in the arse for communications, but a golden opportunity for what I had in mind.

The sense of urgent purpose worked like a shot of amphetamine. I swear he stood several inches taller than before as he flicked on the kettle and spooned heaps of coffee into a mug.

"So, can you do it?" I asked.

"Depends what's on those fakes. But…" he smiled for the first time in days, "if anyone can do it, I can."

His good mood didn't last long. There was nothing of any use on there.

"It's a fucking graveyard." Kyle sighed, his pupils darting wildly behind the counterfeits. "It's just his personal emails and messages. Nothing I can use. He called you his mistress in one of them, at least I assume it's you? I haven't seen your arse, so I don't know if it's smoking or not…"

"Give me that!" I snatched the fakes and surveyed the message. To someone called JH, it can only have been Heath.

Those two were thick as thieves. I tried not vomit at the text exchange.

JH: Good job today. Shall we meet to discuss next steps?
Cole: Not today. I've already got a meeting with the mistress.
JH: The one with the smoking arse? Lucky you. Send her my way when you're done.
Cole: Give me good coverage at the press conference Wed and I just might!

This was good though, aside from the slimy misogyny. He'd talked about me to Heath, called me his mistress; that meant he wasn't planning on stopping our rendezvous any time soon.

"He obviously keeps his work accounts locked down, which is only to be expected," Kyle said.

"I know," I sighed, "but when I realised how cocky he is, I dunno. I thought maybe he'd be lax and keep his Shades logged in."

"No such luck. But he seems quite taken with you."

"I should fucking well hope so," I shuddered at the memory of his sweaty body, "after everything I've let him do!"

Kyle screwed up his face. "Please. No details. No torture the ERP could devise would be worse than the thought of him mid-coitus."

I laughed. It was good to see Kyle's humour coming back, it meant he had ideas. "Yeah, well, remember that next time you dismiss my role in all this. Talk about taking one for the team."

He grinned. "You're right. I am sorry, Terri. I've been a shit recently."

I shrugged. "It's been a shitty week."

"I am actually quite surprised you haven't kneecapped me for my mouth."

"Contrary to popular belief, I'm not completely psycho. I

don't go around incapacitating my allies." I smirked at him. "But if you let on to anyone, I will have to kill you."

"Your secret's safe with me." He crossed his heart, and smiled wide. "You know, there might be a way to get in after all."

"I'm all ears."

"You've exchanged email addresses, yes?"

I nodded. "Pretty much. He got me to set up a separate one, it's how we arrange when to meet."

"So... he'd trust your address and open an attachment?"

"What kind of an attachment?"

"A Trojan. Malware that installs an OMR logger, and allows us to stream directly from his Shades onto these counterfeits. If he accesses the National Grid we'll have his password."

"And then he'll know he's been hacked and trace it straight back to me! No dice, hotshot."

"What do you take me for? We won't hack the Grid until you've had another little midnight appointment, so you can remove the Trojan from his Shades before we hit them. I can cover your tracks, encrypt everything. Untraceable."

I thought for a moment. It was risky. I wasn't one for risky. But getting chipped was an even bigger risk. And Kyle would be just as screwed as me if this went tits up. He wasn't one for risks either; both of us were only here because we'd made the decision *not* to risk our own arses. I could count on his desire for self-preservation if nothing else. Hanging me out to dry wouldn't end well for him, so he was just as invested in my safety as I was. That's about as close to trustworthy as a person can be.

"Okay," I said. "If you think it's safe, I guess I have to trust you."

"Great! Now, I can handle the Trojan, but I need you to provide the, er, attachment."

"Yeah, what kind of attachment? It's got to look legit."

"Well, given the nature of your, erm, relationship... I was thinking a selfie."

"We're not exactly a cute couple," I snapped. "We don't

send each other kissy lips and *I miss ooo, snugglebum* messages!"

He cleared his throat, and dropped his voice to a whisper. "A different kind of selfie."

The penny dropped.

"Oh, good God! Really?"

"It'd get his attention. I could take it for you if you prefer... Maybe that 'smoking arse'..." He was almost giggling now.

"Fuck off!" I grabbed the fakes and stood up. "I'll do it myself."

"Do you want me to help you with the lighting?"

"No! I'll use the bathroom."

Kyle rarely ventured outside his room to the shared bathroom, unless he had to take a shit. He said he was too paranoid. He preferred to piss in a bottle and empty it down the sink. Frankly, when I saw the state of the facilities I couldn't blame him. Someone had left the seat up, and the stench from the shit stains streaking up the sides was noxious. I knocked the lid back down with my elbow, and it clattered and split. Silverfish scuttled across the lime green linoleum, the unshaded light bulb swayed from a frayed cord that looked as though it might snap. The small vanity sink wasn't even plumbed in properly, only one tap was actually attached, and the waste pipe was being held together by a combination of grime and ancient duct tape. Yeah. The illegals really were coming over here and living in paradise.

The door didn't fucking lock. There had been a working bolt at some point in history, but all that remained was the metal casing. I'd be squatting over Kyle's bottle myself if I needed a piss while I was here. I rested my Shades on the edge of the cracked, mildew-ridden bathtub and knelt down in front of them, laying tissue beneath my knees so my trousers didn't catch hepatitis from the floor. I pushed my back against the door, so no one could fling it open.

I'd never done a glamour shot before. And this one couldn't be less glamourous if it was in an abattoir. I unbuttoned my shirt, set the Shades timer and posed. I tried to look friendly, and yet sexy. It didn't work. The pictures were dreadful, all grimace and nipple. I decided if I couldn't keep the disgust off my face I ought to keep my face out of it altogether. I wrenched my trousers down to my ankles and took another shot, this one from the neck down and the knees up. I could barely look at it, but it was done.

I went back to Kyle's room and handed him the fakes.

"There," I said. "Not exactly a page three boudoir shot but it's got enough."

"Nice," he said, putting them on a little too quickly.

"Don't look at it."

"How am I supposed to encrypt a Trojan into it without... whoa! Nice assets, Terri."

I kicked his shin.

"A little bit of professionalism please, you primordial slime."

"Sorry." He rubbed his leg. He'd have a bruise tomorrow. Good. "I'm only joking around. I promise I'm taking no notice whatsoever. It's all just pixels to me. Think of me as a doctor, just another day at the office. It's not exactly the first time I've looked at naked ladies on Shades."

I glanced at the waste basket full of tissues and felt queasy. "Just fucking get on with it."

He nodded and sat in the armchair, concentration etched on his face. He muttered about encryptions and reroutes, but it all sounded like a foreign language to me. I fell asleep on the sofa, dreaming about armies of electrons surging through the air toward the Ever Cloud. When he shook me awake a couple of hours later, the grin on his face told me Cole had taken the bait.

"Terri, Terri! We're fucking IN!"

I tried to smile back, but I felt woozy. "I knew you could do it," I mumbled. He thrust a black coffee at me. I was notoriously disinterested in anything without caffeine.

"He's online now. I can see everything he's doing, as he's doing it."

"What's he up to?"

"Well, I think your picture must have got him going... He's watching porn."

Oh, Christ. What a hideous thought. But quite an advantage for me. A little window into his secret desires, something to give me the edge and keep him interested.

"What kind of porn?" I asked, praying it didn't have anything to do with bodily fluids and rubber sheets.

Kyle raised an eyebrow and smiled. "Girl on girl."

I grinned. That I could manage.

"You may as well go back to sleep, I guess," Kyle said. "He could be looking at this for hours."

"Nah," I said. "Six minutes tops. Trust me."

I was right. A few minutes later our illustrious Prime Minister had clearly attended to the job in hand, and activity on his Shades stopped. Kyle was despondent, he thought that was it. But just as we were resigning ourselves to getting nowhere until tomorrow, the feed picked up again. Kyle watched closely as Cole checked all his various accounts.

"Moron uses the same password for everything. I mean *everything*!" he exclaimed.

"Including the National Grid?"

"Worth a shot."

Turned out we didn't have to wait for Cole to log in, he did use the same idiotic code (IX45GGYC) for everything he did. I wondered what it meant, but I couldn't exactly ask him. Kyle jumped up with triumph when the database allowed him access.

"I'm in, I'm in! Jesus. It's all here. All the info, everyone on the Grid. All the names, addresses, even their fucking blood groups. Every single person with a chip, their whole lives laid out in front of me. It's fucking awesome. Look." He handed me the counterfeits. I took a big gulp and set the cup down before scrolling through the database. Millions of names, accompanied by all the private information you could ever want to know. Each one a person, but reduced to a statistic.

"It's fucking appalling is what it is," I said, navigating into a random folder. Lissen, J. She was claiming disability, had two previous marriages, no children, bank account with Lloyds, blood group O-, shit, even her medical records were on there. She'd had cystitis a few months ago. Abortion aged 16. I navigated away, it felt like eavesdropping. Then I saw a name in the list that made me pause.

Lincoln, J: Deceased.

Damn, I'd forgotten the kid had got chipped voluntarily. I didn't go into his file. I'd already used the poor sod posthumously for my own ends. Poking my nose further into his real life seemed distasteful.

"But it's gold," I smiled. "Cole isn't going to want to risk the public finding out about the assorted STDs his cabinet and commanders have had. This should make him think twice about who has to get chipped."

"It's a bit… morally dubious though, isn't it?" Kyle said. "I mean, these are just innocent people. You really want me to leak all their personal details?"

I snorted. Morally dubious? Apparently Kyle had forgotten we were 'terrorists' now.

"Badly," I replied. "I want you to leak it badly."

"I don't follow."

"The information doesn't actually have to get out, Cole just needs to know it could. Put it up on BANtor." BANtor was the Dark Web forum we used to use to spread information. It was being monitored day and night by the PIDs, everyone knew that, which meant that no one was active on it. Not a single thing had been posted since the arrests. Even our armchair supporters knew better than that. "The PIDs will take it straight down, no one will be any the wiser. But Cole will know his system isn't as safe as he thought it was."

“And you’ll be sure to point out the dangers of that.”

“Exactly.” I picked up my work Shades. I had a message from Cole waiting in my inbox, a reply to my degrading selfie no doubt.

“You gotta get that Trojan off, though. ASAP,” Kyle cautioned.

“Working on it,” I snapped, opening the email.

Zara,

Nice preview. When’s the live show? Tonight?

I grinned. It was all falling into place. “Dirty bastard wants to see me tonight.”

“Great,” Kyle said. “And you reckon you’ll get a chance to remove the virus, if I talk you through how?”

“Uh huh. Thanks to your snooping, I’ve got a plan that’ll make sure he’s distracted.”

3
ROSA

It's only now, as I imagine Soheila's eyes watching me from behind her Shades, that I realise how tough her visit must have been. For her, as well as me. It seems I'm as guilty of being selfish as everyone else. There I was, so desperately wanting someone to see *me* in all that was going on, I forgot to do the same for the one person who truly did.

I still hadn't quite understood the repercussions of being known to the public. The reporters abandoned their vigil outside our house the day after the funeral, Mum having delivered the family statement they were holding out for. The PIDS had helpfully penned it for her, and talked us into standing behind her as she read it out. For support, they said. But her words were as insipid, and Jimmy-less, as the funeral had been. She was no longer the harried mum of a real, humanly flawed and complex boy. She was the grieving mother of a hero, a legend. And she played the part beautifully.

It's no wonder they chose her to do the honours. Look at what else there was on offer. A plain, cynical teen, who hadn't even had the good grace to shed tears for the cameras at the funeral, and Dad, whose final sparks of emotion had burned out when he smashed up the shed. He walked, he talked, but all life was gone.

Mum, though, she was the perfect image. Immaculately dressed, cried her eyes out on cue, and, most importantly, she was totally sold on the notion that Jimmy was a hero of the people. Dad and I, well, we were still just grieving for an ordinary boy, one we loved. We were still angry at him for leaving us, for dying from his own stupidity. And we were caught up in something so much bigger than us we didn't know how to fight it, or if we even should. I knew he felt the same as me, but for all my wishing, he never spoke about it. Maybe everything would have been different, if he and I had talked to one another. If he'd come into my room on any of the nights I lay awake and sat beside me. If he'd put his arm around me, cut through all the bullshit with one perfect whisper of observation. One voice of reason, to show me I wasn't alone.

But our paths had fractured. I think at one point, he and I had walked the same trail, my footsteps falling in the indents his had made. But somewhere along the way he'd turned a different corner. It was inevitable, when you think about it, that three people walking different tracks would grow further and further away from one another. I couldn't see it back then, though. Back then it seemed like a bump in the road that would eventually smooth if we just kept walking. I thought that when the madness died down we would find one another. Perhaps we would have, if it ever had.

But on the day Soheila arrived, I was still oblivious to the storm. Out of sight was out of mind. The absence of any reporters outside our house seemed to mean they were no longer interested in us. Mum didn't want me going to the airport. I assumed she was worried about bomb threats or something, but maybe she was more savvy than I gave her credit for. Maybe she knew a public place wouldn't be the best idea. I assumed she didn't offer Soheila a room at ours because she was in still in the disarray of grief. Perhaps I was wrong on that one too. Maybe she did know more about how the media works than I realised.

It was the first time I had left the house, apart from the funeral, since it happened. I felt a rush of excitement, freedom even, as I walked out of the door and into the waiting cab. Guilt crashed down quickly enough. It does that. Lies in wait on the peripheries of your grief, watching for its moment to pounce. Those moments when you start to feel anything other than stomach-gnawing pain. The fleeting moments that start to resemble happiness. It won't let you have them. Not until your penance is paid. A hundred thousand hours, or so it seems, of tormented thoughts.

It's a beautiful sky today. *Jimmy will never get to see the sky again.*

This meal is delicious. *Jimmy would have loved it.*

Maybe I'll go to the movies at the weekend. *Making plans? Jimmy doesn't get to make plans. Why do you deserve life, and not him? It should have been you.*

You can't stop them coming, I'd learned that already. Instead you have to ignore them, like playground bullies. Eventually their catcalls become white noise in the background. But they never stop entirely.

I realise now the cab driver must have known who I was, but was sensitive enough not to mention Jimmy. But I took his lack of conversation to mean I was anonymous, and never credited him with tact. Perhaps, though, I'd have been better prepared for what was to come if he'd made my notoriety known to me.

I was so excited to see my one true friend I didn't take in the faces of the hotel reception staff. Possibly a clue would have lain there. Maybe there were nudges and whispers; I was too preoccupied to notice. I made my way down the luxuriously carpeted corridors with only one thought on my mind. Soheila.

When she threw open the door and I saw her standing there, beautiful and welcoming, I couldn't stop the tears. She didn't speak. She didn't have to. She wrapped her arms around me, drew me close, my sobs soaking her lilac hijab. She swept me gently inside, closing the door without ever breaking our embrace. I let her guide me to the sofa, and we sat, wordless, for what seemed like hours, as she cradled me and let me feel. Safe in the arms of the purest soul I have ever known.

Eventually I lifted my head, looked into those eyes and whispered, "Thank you."

She smiled, and shook her head gently. "Does the moon need to thank the stars for their company? I love you, Rosa, there is nowhere I would be but by your side when you need me."

If I had one last wish, it would be for her to still feel that way for me. Of all I have lost, and will lose, her quiet, patient affection hurts the most. Perhaps, there is some parallel universe somewhere where she and I still hold true. Where we meet after work, both of us successful independent young women, drinking coffee in a bistro full of multiculturalism and sofa-lined booths. Discuss our day, comfort each other from the corporate slings and arrows. Keep each other's hearts pure, hold each other's secrets in our chest. Those last few hours we spent alone were the closest I have come to peace since Jimmy died.

Why did I have to ruin it?

4
TERESA

"Ever heard of non-disclosure?" I turned to the prostitute in my passenger seat. She shuffled forward, reapplying her gaudy lipstick in the mirror.

"Of course," she snapped. "I have had famous clients before, you know."

I sneered. She was pretty enough, but I wasn't keen on the arrogance.

"Let's get one thing straight," I said. "He's not the client, I am."

"But—"

"Oh, it's him you'll be fucking..." I ran my fingers over her shoulder and smirked. "Mostly. But I'm the one hiring you. I'll pay you triple your standard rate for threesomes."

Her mouth dropped open.

"BUT," I continued, "there are conditions."

I had her attention. "There always are." She smiled. "Don't worry, I'm a pro."

"You better be. Firstly, you mention one word of this to anyone – not just the press, even your little call girl chums – I will destroy you."

"Of course I won't. I'm not some kind of media whore. Kiss and tell is bad for repeat business."

"Fine. But there's more. I need you to keep him busy."

"That's kinda what I do."

"Shut your mouth and listen." She scowled, but paid attention. "In the middle of things I'm going to leave the room. To get some champagne from the bar."

"Why don't you order room service?"

"For Christ sakes, do you ever can it? Maybe because I don't want to have to bribe some fucking porter not to go selling his eyewitness account. Or maybe, because I'm the paying customer and you're the hired entertainment and it's none of your fucking business."

"Fine."

"The point is you need to keep him engaged while I'm gone. Under no circumstances is he to become bored, or check his Shades."

"Don't stress. Trust me, when a guy's with me he ain't thinking about anything else. He probably won't even pay any attention to you. I hope that doesn't hurt."

"Just in case you think I'm spouting hot air…" I pulled out my PID badge. She flinched. "I want you to know that if you break these conditions I can, and I will, make life extremely unpleasant for you. I'm fucking serious about this."

She smiled wide, leaned over and kissed my cheek. Her hot sweet breath made me shiver.

"It's okay, hon," she said, "I'm serious about fucking."

I laughed. She was starting to grow on me.

Cole looked like all his Christmases had come at once when I turned up with my little 'present' in tow. Thanks to Kyle's monitoring of his porn-watching habits I had exactly what I needed to make sure he was too consumed with excitement, and lust, to worry about silly little things like leaving his Shades unattended on the table.

Our glorious leader was even more of a flash in the pan than usual, so the girl and I had to amuse ourselves with each other for the most part. I began to worry that his lack of stamina might mean she couldn't keep him engaged long enough for me to carry out my task. My concern must have been obvious on my face because she leaned in and whispered in my ear, "Don't worry, honey. I'll go slow on him."

I nodded, and she replied with a wink. Standing up, she stretched out and sighed, showing her curves and flawless body in all its glory. I almost forgot the job in hand. She glanced sideways, checking his readiness.

"Oh," she said, when it became obvious round two was imminent, "I am so *thirsty*..."

I don't know why I doubt other women's ability to deceive so much.

Cole reached out for the phone by the bed. "Shall I get us some room service, ladies?" He smiled. God, he looked like the king of the greasy sloths, laid back on his silk pillows, everything on full display, as he grinned at his 'subjects'.

"No," I replied hastily. "I don't trust the staff. I'm sure we've had to stop leaks from here before. Some judge or something had a Thai boy on the go I seem to recall. Nearly blew right up, and he was ERP. No, don't worry. I'll go down to the bar. I need to check my email anyway, Mills has an assignment for me. You two carry on, I'll be back with a bottle in a minute."

I pulled my dress on, without bothering with underwear. Cole reached out and grabbed my hand, bringing it to his fat, slimy lips.

"So dedicated, Zara. Such a treasure. But, it seems rude for me to enjoy your present without you..."

Oh God. I leant in, kissed him deeply, trying not to gag. "I think it's the height of bad manners not to play with a new toy you've been given," I said, gesturing for her to come closer. "Especially when it's already unwrapped."

"Well, I'd hate for you to think me ill-mannered." He reached out and gently pulled her onto the bed. "I'll keep her warm for you."

I doubted that.

She climbed on top of him, making exaggerated moans. I grabbed his Shades and slipped them in my pocket as he buried his head in her double Ds. She saw me, over his shoulder, but winked again. I wasn't sure how much a whore's promise of silence meant, but I figured she couldn't be less trustworthy than the politician himself.

Out in the corridor, I followed Kyle's instructions to remove the Trojan from Cole's Shades, then raced to the bar to grab the champagne. Tomorrow we could leak the info, show Cole the flaw in his plan and I could avoid getting chipped. Now that was something to celebrate. I might even be able to enjoy the evening now, if I focused one particular person rather than the other.

But as I waited to be served I made the mistake of switching on my own Shades to check my messages. Fifteen missed calls from Greyson. You can't ignore that many, however much you want to. I had to call him back.

"Jinks!" He was almost spitting at me when he answered. "Where the fuck have you been?"

"Sleeping," I lied.

"Well, for fuck's sake get here *now*."

"What's going on?"

"Major damage control, that's what. Mills is gunning for you. That fucking girl—"

My heart pounded. What the fuck? Had the girl upstairs betrayed me already? I'd only been out of the room five minutes. I tried to sound nonchalant.

"What do you mean?" I asked as coolly as I could.

"The fucking Lincoln girl!"

Rosa?

"What are you on about?"

"How can you not have seen it? It's fucking *everywhere*!"

"I was sleeping."

A link flashed up on my screen and I clicked it. *Dear fucking God*. I abandoned the champagne on the bar and ran. I told the barkeeper to ring up to the room, tell Cole I had to leave on urgent business. I was halfway across the car park when the cold breeze made me realise I'd left my knickers behind.

Fucking Rosa.

5

ROSA

After my initial outpouring I felt euphoric. Talking so openly was like a warm bath, soothing away my aches and invigorating my senses. Soheila ordered us coffee and cake from room service. We moved on from talking about Jimmy and started discussing the sorts of things normal teenage girls concern themselves with. Exams, clothes, boys… and I didn't even feel guilty.

When someone really sees you, really knows your heart, you don't have to make a display of your emotions. Giggling with Soheila about some boy who'd made a pass at her didn't mean I wasn't grieving. And she understood that. But somehow, to the rest of the world, the ones who don't care to look beneath appearances, you have to wear the expected feelings like a badge.

Being slated for not crying at Jimmy's funeral taught me that. The world doesn't see how you feel, it only sees how you act.

That safe haven, that catharsis, should have been enough. But I felt high on normality. Sometimes after you've had the flu, or some nasty infection, normal health feels like a superpower. You don't just feel okay, you feel on top of the world. It was kinda like that. The simple act of sitting and chatting, of being Rosa instead of 'Jimmy's grieving twin', released far more serotonin than it should have. I felt invincible with Soheila by my side. Normality was intoxicating. I wanted more of it.

"Shall I ring for more coffee?" Soheila asked as we drained our cups.

"No," I stood up, feeling determined, "let's go out!"

She looked shocked. I've wondered ever since if she knew more about the country we were in than I did. Perhaps she was trying to tell me, but I batted her concerns aside without giving her a fair chance to voice them.

"Rosa, I don't know if that's such a good idea."

"Oh, c'mon! Just a coffee somewhere, maybe some shopping? *Please*. I haven't left the house since..."

She sighed. Fiddled with her hijab. I didn't even think to credit her with any insight. "I... Rosa, this isn't my country anymore."

Why didn't I listen? I pressed on like a freight train, mowing her objections down.

"I need this, Soheila. I need to do something normal, to feel human again. I can't do it on my own. I'm not strong enough. But you being here, it makes me feel alive again. Please, I need you. I don't have anyone else."

"Okay." I'd railroaded her. She was too kind-hearted, too concerned about me and my needs, to say no.

"It'll be fun, Soheila, just like if you'd never left, and we were still hanging out."

"Yeah. Just like how it would be if I never left," she said slowly.

"Don't you wish that?" I asked. "That you'd never left?"

"No." She pulled on her coat. "I wish the opposite. I wish you'd left too."

"Well, same difference. I tell you what, we can pretend this is Sydney, not London, if you like. Except for the weather."

She laughed. We walked through the lobby, and into the crowded streets, arm in arm. My heart, my soul, my star. I felt ready to face the world, ready to start healing. I felt safe, sheltered by the greatest friend I have ever known.

But the world doesn't see how you feel. It only sees how you act.

It all descended so quickly. One moment I was walking along, feeling the kind of sense of belonging, and pride, I see other teens exude when they troop with their peers. The next, it all started to go wrong.

I noticed the stares first. There's something very eerie about the British letting their façade slip. There they were, all walking next to one another, but pretending to be alone. No one wants to seem as though they're anything other than consumed with their own business. But once one or two break character, some kind of animalistic instinct rolls through the crowd like a tidal wave.

It started with whispers, little billows on the breeze. Too soft to be distinct. Soheila gripped my arm, and it crossed my mind how out of place she must have felt in her hijab. But still I was selfish. A few whispers and nudges wasn't a big deal, surely? Not compared to what I've been through.

But then a word came gusting through the rabble and hit me like a suckerpunch.

"Jimmy."

It was me. I was the reason for the rumble of disquiet brewing all around. They recognised me. It was a shock, I admit. I thought I was yesterday's news. Oh, I knew people were still talking about Jimmy, but I didn't think I was important enough to be remembered. Certainly not distinct enough to be recognised out of context. Still, I pressed on, my face set in a stare of feigned ignorance. They recognised me, so what?

A big fucking shit storm, that's what.

The whispers gathered momentum. That little breeze became a tornado swirling all around us. The shock on their faces turned to sneers, the nudges to jibes, the mumbles to shouts.

"Traitor!"

"Your brother's turning in his grave!"

"Selfish little cow!"

They were still buying that crap about how I was heartless, all because I couldn't cry with a dozen cameras in my face. We quickened our pace, heading for the cafe a few shops down. My heartbeat became a thunder in my ears. I moved my feet to match its rhythm. *One, two, three*. Block out the voices, get through the door.

But as Soheila's hand reached out to push the glass open, I heard a yell that drowned out my own percussions.

"Fucking Muzzie lover! Fucking terrorist!"

Shit. It wasn't the funeral they were angry about. It was Soheila.

"C'mon, Rosa!" She wrenched me through the door. We turned back to see the shop front lined with passers-by, staring at us from behind their Shades. They were filming us. The barista moved quickly, locking the door and turning the sign to Closed. The mob outside banged on the door, shouting obscenities. The manager came hustling over, waving his hands in the air.

"You can't be in here," he shouted. "Don't bring that rabble to my shop! I don't need this kind of publicity!"

"Please," Soheila's tears rolled down her cheek, and her arm shook beneath my palm, "we can't go back out there."

He exhaled through his nose. The rest of the patrons were staring. Maybe they were sneering too, but they all looked blurry through the stinging water forming in my eyes.

"No," he said at last, "I suppose you can't. Very well, follow me."

He led us past the tables full of blurred shapes drinking their coffees. Someone shouted *Bitch* at me, or maybe Soheila, as we walked by, but the rest just muttered and tutted. He showed us to his office out the back, and closed the door on the world.

"I'll have to call the police," he said.

"But we haven't done anything wrong." I protested.

"Yeah, well. Do you fancy going out there and trying to explain that to them?" he said, gesturing to the shop front.

I shook my head. He was right. We needed help.

He left us alone and I joined Soheila in her sobs.

"I'm so sorry," I said. "I had no idea. I just didn't think."

"No," she said, taking my hand. "I had a bad feeling about it, I should have said no. But I never expected this. Such hatred, Rosa! I mean, I see it on the news sometimes, and Dad always says we should thank Allah that we got out when we did. But… to be in it, to see their faces, hear their words. I can't understand how people can behave in such a way."

The tabloid lying on the table caught my eye and I unfolded it. On the front page were the mug shots of two Middle Eastern-looking men. The headline above read: *The Islamic Face of Gridless*. I grimaced. "Maybe this has something to do with it."

Soheila let out a sound that was half guffaw and half sob. "Oh, your news, Rosa," she said. "This is shameful. I've been following the whole thing back home. Twelve people were arrested from Gridless. Ten of them were white."

"I don't suppose that matters to many people," I said.

"You should not stay here, Rosa," Soheila said. "This is not a country for someone with a heart, and brains. It will destroy itself, and take you with it."

"How can I leave? I've got no money, no career yet. And my family is here!"

"Just promise me you'll find a way, as soon as you can. I can't bear to think of you here."

"I promise," I said. And I meant it, at the time.

When the PIDs had entered my home, and upturned Jimmy's online life, they felt like an invading force. But when Officer Greyson walked through the door of the small, cluttered office, I felt only relief. His was the friendliest face – aside from Soheila's – I had seen that afternoon. He must have been pissed off, but he hid it behind layers of professionalism and congeniality that soothed my anxiety.

"Miss Lincoln." He smiled, and shook my hand. As though I were a respected peer, not a naive teen who'd got herself into a fix. "Lovely to see you again, Rosa. And this must be Miss Afzal?"

He offered his hand, but Soheila didn't take it. He pretended not to notice. "Charmed to meet you," he said, pulling up a large box and squatting on it as there were no more chairs.

"Now, you seem to be having a little situation, ladies. But don't worry. My officers are dispersing the crowd, and we've a car waiting to take you to safety. While that's being sorted out, why don't you tell me how this happened?"

Soheila glared at him. I guess she'd heard about Cole's new branch of the police force, and made her own conclusions. I'd never been a fan of the Public Information Department myself, but since Jimmy's death its officers (with the exception of call-me-Zara) had treated me with more kindness than anyone else. Even if that kindness came at a price, Greyson had a way of making me feel everything would be okay. As though he was on my side. So, I blurted it all out. How alone I'd been. How nobody in the world seemed to understand me, except Soheila.

"That's why she came," I explained. "I needed a friend, and she's the best one in the world. But, I didn't know how people would react. I'm sorry, I never meant for this."

"No, Rosa," Greyson said. "I'm sorry. We failed you. We should have realised you needed more support. I confess, we've been busy managing all the public interest in your brother, and bringing Gridless to justice. We neglected to give you the help you needed. You should've had someone to talk to about all this."

"I've had counselling," I said. "I just needed a friend."

He shook his head. "No, I meant practical advice. How to deal with the media, and the public. What not to do, who not to be seen with…"

"What do you mean?" Soheila piped up. "She's not a criminal! Why shouldn't she do whatever she damn well pleases?"

Greyson gave a wide smile. "If only it were that simple, Miss Afzal. You're right, of course. Obviously, *we* have no objection to your conduct, Rosa. As your friend so pertly asserts, you're a free woman. But I think you may have discovered that doing as you please, even though you have a legal right to do so, can end up badly."

I couldn't argue with that. I was still shaken by the force of what had happened.

"You see, Miss Afzal," Greyson continued, "my goal here is one of protection, not restriction. If I could police the actions and opinions of the great unwashed I would. But, you must see that is impossible. Sadly people will, for a time, scrutinise you, Rosa. I can't prevent that. But if we work together we can educate, and empower, you. Help you navigate this media storm. Trust me, if you play the game, just for a little while, they'll lose interest. But if you keep courting controversy before the dust can settle... well, you'll never be left alone."

"I didn't know I was courting controversy," I protested.

"I know," he said. "That's why this is our fault. We should have realised you wouldn't be aware of all the issues. You are only eighteen after all."

That stung, but I couldn't disagree. The afternoon's events had proved to me that I didn't understand the climate at all. I may not like it, but I had to live in it. For all my behind-closed-doors notions of subversion and rebellion, I knew I was a vulnerable young girl. A rabbit caught in the headlights. And I never wanted to feel so hounded, so trapped by my own notoriety, ever again. If I had to take their advice in order to survive the storm, so be it. It wouldn't be for ever.

By the time we were escorted to a waiting car with blacked out windows, the police had moved the crowds along. Greyson said going back to the hotel would be a bad idea; one of the reception staff had already tipped off the press. The whole place was surrounded by reporters, hoping to pounce on Soheila if she returned. He'd already sent a lackey to collect her things. So we were taken to PID HQ, a huge building fronted by frosted glass that gave the illusion of transparency.

Not that there's much to see, at least not on the surface. It looked like any other office building. Secretaries bustled back and forth carrying papers. Middle-aged men wearing striped shirts stomped about barking orders. Wiry young officers strode down polished corridors, entering locked doors by virtue of their fingerprints. I figured if there was something interesting here it was behind one of those. And we would never see it.

Greyson led us down a long hall, and stopped outside a door marked B.

"Rosa," he said, "why don't you come in here with me? We'll have a little chat, take a statement, just for the record, and then work out what help we can get sorted for you."

"What about Soheila?" I asked.

"Miss Afzal, please take a seat in the room opposite. My colleague will be along shortly. We'll just need a quick statement from you too, then we can get your belongings back, and sort out somewhere for you to stay."

"Can't we do our statements together?" she asked.

"'Fraid not. Policy you see. We have to take them separately."

"Okay," Soheila said. "I'll see you in a bit then, Rosa."

I nodded. "Yeah, see you." I gave a small wave.

She turned and walked into the small room opposite. I never saw her again.

6
TERESA

She couldn't have timed it worse if she'd fucking tried.

The PIDS couldn't get around the fact that Daniel and Kyle were white. But it wasn't too much of an issue. Every nut job white terrorist for the past five years had been proclaimed to have 'links to Islam'. (Even if that link was just buying the odd kebab from the Muslim-run takeaway down the road; the public never ask.) Several Asian members of Gridless had been arrested, so those were the ones whose photos appeared in the top right corner whenever the news was on. Schyler and Kimmy, with their bleached blonde hair and decidedly Western dress sense, never got their five minutes of fame.

On that particular Tuesday, the buzz had been about the preliminary hearings for the captured terrorists. So Sayid and Khal, being the most 'Muslim looking' of the bunch, had their mugs all over TV again.

Yet Rosa, in her infinite fucking wisdom, had chosen this day to walk through the middle of London arm in arm with a hijab-wearing foreigner. Which meant my evening turned into a nuclear shit storm.

I raced into the offices and barked at Belinda.

"Where's Rosa?"

Belinda tried to ignore my obvious mood and smiled sweetly. "She's in interview B with Greyson."

"Right." I started to stride down the corridor, ready to murder her – or at least give her a piece of my swirling mind – But Mills stopped me in my tracks.

"Oh, no you don't, Jinks. *You're* not going anywhere near her."

"But—"

"You were supposed to have sorted her. You were the one we trusted to talk the kid round. You were supposed to make sure she'd toe the line. Well, how did that go, eh? Do we have a compliant teen giving credence to our story, or do we have a giant fucking clusterfuck?"

"Sir, with all due respect, how was I supposed to know she'd cosy up with a Muslim?"

"Oh, I'm sorry. Here I was thinking anticipating people's actions and covering them up was part of your fucking job! How silly of me." Spittle was starting to form in the corners of his mouth. I calculated that it wouldn't be wise to argue. "Have you seen the footage? Have you read the public reaction?"

"Yes, but—"

"*You* were assigned to her. So why is she making such great big fucking gaping holes in her judgement?"

"She's just a kid, sir. She's eighteen."

"Oh, right. Right. Let's just make that statement, shall we? Sorry, Mr Joe Public, we know you're all upset about the callous, uncaring twin of our great nation's hero getting chummy with a terrorist, but y'know, she's only eighteen so, oh, well."

"Well, that's not actually the case..."

"And Jimmy Lincoln isn't really a hero, he was a drugged-up prick. If truth meant sweet Fanny Adams, we wouldn't have a job! The fucking vloggers have already claimed she's been radicalised! This was your baby, Jinks, your bright idea to save our skins. You told me once you'd stand by it, so why the fuck weren't you here protecting your own house of cards?"

He was right. I could have flayed myself. I even saw the fucking photo on her desk. I'd done the digging, I knew the

Lincolns had links to a Muslim family abroad. I should have thought of every eventuality. Constructing a legend means tearing down anything that might shake its foundations. If there's one thing you can count on it's that people will find a way to fuck up your plans. Part of being a PID is anticipating human fallibility, and hiding it from public consumption.

"I'm sorry, sir. Really, I am. Please, can I have a word with her?"

"Oh, no. That ship has sailed. Greyson's doing just fine; let's leave it to someone who was actually here when the shit hit the fan, eh? You'd do best to get out of my sight. Take that fucking Muzzie to the airport, and make damn sure she never comes back. Can you manage that much?"

"Yes, sir."

I was seething, but mostly at myself. I'd have to just suck it up and wait for things to blow over. I knew Mills would calm down by the morning. I found the little Muslim girl in Interview C, crying all over the table. No wonder she was so pally with Rosa, they were both pathetic. She didn't say anything as I led her out the back door and into the car. But as we pulled away she found a squeaky, nasal voice.

"Where are we going?"

"Airport," I replied. "You're going back to where you came from."

"You don't need a plane to get to Kent," she said.

Oh, a little sass in there after all then.

"Australia, smart-arse. But watch your mouth or I might accidentally drop you in the Middle East."

"But I have to see Rosa. I have to see if she's okay."

"Not gonna happen, chicklet."

She shuffled, straightened up and tried to look assertive. "Then I demand you take me to the Australian embassy."

I nearly choked. "Embassy? Jeez, you *have* been gone a long time, haven't you?"

"Since before the ERP came to power, thankfully."

"Yeah, well, wise move. Just you stay put this time, get it?"

I pulled at the scarf around her head. "And take this fucking turban off before we get out."

She scowled. "It's a hijab."

"I don't care if it's the crown fucking jewels, it's got you in enough trouble today. You really want more public harassment?"

"No. But it won't make any difference. I'm all over the internet, they'll recognise my face."

"Sweetheart, no one was looking at your face. No one sees past that rag."

She stared at me, and I felt a little shiver. Rosa always says she has eyes that see who you really are. I'd not have believed her if I hadn't felt it too. Not that I ever told Rosa that. She has no clue I ever met her precious 'star'. But I had an uneasy feeling that she saw through the PID front. And that she understood.

"And is that how things should be?" she asked me, still staring.

"It's not about what should and shouldn't be, honey. It's about what is."

She smiled, and nodded. It was eerie.

"I understand. But I must speak to Rosa."

"You really care about her, don't you?"

"Of course. She's the best friend I've ever had."

"Well, then I'm going to level with you. You being seen with her caused a shower of shit for us. We can deal with it; we can protect her even. But only if you're not in the picture."

"What do you mean?"

"Let me put it simply. That thing on your head makes you a terrorist as far as almost everyone in this country is concerned. If you continue to keep in contact, her life will be ruined. Some armchair warrior somewhere will find evidence you're in touch. It'll go nuclear. There'll be a level of public outcry even the PIDS can't control. Someone might even decide traitors like her need a bit of vigilante justice. If you care about her, stay away. Because while you sun yourself on your nice Australian beaches, she's gonna be here. Dealing with this shit."

She turned toward the window and said nothing, for at least fifteen miles. She was pissing me off. Partly because I couldn't read her, and partly because I respected that. I hate manipulating people I respect. Luckily, I don't come across very many of them. Eventually she broke her silence.

"I understand where you're coming from. Things here are much worse than I knew, and our news doesn't shy away from its condemnation of your government. I accept that, although I am free from it, Rosa still has to make a life here. And for all the world I would not make that any harder than it has to be. So, for her sake, I will do as you suggest. But I need to ask you, will you do one thing for me?"

I wasn't happy with this turnaround, but whatever it took to get her to play along was what I needed to do.

"And what would that be?" I asked.

"Tell her. Tell her why. I will not contact her again, at least until your Prime Minister is on the scrapheap where he belongs. But only if you promise me you will tell her it is for her sake. Tell her I love her, and she will always be welcome to leave this cesspit of a country and come join her friends across the world."

Yeah. Like hell I would.

"I promise, Miss Afzal," I said. "It will be the first thing I do."

I was worried for a split second that those eyes really did have some way of seeing truth. But she seemed satisfied, so I guess she wasn't the all-knowing benevolent oracle Rosa built her up to be. She was just a teen. Less easily played than Rosa, but playable nonetheless. She even took her hijab off when we reached the airport. No one recognised her without that. I babysat her until she boarded, then headed back to the car, confident that was the last I would ever see or hear of her.

All in all, the evening had turned out all right. This little mess could be easily fixed with the girl out of the way. Some public gesture by Rosa ought to do it, along with a few articles suggesting she had been targeted in her vulnerable state. We could get the public feeling sorry for her easily enough. And, most importantly, the Trojan had been removed. Now Kyle could go ahead and leak the info.

I was just about to set off for HQ when my Shades beeped, a number I didn't recognise, but I answered.

"Zara..." It was Cole, "Where are you, this is an emergency!"

"Don't worry, I know. That's why I rushed off, remember? I've got it all in hand."

"What are you talking about? How could you know, I've only just realised myself."

"Well, you were... busy. But it's done. I've got rid of the Muslim girl."

"Muslim girl? What Muslim girl? I'm talking about that damned prostitute! She's stolen my Shades!"

Oh, shit. I reached into my pocket. I still had his Shades.

I sped across town to the area just outside Camden where I'd picked up the girl earlier, praying she'd be back touting for business. It didn't take long to spot her. She was leaning through the window of a Ford Focus, negotiating her next encounter. I pulled over on the red line, switched on my hazards and dashed over to her. The chill of the night air reminded me I was still going commando.

She looked up from her greasy potential punter and smiled when she recognised me.

"Back for more so soon, honey?" she asked. "I'm afraid I'm doing business with this fine gentleman right now. But I've an opening tomorrow."

"Come with me. Now," I hissed.

"Hey! Back off," the fat, ruddy-faced guy in the Ford yelled at me. "She's dealing with me. She don't want no skinny lezzo. She's about to get some real meat, ain't that right?"

The girl smiled. "Sure is." She reached through the open

window and stroked his chin. I didn't have time for this shit. I pulled out my PID badge and flashed it at him.

"Shit!" He sped away so fast he nearly took her arm off.

"Well, fuck!" She glared at me. "What did you do that for? He's a regular and you've gone and spooked him. I gotta make a living, you know."

"You'll be compensated," I snapped. "Just get in the car."

"Well," she softened, "it seems my schedule just opened up, so I guess I could squeeze in a return trip to the Plaza. Perhaps you'll actually come good on the champagne this time?"

"We're not going to the Plaza."

"Well, where are we going then? I know you missed out earlier, honey, but I don't usually do girls as a rule. Only as part of a threesome."

"I don't want to fuck you," I said. "We need to go see a friend of mine."

"All right," she strapped herself in. "You seem to have some rather high-flying friends, with deep pockets, so I'll trust you. I usually like to know where I'm going though. You gotta be careful in this game."

That's fucking logic for you. It's fine to get in a stranger's car, but only if they tell you where you're going. I wanted to point out that her safety plan had a bigger hole in it than she did, but I gritted my teeth and just kept driving.

When we pulled up outside the dilapidated terrace where Kyle was hiding out she screwed up her nose.

"Here?" she asked.

"I'm sorry, princess," I said. "I didn't realise you had such high standards."

"All right," she said. "No need to get pissy. I was just expecting something else, that's all. But as long as I get paid I don't really care."

"Good," I said. "Now follow me."

Kyle jumped up from the sofa when he heard me open the door.

"Terri?" he called out.

"Yeah, it's me. But there's something you should—"

"Terri?" The girl followed me inside, pulling her coat a little tighter around her as she surveyed the filthy walls. "I thought your name was Zara?"

Kyle was only wearing his boxers. Not an appealing sight at the best of times. Combined with the open-mouthed shock it looked almost comical.

"What the fuck, Terri?" He picked up a blanket and chucked it over the laptops and Shades scattered all over the kitchen side. "Who is this? What the hell are you doing bringing someone here?"

"Is this the client?" She plastered a smile over her disgust. "Great to meet you, stud."

"You bought me a whore?" his face was red now. "What the actual fuck? Have you lost your fucking mind?"

"Right," I said, "both of you sit down, shut up, and listen to me. We are in deep shit."

They both sat down slowly, staring at me like naughty school children.

"Kyle," I said, "I need you to sort out a fake passport for this... working girl. She needs to get out of the country. Now."

"What are you talking about?" The girl stood up. "I already told you I won't rat on your precious PM."

"It's not about that." I sighed. "Unfortunately, the Prime Minister believes you have stolen his Shades."

"What?" she said. "*You* stole his Shades, I saw you do it!"

"I know," I said. "But he can't know that, so I'm afraid you're going to have to take the rap for it."

"Wait," Kyle said. "Back up, why does he think his Shades have been stolen?"

I pulled them out of my pocket.

"Fuck, Terri! Couldn't you get the Trojan off?"

"Of course I could! I'm not stupid! But... there was an emergency at work, I had to go. And, well... I forgot I had them. So after he was done with missy here, he went to make a call and discovered they were missing. So he put two and two together and came up with a thieving prostitute."

"Oh, shit." Kyle started pacing. "Who knows?"

"No one," I said. "Only me. Funny, he doesn't want anyone knowing about his little recreational sport. I told him to give me a couple of hours to sort it, but if I don't get them back to him soon he'll have to get the PIDs involved."

"So, what the fuck do we do?"

"I go take these back to Cole, I'll tell him I took care of her. Meanwhile you get her some papers and then we get her on a plane."

"I don't want to leave!" she protested. "Why the fuck should I? I'm not a thief!"

"Well, he ain't finding out it was me, honey," I snapped. "So I'd say emigrating was your best option."

"Are you insane, Terri?" Kyle said. "What's to stop her selling her story to the press once she's out of the country? How the hell can we trust her?"

"I'll pay her for her silence," I said. "Seriously, Kyle, what other option is there?"

"Who are you people?" The girl was getting hysterical. She stared at Kyle. "I know you, I fucking know you! I've seen you in the papers! You're that guy, the one they're after." She started backing up toward the door. "Holy shit! You guys are Gridless!"

"Shut up!" Kyle launched forward, grabbed her by her coat and threw her down on the sofa. "Well, that's just fucking great, Terri! Why didn't you just call the cops on me yourself?"

My Shades beeped, fucking Greyson. I had to take it; I'd already been AWOL when it kicked off earlier. "Just calm the fuck down, both of you!" I snapped. "I'm going to take this call, and when I come back we're going to sort this mess out, right?"

I left them scowling at one another and stepped outside to answer Greyson. I wish I hadn't. He was only calling to big himself up.

“I thought you’d want me to keep you in loop, Jinks, even though Mills took you off Rosa.”

How fucking thoughtful. All he really wanted to do was brag that he’d talked her round and we wouldn’t get any more grief from her. He even got her to agree to get chipped for the cameras, to try to repair her public image. I gave him the ego stroking he was angling for, and got off the call as quick as I could. But not quickly enough.

The girl lay motionless on the couch. One arm dangled down toward the floor, the other slumped across her ample chest. Her eyes were wide, he mouth set open in a silent scream. Her skin looked like plastic, more sex doll than sex worker. Behind her, Kyle stood panting with a scarf wrapped round his clenched fists. The steely look on his face was almost as frightening as the corpse he stared at.

“You shouldn’t have brought her here, Terri,” he said in between gulping breaths. “You gave me no choice.”

“Jesus, Kyle!” I pulled the door shut behind me. “There’s always a choice. I was taking care of it.”

“Well, excuse me if I don’t feel like trusting my life to a hired slut.”

“You didn’t have to kill her!”

“Yes, I did. If you could take your head out of your arse for two seconds you’d see that’s exactly what I had to do.”

“She wouldn’t have turned us in, I’d have made sure of it.”

“And how do *I* know that? Her word? Your word? Sometimes I think you’re a bit too fucking sure of yourself. There was only one way out of this, Terri, and you didn’t have the balls to do it.”

“We’re not killers, Kyle! Murdering innocent people is not the aim of the game here.”

“Well maybe the stakes got a little higher when you fucked up and let everyone get caught, eh? Or maybe you should have taken care of your own mess and not brought it to my fucking safe house! I am not risking jail for the sake of some fucking whore. Get your head in check, surely you can see what a risk it would be to let her walk away?"

He was right. I knew it deep down. We'd never really be sure, even if she was on the other side of the world. Maybe some reporter somewhere would offer her more for her story than I could for her silence. It was the cleanest solution. The mission not the man. I guess that holds true for innocent bystanders too. Collateral damage. But I was never that ruthless. Never could write off life like that. I never wanted us to be like them.

And I was shocked. I never knew Kyle had it in him. To me he was just the hacker geek. I suppose I've got a reputation for being more ruthless than I really am, and maybe no one ever realised just how ruthless he could be when it came to saving his own skin.

So now we had a dead body to deal with. Not a major issue in itself, Cole had plenty of contacts who could help. But I couldn't have government workers coming here. We'd have to get the body somewhere else. At least there wasn't any blood. Kyle's method of despatch had that going for it.

"Okay," I said. "I'm sorry, you're right. I wasn't thinking straight, been a hell of a night. But we've got to get this corpse out of here, and I can't carry her on my own."

"I can't leave! You know that."

"There's no CCTV on this street, let's just get her to the garages round the corner. C'mon, it's past 2am. Shove a hoody on, keep your face down, it'll be fine. It's either that or she stays here and decomposes in your living room. Besides which, if I don't contact Cole within the hour he's going to get jumpy, he's freaking out already. I promised him I'd sort this."

He reluctantly agreed. We rolled her up in the large, vomit-stained rug that lay wonky on the cracked wooden flooring. We couldn't have looked more suspicious, two hooded figures hauling a mass wrapped in carpet down the street in the dead of night. But the only people out at this time round here were up to their own crimes. More concerned about not being caught themselves than what anyone else was up to.

We reached the garages and unrolled the rug. She fell face down on the gravel and I couldn't help but pull her skirt down to cover her modesty. She should at least have some dignity in death, even if she didn't in life. I took the scarf from Kyle and shoved it in my pocket. There'd be no fingerprinting to worry about. This murder would go unreported. Cole would make sure of it.

"Right, get going," I snapped at Kyle. "I'll give you two minutes to get back, then I'm calling in."

"Okay." Kyle struggled to secure the rug under his arm. "You got this straight?"

"Of course. I found her on the corner there, touting for business. Demanded she gave Cole's Shades back, which she did. But she threatened to go to the press, so I had no choice but to silence her. Don't worry, he'll buy it. But it goes without saying that we'll have to delay the info leak. Can't have him thinking it had something to do with the theft."

Kyle nodded. "All right. I'll sit on it, but not for too long, eh?"

He left, jogging as fast as he could with the cumbersome rug under his arm.

I waited a few minutes. Then I made the call.

7
ROSA

When I finally left the interview room, Soheila was on a plane home. They made sure of that.

But Greyson was good. So good that by the time they told me my star was somewhere over Europe, I believed it was a good thing. Yet again, I got played. A person in shock is very susceptible to suggestion. And boy was I in shock. Even after several warm drinks, and hours spent in the quiet, secure and sparsely furnished room at PID HQ, I was still trembling at the memory of the crowds, and the violence of their voices.

No matter how much you want to believe that people are your allies, and the establishment your enemy, when you see the hatred in their eyes you can't help but question yourself. The common people had pursued me, debased me, humiliated me. Greyson had been my knight. He took me to safety, let me speak all the things that were in my heart, without ever once checking the clock.

He showed me the footage. Said he wanted me to be prepared, wanted me to see it while we were in a safe space. Now I know it was just his way of reaffirming what he was telling me, making sure I was conditioned by his words. It wasn't so much the sight of myself, running like a hunted rabbit into the coffee shop, that got to me. It was the comments below.

Filthy fucking turban lover.

She's a disgrace!

If she loves muzzies so much she should be treated like one. Someone should rape her and cut her fat fucking throat.

It felt like the whole world hated me.

"I know it's upsetting, Rosa." Greyson handed me tissues and put his arm around me. "But you need to understand what people are really like. It's like we were saying before, remember? After your brother died? We talked about heroes and villains, and how the public need both? Even if there are none, they'll create them. That's why we do what we do, to try to control and direct that instinct. To protect the innocent."

"That's why you made Jimmy a hero?"

"Exactly. If we have a villain, in this case the terrorists, then we need a hero. Unfortunately, the public tend to overextend in their thinking. And, well, after this morning's headlines... let's just say you and Miss Afzal picked a bad day to go for a stroll together."

I couldn't stop the tears. "It was my fault! She didn't want to go out, I practically forced her."

"How could you know, Rosa?" He spoke so gently. I felt protected, understood. "No one expects you to be keeping up with the news, you're grieving after all. And it isn't Miss Afzal's fault either; not being a resident of this country she wouldn't know the etiquette surrounding religious dress."

There was no law against wearing a hijab in public. There didn't need to be. Those few Muslims who had remained in our country had abandoned wearing them. Being spat and sworn at in the streets will do that to you.

As much as he told me it wasn't my fault, I heard something different. Which I'm sure was the intention. Soheila wasn't a resident of this country, but I was. I should have known better. Now she was all over the internet too, and all because I was too selfish to consider things from her point of view. He told me Zara had escorted her to the airport. I was upset that we hadn't got to say goodbye, but happy that she was away from the mess I'd landed her in.

"You've had a terrible time, Rosa," he continued, "but we need to think about the future now. Your future. And I promise we will not leave you to fend for yourself again. I'll be there with you, to guide you. You can call me anytime."

I nodded, and tucked the number he wrote down into my pocket. But I couldn't see a way past this. How could I ever leave the house again? How could I have a life at all? He seemed to read my mind, because of course I was still labouring under the delusion that I wasn't as transparent as cling film.

"Now, there are two ways we can go from here," he said. "I know which one I think would be best. But it's up to you. The first option is to lay low. Stay away from public places, keep your face off camera and wait for all this to die down. Now, that's the course of action I would recommend if you weren't the strong, intelligent young woman that I know you to be. But you have a bright future ahead of you. If you can just tackle this head on it'll go away faster, and you'll be free to pursue your goals. So, with that in mind, I would strongly advise you go for option two."

"Which is?"

"Own this. Put yourself forward. Make a statement giving your side of the story, then back it up with some public gestures designed to rebuild your reputation."

"Like what?"

"Oh, anything you like really. Make a donation to the veteran's hospital in Jimmy's name. Or you could sell some stories about your childhood together and give some of the proceeds from that. Write a memorandum blog, our guys can do it for you if you like. People would go mad for that. Everyone wants personal stories about their heroes. And I think it would help if you got chipped."

"But I don't agree with the chips."

Greyson just laughed. "I don't agree with income tax, Rosa, but it doesn't mean I can choose not to pay it. The law is being rushed through as we speak. You'll have to get chipped sooner or later, no matter what your views are. All I'm saying is turn it to your advantage. Go to one of the voluntary chipping stations before it becomes mandatory. With a camera crew in tow, of course. Do it in honour of Jimmy. The public will lap it up."

When you're drowning you grab the lifebuoy, no matter who throws it. Greyson was giving me a plan, a way to navigate the waters. If the day's events had taught me anything it was that I knew nothing. I needed guidance, and he was the only one offering it. So I agreed to his scheme.

He proved himself to be a useful asset almost immediately. When my parents turned up, he fought my corner. My mother made the whole incident about her, of course, and how much distress I had heaped on her already overburdened shoulders. But Greyson leapt to my defence. He insisted it was the PIDs who were at fault, and talked about how much I had suffered. But she didn't care, so he changed tack. Told her about the planned publicity stunts. Her burning martyr act faded, and I thought I could see pound signs flashing in her eyes.

She was already a pro. Less than a month had passed, but she was an expert at the media relations stuff. When I think back to that time, it's the evenings that stick in my mind. Dad would mope around in PJs, dropping pills that fizzed and bubbled into half-empty glasses of water. But she wafted through the house and out the door, leaving us with nothing but the fug of hairspray and Chanel. Off to some appearance where she would receive endless adoration.

I guess she needed to keep busy. She kept Jimmy in the spotlight, so he didn't fade from her life and leave her with nothing but the abyss my father had succumbed to. But to me it felt callous. As though she was flaunting her grief.

So I was to be a show pony, rolled out for the cameras.

I would have to accept my public flagellation if I were ever to have a normal life again. The spark had come back into Mum's eyes, and she chatted with Greyson about schedules and stylists. I just wanted to go home and call Soheila. I needed to apologise. I knew I could handle it all, the public scrutiny, the cameras and interviews, even the chip, if only she forgave me.

But she never did. The night turned to day and I called, and called. But each time my request was declined. At first I thought she hadn't got home yet. Then I thought she must be sleeping off jet lag. Then came the sickening realisation that she must be deliberately ignoring my calls. I tried to pacify myself with a thousand excuses as to why she couldn't answer, but I didn't believe a single one of them. Eventually, after two days of torment, the endless ringing tone that had become the soundtrack to my misery was replaced by something worse.

You do not have permission to dial this number.

She'd blocked me. My star had gone from my life, leaving only darkness.

8
TERESA

"People are stupid, Zara." Cole scraped the last of his feta salad from the plate with a piece of bread, and shoved it into his mouth. "Heath taught me that."

He'd been delighted with how I'd taken care of our little prostitute problem. As I suspected, he'd had no trouble despatching some goons to dispose of the body. A quick DNA analysis revealed her name was Heidi Jones. She had plenty of previous and no close family to mourn her absence. People like that can disappear easily. I had worried the whole incident might make him think our liaisons were too risky, but the opposite proved true. He admired my loyalty and resourcefulness, so he said.

I guess a woman who can take care of dirty business when the need arises was a welcome change, after twenty years married to his insipid wife. She'd funded his early campaigns, but never stoked his desire. Lucky her. So, instead of backing out of our affair as I had feared, the shared secret brought us closer. He invited me to his summer house in Kos, having ensured that Mrs Serena Cole was otherwise engaged with charity functions for the week.

A chance to have his ear for a whole week (even if it did have the unfortunate drawback of having to share his bed) was too good to pass up. I figured it would be the perfect time for Kyle to release the information we were sitting on. I'd be right there with Cole to point out the implications, with no one around to contradict me.

We spent the first few days lounging on the beach, drinking cocktails and fucking. Cole blissfully unaware that back in London a drunken, unwashed hacker-turned-murderer was set to point out a fatal flaw in his grand scheme. Eventually, after the novelty of relaxation began to wane, our conversations had turned to work.

"I'm not telling you anything you don't already know, of course," he continued, washing his starter down with a large slug of beer. "As a PID I bet you could tell stories of public stupidity that would surprise even me."

I nodded. "We kinda rely on it most of the time."

"Yes. Yes I suppose you do," he said. "It was a shock to me at first though. You'll think me naïve when I tell you that, I expect. But I spent my formative years among the highly educated classes. I didn't have the benefit of experiencing the daily life of the working classes like you did."

I wanted to smack his self-satisfied face, but I just nodded politely.

"In many ways, my dear," he continued, "you are the more educated of us both."

Condescending twat.

"I suppose, if you're referring to the school of life." I tried to sound congenial.

"Precisely, my girl, precisely. And that's what I was missing. That's what they were *all* missing. Taking the time to understand the mind-set of the common man, and create policy accordingly, that's what won me the election. It's not a pretty place to wallow in, but the psyche of the masses is where you find the key to unlock Number Ten."

"I guess you have to understand someone in order to manipulate them..." I realised what I'd said the moment it was out. "I mean, that's how it works in my job," I added quickly. "Knowing how a person thinks and feels, that's how you can appeal to them."

"Exactly!" It seemed he was so caught up in self-congratulation he hadn't noticed my barbed comment. "I had to respond to what the people believed were the problems in order to achieve my goals. It's no good talking about deficits, international commitments and balancing books, they don't care about that. Don't even understand it. They care about what they can see, and feel."

"Which is?"

"Which *was*, Zara, which *was*. They cared about making the streets safer, about not being able to find a job, about people getting something for nothing while decent folk worked their fingers to the bone and couldn't even make ends meet! I knew I could do it; I could make us great again. But if Heath hadn't shown me the way, well, I'd never have been given the chance. He knew how they really felt. His reporters were out there, day after day, listening to the real stories, the real people. He knew they craved a true leader. Someone who actually listened, and would take action. He gave me the platform I needed to reach the people, and I used it to give them hope, and direction.

"Now look, crime is dropping, employment is rising, fewer people claim benefits than at any time in the last three decades! And all because I knew how to speak their language, knew the issues that were important to them."

"So what was the big secret then?"

"What it always is. Heroes and villains. People can't point their fingers at arbitrary concepts; balance books and GDPs are as ethereal as ghosts and myths to them. No, they need real things, flesh and blood things, to hold to account. They had already decided who their villains were, but no one seemed to be listening."

I put down my glass and stared at him.

"So," I said, "are you saying that your stance on immigration was pantomime?"

"In a way. Insomuch as I believe I could have achieved these levels of security and prosperity with or without those policies. But I am a public servant. That's what the rest of them had all forgotten. It wasn't down to me to tell the public what was best for them; it was my job to represent their views. In doing so, I have been able to deal with the real issues by giving them what they want first."

"So, you… you personally, didn't want to expel all the foreign nationals? Or stop immigration?"

He shrugged. "To be honest, it was neither here nor there. I wanted to make Britain great again, to make life fairer for the hard-working man. Increase security, reduce terrorism. I believe my chips are the way forward on that score, but I had to deal with what the public wanted first. I was elected for my promise to act, when no one else would take the hard line they wanted to see."

He was saying he wasn't racist? Saying he didn't care about immigration? For a few moments I questioned myself. Was it really the masses that had imposed their hatred onto the establishment, not the other way around? Had we, in fact, got the government we deserved?

But as he tucked into his moussaka, he quickly put an end to any sympathy I felt for him.

"Then, of course, there was Dover. Someone had to do something about Dover."

I just smiled, picked up my knife and fork. I couldn't trust myself to reply.

Someone had to do something about Dover.

Don't worry. Someone will.

9
ROSA

They didn't waste any time getting my public acts of contrition set up. That's how they work: strike while the iron's hot. Or before the victim of their schemes has time to change their mind. Because I *was* a victim. I know that now. Hindsight is a frightful, frustrating thing. Sure, they were getting me out of a mess. But not one of my own making, as I believed. When you look at the big picture, it was all their doing. I wouldn't have had a public reputation to repair if they hadn't first used my brother's death for their own ends. And yet at the time I was grateful to Greyson and his colleagues. Like a feudal peasant thanking the gracious king for a scrap of bread, when it was his taxes that left him destitute in the first place.

But I had my own agenda. I was still smarting from the blow of Soheila's block. They'd promised me a chance to tell my side of the story, and on camera. She'd told me she watched our news, that Kadeem used it to reaffirm to himself that he'd done the right thing in whisking his family across the globe. If she wouldn't let me apologise to her in person, at least she might see my interview. Maybe then she'd forgive me. They wanted remorse? Oh, I was full of it. But not for betraying the values of my country. For something far more important. For hurting Soheila.

So I let them take me to the studios. Let them snip and

spray my hair. Let them douse me in powder and paint, shove bits of silicone that looked like wilting chicken breasts in my bra, and tell me how to place my legs for the most flattering angle. All because I was to be unscripted. I could say what I needed to say, live on TV.

I sat in the pastel green armchair with cameras, lights, and microphones all trained on me, waiting for Charlize Chambrody. Remember her? She was a big deal news anchor a few years ago. Botched botox put an end to her career faster than the aging she was trying to mask would have done. I hear she's an alcoholic now. Good. I heard her before I saw her, that slightly nasal voice was very distinctive. She waltzed into the room surrounded by lackeys, moaning about her schedule. Greyson tapped me on the arm and whispered in my ear.

"Rosa, exciting news! This is going to be broadcast on Thursday, just before you get chipped."

I was half entranced by the lithe, bristling figure of Charlize striding my way, but I still found his news unsettling.

"What? I thought it was going out live?"

Greyson shook his head, beaming wide. "No. Change of plan. HQ think it'll serve you better if it gets combined with Thursday's footage. Brilliant idea when you think about it. Plus it means less pressure. If you stumble over your words or something like that. You can take your time, really make sure you get your points across."

"I, I don't..."

Someone shouted from behind a camera, "And places! Rolling in five..."

"Oops, gotta go," Greyson patted me on the shoulder. "Knock 'em dead!"

"Four..."

"But I..."

"Three..."

Charlize snaked into her chair and handed her coffee to an assistant who scuttled away, half bent like a Wimbledon ball girl.

"Two…"

"Charmed." Charlize greeted me, without making eye contact. "Ready?"

"One…"

"Not really."

"And… rolling."

Charlize's smile flicked on like a light switch. "Good morning! Welcome to *Sunshine Britain* with me, Charlize Chambrody. I'm joined today by a young lady who has found herself thrust into the public eye, under truly tragic circumstances. She is, of course, the twin sister of the famous James Lincoln, whose death has saved the lives of hundreds, and touched the hearts of so many more. Rosa, welcome. It's so kind of you to join us today."

"Hello."

"It's been a very rough time for you, hasn't it?"

"Yes."

"First the death of your twin, then all the media interest. No wonder you have… made some errors, shall we say?"

"Well, that's why I'm here. To set the record straight."

"Of course, of course. The press have been a little unkind to you of late. That must be quite hard to deal with? I mean, people can be judgemental, but we none of us really know how we would act in your shoes. So, can you tell me, in your own words, why you were so distant, unmoved even, at your brother's funeral?"

"It was just so… overwhelming. I loved him. I loved him so much. But I couldn't even believe he was gone, and then there were so many cameras, so many people. It didn't even feel real. I think I was just overwhelmed. That kind of shock, that kind of pain, you know? You don't know what's real, or right, anymore. You don't know how you're going to make it through the day, or who you can turn to. You just can't think straight."

"Of course. I think we can all understand that. So, there you were, trying to come to terms with the loss of a beloved brother, a *twin* in fact. Someone that you have literally shared your whole life with, and on top of that you've then had to deal with people criticising you. I can't even imagine how hard that must be. You must have felt very isolated."

"I did. That's exactly how I felt. That's why I wanted to see Soheila."

"Ah, yes," Charlize shifted in her seat, leaning forward. "Miss Afzal. Another reason you have come under scrutiny. You feel your friendship with her has been twisted by the press?"

"Completely. You have to understand, we've been friends since we were toddlers. She's the best person I've ever met. She was the only one who really listened, who seemed to care and understand."

"Mmm-hmm. And she's not currently a resident of this country, is that correct?"

"Yes. The whole family moved to Australia a few years ago, to get away."

"So just walk me through this, Rosa. You and Miss Afzal had been chatting online, for quite some time?"

"Ever since she left."

"And whose idea was it for her come and visit you?"

"Hers… I guess. She knew I needed a friend."

"So, what you're saying is that Miss Afzal, your childhood friend, came here simply to support you? That having not being a resident here for many years, she would have been unaware of the changes in our culture?"

"Well, she does still try to keep up with the news in our country. She's very well-informed, very intelligent."

"So what possessed her to walk through the centre of London with you, in full religious dress, on the same day the link between Gridless and Islamic extremists was confirmed? An act of defiance?"

"No! It was my fault. I insisted we go out. I know now that it was a bad idea. I was wrong. I was so confused, I was hurting so badly. I wish we'd never left the hotel. I've never seen so much hate for innocent people."

"You're talking about the crowds that pursued you, harassed you?"

"Yes."

"How did that make you feel?"

"Scared. Alone. Trapped, I guess."

"And how do you feel about the people that harassed you in the street?"

"They're animals. They just want someone to hate. They didn't see us as the human beings we really are. They wanted to punish us; in their mind we were villains."

"Why do you think that is?"

"Because they're brainwashed. By the media, by their own intolerance."

"That's a bold claim. Can you not see things from the public's point of view? The sister of a national hero, flaunting her friendship with a defiant Muslim?"

I sighed. "I can understand how it must come across if you believe everything you read in the papers. But once you have the facts things are a little different. And she wasn't being defiant. In her country lots of Muslims wear hijabs, she didn't realise how much things had changed here. She was just being a friend. It wasn't an act of aggression. It wasn't a statement of hatred toward our country like some of the journalists have twisted it to be. It was just a friend being there for her friend in her time of need."

"So there we have it. A young girl travels halfway across the world to comfort her grieving friend, and ends up in the centre of a media storm, through no fault of our own. Thank you, Rosa, for setting the record straight. Perhaps now people will think a little harder before they rush to judge, eh?"

"I hope so."

"Now, is there anything you would like to say to Miss Afzal, should she be watching?"

It was my chance. Maybe my only chance to make Soheila

listen to how sorry I was. Maybe even win her forgiveness. I looked straight at the camera. I tried to keep my composure, but I couldn't help the tears that rolled slowly down my cheek, or the wobble in my voice.

"I'm so sorry. You have to believe me. I never meant for this to happen. I was wrong. I thought I knew best, but I didn't know anything at all. I swear I'll make it up to you. Please, please forgive me."

"And… cut!" The guy behind the camera yelled. "Perfect. Wonderful job, ladies."

Charlize was already out of her chair and pacing around on her Shades before I could register what was going on. "Is that it?" I asked Greyson, who had come rushing over with a tissue for me.

"Yes," he said. "Great job, you did so well! I'm proud of you. It's going to be great. I've seen the schedule, they'll broadcast this alongside the 'behind-the-scenes' look at you getting your chip, and the memorial blog will go live at the same time. Triple whammy! You'll be the nation's sweetheart by 8pm on Thursday."

"I don't want to be the nation's sweetheart. I just want to be left alone."

"Trust me. The pendulum has to swing both ways before it can settle. There'll be a flurry of attention for a week or two, but at least it will be positive attention this time. Then it will all die down. You've done the right thing for your future, I promise you."

What a crock of steaming shit.

10
TERESA

I don't do regret. It doesn't get you anywhere. In fact, it sends you on a skyrocket to nowhere. Just look at Rosa. You can't change the past, only the future. If I sat around dwelling on every mistake, every bit of shit luck, every time I did something I'd prefer not to have done, I'd never manage to drag my arse out of bed in the mornings.

No, I don't regret anything I've had to do to get us here. But still, I'm fucking glad I had nothing to do with that interview.

I've screwed her over lots of times, I know that. It was never my goal, just like sacrificing a pawn is never the sole aim of a chess move. There's always a bigger plan, a few steps down the line. And really, what glory is there for a pawn still standing on the board once its king is checked? Her life would have been miserable with or without my input. At least now it will mean something. But I do feel a little bad for her. Sitting there, waiting for the final moment. I can see the fear in her eyes. But it's the sadness that really shows. She's about to give her life for a higher cause, and she's going to that martyrdom believing the only true friend she ever had hates her. I wish I could have told her the truth about Soheila's silence, I honestly do. But it might have changed the playing field too much. Might have given her another option. I couldn't take that risk.

The mission not the man.

But for all the wrong I've done her, at least I wasn't in that fucking editing suite.

We were still in Kos when the broadcast went out. Cole was like a pig in shit, practically bouncing up and down with anticipation when we settled on the villa's sofa to watch. It was less than a week before the chips became mandatory. He knew how fickle the public could be so he was pushing it through at lightning speed, before the knee-jerk approval could fade. Rosa's interview, and chipping footage, was to be the icing on the cake, ensuring those on the fence would be won over. I was equally excited, but for a different reason. Kyle and I had decided that just after the broadcast would be the perfect time for our little info leak. With me in another country, and sat right next to the man himself, there could be no hint of my involvement. Plus, I'd get the pleasure of seeing his pride turn to a fall.

It didn't matter that I seemed jumpy. Cole took it as dedication, and concern. He poured me a beer and put his arm around me.

"Don't worry, Zara," he kissed the back of my neck, taking my shudder for a shiver of pleasure. "I'm sure they've managed fine without you."

"I hope so." I was thinking of Kyle.

"It's always tough, relying on your colleagues. No matter how good you know them to be, there's always that part of you that wonders if you ought to have done it yourself. Believe me, I feel the same every time one of the cabinet makes a statement. It just shows how dedicated you are, how passionate. But we must learn to delegate, my dear. Trust in our teams. We're allowed a holiday after all."

Trust in my team. I did. Kind of. But my 'team' was just one guy, and I hadn't been able to risk any contact with him since we left England. The only thing I knew for sure was that he hadn't been captured. Cole would have heard if he had.

"Anyway," Cole continued. "I have it on good authority that it all went swimmingly."

I frowned at him.

"I'm sorry," he said. "I know we swore no non-urgent calls this week… but you'll have to forgive me. I couldn't resist checking in. You were having a snooze, so it's not as though I was ignoring you."

I smiled. "You're forgiven," I said. "Neither of us are very good at switching off, are we?"

"People with our drive and ambition never are," he said. "That's what makes us great."

He waved an arm, in an unnecessary call for hush, as that awful Charlize woman appeared on screen. She annoyed me even then, with her nasal voice. Too big for her boots, just like that tosser directing *The Raids*. A couple of years ago she tried to publish her autobiography, which was basically just an expose of the industry. She was pissed because she thought she was a rare talent, not just a pretty face and big tits. She was wrong of course. When the wrinkles started to become too deep for the make-up team to conceal the producers told her, in no uncertain terms, it was surgery or sack. Funny, she only actually objected to the surgery after it went wrong. Being too ugly to ever be on screen again, she thought she'd make a quick buck selling secrets. The reality behind Rosa's interview being one of them. Needless to say, we shut her down and stitched her up. The arrogance astounds me. She knew exactly how things worked, why did she think she'd be an exception? Delusions of grandeur, I guess. Not much of that left for her now, stupid cow. I heard the alcohol got her in the end.

But I have to admit she did a damn good job on the interview. From the establishment's point of view, at least. She began with her usual inanely chirpy greeting, but then went straight for the jugular.

"I'm joined this evening by the twin sister of national hero Jimmy Lincoln. She's come to tell us about her recent experiences with Islamic extremists, and the tactics they employ. Tactics that almost led to her becoming radicalised herself. Rosa, welcome. It's very brave of you to come on national television to speak on such a sensitive subject. I understand that you yourself requested the chance to speak to the nation. You feel that by opening up on this matter it may help others avoid the trap you almost fell into?"

"I hope so." Rosa almost whispered. She looked pathetic, like a bedraggled rag doll. They'd made her up, but then stuck her under a sickly yellow light that emphasised every shadow and blotch. The very picture of shame and contrition. A cautionary tale indeed. I have no idea what questions she was actually answering, but it didn't matter. The editing was flawless.

Charlize went on to quiz her about her friendship with the Muslim girl.

"So, you'd known her your whole life?"

"We've been friends since we were toddlers."

"Indeed. In fact, your fathers were once business partners, correct?"

"Yes."

"But a few years ago that relationship broke down. There were... allegations. Mr Afzal was suspected of having links with terrorists, so your father wanted to distance himself, is that right?"

"Completely."

Cole was beaming. I nodded along, in perfect PID style. This was perfect, from my professional point of view. But even though I couldn't stand the Lincoln girl and her self-indulgent pity, I couldn't untwist the knot in my stomach. Maybe it was because I hadn't been the architect of this particular stitch-up. I didn't have all the bullshit justification to do to myself. I can always convince myself my own actions were, ultimately, for the greater good. But this time there was no double agent involved. No undercover martyr playing the game for appearances' sake, but secretly for the demise of the system. This was just exploitation, pure and simple.

Charlize pretended to check the paperwork in front of her.

"I understand there was a police investigation, but it came to nothing because the Afzals fled?"

"The whole family moved to Australia a few years ago, to get away."

"But you kept in contact with Miss Afzal. Why was that?"

"She's the best person I've ever met."

"Or so you thought?"

"Yes. I was wrong."

"So, the two of you have been talking online for quite some time?"

"Ever since she left."

"And can you tell me, was she always interested in what was happening here? Perhaps, even, unusually so for someone who no longer lives here?"

"Well, she does keep up with the news in our country. She's very well-informed, very intelligent."

"And what sort of opinions does she have on our culture? Our freedom and way of life?"

"I've never seen so much hate for innocent people."

"So, this is what's confusing me, Rosa. I hope you'll explain. You were aware that the Afzals were suspected of having links with terrorists, you knew that your friend had some very intolerant views toward our country… how on earth did you get sucked in? From what you've told me earlier, she took advantage of your grief? How did that come about?"

"I loved him, I loved him so much. But I couldn't even really believe he was gone. I think I was just overwhelmed. That kind of shock, that kind of pain, you know? You don't know what's real, or right, anymore. You don't know how you're going to make it through the day, or who you can turn to. You just can't think straight."

"And then, of course, just when you needed support the country seemed to be against you? All those ridiculous comments about your lack of tears at James' funeral. I suppose, you just needed someone to be there for you?"

"She was the only one who really listened, who really seemed to care and understand."

"So you were vulnerable, and felt alone. And she used that to her advantage. Whose idea was it for her to come and visit?"

"Hers."

"And it was the public reaction, and the support of the police officers that finally made you see her for what she really is?"

"Yes."

"And how do you feel about the extremists now, Rosa? About all the things she said to you? About the intended plot that your brother thwarted?"

"They're animals. They just want someone to hate. They didn't see us as the human beings we really are. They wanted to punish us, in their mind we were villains."

"Why do you think that is?"

"Because they're brainwashed, by their own intolerance."

"Thank you, Rosa. It must have been very difficult to come here and say these things. I think we can all understand that grief made you vulnerable, and susceptible to suggestion. Perhaps we ought blame our own media. After all, here was a young girl in terrible pain, and instead of supporting her we, as a nation, condemned her. No wonder she took solace wherever she could find it. Now, you have of course followed your brother's fine example, and signed up for the chipping scheme ahead of its mandatory rollout, as a symbol of your loyalty to this country, and its people. In just a moment we'll be showing the behind-the-scenes footage of you joining thousands of others of loyal patriots in this act of solidarity. But before we go, is there anything you would like to say to the people of England?"

"I'm so sorry. You have to believe me. I never meant for this to happen. I was wrong. I thought I knew best, but I didn't know anything at all. I swear I'll make it up to you. Please, please forgive me."

Charlize turned to the camera. "I know I can, can you?"

Cole clapped, and picked up his Shades.

"I'm sorry, my dear, I feel compelled to congratulate your superiors on a job well done. Will you indulge me, just for a moment?"

I nodded, "Of course."

They cut to the footage of Rosa being escorted to a chipping station, guards on either side. I suppose it was for her protection, but it looked more like a prisoner being escorted to their execution.

I felt sick. The same pang of shame I had felt when I saw the Gridless sticker on her brother's door sat in my stomach. But there was no time to dwell on the Lincoln twins. Any minute now Kyle would leak the info, and I had to be on top of my game.

11
ROSA

In my final year at school we had studied *The Crucible*. Despite her best efforts, our passionate but somewhat drippy teacher couldn't get the point across to the more oafish students. They couldn't understand John Proctor's motivation.

"He's a whiny pussy," Kurt replied when asked for his character analysis.

Ms Hule turned a little pale. But she prided herself on encouraging freedom of opinion in her classroom, so she didn't chastise him.

"What makes you think that, Kurt?"

"He seriously went and got hung, rather than confess?"

"But he wasn't guilty, Kurt," Mrs Hule tried to reason. "Why should he have confessed?"

"To save his life, Miss!"

"Perhaps, to John Proctor, there are some things in this world that are more important than mere physical existence? Honour perhaps? Truth? Justice?"

"Yeah well, none of that's much good to you when you're swinging by your neck, is it?"

As hard as she tried, she couldn't make them see. To the oafs, Proctor wasn't a great and noble hero of literature. He was an attention-seeking cry baby.

They didn't understand. But I did. And never more so than when I sat and watched the farce that was my edited interview.

Sometimes it isn't death that destroys a person.

They spun me, cut me and left me reeling. I can't describe how I felt. Words like anger, betrayal and despair would best suit, I suppose. But I can't feel that now, in retrospect. All I feel is stupid and ashamed. That old sadist, hindsight, flagellates me, until it feels like my fault. Ignorance is no defence, they say, so perhaps neither is naïveté? Dad certainly didn't think so.

I looked to him, with my world and all I held dear in tatters all around me, as the one person I thought would truly understand. But as my tears fell, and I stared in disbelief at the screen, he just got up. Walked out on the spectacle, left me alone.

I followed him into the kitchen. "I didn't say that, Dad. Those weren't the questions she asked me."

He stopped for a second and looked down at his wretched, snivelling daughter. I waited for words of comfort and wisdom.

"What did you expect, Rosa?" he asked. "When you dance with the Devil you don't get to pick the tune."

He'd finally broken his silence, to offer me condemnation. All the time I had been desperate for an ally, for advice, and he'd said nothing. Didn't he know that if he had cautioned against the PIDs' plans I would have abandoned them in a heartbeat? But he sat in judgement without ever first offering counsel. Of all the betrayals in my lifetime none ever cut so deep.

Mum was the epitome of hook, line and sinker. Trying to get any understanding out of her was pointless. In her eyes the PIDs could do no wrong. They had given her son a hero's immortality, after all. I tried to explain why I was so upset, that I had been manipulated, misquoted. But she wouldn't hear of it. She was three-quarters of her way through a Cabernet. Empathy for her wayward daughter wasn't on her agenda.

"Of all the ungrateful little... Honestly, Rosa! Do you

know how much work has gone into sorting out that little mess you got yourself into? All those man hours, not to mention everything I've suffered, on top of all this family's already been through! And all you can think about is that you don't like the editing job? I've never heard anything so selfish in my life!"

"But Mum, they're saying the Afzals had terrorist connections."

"Oh, and you suppose you know better, do you?" She slammed her wine glass down on the table. "All those highly trained professionals, all that research, but *oh no!* A silly little teenage girl with a chip on her shoulder knows better?"

The lines around her mouth were more pronounced than I had ever seen them. Eyeliner started to smear under her lids, wide eyes locked me in a gaze that I could swear held hatred. I felt the blood in my veins turn cold at the unmasked scorn she shot at me.

"You're not saying… You don't think that, surely?"

"Left in a bit of a hurry, didn't they? I always thought that Kadeem was a bit dodgy."

"No, you didn't!"

"Now you know what other people *think*, do you, Rosa? Well, it'd be the first time anyone in this family paid attention to what I think, so I suppose I should be grateful. Yes, I always thought he was dodgy. But I had to be the good wife, didn't I? Couldn't go having my own opinions, not when princess Rosa finally had a little friend, and Daddy dearest had a business to think of. No, doesn't matter what *I* think. Just as long as I cook the meals, play nice and say all the right things. Well, I was right. So you can both stick that in your pipe holes and bloody well smoke it!"

The front door slammed. Dad had gone. Left me with her.

She was so pissed, so aggressive. There was nothing I could say or do. I wanted to be a thousand miles away, but I was too scared of the world outside to even storm out. So

I did what any teen would do in my situation. I ran to my bedroom to cry.

The throbbing in my right arm, from the chip insertion, seemed amplified. Yes, they really had stitched me up. Physically as well as emotionally. Alone in my room I remembered Greyson saying I could call him anytime. Once again it seemed I had nowhere else to turn but to the enemy. Perhaps he hadn't known either? Perhaps he could at least help me see a way forward.

So I picked up my Shades and called him.

"Rosa!" He was cheerful when he answered. For a moment I wondered if he hadn't seen the finished interview. Surely he would know how upset I must be if he had? "Great job, huh? You must be thrilled!"

Apparently he chose to ignore the stark evidence to the contrary that was my blotchy, tear-streaked face.

"How dare they?" I tried to sound assertive and pissed off. But my voice was high and squeaky. "Those aren't the questions I was asked."

"I know, right?" Greyson wasn't even looking directly at me. His eyes kept darting to the sides, looking at something that was far more interesting than me. "Genius those editing guys. It was a bit of a car crash originally, when we watched it back. I thought we'd have to get you in to reshoot. But they didn't want to put you through it all again, with all you're dealing with. Honestly, the work that goes into these things is immense. I'm stunned. You must be so pleased."

"Pleased? They've twisted everything I said. Everything I believe, everything I am! You have to make them retract it, make them show the original. I'll go to the press. I'll upload my story everywhere! I demand—"

"Rosa." he stopped his distracted glances and focused right on me. I wished he hadn't. The congeniality I was used to, the façade, was gone. "You're in no position to be making demands. We've gone above and beyond for you, to rescue you from your own mess. You came to me for help and you got it. We could have left you to fend for yourself, to play the role of 'bad twin' to your brother's good. It isn't our job to rescue headstrong teens from the shit piles they create for themselves, you know. We pulled out all the stops because of the respect we have for your family. You have no idea what it takes to reverse public opinion. We do. Thanks to us you have a bright future. You can write your own ticket. I advise you to accept our generosity graciously. Move forward with your life."

"But I don't care about money!"

He shrugged. "That's your choice, Rosa. I think we've done all we can for you. You'll be fine from here on in, as long as you toe the line. There's no need for us to impose on your life any further."

"I thought... I thought you said you'd be there, for whatever I need. For as long as I need?"

"And I have been. I've given you all you need to put this behind you. Now it's time for you to stand on your own two feet. You're ready."

"But—"

"Goodbye, Rosa."

I'd been used. Chewed up and spat out. But now I had a 'life'?

I knew, in that moment, that I was a puppet. That hasn't changed. I'm not so stupid that I can't see my place. Teresa, Kyle, even Greg. They're using me. Just like the PIDs did. The difference is this time I'm going into battle with my eyes wide open. This time, I get to choose who pulls my strings. Sometimes that's the only choice we have.

Just like John Proctor, I know that there are more important things than mere physical existence. Things worth dying for. Like truth, honour and justice. Like refusing to be a poster girl for all the things I find abhorrent in this rotten, stinking world Cole has created. Like setting the record straight.

12
TERESA

I guess she sees herself as some kind of tragic misunderstood heroine. She's more use to me dead than alive, so it's a delusion I've been happy to fuel. She never got over the interview. She couldn't stand being thought of as a Reclamationist. Me, I've spent my whole life publicly promoting values I despise. It's the mission that matters, not my image. What people think of me doesn't bother me. I'm above all that. That's the difference between the glory-hunters and the real soldiers. I don't need someone else's understanding, or validation.

I'd seen enough of her self-indulgent, pity-party nature to know how much that interview must be tearing her apart, but I didn't dwell on it. Greyson had done his job by the book, and I probably would have done the same in his shoes. PID business wasn't on my mind that evening; I was waiting anxiously for more important news.

Cole finally got off his call to Mills, after blowing plenty of smoke up his arse. I could just picture him on the other end of those Shades, getting more puffed up with each word of praise. He'd be intolerably smug when I got back.

When he put his Shades down, Cole came over and rubbed my shoulders.

"Duty done," he said. "Now to relax."

His Shades started to ring.

"Hadn't you better get that?" I asked.

"No. Leave it. I've already neglected you for too long."

Oh, please. Neglect me some more.

The call rang off, and he started tugging at the cord on my dressing gown. He mistook my nerves for excitement, chuckling as he ran his hand up my thigh.

The Shades rang again.

"I really think you ought to get it," I said, trying not to sound too urgent. "It must be important."

He sighed, and stood up. "I suppose," he said. "If you don't mind?"

"Not at all."

"You're a remarkable woman. So few understand the pressures I am under."

"We're both slaves to our profession," I replied.

He laughed, and answered the call. As he paced around the bedroom his expression, and his erection, went south. I grinned. This must be the news I was hoping for.

"God damn it!" His face was even better than I had imagined. He was almost beetroot. A mixture of red anger and blue shock that accentuated his capillaries so it looked as though he had a map of obscure B roads tattooed across his cheeks.

"What's the matter?" I curled up next to him on the edge of the bed with my eyes wide, egging up my concern.

"Damn hackers. Damn lowlife bottom-feeding scum!"

"What's happened?"

"Some bastard... some ignorant, good for nothing bastard has hacked the Grid!"

"Oh my goodness." I sat up straight, looking as professional and intelligent as I could manage in a fluffy white dressing grown. "Have they done any damage?"

"Leaked all the data. Published all of it!"

"Oh good God!" I reached for my Shades. "Where? The broadsheets? Oh, shit, it's the left-wing tabloids, isn't it? I should call in. Hell, I should fly back. This needs to be contained. I'll pack right now."

"No, no, my dear. No, not the papers; not the press at all, in fact. Just some corner of the Dark Web where the lowlifes and good for nothings waste their worthless little lives with petty criminality."

BANtor in other words.

"Has it been dealt with?"

"Yes. Yes, it's all been taken down. I suppose there's no real harm done. We'll have to review our security and so forth, but the leak has been contained. It's just… I thought it was watertight."

"Nothing ever is. Not really."

"I suppose you're right. You'd know better than me. I just can't fathom it. Why? Why would someone do it?"

"To prove they can?"

"That seems a shallow motivation."

"Most motivations are. It's good it's been contained, though," I said. "No real harm done. But… Oh, I'm probably just being paranoid. If your advisors think everything is fine, I'm sure it is."

He frowned. "What? What is it?"

I smiled, and reached for the bottle of wine by the bed. "Oh, nothing. I'm sorry. I've gone into PID mode. Y'know, the kind of ultra-paranoia and thinking through every possible thing that could go wrong that I have to engage in to do my job. Forgive me, we're supposed to be relaxing. And trusting our teams. I mean, if *I've* thought of a potential problem then they must have too, so there's no reason for me to doubt that—"

"Zara," he took the glass out of my hand and set it down gently on the bedside table, "I know we said no work. But, if something's troubling you, I want you to share it."

I exhaled loudly. "Well… It's just that… If someone's done this once, then it just proves it *can* be done, right? I mean, all that's happened right now is they've leaked the info of the benefit claimants and a few volunteers. No harm, no foul. But, when the chips are mandatory. When we've *all* got one, all the ministers, all the secret operatives. I just… I don't know. It would worry me, I guess. Being undercover, say, and then someone hacking and finding out who I really am. It could be dangerous. Plus, knowing *where* high profile people are, all the time? I mean, this lot just wanted to show off, leak the info for an ego trip. What if a smarter outfit managed it? A terrorist group, perhaps? They'd know exactly where everyone was, all the time. Even you."

He turned a little pale. The thought of some highly trained assassin tracking your every move with GPS will do that to you.

"I've been assured," he said, "that security will be increased, that this can never happen again."

"And I'm sure they're right," I said. "But… didn't they say that before?"

13
ROSA

Dad didn't come home that night. Or the next. I didn't know where he was, and I didn't care. It was irrelevant because he wasn't where I needed him to be. With me, giving me support. Instead he had condemned my actions and walked out the door. He may as well have let go of my hand and let me fall from a cliff.

Thanks to the PIDs' little editing stunt I had public support, but parental disapproval. Dad because he thought I'd compromised myself by playing their game, Mum because I hadn't played the game well enough. That's what you call a no-win situation as far as home life is concerned. No matter what I did, one of them, if not both, would disapprove. My sanctuary had become a battleground, as well as pit of grief and despair.

When Dad did return home, there was no attempt to reconcile. A flutter of hope briefly danced in my belly when I heard his key in the door. Maybe being away, doing whatever it was he was doing, had given him time to reflect. Would he rush up to my room, eyes full of tears, strong, warm arms outstretched, and finally tell me all the things I needed to hear? Like how he knew I'd been manipulated, how proud he was of me, how we were on the same page. Him and me against the world. Always.

Not a bit of it.

When he didn't come up the stairs, I crept out of my room onto the landing. I hid in that one perfect spot kids always find. The one where you can hear, and sometimes see, your parents, but they can't see you. He wasn't heading my way. He chucked his coat over a dining room chair and headed straight for the study. Mum was chatting on her Shades; she didn't stop to greet him. Instead she pulled a face, as if she'd caught a whiff of something noxious, and carried on talking.

"He's back, apparently," she said, a little too loudly, when he shut the study door behind him. She always did that. She waited until you were far enough away that it seemed as though she didn't want you to hear, but then raised her voice to make damn sure you did. She didn't fool anyone. 'Passive aggressive', Jimmy used to call it. He didn't know how much it stung, though. She never did it to him.

Usually Dad just pretended he didn't notice. He'd let her rant on to whichever harpy she was gossiping with, refusing to dignify her with any kind of reaction. Not this time.

"Oh, I don't know," she said, walking close by the study door. "I don't care to be honest. It's not like he's been *any* help or support anyway. Just leaves me to deal with everything, as if I'm not grieving too! Not much of a man really when you think about it."

She nearly jumped out of her skin when Led Zeppelin came on full blast from behind the door. So did I.

"Dave!" She banged on the door. "Turn that down, it is far too loud!"

Dad flung the door open. "On the contrary, Jane, it is clearly not loud enough because I can *still hear you*!"

She wasn't used to him reacting to her. Come to think of it, maybe that was part of their problem. I'd been on the receiving end of his unresponsiveness for a while, so I can kind of sympathise. She didn't miss a chance, despite the shock of his retaliation, to play martyr though.

"You see?" she said to her confidante as she turned tail and headed for the lounge. "You see what I have to put up with? How am I supposed to keep it together? Neither of them care about anyone but themselves!"

Nice little pop at me there too. I'd heard enough. There was no solace to be had, no reconciliation. I went back to my room and switched on my Shades. I scrolled through all the recent articles about me, more concerned with the public comments than the content. It seemed Greyson was right, they did know how to change opinions. I was no longer a villain. I was praised for my courage in speaking out against the 'Islamic threat', exalted for my willingness to admit I had been manipulated, and ultimately seen as the grieving twin of a hero who had been taken advantage of.

Jimmy would want the English people to look after her.

Fuckin terrorists trying to insult a hero's memory by converting his sister! Good on ya, Rosa. Stay strong.

Thank you for sharing your story, Rosa. You're an inspiration.

It was all built on lies, but it was nice not to read people calling for me to be raped and stoned nonetheless. At home I was a disappointment and a disgrace. A burden to my mother, and a source of shame to my father. Out there, though, if the web was to be believed, I was indeed a sweetheart of the nation.

I didn't want to be either. I had to get out, but I didn't want to be recognised, even for positive reasons. I crept into Jimmy's room and took a hoodie from his wardrobe. I knew he wouldn't mind. He'd often lent it to me. There was something so much more comforting about a large, soft garment made for a man. I could disappear into it, and it felt like being hugged by stronger, more assured arms.

Mum heard me coming down the stairs, but didn't look at me. Not even when I yelled that I was going out. She didn't ask where, or when I'd be back. Not that I knew the answer to either of those questions anyway. Still, shouldn't a mother want to know them?

Turns out, I never did come back. Not really. I may have returned in the flesh, but after I closed the door behind me that day I never called that house 'home' again.

I pulled the hood up and kept my head down. At first, as I walked to the Tube station and onto the busy platform, I was constantly braced, expecting someone to shout something. But after a while, when no one seemed to be taking any notice of me, I began to relax. Being wrapped up in Jimmy's jumper kept me inconspicuous. Not walking arm in arm with Soheila probably helped too. I had no intended destination, no purpose even, except to be away from home. I rode the Tube until I felt claustrophobic. I got off at Tottenham Court Road and wandered into Soho, for no reason other than that was where my feet seemed to take me.

If I'd taken different steps, turned down different roads, perhaps my life would have worked out differently. But by that point I honestly believe the chance for things to be any better was gone. I could have returned home that night, picked a side in the parental war, continued to toe the line. But I couldn't have made things better. Not for them, and certainly not for myself. The damage was already done. You see, I've never really been in control. It wasn't my choices, wasn't the steps *I* took, that shaped my life. It was always other people's. From my parents', to Jimmy's, to the PIDs'. Until today, until this moment, sat upon this stage with my finger tracing circles on the button in my pocket, I've never had control over my own destiny. Even the decision to walk into Ted's Bar that day was the result of someone else's actions.

Perhaps I'd relaxed a little too much. Walking unnoticed through the London streets had soothed me a little. The oppressive grief and fighting at home seemed far away, and I felt a sense of freedom in my apparent anonymity. When I spotted a pair of jeans on sale at a market stall I pulled my hood down, without thinking, to get a closer look.

The woman riffling through floral dresses on the rail opposite gasped, and I immediately regretted my actions.

"Oh my gosh." She waddled around to my side, laden bags hanging from her pudgy wrist. "You're Rosa, aren't you?"

"I—"

"Yes, yes, you are! I'd recognise you anywhere. Oh, my little lamb. What a time you've had."

The man running the stall picked up on what she was saying. "Hey," he said, "you're Rosa? Rosa *Lincoln*?" He grabbed my hand and shook it vigorously. "Half price for you," he said. "Anything at all from my stall is half price for you. My wife travels the Circle line, you know, every morning. Anything for the sister of Jimmy Lincoln."

His emphatic tones drew the attention of other browsers and, just as it had before, the crowd buzzed around me. At least this time they were shouting support, not threats. But the same sensation of being trapped, and hounded, came over me.

I didn't want to piss anyone off. I'd seen how quickly a crowd turns nasty. But I had to get away. I excused myself, backing away, weaving through people, quickening my pace. They didn't pursue me; this wasn't a pitchfork mob but a gaggle of coo-ers and onlookers.

I darted down a side street, feeling like my cover had been blown. The open air didn't feel soothing anymore and I craved indoor solace. I noticed the chalkboard on the pavement, the only thing that gave hint to the fact there was a bar among the houses.

Ted's Bar was down a small flight of cracked concrete steps, in a basement beneath a three-storey town house that had been converted into flats. Under normal circumstances the dark, windowless door and overflowing rubbish bin would have been off-putting. I hadn't yet begun to frequent drinking establishments, but I'd always envisioned hanging out in bright, modern cocktail bars, not dark and dingy underground dives. But, right there and then, I needed to get off the street, and the obscurity was perfect.

When I pushed open the door the stale odour of hops and dried piss hit me immediately. Ted always says having the gents right next to the front door drives away business, but at least it stops the snobs coming in. At first I didn't think anyone was in there. Frankly, I couldn't see why anyone would *want* to be. The lighting was so low it took my eyes a few moments to adjust. The bar was just one big room, old cracked-leather sofas lined the edges, and outdoor picnic tables were dotted around the centre. Most had folded up beer mats stuffed under at least one leg. A huge, frayed floral carpet with tracks to and from the bar worn in, covered the middle of the floor, but didn't reach the edges, which were just bare concrete. This wasn't the kind of place you came to for the ambiance.

"Be right with you, hold up." A voice made me jump.

"I—" I didn't know who was I talking to, or where they were. "I'm sorry, I think I've got the wrong place."

A throaty chuckle rang out, then I noticed a messy head of curly hair bobbing about behind the oak bar. "You and everyone else." He stood up. A giant of a man, six foot six at least, there was barely a hair's breadth between the top of his long dark curls and the low-beamed ceiling. But the smile on his face had that same warm, open quality that Soheila's had.

"Well, hello there, little lady," he said, wiping grease from his hands with a bar towel and setting his spanner down. He rested his arms on the bar and leaned forward, focusing on me as though I were the most important person in the world. "What can I do for you?"

"Like I said, I think I'm in the wrong place."

"Well, that depends," he said. "If you're supposed to be somewhere else and you've got lost, then let me give you directions. But... I've a feeling you've wandered in here because you need a drink, and I've gone and put you off with my shoddy decor and ape-like appearance. In which case, please let me make it up to you with one on the house."

He was grinning. His easy nature was so disarming, I found myself smiling a little.

"It's neither, honestly," I said. "I just... I just needed to get off the street for a bit. But I wasn't looking for a drink, I'm sorry. I shouldn't have come in."

"I don't have a minimum drink policy." He winked. "In fact, I don't have any policies at all. I would add 'young women who don't want to buy anything but just want to get off the street welcome' to the board out there, but I don't think it'd fit."

I smiled properly now. "You're very kind. But, I shouldn't disturb you."

"Well, yeah..." he said gesturing to the empty bar, "I am swamped as you can see. Seriously, Miss, if you wanna just sit here while whatever it is you're avoiding goes away, I swear I won't even talk to you if you don't want me to. I'll even make you a coffee or something if you don't want a real drink. Might have to be in a pint glass though. Don't get much call for non-alcoholic drinks in here, and I appear to have misplaced the good china."

"I don't think what I'm avoiding will ever go away," I said. He tilted his head, and looked at me a little closer.

"Do I know you?" he asked.

"No," I said. "Nobody does. But everyone thinks they do."

"I hear that," he said. "That's very insightful. And you're right. I don't know you, not one little bit. But I reckon I know why people *think* they do. You're that kid's sister, right? I mean, that's not *who* you are, but it's why I know your face."

I just nodded. Even in the darkest, most obscure corner of London I couldn't find anonymity.

"And I'm guessing you just want to be left alone, but you keep getting hassled?"

"Something like that."

"Do you want me to call you a cab? Get you home without having to face the plebs out there?" He opened the till and started pulling out notes. "My shout."

"I don't want to go home. I don't know where I want to go. I don't *have* anywhere to go." I felt my eyes sting.

"Sounds like at least seventy per cent of my regulars, then," he said, chivalrously ignoring the tears I tried to blink back. "Fortunately, I'm an expert with people who don't want to go home. Usually it's cos of their wives, or cos of their *lack* of wives. Funny how it works both ways. So, as a bonafide professional in helping people with your particular predicament, I can give you a prescription for that..." He grabbed a pint glass, pulled a pint of lager and then dumped a shot of clear spirit into it before handing it to me. "Now, you have that. On the house of course. Maybe afterwards you'll feel like telling me about yourself, maybe you won't. It's all good."

14
TERESA

"Wakey, wakey—" I waved a bottle of Jack in front of Kyle's sleeping face, letting the liquid slosh back and forth. He opened his eyes and grinned.

"It worked then," he said, reaching for the bottle.

"Like a charm," I replied. "You are now looking at a chip-exempt member of government services!"

"Happy days. And it looks like you've got yourself a nice tan to boot." He took a big slug. "I should've been a woman."

"Don't get grumpy," I chided. "This was mainly about you, about keeping you safe. And fed."

"And it just so happened to involve a nice little beach holiday for you." He smiled. "I'm only teasing. It's great news. I've just been going a little stir crazy here all by myself. Powdered milk and pot noodles don't really do it for me."

"Which is why I've been shopping." I pulled some steaks and sausages out of my grocery bag. "Ta-dah! A little token of my appreciation. You're a fucking genius, Kyle."

"Yeah, I know. Reckon being a genius is overrated, though. So, you worked your womanly wiles, eh? No suspicion?"

"None. They know his login was used, but they've no idea how. They think his account must have been hacked remotely."

"You could still be considered?"

"Not unless Cole blabs about us… and he's not likely to do that."

"At least not all the time he trusts you." Kyle sparked up a joint.

"He's got no reason not to."

Kyle laughed. "I'd say he's got every reason not to, he just doesn't have the brains to see it."

"Fair play. Anyway, the point is he saw sense. He knows now how dangerous having high-security personnel on the Grid could be. So all secret service, PID officers and undercover cops are exempt. As well as the whole of the cabinet of course."

"Of course." Kyle grinned. "And fugitives such as myself."

"Yeah… well. Just don't get ill, okay?"

He snorted. "I'm screwed on that score, with or without the chips," he said. "I'll never be able to see a doctor, or buy a pint, or even take a fucking walk in the park again."

I didn't know what to say. He was right. He was in a shitty situation. Even our comrades in jail got to walk in the sunshine, albeit behind a barbed wire fence. I couldn't do what he was doing. Hiding out in this shit hole would drive me insane. But I'd hoped the success of our first mission as a duo would have cheered him up.

"I'm sorry," I said at last. "I know this sucks for you. I'll come over more often, bring more stuff."

He shrugged. "I knew the risks. I've done the 'crimes'. But… I just don't see how we can move forward, Terri."

"What do you mean?"

"In a few months you'll need a chip for everything. Healthcare, jobs, travel, even shopping, right?"

I nodded. "They're not saying it yet, but that's what coming."

"So how do you expect to get recruits? Who's going to voluntarily put themselves in my position? And if anyone was fool enough to do it, how the fuck do you expect to keep them alive when they can't earn money, buy food, get medicine? Face it, we're on our own. And we've gone as far as we can go. We're not behind bars, and that's a miracle in itself. Maybe we should just be happy with that."

"Give up? After everything? Shit, Kyle, no one said this was going to be easy! It's bad enough the others are rotting in jail, you want that to be for nothing?"

"We lost, Terri. Face it. We've gone as far as we can go. If it all went tits up with the team and the facilities we had, then what the hell chance do we have on our own? You're not getting chipped. That means we can survive. We've been lucky, but if we carry on our luck will run out eventually. We should stop this, now. While we still can."

"I don't lose!" I snapped.

"No. Just everyone you come into contact with."

"Fuck you, that's not fair! Don't you see we have a chance? We only have *one* chance. Take down Cole, get the truth out there. That's the only way you'll ever be free. That's the only way anyone will ever be free."

"Nice speech. But we don't even have a fucking plan."

"It starts with us. It starts with rebuilding, recruiting. People will join us if they know the truth; we had plenty of support before. There's people out there speculating right now, saying they don't believe the story Cole's put out, saying they don't believe we're terrorists. Trust me, I know because I have to spend half my life shutting them down."

"Which is exactly the fucking problem. How are we supposed to communicate, to organise? Yeah, there's plenty out there who agree with us, but we can't reach them."

"You're the best hacker there is. You must know a way to get around the web surveillance?"

"I do. But they don't. That's the issue, Terri. Remember the USB? The one I became a fugitive to protect? There are names on there, email addresses, even numbers. Some of our biggest supporters, and some of them would be damn useful right about now. There's doctors on here, engineers, even some government workers like you. But every communication is being watched, much more so than before. Sure, I could get encrypted messages out there, but most of our sympathisers wouldn't have a clue how to access them. It doesn't matter how many support our cause, if we can't reach out to them they may as well not exist."

"So… we visit them in person."

"Are you fucking mad?"

"C'mon, are you telling me you can't track people down from their email addresses? I know you can. So start with the most useful. The ones who donated, or the ones with skills we can use. Find me potentials and I'll scope them out."

"Terri, we can't possibly coordinate any kind of operation like that!"

"Maybe not. But it's a start at least. If nothing else it'll give you something to focus on other than your own self-pity."

"And then what? Even if you do manage to find a few people willing to join, what the hell do we do then?"

"Something will come to me. It always does."

He wasn't impressed with my arrogance, and he made no attempt to hide it. But he made a start anyway, so I was happy I'd given him a task to pull him out of his slump. I don't believe in fate, or providence. I don't think opportunities, or people, come into our lives for a reason. I think the winners are the ones who turn circumstances, and people, to their advantage. That's why I knew something would come to me. Not because of divine intervention, but because I've spent my whole life making something out of nothing.

As it turned out, something did come to me. Or rather some*one*. But it wasn't destiny that delivered Greg to me. It was Greyson.

When I got back to work a few days later, Mills was just as smug as I'd predicted. He couldn't wait to brag about his conversation with the Prime Minister. He still hadn't forgiven me for Rosa's little lapse in judgment. I don't suppose jetting off to my sister's wedding (that was the cover story for my week away) helped my cause much either. So I had to sit and listen while he regaled me with tales of how outstanding Greyson had been, and bragged about his personal congratulations from Cole.

What he didn't know, of course, is that I'd heard every word Cole said to him. And Mills' retelling was exaggerated to say the least. I smiled in all the right places, all the while smirking inwardly. According to him, Cole had told him he was 'the best of the best'. What he actually said was that he 'had carried out his duties admirably'. But hey, Mills is a PID. Reality doesn't come into the equation. When someone lies for a living you can't ever expect truth from them. Hell, just look at me.

He was trying to make me jealous. So I decided to be gracious. I figured that'd piss him off more. I congratulated him, told him how proud I was of the team, said I knew I needed to keep my eye on the ball more from now on. He wasn't expecting that. I smiled sweetly, and left him in his office, looking somewhat perplexed.

I was so amused by his reaction I decided to employ the same tactic with Greyson. When I saw him strutting toward me, oozing self-satisfaction, I wanted to burst his bubble. Normally I'd have insulted his hair, or told him his flies were undone or something. Anything to wipe the smug look off his face. But I didn't. Before he could even speak I smiled wide, and clapped him on the back.

"Sweet job, partner," I said. "I watched it go out live, you really pulled that one out of the bag. Thanks for cleaning up my mess, I owe you one."

That did it. The grin faded into confusion.

"Okay," he said. "Who are you and what have you done with Jinks?"

I laughed. "Maybe the sun chilled me out a bit," I said. "I mean it, I appreciate it. I think I needed a break. It's all been a bit intense lately. You did good, really good."

"I thought you'd be pissed off. Like I'd shown you up or something."

"Hey, we're on the same team, right? You had my back, I can see that. If there's anything I can ever do..." I picked up my case files and started walking toward my office.

"Actually," Greyson called out. "There might be."

Oh, fuck. It was clearly an empty offer. "What?" I asked.

"Would you… well, it's a little bit unusual, but would you…"

"Spit it out then."

"Would you have a drink with my brother?"

What the fuck?

"I'm not into setups," I said. "I'm sorry if your brother's having a hard time getting laid, but when I said I owed you one I meant workwise."

"Oh, no. Nothing like that. I'd be there too."

"That sounds even more dodgy."

He sighed. "I'm not going about this very well. Let me start again. My brother, he's a lot younger than me. Just turned twenty-three. He's just finished his computing degree, and Dad talked him into taking the service tests."

The service tests were aptitude tests anyone who wanted to work in the intelligence sector had to take. From PIDS, to military intelligence, to the secret service. They were designed to help assign recruits to the best branch of our family of public deceit organisations.

"Yeah, and? Did he fail? I can't help him with that. You gotta wait six months and retake." Trust me, I know.

"No. No he didn't fail. He scored three hundred twenty-seven."

I whistled. I'd got 245, on my second attempt. "Shit. That's impressive. That's—"

"Security level, I know."

Security was the branch reserved for the most gifted. The best encrypters, hackers and programmers. They dealt with the highest level of secure information. Military information, the Grid, even the Ever Cloud.

"Okay, so your brother's a genius. Must piss you off, but what has that got to do with me?"

"He doesn't want to work in service."

I shrugged. "Can't blame him."

"I know. It's his life, right? I don't care what he does. But

Dad does… Jinks, my dad isn't well. I don't want to go into it but he's only got a few months left. A year tops. He wants him to be settled, have a good job. He thinks service is the best path. It'd mean so much to him. He's worried about him."

"Why is he worried?"

"My brother, well, he's a bit wayward. He's a bit of a lefty, truth be told. Hates the establishment. It's all just student day rebellion, if you ask me. But, well, he was a big supporter of Gridless."

Now my interest was piqued.

"Really?"

"Yeah. I mean, not now. Not after we've proved they're terrorists. He's not radical or anything. But you can see why Dad's concerned about him. He wants me to get him on the straight and narrow, make him see sense. A job in security would set him up for life. But he keeps harping on about the ERP being fascist."

Good man.

"I'm sorry, Greyson, I still don't see what this has to do with me."

"He thinks I'm a stiff. He can't relate to me. But you, you're more on his level."

"What do you mean by that?"

"Oh, c'mon, Jinks. You know. You're vibrant… attractive. You're not some government yes man like he thinks we all are. You could make him see that you don't have to be a sell-out to work in service. You can make it work for you, not the other way around."

My mind was racing. A Gridless supporter with the chance to work in the highest level of national security? Okay, there were a million hurdles, but it seemed too good not to at least scope out.

"Fine," I said. "Set up drinks. I'll turn on the charm, see if I can get him onside. I can't promise anything, though."

15
ROSA

By the time I'd finished my fourth concoction, Ted had offered me a job, and a home.

Ted's Bar was the kind of place where nobody cared who you were. Nobody asked about your life because they were all there for the same reason: to escape theirs.

By the time the regulars started drifting in through the door, Ted was almost as pissed as I was. We'd spent the afternoon drinking and talking. He didn't ask me any of the usual questions – what was Jimmy like? How are you coping? – in fact, he didn't ask me anything at all. Instead he talked about the bar, about his van that needed new suspension but was 'Okay as long as you floor it', about his brother's band. All the small stuff. The type of inconsequential chatting for chatting's sake that had been absent from my life for so long.

He didn't ask but, after enough of his free-flowing drinks, I told. Eventually, somewhere in between his anecdotes of what seemed an idyllic, carefree existence my mouth started moving, and I couldn't stop it.

I confessed it all. How trapped I felt by my brother's memory, how awful things were at home, how alone I was, how unseen. He didn't seem shocked, or even concerned. He just shrugged his shoulders, and poured another drink.

"Hey, I could use some help here if you're looking for a

change of scene. I can't pay you properly, but there's a room upstairs sitting empty. You could stay here. If you want to get away from all that crap for a while."

"I... I don't know. I don't know anything about working in a bar."

"Well, that makes two of us then. To be fair, this place pretty much runs itself. Think about it. Stay a while, meet the punters. Let me know what you decide. I'm easy either way."

That's the thing about Ted. He's easy. So laid-back he's practically comatose. I'd never met anyone quite like him before. On the surface it might seem odd, suspicious even, for someone to offer a near stranger a home and a job so quickly. But that's just how Ted is. He lives in the moment, doesn't think too hard about tomorrow. Doesn't concern himself with consequence or convention. I admired that. Still do. I don't blame him for anything. He was only ever living for the here and now.

And he wasn't kidding when he said the bar ran itself. When I heard the door open, and the first patron arrived, I wondered how the hell he was going to manage his shift when he was so inebriated. It was simple. He didn't. To start with he pulled the pints, but as the evening went on he just moved round the bar, chatting with the regulars. People helped themselves, pulling foamy pints and dumping their coins on the counter. It was always that way. If a barrel ran out, and nobody was sober enough to change it, everyone just made do with whatever was left. That was the kind of place it was. No airs, no graces. But most importantly, no judgment.

The clientele weren't exactly sophisticated: an eclectic mix of unemployed layabouts, blue-collar alcoholics and illegals. But they were friendly and accepting. A couple of them recognised me, but were more concerned with what I was drinking than who my brother was. My mother would have had a fit if she'd seen me consorting with such types, which only made it seem more appealing.

By the time Big Mikey (a huge guy with a squeaky laugh

who looked like an aging eighties rocker with a greasy mullet and tattooed knuckles) had set fire to his fifth Sambuca, I'd made my decision. I had never felt so free and easy before. Granted, with the exception of the night I threw my virginity away, I'd never been so drunk before either. But facing the reality of my choices sober wasn't something I'd ever need to worry about at Ted's.

"I wanna stay," I said, handing Ted a badly poured pint in my drunken attempt to show him I was keen.

"Cool." Ted smiled. He stood up and grabbed my hand, holding it aloft. "Hey, guys," he yelled, and the whole bar settled to a dull roar to listen. "Let me introduce my new barmaid, Rosa. C'mon, let's make her welcome."

Everyone cheered. Glasses chinked, big burly guys clapped me on the back. I was the girl of the moment. And for once, the attention I was getting was nothing to do with Jimmy, or Soheila, or some PID arranged publicity. They were clapping for me… just me. I was enough.

I had found a new home.

Needless to say, Mum went bat shit when I rolled up with Ted, in his battered van, to collect my stuff the next afternoon. I think I was still a little drunk from the night before because I simply didn't care. Something had shifted within me. Perhaps it was the euphoria of finally having a choice in my own destiny, albeit not a very glamorous or constructive one. She ranted and raved, calling me ungrateful and stupid. But her words no longer hurt me. I had seen another path, a different way to live. A way that didn't include her. I didn't have to stay here, didn't have to be who she wanted me to be. Didn't have to spend every waking moment of every fucking day surrounded by Jimmy's distorted legacy. And that meant she had no power over me anymore. Even when she realised her venom wasn't hitting its target, and switched to crocodile tears and pleading, I was unmoved. It was too late to pretend she understood me.

When I loaded the final bag into the van, she knew she'd lost the battle. But she couldn't resist a parting shot.

"I wish it had been you, not Jimmy!" she yelled. Tears streaked down her face, leaving tracks of mascara.

I just smiled. "Tell me something I don't know," I yelled back.

At least she'd finally said it. I hope the neighbours heard.

My room above Ted's consisted of a mattress on the floor and a broken cupboard, but I didn't care. All the luxuries I had grown up with seemed tainted and poisonous to me now. They were simply products of a world that turned on lies and spin. The raw, minimal nature of my new surroundings was the antidote I needed. We shared a (filthy) bathroom, and Ted said I could watch TV in his room whenever I wanted. I never did.

The university had already suggested I defer my place for a year, given my notoriety and all I must be going through. I fully intended to take them up on it. A year seemed like forever back then. I thought when the time came I'd be stronger. A few months at Ted's, and I could seek a better paid job somewhere else. I'd save up and get a student loan so I could live on campus and never have to go home. That was the plan.

The trouble with plans is it isn't enough just to have them. You have to actually act on them. That was the bit that tripped me up.

I fell into the routine of waking around lunchtime, staggering down to the bar and helping Ted open up. The regulars poured in as the afternoon turned to evening, and Ted encouraged me to drink with them.

"People come here for the company, and the friendly staff," he said. "Knowing someone will always be here to chill with. That's our selling point."

I wondered how he turned any profit, when he and I sank so much booze ourselves. It didn't take too long to find out.

16
TERESA

Greg Greyson was nothing like his brother. So he had that going for him at least.

I got Kyle to do some digging. He was cautiously excited at the prospect of a potential supporter in Security, and wasted no time uncovering Greg's online life. He had been a supporter, Greyson was right. Not just an armchair one, either. Once Kyle uncovered his BANtor alias, it was clear why his big brother was so embarrassed. He'd been the ringleader of several protests at his campus, and hacked their computer networks so that Gridless' logo, and latest message, played whenever someone tried to boot up their PC. He'd applied several times, via the Dark Web, to join our team for real. But Daniel had declined his requests, saying we had enough hackers already. Greg (under the alias Hawkfish) had begged to be considered, should we ever need more.

But that was before Daniel was caught, before the PIDs painted us as mass murderers. Would he still feel that way now? I had to find out.

We'd arranged to meet in Floren's, a cocktail bar in the West End. I'm not sure whether Greyson was trying to impress me with his choice of location, or suggest to his brother that a career in Services would give him the wealth to hang out in such exclusive places. Either way he failed. Neither of us are the type to be wooed by such bourgeois extravagance.

But that's Greyson all over. Suited, booted, slick and groomed. The perfect cog for a corporate machine. If he hadn't gone into the PIDs, he'd have made an excellent junior executive for some faceless conglomerate. Greg was the total opposite. He looked out of place, sitting on a white leather bar stool in ripped jeans and vest top. He hadn't shaved for a few days, and his slouched stance showed he wasn't concerned with 'power posture' like his brother was.

Greyson did the introductions, looking slightly embarrassed at his brother's lack of effort.

"So, I hear you did really well on the entrance tests?" I didn't waste time on pleasantries. If Greg was as smart as Greyson said he was, then he already knew there was an ulterior motive to our little get-together.

"Yeah, well." Greg shrugged.

"Don't be modest!" Greyson clapped his shoulder. "Smashed mine out of the park, didn't you, bro?"

Greg and I both winced at his attempt to sound casual.

"So they got you lined up for Security?" I took a swig of the neon blue cocktail Greyson had bought me. "Pretty good deal."

"Only if you want to spend your life propping up neo-fascists," Greg said, "which I don't. But brother dearest seems to think money is more important than principles."

Greyson scowled. "I know you don't see it, but that's because you're young. You don't remember how it was before. The ERP have done more to make this country safe and—"

"Oh, spare me." Greg rolled his eyes. "Guess you can only read the script so many times before you start to believe it, huh?"

"Not necessarily," I said. "I don't vote ERP."

Greyson's mouth fell open. I guess he'd always assumed that his PID colleagues were supporters of Cole's agenda in private as well as on the job.

"What?" I asked. "It's not a condition of employment y'know. Anyway, the point is you don't have to eat cake to work in a bakery. The PIDs pay me well for my skills, I get plenty of perks, and I like the job. You gotta get your living from somewhere. Who cares who the boss is as long as the deal's good?"

I was being deliberately provocative. I wanted to see if Greg would bite. He did.

"That makes you worse than him, as far as I'm concerned," he said. "He believes in their crap. I fundamentally disagree with everything he stands for, but at least he's standing for something. To help promote a regime you don't even believe in? Just for money? That makes you a sell-out in my book."

Greyson snapped at him and flushed red. But I smiled. The image of Rosa, mouthing off at me in her middle-class bedroom, flashed through my mind. He was just like her. A spoiled little rich kid with delusions of rebellion. No wonder they hit it off so well. But, unlike Rosa, this kid had skills I could use. Time to up the ante.

"I'm not saying I disagree with the ERP," I said, "just that I didn't vote for them. You've got to admire the way they're dealing with threats like Gridless though…"

Greg laughed. Not a real laugh. One of those sarcastic, forced chuckles people give when they want to imply your argument is so stupid it's actually funny.

"Threat? What fucking threat? You don't actually believe your own hype, do you?"

"What's not to believe?" I asked. "Gridless were going to blow up the Underground. I've seen the blueprints myself."

"You don't know how deep the rabbit hole goes, do you?" He was getting cocky now. "I actually pity you guys."

"That's enough!" Greyson snapped. "Jinks, I'm sorry. I didn't realise he'd be such an arse."

"No worries," I said, downing my drink. The place was filling up. I glanced at the bar; it was ten deep. It'd take ages to get served. "I like a passionate debate." I waved my empty glass at him. "Get me another, would you? I've got a thirst on now."

He looked a bit put out, or perhaps worried about leaving me alone with the black sheep of his family. It's hard to tell with Greyson. He mouthed something to his brother (probably telling him to be nice) and walked off to the bar, leaving me and Greg by ourselves.

"You think you're pretty smart, don't you?" I leaned across the table and hissed at him. "I know your type. Good at mouthing off, not so good at standing up. Got all the ideals, and the precious principles, but only from a distance. Don't see you putting your arse on the line for your cause. Do you even have one?"

"I think that's my business, not yours."

"On the contrary, if you're planning on consorting with terrorists, it's absolutely my business."

"Gridless were *not* terrorists!" He slammed his fist down on the table.

"You're wrong," I said, "but at least you've admitted you support them."

"Yeah. You know what? Fuck it. I did support them. And I don't believe all this crap you guys have been brainwashing the country with. No matter what you say."

I stared at him. Could I take the risk? Kyle had cautioned me to play it safe, not give too much away. Even to a supporter. But he wasn't witnessing his own decline. Every time I walked into that shitty little hideout I wondered what I'd find. The solitude, the fear, it was getting to him. Suggesting we throw in the towel? Kyle was losing it. Sometimes, taking a risk is less dangerous than sticking with the status quo.

"You misunderstood," I said. "I said you were wrong, and you are."

"Then we'll have to agree to disagree."

"I'm afraid I can't do that. Not when it comes to Gridless. You said, they '*were* not terrorists', but I'm afraid the correct statement would be 'we *are* not terrorists'."

He sat back, staring at me. For an intelligent guy he didn't seem to be getting the point as quickly as he should.

"Have you ever considered," I said, "that the best way to take down a city is from within its walls?"

"Are you saying…?"

"Take. The. Fucking. Job," I said. "If you want in, that is. Or you could just sit there watching BANtor, hoping for some glimpse of us that won't ever come. Because without someone in Security, me and Kyle are pretty stuffed when it comes to communications."

"Kyle?" he asked. "Kyle Redwood?"

"The same," I said.

"Oh my fucking God! I don't believe this. This is so exciting. How many are left? What are you planning?"

"I've said too much already," I replied. "Right now all you have on me is your word against mine. Say anything to anyone and I'll just deny it. And use my PID perks to make your life extremely uncomfortable. I need to know I can trust you. I'm saying nothing else until you take that job. Show me you're committed, and I'll show *you* where that fucking rabbit hole leads."

He just nodded and stared at me with doe eyes like I was a film star. Greyson returned with my drink, frowning at the silence between us. I kicked Greg under the table.

"You two alright?" Greyson asked. "Haven't killed each other, I see."

"I think you underestimate your brother," I said. "He's not as closed minded as you think."

"How do you mean?"

"I'm going to do it," Greg said. "Take the job. Jinks here talked me round."

"That's fantastic! But how the hell—"

"She made me see that it's no good bitching and moaning," Greg said. "You've got to be *in* the system to make things better."

He wasn't very convincing. I stepped in to help.

"Exactly," I said. "You can't just whinge about things you have no clue about. I told him, if he takes the job he can see for himself what we really do. I'm sure he'll realise the ERP isn't the enemy he thinks it is. But, even if he doesn't, at least he'll be in a position to challenge things."

"Well," Greyson said, raising his glass. "I don't care why you agreed, I'm just stoked you did. Dad'll be so happy to see you settled. That's all I really care about."

I was a little surprised he bought the total 180 in Greg's attitude so easily. But people tend to believe anything if it means they get what they want. Another thing the PIDs taught me. 'People don't check gift horses for tooth decay,' Mills always says.

I finished my drink and said a hasty goodbye. The hardest part was still to come. I had to go and tell Kyle I'd given away more information than we'd agreed to. I figured I'd better stop by the off-licence on the way.

I practised my argument all the way there, expecting Kyle to go ballistic at my lack of caution. But when I arrived he was in a good mood and sober. Two states I hadn't seen him in for a long time. He'd managed to trace the names and addresses of several useful supporters from their email addresses, and was feeling pretty pleased with himself. I let him ramble on about what he'd been doing, even though most of it sounded Greek to me, because watching him so animated and passionate was refreshing. Plus people like, and trust, those who let them talk about themselves. So it was a good way of buttering him up for my admission.

"Of course," he said, as he finished his detailed account of all his hacking exploits, "we can't *do* a hell of a lot with the info yet. Certainly can't risk sending out a message. But I was thinking about your idea of visiting a few of them in person, and it's not as ridiculous as I thought. I mean, given that we can't contact them electronically, it might be the only thing we can do... unless you managed to get anywhere with that Hawkfish guy?"

Good things come to those who let people talk.

"Actually," I said, unscrewing the new bottle of Jack I'd just bought. He didn't seem to need a drink, but I sure as hell did. "I think he's the answer to our prayers. He's still a passionate supporter, just like we hoped. Bit of a fanboy, actually, he practically swooned when I mentioned your name. And he passed the entrance tests for Security, but he wasn't going to take the job. Principles and that. I had a good feeling about him. So, we had a little chat, I explained our communications problems, and I'm pretty sure he's going to go undercover for us."

I braced for the backlash, expecting Kyle's elation to turn to fury at my recklessness. But he surprised me.

"How much did you tell him?"

"Next to nothing. I said he had to prove himself by signing up if he wanted in."

"So he's got nothing on you?"

"Nothing but his word against mine."

"And you think he'll go for it?"

"He's a middle-class rebel without a cause, we can give him one. Yeah, he'll go for it."

"That's fantastic. Christ, Terri. A mole in Security? That's like the fucking Holy Grail."

I hadn't expected it to be so easy. I guess he'd started to realise that nothing good comes without a little risk. Being stuck in hiding was no life, and rebuilding Gridless was the only way out for him.

"I gotta say," I said, "I was expecting Mr Paranoia. It's not like you to trust my judgment."

Kyle took a swig and sat down beside me. "I know I'm an arse most of the time. But I do trust you, Terri. I've been thinking, a lot. Hell, not much else for me to do stuck here. You were right. We need to make things happen for ourselves. The only way I'll ever be free is to finish what we started. That's not gonna happen unless we take a chance on people. If this guy… What's his real name again?"

"Greg. Greg Greyson."

"Greg. Well, if this Greg can cover my tracks, I can rally the troops in no time. If there's still anyone out there who hasn't been turned against us."

"Oh, they're out there." I said. "For every wacky conspiracy theorist we let have their little vlog there's dozens of more intelligent ones we shut down."

That's PID operations 101. You can't silence all dissent, it's too suspicious. There will always be people who don't believe what they're told. You have to let some of them speak. The trick is to make sure it's the looney tunes ones who get to have a voice. Anyone credible needs to be stopped.

"Well then..." Kyle topped up my glass, "it seems we're back in business."

17
ROSA

Days turned to weeks. My hours were lubricated with booze, so they glided seamlessly by. For the first time in my life I was sedated by a lack of stress, a complete absence of commitment. Ted didn't care about things like time, or schedules. Between us we managed to keep the doors open, and the punters served, without ever doing anything as organised or conformist as taking shifts. Sometimes I rolled out of bed at lunchtime and Ted was nowhere to be seen. So I just opened up in my PJs, eating Cheerios and drinking Alka-Seltzer at the bar while the regulars pulled their own pints.

I didn't think beyond the here and now. Didn't think at all in fact. I was utterly numb. Until one afternoon Dad turned up out of the blue.

I was in my customary position, sitting on the bar drinking cider and chatting to the lunchtime down-and-outs, when he stepped through the door. I wonder what he must have thought when he saw me. His little girl, swigging from a pint glass at one o'clock in the afternoon, laughing with unwashed, unemployed, middle-aged men. But if he was appalled he kept it to himself. I guess he knew he'd already lost his right to judge me.

I pulled down my skirt and hitched up my top when I saw him standing there. Looking back, I feel embarrassed.

But at the time I felt defiant, rebellious. I was surrounded by my people, as pathetic as they might be, and in this place I was respected, beloved. People listened when I spoke, people actually *wanted* to converse with me. They paid me attention (perhaps the wrong kind of attention, but attention nonetheless). I wasn't a pathetic, snivelling little girl begging for crumbs of my daddy's affection anymore. I didn't have to listen to his rules. He'd walked into my territory. Here, I was in charge.

"What are you doing here?" I asked, striding up to him. "I'm working."

"I can see that," he said. "I'm sorry. But... please can we talk? Privately?" He was shuffling his feet, looking down. He was awkward, uncomfortable. Thanks to the cider buzz I viewed the world through a veneer of egotism, so I read all sorts of things into his demeanour. I figured he'd finally realised how useless he'd been, how he'd driven me away. I thought he'd come to apologise, and beg me to come home. I was already rehearsing my 'It's too late for that. I'm never coming back' speech in my head as I led him through to the kitchen.

But that wasn't it at all. The last conversation I ever had with my father had nothing to do with apologies or bridge-building. It held no words of wisdom for me to hold onto. It had nothing to do with me at all.

"Rosa," he said, still not making eye contact. "I'm leaving."

I wasn't expecting that. I didn't know what to say.

"I thought you should know," he continued.

"Why?" I asked, though it seemed a stupid question even at the time. Had I been so self-absorbed that I hadn't realised I might not be the only one finding home life unbearable?

"You know why," he said. "Your mum and I... well, things haven't been good for a long time. You know that. We tried to hide it, tried to make it work and be a family. But now..."

He didn't need to finish. I didn't even want him to, because I knew whatever came next would be bullshit. He couldn't say what he really meant, so he'd have to spout some rubbish.

Probably about how I was independent now, or mature enough to handle it. But we both knew the truth. It was Jimmy. Jimmy was the glue, the golden boy. The pride and joy that united them. I wasn't enough.

The sweet numbness I had been wallowing in was sucked away like water down a plughole. All the grief, pain, and anger I had gone to such lengths to avoid hit me again. I felt my guts churn, spinning a lump of bitterness that sped through me and lodged itself in my throat. I wanted to cry, but not in front of Dad. He wasn't my refuge anymore. I didn't want to be that weak, needy, pathetic. I didn't want to be Rosa. So I rode the wave of Dutch courage, and spoke as matter-of-factly as I could. I guess some part of me was still trying to win his respect, show him I was an adult. Show him I had value, even though I didn't believe I did.

"So where are you going to stay?" I asked. "There's some rooms to rent a few buildings down from here. Not great, but they'd work as a stopgap while you get the finances in order."

That's how I thought adults handled things. Leave emotion aside, just focus on the practicalities.

"Rosa..." He tried to look me in the eye at last, but I looked away. If I locked my gaze on his face I wouldn't be able to hold it together. I'd weep for all that was, and all that could never be again. "I'm going to Australia."

"What?"

"You know I've been wanting to, ever since Kadeem moved out there. But your mum... well, she thought you and Jimmy would be better off here."

Yeah. Look how well that worked out.

"But now," he said "well, I just need to get away, from everything. The offer's still open so I decided to take it."

"Kadeem?" I asked. "He still wants you to be his partner?"

"Yes. And he speaks so highly of the place."

So Dad was still in contact with the Afzals, even though Soheila and I weren't talking. No wonder he was so pissed at me; I had dragged his friend's daughter into a mess. They probably ran me down together.

"When do you leave?" I sounded cold. Which was ironic considering heat of the humiliation running through me.

"Tomorrow. I wanted to come and see you, to explain."

"You don't need to explain. I couldn't live there anymore either."

Except *I* had no money, so my options were vastly less impressive.

"I never wanted it to be like this, Rosa. All my life I've tried to do the right thing. I stayed at a job I hated, in a country I've grown to despise, because I believed it was best for the family. Everything I've ever done, it's always been for you and Jimmy."

"Jimmy's gone," I said, taking a little satisfaction in the tears that formed in his eyes. Why shouldn't he feel some pain too?

"I'll still cover your tuition, Rosa. I'll send the cheques."

So that was it, was it? That was his responsibility to me absolved? He'd send some fucking cheques? Like I was a debt that needed repaying. A mistaken purchase. He'd gone into the store only wanting one, but somehow ended up with an inferior extra product. When you're a twin you always know that only one of you was planned. When it came to me and Jimmy, it was pretty fucking obvious who the accident was. Now Jimmy was gone he was off to live his own life, and I amounted to nothing more than a financial millstone.

Cheques for tuition. Not for plane tickets to go visit.

He didn't even ask me the question. The one that might have saved me, even that late in the game. Because I would have. I would have gone with him if he'd asked. Despite the anger at him, despite the fear of Soheila's reaction. Because there was hope, away from here. Hope that those wounds could be mended.

But I wasn't going to ask. I wasn't going to plead. A child shouldn't have to beg to be included in their parent's life.

"Have a safe flight," I snapped at him, and headed back to the bar. He followed, grabbing my arm. I pushed him off.

"I just want to say—"

"There's nothing left to say. I need to get back to work."

I didn't watch him leave. I couldn't. I turned my back, pretended to rearrange the spirits behind the bar, anything so he couldn't see the tears that rolled down my face. It's one thing to leave the family home in a fit of rebellion. It's another to watch it crumble behind you. Suddenly my new life didn't feel free and easy anymore. All the time it had been a choice, *my* choice, it seemed idyllic. Now it was a necessity, I started to see everything that was wrong with it.

There was only one safety net remaining. Mum. But the last time I saw her she had made the dark secret of her heart known. And she hadn't once tried to call to apologise. When your own mother tells you they wish you'd died in place of your sibling, you'd have to be a special kind of weak and pathetic to make the first move toward reconciliation. You'd have to be desperate, an apologetic worm of a person with no self-esteem.

You'd have to be Rosa.

I don't know what I was thinking. Perhaps I had some deluded notion that she was too embarrassed to call me, and if I contacted her she'd be grateful, maybe even weep with remorse. Or maybe it was the pure fear that my way back out of my own decisions was slipping away. Either way, calling her just made things worse.

"I suppose you're calling to tell me you're leaving too?"

Seriously, that was how she answered the phone. No relief to hear my voice, no 'I miss you', no 'How are you?' even. Just attack. An instant need to defend myself, even though hers had been the indefensible action.

"No. I'm not… I called to…" *To hear you apologise, to hear you beg me to come home, to hear that I still have a home*. "See how you are."

Big mistake. She wasted no time lamenting her situation.

She waxed lyrical about how we had both abandoned her. It was clear that she had drawn her battle lines, lumping me and Dad together as her foes. Her strategic manoeuvres involved using the 'grieving mother' missile to its full advantage, then employing the scorched earth tactic of selling the house.

I came away from the conversation without any comfort. Not once did she ask how I felt, or even if I was okay. Worse, now I knew there was nothing between me and freefall, because she never mentioned any possibility of having a home with her.

I tried to block the day's events out with the method I had begun to rely on. But no matter how much I drank, I couldn't escape it all. My refuge had been contaminated. When Dad walked in he brought all the memories, all the grief, all the humiliation, into my fortress. I hadn't 'dealt with' anything at all; I'd just been ignoring it. Now it all came crashing back into my life, and there was nowhere to run.

Jimmy. Every thought turned to Jimmy. Everything had happened because of him. Or, more accurately, because of the lack of him. I wasn't enough to keep the family together, but he would have been. If I'd died he would have had the strength, and the words, to comfort them. He would have had the charisma, the charm, and the savvy to woo the media. He would have glorified my memory, not brought shame and scandal to our door.

I drank. I wept. I screamed. I raked my fingernails down my forearms leaving red roadmaps of my pain. And I wished. I wished what my mother wished. I wished it had been me instead. I wished I was dead.

And from that moment I was always travelling here.

Oh, I tried to forget it. When Ted introduced me to SIGHS I even thought I could. But that one white-hot moment of clarity had burned itself into my very identity.

I am Rosa and I wish I was dead.

It beats, it breathes. Steady, constant. Like the cornerstone upon which all else rests. The violin meanders, the flute weaves and dances, but beneath them the percussion stays the same.

I am Rosa and I wish I was dead.

There's a certain kind of perverse freedom that comes with that realisation. Once you decide that your life holds no value to you, the need to protect it from harm dissipates. It's hard to care about anything long-term when deep down inside you just want out. So when Ted found me that evening, crying in my room, suffocating under the weight of all the crap I'd been trying to forget, I could find no rational reason to object to his offer.

I'd tried to sleep, but even the drink couldn't numb me enough to stop the dreams of Jimmy getting through. Ted opened his palm and there it sat. A small white pill. G-Star. The very thing that killed my brother.

"Trust me, you ain't dreaming about anything but sugar plums and rock and roll if you take this," Ted said.

I started to shake my head, but then I remembered I had nothing to live for, and consequence scurried away like a chided puppy.

"Fuck it," I said, washing it down with the last of the absinthe.

18
TERESA

The whole room falls to a hush now. Everyone's twitching with a nervous buzz that has nothing to do with the coffee Greg supplied. Even I'm jittery. Just a few minutes now. The Archbishop leads the crowd in a rendition of 'Amazing Grace'. There's not a churchgoer among us, as far as I know, but we're all transfixed.

It's Rosa's turn next.

My mind races, searching every potential problem for the thousandth time, making sure I've covered every base. There's nothing left to go wrong. Apart from the device itself, but that's been checked and rechecked. There's not a single thing standing between us and our goal, not any more. I see Kyle's eyes flick to the remote detonator on the desk in front of me. He's jiggling his knees, running through the same mental checks as I am, no doubt. It's impossible not to worry. We've worked so hard.

We've come such a long a way. It's hard to believe now, when I look around at the faces of the bright and brilliant people stood beside us, that it all started with just the two of us, in a piss-stained hovel. Just when I thought I might lose Kyle to drink and disillusionment, I'd managed to pull him back from the brink by taking a chance on Greg.

Turned out, it wasn't decent food, or even the freedom to

walk outside, he needed. It was the company and conversation of another male as tech-obsessed as he was. Go figure.

Greg took the job, of course, and to my surprise Kyle agreed to meet with him. I guess even paranoia has its limits. They hit it off straight away. Greg viewed Kyle as some kind of hero, and Kyle loved having his ego stroked just like any other male. I have to admit, Greg was a hell of an asset. Growing up with Greyson meant he knew exactly how to imitate his brother's 'efficient lapdog' demeanour. He was able to schmooze like a pro. Brown-nosing, combined with his undeniable skill, meant he rose through the ranks at Security exceptionally quickly. It was only a few months before he was in a position to manipulate the Ever Cloud for us.

Not just the Ever Cloud, in fact. Between them, Kyle and Greg were able to keep all our communications hidden. It was all gibberish to me, but listening to them chat about encryptions and VPNs made me smile. Kyle even started shaving again.

Once we could reach out, we did. Greg managed to redirect the PID surveillance of BANtor to an earlier cached site, just long enough for us to broadcast our first message. It was simple and swift. Just graphics; we decided the time for dressing up and being funny was over. No more suits of armour, no more posting politicians' dodgy browser histories in order to poke fun at them. This was serious. There were plenty of people watching for a sign, and we needed to give them one. Our logo, followed by the message:

Arise. The truth will out. No chips, no chains.

At the bottom, a Dark Web address that Greg had cloaked from all government surveillance. It only stayed online for a couple of minutes, any longer and the PIDS monitoring might have realised they were watching a cache. But within seconds our new communication site had dozens of hits.

With Greg and Kyle taking care of our security, we were

able to talk online in a way we never had before. At first we were joined only by those who had been staunch supporters before. But as the chips rolled out the recruits rolled in. That's when we became more than just activists. It soon became clear that we needed to fill a humanitarian role too. With the unchipped unable to get healthcare, there were many altruistic members of the medical profession who objected.

"It's not my job to ask someone's circumstance," David had said, "I came into medicine to treat the sick, not question their ancestry." It was a sentiment many of his colleagues agreed with, and we soon set up secret clinics where those who could not, or would not, get chipped could receive treatment.

Greg found us a new HQ, this time on the outskirts of London where there was less surveillance. Reality began to bite for the masses. Everyone started to hear stories about how their brother/mother/best friend's auntie almost died waiting in A&E, while the rich from the posh side of town went straight through with a splinter. Or how their friend's little girl is a genius, but her thick, affluent friend got the better school. The fact that the information on your chip had a direct impact on the quality of public service you received began to dawn on the public. As the memory of the horror they had been told almost happened faded, the security the chips provided didn't seem worth it anymore.

People started cutting them out in protest. That's when the shit really hit the fan for Cole, and for me.

I was getting it from all angles. Both my identities were under pressure. On the one hand I was a PID officer, and the mistress of a Prime Minister who was plummeting down the opinion polls. On the other, I was the leader of a resistance movement that had all the unchipped – and therefore poverty stricken – looking to us to save them. And I didn't have a fucking clue what do about any of them.

The ERP had figured out there was a resistance. It was impossible to keep that under wraps as the number of supporters grew. But Greg and Kyle were manufacturing leads that went nowhere. Plenty of 'sightings' of Kyle abroad came through to the PID offices, leading them to believe this new movement may have been inspired by the old, but was not affiliated. They thought there were simply pockets of dissent, small groups that couldn't possibly unite because all communications were monitored.

Against Heath's advice, Cole decided to launch a war of words against those he knew must be helping the unchipped to survive. Doctors, nurses, shop keepers trading food for illegal cash and the like. He called them traitors, criminals. Declared they were aiding and abetting terrorists. The public didn't like that. There had been no serious terror threat since the supposed Underground Plot. Out of sight, out of mind. Without a climate of fear to fall back on, Cole was simply calling people traitors for having the human decency to help others.

The left wing press went nuts over 'Cold-Hearted Cole', and Heath's newspapers and networks couldn't find an angle strong enough to win back hearts and minds. Cole's reputation was in tatters. Every day more and more people removed their chips. Which meant that every day more and more people looked to Gridless for some sort of end game. Some form of plan, and we didn't have one.

We'd put all our energy into rebuilding, recruiting. Now we had more support than we could handle, and as many differing opinions on what to do next as there were members. Plenty wanted Cole dead, but what would that achieve? By removing their chips our supporters had disenfranchised themselves. There was no hope of voting in a better leadership. Not unless we got the truth out there at the same time.

Cole was equally desperate. He was convinced he needed Heath in the cabinet; both for his ability to spin shit into gold, and to keep a close eye on those who coveted his position. So, he created a post for him: Minister of Public Information. This made him Mills' direct supervisor, and my boss.

It was a bold manoeuvre. Although Heath was widely

known to be Cole's unofficial advisor, he wasn't an elected politician. The public were outraged. Briefly. Until Heath's papers and news channels told them not to be.

Our sexual liaisons had become less frequent. Cole's flop in the opinion polls led to a similar situation in the bedroom. Yet he must have enjoyed my company, because he continued to invite me to his hotel rooms even when his libido was in the gutter. I hadn't expected him to develop feelings for me, but it seemed he had.

Often Heath was there when I arrived, the two of them plotting and drinking together. They were an odd pairing. An alliance initially based on mutual self-interest, which had grown to be something resembling friendship. Cole was an ex-public school boy, trying to portray himself as a working-class hero. Heath was from the gutter. He'd clawed his way up through the ranks of the shit rag tabloids, by virtue of his ruthlessness in pursuing exclusives, then married into enough money to launch his own empire. Now he wore the outward trappings of the rich elite, but behind closed doors his rough edges still showed.

He was always friendly to me. But he made me nervous. Not just because he was technically my employer, but also because his reputation for dirty tactics was second to none. The out-of-court settlements paid to victims of his illegal methods of 'investigative journalism' ran into the billions. So, whenever he joined us for the evening, I played nice but kept my guard up. It was on one such night, just after the latest opinion polls were released, that Heath unwittingly set today's events in motion.

"I just don't know what to do, Zara." Cole poured me a Scotch and continued pacing the length of the suite. "How do I make people see?"

He looked as though he hadn't slept. Dark circles framed his eyes and he hadn't bothered to shave. I almost felt sorry for him.

"People are fickle, Jeremy, you know that," Heath called out from his seat on the balcony. He puffed on a cigar, tapping the ash carelessly on the side of an ornate glass ashtray. "We can turn the polls around. It's not a crisis."

Cole ignored him, and spoke directly to me. "I'll never understand the public the way you do. How can they forget so quickly? I've made them safer, given them their national pride back. What more do they want?"

"I guess the grass is always greener..." I replied, not really knowing what to say. Heath just laughed.

"Bollocks," he said. "Jeremy you're a good man. The best. But you just don't understand how people think. The public are ignorant, directionless morons. They bumble about from one distraction to the next. They're more concerned about the colour of a celebrity's knickers than domestic policy. It's no good trying to give them what they 'want', they don't have the slightest clue. Left to their own devices, today they'll want one thing, tomorrow the opposite. You'll never get anywhere by trying to please them."

"I beg to differ, sir," I said. "With Jeremy's rivals looking for an excuse to bring him down, surely what the public want is of utmost importance?"

Heath snorted a laugh. "You're almost right, but you're forgetting the most important thing. It's easy to give the public what they want; the trick is to be the one that tells them what that is. Even better, tell them what they don't want. What they should be afraid of. You're a victim of your own success, Jeremy. The electorate have no grudges left, no one to fear. And that's the problem."

"Heroes and villains?" I asked.

Heath nodded. "If there's one thing I know, it's stories. I know how to tell them, and I know how to sell them. But, there has to be a narrative. A motivation. I can't just harp on about Jeremy's achievements, not without a reason. He can't be a hero if we haven't got a villain."

"So..." I thought hard. "Maybe remind them? About the plot, about the kid. Maybe a memorial thing? Some kind of celebration on the anniversary. Big media coverage, saturate prime time with it."

Heath rolled his eyes. "Look, it was a great plan of yours, darling. Genius, in fact. But we can't keep rehashing old ideas. Don't want to come across like a one-trick pony, do we?" I seethed at his patronising tone, but kept quiet. "We can't just roll out past glories every time the polls don't go our way. What we really need is an enemy."

"I've tried that," Cole sighed. "No one bit."

"You were gunning for the wrong people," Heath said. "Doctors, nurses and such… even if they're whacko socialist types, they're too relatable."

"So… the illegals?" I said. "Increase our coverage?"

"God, no." Heath screwed up his nose. "Why do you think we've cut *The Raids*? Think about it. If illegals are still a problem then the chips haven't worked and Jeremy's policies have failed. No, we need a new target."

Cole's Shades rang. He excused himself and went into the other room to take the call.

"Must be the wife," Heath said with a grin and a wink. He gestured to me to come out to the balcony and sit with him. I complied.

"Doesn't it bother you?" he asked me. "Living a lie?"

I felt all the warmth drain from me. Had he figured me out? My heart raced, but my head told me it was impossible. So I kept my composure.

"What do you mean?"

"Being the 'other woman'." Heath smiled. "I thought mistress was usually a short-term position. After a while they demand a permanent contract, or quit altogether. But you're still here. On zero hours with no pension plan. What's your angle?"

I was being interrogated. I shouldn't have been surprised. In fact, I was shocked it hadn't happened sooner. Heath lived for Cole's image and reputation. For me to be in his life for so long without scrutiny was an unusual oversight.

"Angle?" I replied. "Why should there be an angle?"

"There's always an angle," he said. "Do you know how I got where I am today?"

"You systematically destroyed the credibility of your opponents?" It was a provocative question. I was trying to deflect. Everyone knew that when Heath first started his own paper he'd leaked 'exclusives' to his rivals that turned out to be libellously fake, after they'd run them on the front page. But he had always publicly denied it.

He laughed, and held his hands up. "Seems you have me bang to rights. But that's not what I was driving at. Before that. Before I was on top. I clawed my way up by doing what others wouldn't do. I worked harder. I went further. And yes, sometimes lower. And when I reached the limit of what I could achieve by myself, I formed alliances. Business ones and personal ones. There's no shame in it, Zara, it's what winners do. We use every advantage we can. Not everyone is dealt aces. Some of us have to bring them to the game ourselves. I don't give a shit if you're using Cole for money, or your career. He's happy, you're happy. It's business. But be honest with me. I know you want something, I just want to know what. Call it professional curiosity."

"You're asking what's in it for me?" I said, taking a deliberately long, slow sip of my Scotch, and keeping my gaze firmly on his. "I'd suggest you hang around after dark to find out, but… I don't think Jeremy feels that way about you."

He flushed a little, but laughed and gave a slow nod that I took to mean 'well played'. I'd shut down the question, but not necessarily his suspicion.

"We don't all want diamond rings and picket fences," I said. "Some of us want to work, and fuck. In my experience, it's the men that ruin affairs by leaving their wives and expecting you to pick up where they left off. Jeremy doesn't want that scandal, and I don't want that life. Serena can keep it."

"Well," he said. "Lucky Jeremy, eh? If I'd known women like you truly existed, maybe I'd have been tempted myself, if I didn't have so much to lose." He seemed satisfied. For now at least.

"So," I changed the subject, "he seems very down. I take it you've got a plan?"

Heath shrugged his shoulders. "I've got dozens of them. The problem is Jeremy. He's too bloody principled."

Principled? Was he high?

"What do you mean?"

"Oh, come on, you know what he's like. You know how much he cares about his policies, about public safety."

For all I wanted to, I couldn't disagree. I had come to realise that, as heinous as his ideas were, Cole truly did believe in them. He actually thought taking away people's liberties, keeping all their data under constant surveillance, made the country safer. I knew he was passionate, I'd just never thought of him as principled before. I guess we only see people as having principles if their ideals match our own.

I nodded. "Yes, it's one of things I admire most about him," I lied.

"Yes, yes. It's all very *admirable*, I'm sure. But not always practical. You're in the same line of business as me, pretty much. You know how it goes. Sometimes you have to do things that are perhaps a bit dodgy. But necessary. For the greater good?"

He had no idea.

I conceded, and he continued. "But Jeremy ties my hands. I could do so much more for him. For all of us. If only he would agree to a little collateral damage."

"What do you mean?"

"Well… hypothetically… take this resistance nonsense. That could go away in the blink of an eye if I had a real reason to paint them as dangerous."

"You don't think they are?"

"Christ, no. They're a bloody fiasco. Little pockets of disgruntled plebs? Please. They've no leadership. Not like before. As awful as he was, Knight was a genius."

Prickles snaked up my spine at the mention of Daniel.

"In what way?" I managed to say.

"In almost every way. Shame he wasn't a politician really. *Him* I could have worked with. There was a man prepared to sacrifice anything, anyone, to maintain his position. I interviewed his team, the ones in prison. But the only thing I learned was how shrewd Knight was. Absolutely ruthless. Not one of their stories matched, he had them all believing different versions of things. I don't think a single one of them really knew anything about him, but every one of them thought they were his right-hand man! And not one of them would betray him, even under torture. That's the type of loyalty you only get through manipulation."

I felt sick. I knew he was lying. He couldn't get a straight story because everyone kept their mouths shut. They had to have done, or else Kyle and I would be behind bars too. But to hear him say such ugly things about Daniel turned my stomach.

"Anyway," he continued. "What we really need is for these so-called resistance nutters to do something heinous. Then we'd be able to get the public back on side. Show them that turning your back on the chips leads to dangerous, radical thinking. Grant an amnesty, perhaps, let people get re-chipped, no questions asked. Show them *we* are the merciful, moderate path. But they don't have the intelligence or the man power to coordinate anything, so here we are. Were I able to manufacture a disaster, Cole would be back at the top of the polls by teatime."

"Manufacture a disaster?" I couldn't believe what he was saying. Not because I didn't think him capable, I knew he was. But it seemed reckless to admit that to me. Either he felt I could be trusted, or he knew I could be squashed.

"Oh, don't look shocked," he said, downing his drink, "I'm not talking a major incident. Just a small attack. Something that would get people scared, but without too much harm. A small amount of damage, for the greater good. But he won't have it. So all we can do is hope those goons manage to raise their knuckles from the ground and bloody well *do* something. It's frustrating."

Cole returned from his chat with his wife, looking even more downtrodden than before. Heath left us alone, after reassuring Cole there was plenty of time to sway the tide yet. We didn't fuck that night. I lay awake next to the restless PM with my mind racing.

The resistance needed to do something heinous.

Was he right? We needed to make a statement, and to do that we needed to grab attention. The way things were going, Cole would just fizzle out and be replaced. But that wasn't good enough. Unless we made an example, put the real truth out there for everyone to see, then his successor could be worse. We had to be ruthless. We needed Cole to go out with a bang, not a whimper. I needed to get him back on top, then bring him crashing down.

But how?

That was when, for the first time in her miserable life, Rosa managed to time things perfectly.

19
ROSA

The first night I took G-Star I wept with happiness. Ted was wrong. It didn't take my mind away from things; it changed my perspective on them.

It was like turning the dial on a kaleidoscope. All the elements remained the same but, as the light shifted, the pieces moved and the patterns became beautiful. Jimmy was still dead. But, instead of mourning that fact, I was moved to tears by the knowledge he had truly lived. I knew now how he had felt just before he died, and it was glorious. No fear, no pain. Just a euphoric sense of unity and peace with the world around him. Suddenly I felt I understood him, was one with him again. I had no more anger at his stupidity, because it didn't seem stupid anymore.

Everyone else worked, worried, scrabbled for a future that would never be, *could* never be, as wonderful as this feeling. What good was a career, a family, money in the bank, if it couldn't get you anywhere close to this nirvana? Long, healthy, conformist lives ended every single second with their owners never having felt this pure bliss. I had been the ignorant one.

Topped on G-Star, I was finally peaceful. I cried sweet, sharp tears in Ted's arms as I described my life, and Jimmy's, as I now saw them. We laughed, we danced, we fucked. I didn't feel hung up about my body, or about what our physical actions meant. Because I finally got it. There was no more yesterday, and tomorrow may not come. Nothing meant anything, and that was true freedom.

The only problem I had left was the comedown.

When I woke from the dreamless sleep that came after the high, it was like I'd fallen asleep wrapped in the silk sheets of an emperor's palace and woken in a gutter. All the things that seemed so sure, so certain, now filled me with doubt and guilt again. The notion that Jimmy had died in bliss seemed moronic. The cold, hard reality of unyielding tarmac and severed flesh beat at my brain. My body didn't feel lithe, slender, and gorgeous any more. I looked down at my pudgy waist and stubbly legs and felt a hot flush of shame. God, what must have I have looked like naked? What must Ted think? Did I even use protection? The reality of my choices was too heavy, and embarrassing, to bear.

The only way out of the mire was to take more. Ted was happy to oblige.

I got hooked on G-Star about two months before it officially became illegal. Which is just my luck. Nothing was ever said in the press about Jimmy's little habit, but the loopholes that allowed SIGHs to fly under the radar of classification were quietly closed. Ironic, really. If Jimmy hadn't been topped he'd never have taken that dare. Hell, Kinga never would have dared him in the first place. G-Star use saved Cole's life. If anything, the drug was more the hero of the hour than Jimmy was. Yet the ERP cracked down nonetheless.

It wasn't any harder to get, so the supply was still plentiful. But its sales couldn't go through the books anymore. And I became a criminal overnight. I didn't equate the two things at the time (I was perpetually topped) but the phasing out of cash as legal currency forced more and more illegals into the, now criminal, SIGH trade. You couldn't buy SIGHs legally. You couldn't buy *anything* legally if you didn't have a chip. Even

Ted had to get one of those scanners to avoid prosecution. You couldn't get a bank account without a chip, so cash was the only thing you could deal in.

Needless to say, there was plenty of cash coming in and out of the bar. We became a dealership, not just for SIGHs but also for all illegal goods. Anything purchased with cash was 'black market', so it wasn't long before illegals were swapping drugs for food. Suddenly the kitchen, which had once been bare save for a few pot noodles and a lump of mouldy cheese, was stocked high. Ted bought foodstuffs legally, under the guise of being a pub-restaurant, and traded them for SIGHs or cash (with which to buy more SIGHs). We sold G-Star over the counter, scanning customers for the cost of a round of beers. It didn't matter that we were recording more pints than were sold; the regulars drank enough for free to cover the difference.

Somewhere, in my addled consciousness, I believed we were being altruistic. The illegals needed food, and we were giving them a way to obtain it. It was exploitation of course, but that's what the world turns on. The irony was that, for the most part, the illegals themselves didn't use SIGHs, yet they were the driving force behind the booming drug trade. Off they went with their boxes full of potatoes and meat to feed their children, leaving us legal patriots to throw away our privilege on fleeting highs.

I had become the very thing Jimmy told me not to. A fuck-up. And I didn't care.

Weeks turned to months. Little white G-Star pills turned to dirty syringes full of Krenom. Principles and plans turned to 'Who did I fuck last night? Shit. Gimme another hit.'

The time for me to take up my place at university came, and went. I vaguely remember glancing at the nicotine-stained calendar on the wall, where I had circled 12th September in red biro, as Ted pulled the tourniquet tight and shot liquid heaven into my veins.

I existed in an endless cycle of injecting, topping out,

crashing and injecting again. Ted and I were running the bar, somehow, and even making a tidy profit. Not that we saw any of it, unless you count that fleeting moment where you watch the amber liquid disappear into your skin.

The world was moving outside our walls, and I was glad not to be a part of it. My Shades stopped working and I didn't even care. Occasionally a regular would tell me they'd seen my mum on TV again, promoting some cause. I would just shrug and walk away.

And so life continued, month after month, hit after hit.

You should never let someone shoot you up if they've taken their hit already. That's topping 101. And it's a decent rule to live by. Trouble is, like all decent rules, it goes out the window when you're high. Why would you be shooting up when you're already topped? Because you're a fucking addict.

We were going for a double-hitter, me and some guy whose name I can't remember. I'd shot him up with Krenom, but he was having a little problem in the trouser department. In our drugged haze we both agreed that a second shot was what was needed to raise the beast. The last thing I remember about that evening was him kneeling between my legs, pushing the syringe into my thigh.

I woke up three days later to the sound of beeping machines and the feeling of choking. Panicked, I clawed at my throat.

Someone in the blinding brightness of the room rushed over. "It's okay, sweetie, it's just the breathing tube. Hold on."

Her name was Sadie, it said so on her nurse's ID. I remember because I was in the unusual state of sobriety. She calmly explained to me why I was no longer in the dark comfort of my room. I had overdosed, nearly died in fact. That didn't overly bother me. What bothered me was that I wasn't topped. Reality with all its floodlit sharp edges was inescapable. For now.

"I know it's a shock," she continued. "Just rest and take deep breaths, hon. I can give you a while to come to, but there's a lot of people waiting to hear how you're doing."

A lot of people?

"Like who?" I croaked.

She smiled, "Your boyfriend for one, he's been hanging round the whole time."

"I don't have a boyfriend."

"Oh," she said. "My mistake. Well, whoever he is he sure cares about you. He's the one that called the ambulance, said he found you alone and unconscious in your room. Tall guy, really tall... wavy hair."

"Ted?"

"Yeah, that's it. Ted. He's around somewhere."

Ted had called the ambulance? So that fucker who shot me up must have done a runner when it went wrong... I wondered if he'd banged me first. I thought about tracking him down, then I realised I didn't have the faintest clue who he was. That should have made me reassess my life, but it just made me want a hit.

"Send him in?" I asked. "Please?" He might have some SIGHs in his pocket.

"In a while, my lovely. For now it's next of kin only I'm afraid. Your mother's frantic, you know."

Oh, fuck. My mother.

"There's also police, and press. But we won't let them near you until you're up to it, okay?"

Police and press? I'd never be up to that. I should have known. When you're Jimmy Lincoln's sister you can't fuck up privately. I wished Ted had never called the ambulance.

20
TERESA

"Hey, Jinks, you'll never guess who's in a coma."

Greyson interrupted my train of thought. I was grateful. I'd been back and forth over my conflicting problems (what Gridless ought to do, and what Cole ought to do) for hours, and neither of my identities had come up with a solution.

"Dunno," I sighed. "Hit me."

"The Lincoln girl."

"No shit?" I hadn't thought about Rosa in months, years probably. "How?"

"ODed. Krenom apparently. Would you fucking credit it? After everything we did for her and her family. Some people just don't appreciate what they're given."

I should have predicted it. I knew she was weak. I guess it made sense; she'd crumbled under the weight and turned to drugs. I don't know why I felt a small prick of shock. Somewhere, in the back of my mind, I'd assumed she'd have got past it all by then. Gone back to who she always would have been, got herself back on the middle-class treadmill. She hadn't been on our radar; there'd been no more need to keep tabs on her. She'd been hiding from the public eye ever since the interview. Which suited the PIDs fine. She didn't come across well. The mother had kept herself in the media, and that was enough.

"What's the prognosis?" I asked.

"Dunno," Greyson said. "But the vultures are gathering outside the hospital. Mills is debating whether we need to get involved, if she wakes up that is. She's not exactly got the best track record on camera."

"She won't want to give an interview. Put her under protection, keep them away. Let the mother do the statements. She's more... predictable."

"Sounds like a reasonable plan. But we'll wait and see what Mills thinks, shall we?" There was a sharp edge to his tone that unnerved me a little. Come to think of it, his attitude had been getting colder for a long time. I assumed he'd found a fuck buddy. Men are usually only respectful to their female colleagues if they're trying to sleep with them. "Don't forget, you're not supposed to have anything to do with Rosa. After your cock-up."

"That was years ago," I snapped. "It's not relevant now."

"Yeah. Funny how some people can't let go of the past, isn't it?"

I could tell he was being deliberately cryptic, but I didn't give enough of a shit about whatever whiny point he was trying to make to bother figuring it out. Probably implying the same as Heath had, that I was a one-trick pony. I'd had one big success with the Jimmy spin and now I was resting on my laurels. Given that the whole point of being a PID was to help Gridless from the inside, I didn't care what either of them thought about my job performance.

I tried to concentrate on whatever shitty report it was I was supposed to be working on. But I couldn't get Rosa out of my mind. I was curious. She'd been a petulant, idealistic rebel without a cause, or spine, last time I spoke with her. Then we destroyed her. She didn't have the spunk to come back fighting. Not enough guts to actually stand up, join the resistance. But... clearly not superficial enough to just take the money and run into a life of comfortable mediocrity like I thought she would.

Something had screwed her up so bad she wanted to escape

reality. Losing her twin? Maybe. Losing her friend? Possibly. Family breakdown? Highly likely. But… maybe. Maybe it was more than that. Maybe it was losing her integrity. She was self-indulgent enough to hold her own values in high esteem. The type of person who has the luxury of not having to worry about basic needs, so laments their principles and reputation.

Maybe she still felt the way she did back when I scared her into silence.

And now she was back in the public eye.

Which meant the whole Jimmy story would be too.

Then it hit me.

Maybe I *was* a one-trick pony, but what if one trick was enough?

Mills and Greyson were getting cosy down the hall. I grabbed my cup and headed to the water cooler so I could listen in.

"Well," Mills was saying, "the latest from the hospital is that she's likely to make a full recovery. So I think your plan is the way to go, Greyson. We'll station a couple of officers with her, keep the media away. Mrs Lincoln will read any script we give her."

Slimy bastard.

I downed my water and told Belinda I was taking an early lunch. My heart was racing as I strode through the corridors, trying to keep my exterior looking calm. On the inside, my brain was in overdrive, spinning so much my thoughts came in echoes. Pennies dropped so fast it felt like the jackpot.

Once outside, I called Kyle on the secure connection Greg had set up for us.

"Kyle, I want the Lincoln girl."

"Well, thanks for sharing, Terri. But I'm not interested in your libido."

"I'm fucking serious. We need a van on standby, and at least five, maybe six, recruits… with guns."

"What the fuck are you on about? Is this a wind-up?"

"No, this is what you've been waiting for. This a fucking call to arms."

21
ROSA

I never did get another hit.

The three days I was in hospital (well, the three days I was conscious for) were abysmal. Not only did I have to put up with my mother – who played the concerned, harrowed parent whenever anyone else was in the room, but turned on the blame and anger when we were alone – but there was also the knowledge that my relative anonymity had come to an end. I had propelled myself, and Jimmy, back into the headlines. And all this on top of withdrawal.

Mum forbade Ted from entering my room, which meant the only way I was ever going to make this need stop was to get discharged. Her endless chiding would have been bad enough if I was high. Having to listen to her while every cell in my body itched and crawled was intolerable.

I was relieved when they stationed a PID officer in my room on the second day. Sycophantic Mother was irritating, but preferable to the constant renditions of, "How could you do this to me? To your brother? You are just so selfish!"

I'd been under the mistaken impression that it was *my* veins that had been shot up with enough SIGHs to slay a small whale. *Me* that been clinically dead on arrival and was now going through the physical hell of recovery. But seemingly this was nothing compared to having to sit by my bedside, keep her make-up camera ready and shake hands with well-wishers.

I was at least glad that the PIDs had decided I was not to give interviews. But it soon emerged that I only had two less than desirable choices if I was going to get out. The first was to check into a rehab centre. The second was to go home with Mum.

"Well, of course she's coming home with me," Mum said when the PIDs, in collusion with the doctors, ran through my options. "I've made up the spare room for you, darling. You come back to me and we'll put all this behind us and work on getting you fit and well again."

I opted for rehab. Truth be told, I thought I had more chance of making a break for it, and getting my hands on some Krenom, if I was surrounded by highly trained drugs experts and 24-hour security than if I was under Mum's regime. She wasn't impressed. But the PIDs told us they had been authorised to cover the cost of the best care available, in deference to Jimmy's service to our country.

She started to picture the media mileage she could get out of my little habit. Now she could be a spokesperson for parents of recovering drug addicts, as well as the mother of a national hero. That's double the charity functions and committees.

I couldn't care less what she did. I just wanted out. So I played the game. Professed my desire to stay clean, swore that I had learned a valuable lesson. I had, but not the one they thought. I would never again let a topper shoot me up. I signed the papers and committed myself to a stay in rehab. I'd happily sit around singing songs, sharing platitudes. I'd follow twelve steps. Hell, I'd take any steps they decreed, because eventually they'd lead to my next hit.

"We'll take you out through theatres," the smiley PID officer whose name I couldn't be bothered to learn said. "There's an ambulance waiting out back to transport you to the centre. Less conspicuous that way than in one of our cars."

I just shrugged. Didn't matter to me. So I was going to be led out the back, past the festering waste in the clinical bins, and ushered away discreetly. Whatever. Just so long as I was inching closer to freedom.

Officer Smiley accompanied me in the back of the ambulance. Thank God my mother didn't come too; she'd never have been off the screen again if she'd been on that trip. The PIDs felt it would be a good diversionary tactic to have her exit at the front of the building, giving the impression I was staying in.

"It's all alright, Rosa," Smiley smiled, touching my shoulder as I shuffled in the hard seat. Must have mistaken my withdrawal jitters for fear. "You can relax. No one will bother you. No one has any idea you're here."

He was wrong. Someone did. Someone had a very clear idea indeed.

We'd been travelling for less than ten minutes when we came to an abrupt halt. I had no reason to be concerned. I didn't know where the centre was, and the view from the back of an ambulance isn't exactly panoramic. For all I knew we'd reached our destination.

But Smiley frowned, and peered out of the window.

"Wonder what the hold-up is?" he muttered.

The back door swung open, but it was only the ambulance driver.

"Hey," he said. "Sorry, guys, looks like we've got a flat. Just bear with me, it won't take—"

Two gloved hands appeared from nowhere. One covered his mouth, cutting his sentence short. The other pressed a silver blade against his neck.

Smiley – who was now considerably less happy – reached for his gun. But it was too late. The paramedic was swiftly pulled out of view by the unseen attacker. Heavy boots clattered on the metal steps as a second assailant, wearing a balaclava, entered the ambulance. Pointing his gun at me.

"Hands in the air, officer," he growled.

Smiley stilled his hand, just inches away from the weapon in his pocket, and slowly raised his arms in the air. The two men locked eyes. I held my breath.

A third pair of gloved hands threw a small, round something into the ambulance. I didn't get time to examine it. Before it even hit the floor, the guy with the gun grabbed me by my arm. I was chucked outside, onto the tarmac, with less care than if I were a sack of spuds. I heard the door slam behind me.

The explosion was deafening.

"Get up, Rosa, move it!" I was yanked to my feet. Something hard and urgent was pressed against my back. Everything went dark when one of the other thugs thrust a sack over my head, and pulled it tight at the neck.

I was bundled into a van. The doors slammed. I was aware of people around me, but I couldn't tell how many. They were speaking words, but I couldn't discern them over the roaring tide of my own blood pulsing in my ears.

Who were they? I tried to think rationally. Given that I hadn't done that in quite some time, I was rusty. I was in the news… maybe they were looking to cash in somehow? That had to be it. They were after a ransom. Which meant they wouldn't kill me, right? I must be worth something, being Jimmy's twin and all.

I was cursing Jimmy's notoriety, and wondering whether this might be the sort of criminal gang that has a side line in SIGHs, when the sack was pulled roughly off and I found myself looking into the face of the ambulance driver. They'd taken him too? Why?

"Now, just hold still Rosa," he said. "I'll do my best not to hurt you."

I thought he had managed to slip his bonds, and was going to try to sever the cable tie that was cutting into the already bruised skin on my wrists. But then, he pulled out a scalpel. I became aware of the two other men in the back of the van when they each took hold of me, pinning me where I sat. The paramedic rolled up my right sleeve, and came toward me with the blade.

I screamed.

The two men tightened their grip on me, but the paramedic stroked my cheek.

"Shhhh, Rosa. It's all right. Just breathe."

"What are you doing to me?" I gasped.

I felt the sharp sting, and heard my flesh rip, as he made an incision at the top of my arm.

"I think it's time you had one less chip on your shoulder, eh?" he said with a grin.

Christ. How long had he been waiting to make that pun?

I screamed again as he pulled back a flap of my skin and dove in with his fingers.

A few seconds later he held the chip up in front of me, slick with my blood.

"There we are," he smiled. "Wasn't so bad, was it?"

He handed the device to the guy in the balaclava and picked up a green medical kit. "Now, I'll just pop a few stitches in and you'll be good as new."

"Please..." My arm was throbbing, the sight of my own blood made me queasy. "Something for the pain?"

He laughed. "Oh, come off it," he said, gesturing to the track marks on my arms. "I don't have any local, and I'm not giving morphine to a junkie. Just close your eyes and think of Christmas."

I scrunched my eyes up tight as he got busy with the needle. It didn't hurt that much, but the sheer horror of my situation flooded my body with adrenaline, making every stitch seem worse than it really was.

"All done now," he said at last. "You should be happy, Rosa. You're free."

It was a strange thing to say to someone who was tied up in the back of a van. He must have realised how it sounded because he started laughing.

"Just you wait," he said. "You'll understand."

I was starting to think he might be a screwdriver short of a toolkit. But then he did something that made me conclude he was, in fact, psychotic.

He picked up the scalpel again, and I flinched.

"Don't worry." He started to roll up his own sleeve. "I'm not gonna let you have *all* the fun."

I gasped in shock as he jabbed the blade into his own arm, slicing a neat line before sliding his fingers under his skin and rooting around.

"Wooo!" He grimaced slightly as his grip tightened. I heard a sickening ripping sound. "Yeah, baby! That's the kiddy." He wrenched his own chip out, holding it aloft with a maniacal glee in his eyes.

"Here, bud." He thrust it at Balaclava. "Hold that while I darn my arm, will you?"

I swear I saw the guy screw up his nose, even through the disguise, as he sat with a bloodied chip in each hand.

"For God's sake don't get 'em mixed up!" The ambulance driver (who I was starting to suspect wasn't a real ambulance driver at all) laughed. "Can you imagine?"

I couldn't take anymore.

"What are you doing? What is it you want from me?" I yelled.

"Hush now, don't you fret. It'll all be crystal soon enough. Now, if you'll just sit still and relax, we need to do a little detour then we'll be on our way."

"On our way where? What detour?"

He grinned. "You'll see."

I felt the van was slow, then reverse. Finally it stopped, and Balaclava handed the crazed paramedic his chip back, but held onto mine.

"Now." The ambulance guy bent down in front, his nose just an inch from mine. "We're going to open the back door and you are going to watch very carefully. You will not scream, or yell, but you will watch. Do you understand?"

I nodded. It didn't seem wise to do anything other than

what I was told. This was not a movie, and I was not a lithe and acrobatic heroine. My hands were bound. I had no chance of landing a swift kick to his genitalia and deftly leaping to my feet to sprint out of the van. I'd probably end up falling on my face and breaking my nose.

The door opened to reveal a small car park full of wheelie bins. Balaclava got out and strode over to one of them. Ambulance guy grabbed my chin, pointing my gaze where he wanted it.

"See there, Rosa? See those cameras?" CCTV cameras were trained on the bins. Must be the back of a commercial parade. Though why anyone would want their rubbish guarded I didn't know.

"It's so the illegals don't steal out of date food." He must have known what I was thinking. "They want them dead, not fed. But that's not what's important. Watch what Jake's doing."

So Balaclava had a name. For a split second I thought the paramedic had fucked up. Then a far more chilling notion occurred to me. Maybe it didn't matter to Jake if I knew his name. Maybe I'd never live to speak it.

Jake pulled open the lid of a large bin and turned to face me. He tossed my chip exaggeratedly into the bin before giving the middle finger to the CCTV camera.

"Now just take it in, Rosa, look around, I want you to remember this car park clearly."

It seemed like madness. I had no idea what the hell they were playing at, but I nodded.

Jake got back in and the van sped off. Apparently I was no longer required to take note of my surroundings as the sack was put back over my head. I was a little relieved not to have to keep my facial expressions in check. Or look at the paramedic, who seemed ever more unhinged.

After a while we stopped again, but this time I was ignored. I heard the doors open, and the sound of something heavy being dragged out. When we got going again the paramedic was in very high spirits.

"Finally!" he yelled. "I'm finally free. Jeez, bud, I didn't think Teresa would ever let me get off-grid."

"Yeah, well." Jake's gruff voice chimed in. "Be careful what you wish for. No going back now."

"Come on. Don't kill my buzz, man. Rosa. Hey, Rosa."

I flinched.

"Please," I said. "Please, let me go."

"Not gonna happen I'm afraid. Teresa wants to see you. And what Teresa wants, Teresa gets. But I would like to thank you most sincerely. Thanks to you I am finally where I belong. Somewhere at the bottom of the Thames!" He started cackling so hard I felt the reverberations pass through me.

"Who are you?" I pleaded.

He laughed. "Haven't you guessed by now? You really ought to know. What with your brother being who is… sorry, *was*. I'm surprised you haven't been expecting some… payback, shall we say? Or did you really think a stupid little prick like him actually took us out?"

He got closer. I could feel his hot breath on my cheek as he whispered in my ear.

"We're Gridless, baby."

22
TERESA

"*Zachary*?" Greg exhaled loudly and shook his head. "You sent Zachary?"

I shrugged. "Yeah, I know. But he's desperate to get off-grid. And frankly if he stays undercover much longer, he's going to blow it."

"But he's so…"

"Dramatic?" I offered. "I know he is. But hell, we're breaking cover. Coming out. The more dramatic the better."

"He'll scare the living daylights out of her."

"Greg, she's getting kidnapped. Being scared is par for the course. Besides, she *should* be scared. I have no idea how this is going to end for her yet."

He sighed and went back to monitoring the CCTV network. I knew he found the whole thing distasteful. But he'd made all the necessary arrangements anyway. For a guy who disliked authority so much, he seemed happy to follow my orders.

They all did in fact. I'd found myself in charge of more recruits than I ever thought possible, all willing to do exactly as instructed. But still. This was it. Up until now it had all been clandestine, no real danger. Would they still be so eager to follow me once the police found our calling card and we were notorious again?

Time would tell.

"We're go!" Greg yelled suddenly. I watched his screen over his shoulder. There they were. Sad little Rosa entering the ambulance, Zachary ready to drive her to us, and poor unsuspecting Giles escorting her. I felt a little sorry for him. As PIDs go, he wasn't a bad guy. But, he wasn't a good guy either.

"Collateral damage," I whispered, knowing I would never again bump into him. "No guts, no glory."

"Keeping it together, Terri?" Kyle wandered over and put a hand on my shoulder. He was the only one who knew how out of my depth I really was. Well, we both were. I nodded.

The ambulance pulled away and we exchanged glances. The rendezvous point wasn't covered by cameras seeing as Greg had disabled them. There was nothing we could do now but wait.

Greg busied himself with what looked to me to be pages of unintelligible code. Rerouting and cloaking, so that when the time came to log into the Grid it would appear as though he was doing so from his office. Kyle fired up another monitor and hacked into the CCTV. He sat staring at the pixelated image of the dormant wheelie bin. I just paced.

"How bad will it be," Kyle broke the silence at last, "if the alert goes out first? Before they dump the chip?"

"A problem, certainly," Greg replied, "but not a catastrophe. I'm sure I can disrupt the signal. If I have to."

"Well," I said, "let's just hope it doesn't come to that."

The car park was a ten-minute drive from the rendezvous. It should take longer than that for the Security Department to start tracking Rosa's chip. We estimated. We hoped.

But Greg and I both fingered our work Shades, willing them not to beep. Not just yet.

The minutes seemed hours. Greg's knee jiggled, making the keys in his pocket chink. Finally, Kyle jumped up.

"I see something," he yelled.

We all peered closer. No sign of the van itself. But then

there wouldn't be, not from this angle. We didn't want the reg on camera after all. Not yet.

The tension turned to jubilation when we saw Jake, his swagger unmistakable even in his camo gear, striding toward the bin.

"They did it." Kyle exclaimed. "They only fucking did it!"

Jake held the chip up, then deposited it in the bin before turning to face us (well, the camera).

"What's he doing?" Greg sounded panicked. "Oh Christ, Jake, don't signal us, we don't want them to know we're hacked in!"

But Jake's message wasn't for us. Slowly, and with exaggerated menace, he raised his middle finger.

We cheered. I felt the knot in my stomach turn to liquid. I was so relieved I even hugged Kyle.

"Okay," Greg said, "but come on guys, they need to get out of there."

"Chill." Kyle sat back down, still grinning. "We're golden now. Let them waste time tracking her chip. She'll be back here before they even realise they've been duped."

Greg's Shades beeped first. Guess I should have expected that, he did outrank me at work after all. But mine followed swiftly after.

All Persons Alert. Rosa Lincoln abducted on route. PID officer down. Security to commence tracking. All officers on high alert. Suspects driving a white van. Stand by for intel.

Perfect. No one had caught the reg. There were thousands of white vans driving through London at any given time. Of course, they wouldn't have considered the reg important. They could locate Rosa almost instantly from her chip, or so they thought.

Greg logged into the Grid, now that he could legitimately do so. But he wasn't looking for Rosa's signal, he was looking for Zachary's.

"Okay," he said, "they're on course. Travelling west, toward the river."

My Shades beeped again.

Victim located. All officers on the ground proceed with caution to the following coordinates…

I didn't need to read any further to know they were now all racing to the wheelie bin.

"How long, Greg?" I asked.

"Say five minutes, tops, to find the chip," he replied, "then maybe ten to get the staff roster from the hospital. Maybe fifteen before they're on Zach?"

"Should be enough." Kyle was sounding confident now.

"They're slowing," Greg yelled, "coming to a stop…"

We watched the blinking dot that was Zachary's chip as it moved, ever so slowly now, toward the edge of the Thames. Then suddenly, it was in the river.

"They've done it." Greg was finally starting to relax.

I laughed. "Bet Zachary's thrilled," I said, "never known a man so keen to be pronounced officially dead."

Now the cops would race from one removed chip to the other. By the time they finished chasing dead ends, Rosa would be here, at Gridless HQ. Heath would have the 'heinous act' required to rescue Cole's reputation, and I would have my very own pawn.

The game was on.

23
ROSA

I was convinced I wouldn't be getting out of there alive. I guess I'm not, when you think about it. But this is *my* choice. My chance to put things right.

Like the rest of the world, I'd thought Jimmy had put an end to Gridless. But it seemed he had only hurt them. They had hidden away for a time, nursing their wounds. But now they were back, and after revenge.

Despite my own first-hand experience of being spun to fit an agenda, I had still fallen for the accepted story. Gridless had planned to blow up the Underground, kill untold numbers of innocent people. They weren't a people's movement. They weren't harmless hacktivists trying to enlighten. They were cold-blooded terrorists. Yes, I was still naïve. Although, to be fair, being kidnapped, and having a forced surgical procedure without anaesthetic in the back of a dirty van, didn't exactly give me a benevolent impression.

As far as I was concerned, I'd been abducted by a criminal gang who thought nothing of killing and maiming, and had a personal grudge against my dead twin. It's hard to imagine a scarier scenario. While I still didn't place much value on my life, I didn't want it to end in fear. I wished again that Ted had never found me, that I'd been left to die of an overdose. No pain, no awareness. It seemed a hideously cruel fate. I had been saved only to endure whatever suffering these monsters had in store.

When they finally yanked the sack from my head, I looked around the room in which I was certain I would end my pathetic existence. A basement. No windows, only a small lamp in the corner. No furniture at all. Just one exit, up the stone stairs. I was pushed onto my knees in the centre of the hard floor, wrists still bound. The crazed paramedic circled me, smiling.

"That's you signed, sealed and delivered, my pretty," he said. "Teresa'll be wanting to see you. But be patient. She's a busy woman."

He walked up the stairs and out of view. The door slammed shut and I heard a key turn in the lock. I was alone.

I cried. Not the glistening, delicate tears of a heroine, but the messy, snotty, blotchy tears of a coward. I couldn't even wipe my streaming nose because my arms were bound.

When the tears were spent, leaving me with nothing but a pounding headache for my trouble, I tried to think. Above me I could hear footsteps, all jumbled together. There were lots of people here. Lots of terrorists. Just above me.

I was screwed. Whatever it was they wanted with me, I had no way to prevent it. Unless, maybe… It occurred to me for the first time that they had the wrong idea. Not just about Jimmy, but about me too. I was a victim of the ERPs' spin. They thought I was a Reclamationist. They thought Jimmy had been. Maybe, if this Teresa woman would listen, I could show her we had a common enemy. That my brother was just a topper, nothing more. They didn't need to kill me; they could use me. I was unwittingly famous, and would be more so after this. If I could convince them I was on their side, maybe they'd let me go?

It wasn't much of a plan, but it was the only one I had. I rehearsed my speech in my mind, over and over, while I waited for someone to come. Eventually, I heard the key turn in the lock.

"Please," I called out. "You don't need to do this. Jimmy

wasn't a hero, he never meant to stop you. You've got me all wrong!"

The door opened and through it stepped a tall, slender woman with a jagged fringe. I stopped talking and stared. She looked familiar.

"Have I, Rosa?" She walked slowly toward me, a slight smile on her lips, and suddenly I knew who she was. "Have I now?"

"C-call me Zara?" I was shocked, but relieved. The PIDs had swept in and saved me yet again. But why hadn't I heard any commotion from upstairs?

She laughed. The same disparaging snort of a laugh she'd given when we were in my room, just after Jimmy died. Just before she clawed my wrists.

"Well," she said, "lots of people do. But round here I go by Teresa."

She was Teresa? The one the deranged driver had been on about?

"Zachary mentioned me, huh?" She crouched down so her eyes were level with mine. "It's been a while, hasn't it, Rosa? I can see you're confused, so let me explain. You can save your little speech. I know full well what the PIDs have done to you and your family. I know because I was part of it. No one here blames your brother for what happened. That's not to say he wasn't a pain in the arse, of course. I know what you're thinking, Rosa. You're thinking I'm here undercover. I'm a blue-blooded PID, infiltrating the enemy, right?"

"Aren't you?"

She snorted again. "You're thinking I'll get you out of here, right? As an officer of the law, sworn to protect civilians and everything that goes with it? After all the PIDs have done to you, you still want them to sweep in and rescue you, like the pathetic little damsel in distress you've chosen to be. Well, sorry. You've got it wrong, again. I am undercover, but not here. Zara is my alias. It's the PID persona that's the fake. And you don't need saving from us," she gestured at the track marks on my arms, "you need saving from yourself."

It couldn't be true.

"But when Jimmy died, I told you how I felt about the ERP, about Cole, and you, you—"

"I silenced you." She smiled again, her eyes flicked to my bound wrists. "Come on now, you were a child. A grieving teen. With a middle-class upbringing and a grudge against authority. Did you really expect the leader of an underground organisation to take you into her confidence? Do you think we've survived by giving ourselves away to every petulant adolescent who thinks they want revolution? Surely even you're not that naïve?"

"Well, no. But—"

"Everyone thinks they're special, Rosa. Deep down. Everyone believes they're the exception to the rule. It's everyone's weakness. Did you think that by being uncooperative, or even challenging Cole, you'd have made the blindest bit of difference to anything? Would a witty retort, or a difficult question, have helped the thousands of people who are starving, or the illegals dying without healthcare?"

"No." She was right of course. What would I have achieved by throwing a sulk in front of the PM? What was the point? Except my own principles. "I just didn't want to be… complicit."

"I understand," she said. "Really I do. It might help you to know that something was achieved that day. You *were* important. In as much as, if you hadn't played along, I might not have the connections I do now. But that's all by the by. In the past."

"What do you want with me?"

"To be honest, I'm not entirely sure… but I saw an opportunity, and I took it. I wonder, will you do the same now?"

"What do you mean? How is being kidnapped and threatened an opportunity?"

"Everything's an opportunity. If nothing else you're clean and off the grid."

I didn't want to be either. I wanted to be topped off my fucking head, safe in Ted's bar.

"But of course," Teresa said, "you don't understand yet. Come with me, I have something to show you."

She pulled a flick knife from her back pocket. I flinched. She laughed, but didn't bother to give me any reassurances as she came towards me with the blade. Reaching behind me, she sliced through the cable tie.

"Get up," she snapped. "Follow me."

She walked up the steps and I trailed behind her like a puppy. She didn't restrain me, or even warn me not to try anything. In fact, she didn't even glance behind her to check I was following. She was that sure of herself. Or maybe, she was that sure I was too pathetic not to comply.

She pushed open the double doors at the end of the dark passage, with a force that made them slam back against the walls. There was a huge room beyond, full of desks, computers and people. It used to be a warehouse, but now it was home to the most wanted group in England. I stepped in behind Teresa, all eyes on us.

They didn't look like terrorists. They didn't even look shifty. An eclectic mix of young and old, men and women. Young guys in jeans reclined on their chairs, fingers interlaced behind their heads as they watched their screens. Older guys in shirts and ties chewed biros. It could have been any office in the country. Except for the unmistakable suit of white armour in the corner.

"Just for posterity now," Teresa said when she saw me staring at it. "The time for being light-hearted is long gone. Besides, that was Daniel's gig, and he's no longer with us…"

I know that she wanted to say, 'Because of your brother,' but she didn't.

"Where's Greg?" she asked, not to anyone in particular.

"Small office," answered a rough-looking fat guy, who I later learned was the famous Kyle Redwood. He'd put on a few pounds, and grown a fair bit of facial hair, since his photo had been in the press. Teresa led me though the huge ex-warehouse and into a small room off to one side. It looked more like a broom cupboard than an office.

"Should have guessed you'd be in here," she said to the back of Greg's head.

"Well, can't concentrate out there. Not easy, trying to be in two places at once."

I had no idea what he meant, but Teresa laughed.

"How's the girl?" He was still staring intently at the two screens in front of him.

"Why don't you ask her yourself?" Teresa replied.

Greg spun round, and I was taken aback. I didn't know then who his brother was. In hindsight the sudden sense of familiarity, of comfort even, that I felt when I saw his face for the first time is easily explainable. He has his brother's eyes, and the same charming, confident smile. Greyson had been my rescuer several times (until I realised he was using me anyway).

He stood up. Hastily, awkwardly. He smoothed down his top before offering me his hand to shake. I took it, suddenly conscious of my sweaty, snot-covered state.

"Miss Lincoln." He smiled. A genuine, twinkly-eyed smile. "It's an honour. I'm so sorry for all you've been through. I hope they've treated you okay?"

They hadn't. But for some reason I could only say, "Yes." You don't really expect your kidnappers to enquire about your treatment. It caught me off guard.

"Never mind the small talk," Teresa interrupted. "Greg, I think it's time Rosa here learned a little more about the chips. Would you do the honours?"

"Of course, of course. Rosa, please have a seat." He pulled out his chair and gestured to me to sit. I complied. He handed me his half-drunk coffee, wiping the rim with the sleeve of his jumper. "Here, bet you want some caffeine. It's alright. I've not got anything nasty."

I did want a coffee. I didn't realise how much until I took a big gulp. I wasn't repulsed by drinking from someone else's cup. Until a few days ago I'd thought nothing of sharing needles. Greg put one hand on my shoulder, leaning over me to click on the screen.

"Okay, so I'm going to show you something, Rosa, and it's probably going to come as a shock. But it'll help you to see what we're really about. Recognise this?" The car park with the wheelie bins that the paramedic had been so insistent I paid attention to came up on screen. "I'm hacked into the CCTV right now, so let's just rewind to the time you guys were there…"

The time in the corner read 15:23. I watched as Jake emerged from the van, walked over to the bin and dumped the chip they'd unceremoniously cut from my arm.

"Okay," Greg said, "so you remember that, right?"

"I'm not likely to forget," I replied.

"Course not, sorry. Anyway. Moving on. The alert went out to the police about your kidnapping just a few moments later…"

"15:25 to be precise," Teresa said.

"Right," Greg continued. "So, bear that in mind, Rosa. Now, let's fast forward a little…" The time now read 15:42. Several police cars appeared on the screen.

"How do you think they knew to go there, Rosa?"

I shrugged. "I guess someone must have reported seeing the van there?"

"Maybe. Maybe. Bit quick, though, don't you think? Less than ten minutes after the alert, they've already found a witness and acted on their information?"

"I guess…"

"Okay, so it's quick… but plausible? Keep watching…"

Two uniformed officers exited the vehicle and headed straight for the wheelie bin.

"Suspicious?" Greg asked. I couldn't understand what he was getting at.

"I – I don't really see what you mean?"

The officers threw open the lid, looked inside and pulled out my chip.

"There are seven bins in this car park, Rosa. Let's just suppose, however unlikely, that someone had seen the van drive in there and reported it, *and* they managed to get there in less than ten minutes. Isn't it a bit of a coincidence that they headed straight for the exact bin we dumped your chip in?"

"I guess, but..." I felt like an idiot. They were getting at something, but I had no idea what.

"Nobody tipped them off, Rosa. Nobody had to."

"What do you mean?"

"Rosa," Teresa leaned closer to me, speaking slowly as if I were a child. "Where do you think your mother is right now?"

"I-I don't know. At home?"

"Let's find out. Greg, if you would?"

Greg pulled up the chair next to me and started clicking on the second screen. "I'm a Security guy," he said congenially. "This here is the National Grid. You've heard of that, right?"

"Of course," I snapped, finally regaining a glimmer of confidence. "It's where all the data from the chips is stored."

"Uh-huh. So if I look up your mother... What's her first name?"

"Jayne."

"Okay. So... Lincoln, Jayne..." He entered her name. "What do you think I'll discover?"

I shrugged. "Usual stuff. Employment status, tax payments, medical details."

"What about her location?"

"What?"

He clicked on her name, and suddenly my mother's whole life appeared on screen before me. Not just her basic information, but everything. Bank account activity, blood test results, even the fact she'd bought a bunch of bananas this morning. I fought a wave of nausea.

"It's a bit of a shock, huh?" Greg said softly. "When you see just how much they really know."

I nodded. I knew they had all our information, but I'd never really thought about it that hard before. The idea that every transaction I'd ever made, since the chip was implanted anyway, was on record. I was suddenly glad it was gone.

"Are you ready for the truth?" Greg looked at me with such intensity, I almost laughed. But when he clicked on the small globe icon in the corner of my mother's file nothing seemed funny anymore.

A map of North London appeared, with a small red dot flashing in it.

"Is that—?"

"That's your mother," Teresa said solemnly. Greg zoomed in.

"She's with the PIDs, at HQ," he said. "Probably rehearsing her statement. Would you like me to tell you which room? Interview B by the looks of it."

"It… That can't be true!"

Teresa snorted again. "Oh, it's true, buttercup. I'll prove it if you like."

She pulled a pair of Shades out of her pocket. "Now I'm putting this on loudspeaker, because I'm starting to trust you. If you make any noise at all you'll be dead by your next breath. Got it?"

I just nodded. I had no intention of disobeying. Suddenly getting away from here didn't seem like a priority any more. I was becoming more afraid of the world outside than of my captors. That, and the fact that I didn't doubt Teresa's threat for a second.

I recognised the voice that answered her call instantly. Greyson.

"Jinks," he said, "you on your way in? It's all hands on deck."

"Yeah, I know," Teresa replied, "I got the call to arms. Always happens on my day off, doesn't it?"

"You're jinxed, Jinks." Greyson laughed at his own joke. Teresa rolled her eyes.

"Yeah, whatever. So, you got the mother in or should I swing by and grab her? We really ought to get her to do an appeal."

"We're ten steps ahead of you, Jinks. Mills is with her now."

"So she's already there? At HQ? In the interview room?"

"Yes, she's here. And you should be too."

"On my way."

She took off her Shades and raised an eyebrow at me. "Any questions?"

I had thousands. But I couldn't articulate any of them.

"They're trackers..." I squeaked.

"Give the girl a medal," Teresa said. "Yeah. GPS as standard. Unless you're a government official like Greg here. Or me."

"But..." I couldn't even begin to process all the implications. It was heinous. Effectively spying, on everyone, without consent? "If people knew, there'd be uproar! Surely, all you have to do is get the message out there? The public wouldn't stand for it."

"I used to think that too, Rosa," Teresa said. "Back before I knew how easily they can be manipulated. Do you remember the first time we met? When Cole made that speech?"

"Yes. I couldn't believe he was pushing the chips through, because people were against them. And you said—"

"I told you Jimmy changed the game. And I was right, wasn't I? When people thought they'd come so close to a major disaster, well, they couldn't wait to line up and swallow their pills, could they?"

"But they didn't know about the trackers!"

"No. They didn't. And they still don't. But, even if it we exposed it, all it would take would be another bogeyman. A new threat. Something to make them so scared they would gladly accept anything they were told would make them safer. Trust me, Rosa, I know. I spend half my life helping to keep them afraid. And if there is no new threat, they'll simply invent one. It's how it goes."

"What are you saying?"

"Gridless never intended to blow up the Underground, Rosa. They only ever planned to assassinate the true enemy," Greg explained softly. "Your brother's death didn't save any lives. Except Cole's."

"That's bullshit!" I don't know why I reacted so badly. I

knew Jimmy wasn't a hero, not in the true sense of the word. His actions were accidental, the thwarting of the plot purely coincidental. But still, I had always, underneath it all, held on to the idea that lives *had* been saved. That he hadn't died for nothing. Now they were expecting me to believe that his death helped Cole? I wasn't ready to have that rug pulled out from under me, not yet.

"I saw the blueprints." Even as I said it, I could hear how pathetic a protestation it was. It wouldn't be hard to fake them, would it? It just never occurred to me before.

"All fake," Greg whispered. "But you already know their capacity for lies. That's not the real objection, is it?"

"I just don't believe it." The tears silently fell down my face. "I just can't believe they would make something like that, something so awful, up."

Teresa held my gaze. "It wasn't the first time," she said.

"What do you mean?"

"Come on now." I didn't realise I was shivering until Greg put his jacket around me. "I think that's enough revelations for one day. You need a rest. I'll get you some bedding, and some food."

I was itching, shaking and stunned. I needed to cut myself off from the cold harsh reality around me. I needed to be back in the cocoon I knew only one thing provided. "I don't suppose you've got any Krenom?" I asked.

Teresa just laughed. "Fucking junkies," she said. "You're not touching that shit on my watch, honey. I'm getting you clean, getting you healthy. Then we'll talk some more, and I'll decide what to do with you. Greg, can you take care of her? I need to head into HQ."

"Come on, Rosa, let's get you comfortable."

24
TERESA

She hadn't changed much. A few pounds lighter, probably some organ damage from all the shit she pumped into her body, but otherwise she was the same snivelling wretch she had been at eighteen. Scared, weak and full of self-pity. I knew she'd been through a lot. I'd been personally responsible for some of it – I never let on that the whole Jimmy legend was my idea – but sympathy isn't really my strong point.

I learned a long time ago that there are two types of people. Some, like Rosa, are flowers. They can grow to be proud and pretty, but only if conditions are perfect. A harsh frost, even a careless boot, and they wither to nothing. But some of us are weeds. We find a way to work around adversity. It doesn't matter what you do, how hard you try to crush us; there we are, finding cracks in the concrete, rising from scorched earth. Weeds and flowers can coexist to a point. But make no mistake, the weed will strangle the bloom that stands in its way.

I watched her closely. Her reaction to the revelation about the chips was as close to explosive as I've ever seen her. There was still a defiant spirit in there, not quite crushed. She'd been dulling her senses with drugs, but the anger at all that had happened to her was coming close to the surface now. I still wasn't sure whether she could be more of an asset than just a mere hostage, but I figured having her on side couldn't hurt. If nothing else, it would be easier to hold her captive if she was compliant.

All hell was breaking lose in the media. I couldn't hang around with Gridless too long or my absence at PID HQ would be noticed. I grabbed my coat and went to let Kyle know the latest. He was watching the news avidly.

"Well," he said when he saw me coming, "that's the hornet's nest well and truly kicked. I hope we're ready."

The headlines running across the ticker weren't mincing words:

GRIDLESS abducts ROSA LINCOLN. Twin sister of London Hero Jimmy Lincoln kidnapped and feared dead at the hands of Britain's most dangerous terrorists.

GRIDLESS back and more deadly than ever.

Government issue RED ALERT. Threat level at all-time high. All patriots advised to take extra precautions.

"I guess we'll find out," I said. "By the way, I think Greg should look after the girl."

"Fine by me. I've got better things to do than babysit."

"I have to go. Can't ignore work any longer, and I'm hoping I can get to see Cole later, so I won't be back until tomorrow. Just… hole up. Make sure everyone's gone to ground. No one makes a move until I know what Cole's plans are."

"No problem. Everyone's shitting themselves. It all just got a bit real for the newbies."

"It'll only get worse," I said. "Make sure they keep their heads, alright?"

"Yeah, yeah. I'll keep them sound. But they're expecting a plan. They all assume you've got the next steps worked out, and they're anxious to hear them. Blind trust will only last so long."

"I'm working on it," I said. "Just hang tight."

Things were predictably chaotic at HQ. There was no time for anyone to get weepy over Giles, which I was thankful for. As soon as our logo had been found spray-painted beside the ambulance, Mills had hit the roof. Quite how he kept his job I don't know. There was no spinning the fact that Gridless had been alive and growing, and they'd had no idea. That's the trouble with lies. Sometimes those telling them start to believe themselves. No one had been looking for Gridless, because the whole PID department, with Heath's assistance, had done such a good job convincing the country they had been defeated. They had to have been, or Cole's credibility would have suffered. 'Pockets of unorganised resistance', that was the government stance on any dissenting activities that were uncovered. Now they realised they'd all fallen for their own propaganda.

There was no plan. At least, nothing beyond finding Rosa. No one could decide how to spin this, because no one (not even me) knew if she'd turn up dead or alive.

"We have to play this very smart," Mills said, when he gathered us all together. "We have no fucking clue what these bastards are going to do with her. If we downplay the threat, and she turns up dead, we look like idiots. If we exaggerate the threat, and she comes waltzing back unharmed, we also look like idiots. We can't afford to look like idiots. In short, we need to find the fucking girl. Priority number one is getting the media to focus on the search, shut down any stories about Gridless for now. We'll claim that speculation could harm the investigation. It's a matter of national security, so the press will have to comply. Official line is we are unsure if this is really a terrorist group, or some isolated bunch of thugs using their logo. That gives us the chance to go either way once the girl is found and Heath decides on the angle. What we do not want to do is commit and end up having to backtrack. We're in enough shit as it is. Everyone understand?"

This was good. Very good. As things stood, the PIDs were waiting to see what happened to Rosa. That meant the ball was in my court. Unless of course Heath had other ideas. There was only one place he would be at a time like this: holed up with Cole drinking Scotch and mulling things over. Most likely in Cole's private hotel suite. So as soon as I could get away that's where I went, under the guise of being concerned about my 'lover'.

Sure enough, there they were. Filling the air with cigar smoke and rhetoric. Cole looked pleased to see me; we'd moved into 'my wife doesn't understand the stress I'm under, but you do' territory. He was treating me more like a partner than just a fuck buddy these days. It was useful, but a little sickening.

Heath beamed at me through the cigar haze.

"Zara, I'm glad you've turned up. Talk some sense into him, will you? After all, you must be pleased with this turn of events."

"What do you mean?" I asked, accepting the Scotch Cole poured for me.

"Well, it proves me wrong, doesn't it? It appears we can recycle your idea after all. And now I have something I can use against the resistance. This is lucky for both of us, isn't it?"

"Yes," I said. "I suppose it is."

"Lucky?" Cole scoffed. "It's a damn disaster!"

"No, no, it's far from a disaster. It's a crisis!"

"Same difference." Cole collapsed into the armchair, rubbing his temples.

"That's where you're wrong. A disaster is a problem. A crisis is an opportunity. Now you have a chance to resolve the issue, crush the resistance, and emerge victorious as a great and powerful leader. A magnificent story, and one with a lot of mileage. Your approval rating will be through the roof. Plus, it'll shut down any treacherous whispers in the cabinet. You'll be a hero."

"I wish my department had your optimism," I smiled. "Mills is not a happy bunny."

"Mills is a buffoon," Heath said, "but a loyal one. I haven't given him any instruction yet, that's why he's running around like a headless chicken. I'll meet with him tomorrow, pass on the plan… Once Jeremy's agreed to it of course."

"I thought the current plan was to wait and see what happens to the girl?"

"From the PID point of view, yes it is. For now. But we need a long-term strategy either way. Whatever happens with the Lincoln girl, we're going to come out smelling of roses, I promise you that."

I needed more than that.

"I'm curious," I said. "Forgive me, but everyone but you seems to think this is a disaster. Proof that the chips don't work against terrorism. How are you going to get around that?"

Cole sat forward, sighing. His expression was dark, troubled. "He wants to bring back the death penalty," he said.

"What?" I couldn't believe it. Heath was normally so cunning, so subtle. It wasn't like him to make such a rash suggestion.

"Well of course it sounds ridiculous when you put it like that," Heath chided.

"That's what it boils down to, isn't it?" Cole asked.

Heath chuckled. "You'll have Zara thinking I want Tuesday afternoon hangings in the village square! He's so dramatic, isn't he?"

I smiled sweetly. "He just likes to be honest," I said, stroking Cole's arm. "He's a man of the people after all. They love him for his plain speaking."

"Bullshit!" Heath said. "They love him because he tells them what they want to hear. And this will be no different. You're worried the public will think this means the chips haven't worked? The opposite is true. The problem with the chips isn't that they aren't effective; it's that the terrorists have avoided getting them. Up until now we've dealt with them kindly."

Yeah, right. Letting them starve and die with no healthcare and no means to work or buy goods? How very kind.

"But this new threat just goes to prove that soft politics doesn't work. Not everyone who refused to get chipped is a terrorist, of course. I know that. Some are just tin-foil hat conspiracy theory nutters. They thought they were making a statement, standing up for their loony left-wing principles. They'll also welcome the proposals."

"How do you figure that?"

"By now, they'll have realised their mistake. They thought they were being noble, standing by the illegals they love so much. But a few years down the line, they're starving. Living like rats. Depending on the bleeding hearts to give them scraps of food, and substandard medical aid. So I'm proposing an amnesty. For six months, anyone who was entitled to a chip but refused it, for whatever pathetic reason, can get one implanted, no questions asked. Any illegals can come forward and be voluntarily deported. We'll lift the sanctions and stop prosecutions, for six whole months. Trust me, they'll kiss our feet for it.

"Once the illegals have been removed, and the liberals have accepted defeat, the only people left unchipped will be the terrorists themselves. Therefore, once the amnesty is over, not having a chip will be considered an act of terrorism. And terrorism will become a capital offence, punishable by death."

He sat back, puffing on his cigar, grinning like a Cheshire cat. This was what he wanted all along. Cole looked dubious; he didn't think it could work. But I knew all about manipulating opinions. I knew just how sickeningly plausible it was. If Heath's media campaign was strong enough, the public would indeed welcome the idea.

Sometimes the hype is right. Heath is a genius. How many of my recruits would stay, knowing the death penalty was coming? He wasn't just giving Cole good publicity, he was smoking Gridless out too.

25
ROSA

I didn't see Teresa again for several days. I didn't leave the basement during that time either, but I didn't mind. Greg went out of his way to make it comfortable for me. A real bed, some heating, new clothes, even a pair of Shades, though the sites I could view on them were restricted. Although I was their captive, I got the distinct impression that Gridless did not consider me their enemy. And I wasn't entirely sure they were mine either.

On the second day, a doctor came to see me. Another one of Gridless' surprises. I could only reason that it must be a good thing. They wouldn't be concerned about my health if they planned to kill me. He gave me a check-up and a vitamin injection, which I have to admit did make me feel better.

Greg smiled as he brought my dinner in that evening.

"You look so much better," he said, sitting down beside me to eat his own food. "Your eyes are brighter. It's good to see."

I couldn't help but smile back. Over the next few days, we talked about everything that had happened in my life. Jimmy, my parents, Soheila. Greg told me all about his own upbringing, about being a liberal in a house of die-hard right-wingers. About his reasons for joining Gridless and how he wanted to bring down the ERP.

He had the same easy-going smile as Ted, but in his case it was combined with drive, and an almost intimidating intelligence. After spending the last few years with toppers and down-and-outs, it was refreshing to chat with someone who had it all together. Not only that, but someone who was actively trying to change things.

The world was going crazy outside my prison, over me. Greg showed me the news reports, the public appeals, even my mother's tearful statement. But I couldn't feel anything. They were all searching for someone, and although that someone bore my name, she was not me. They were looking for the sister of a national hero, the daughter of a loving mother, a proud Reclamationist who had denounced her Muslim former friends. I was none of those things, and I never had been.

"We're the same, you know, Rosa," Greg said to me on the fifth night, as we ate pizza.

"What do you mean?"

"We're both victims of our own privilege. Both born into a situation we despise. We could have been like all the others. I could have just toed the line. Got a great job, nice house, just chose to ignore the shit going on. Because it would have been happening to other people, not me. And you could have cashed in. Become a spokesperson like your mother, lived your whole life off the back of your brother's status. But, my conscience wouldn't let me. Neither would yours."

"No," I whispered. "I'm nothing like you. You stand up for what you believe in. You risk your life for your cause. I just fell apart when it got heavy. I'm a pathetic topper waste of space."

I couldn't stop the tears that rolled down my cheek. Greg put down his food and moved closer to me, cupping my chin in his hands and forcing me to look him straight in the eye, even as my shame drew my gaze to the floor.

"Don't you ever think like that," he said. "Look what they did to you! They twisted your brother's memory, tore your family apart. Christ, they even used your own words against you. And you had no one to turn to. Yet, despite it all, you refused to bow down and be complicit. You chose to walk away, to leave a life of comfort and privilege, rather than let them use you anymore. So you got caught up in SIGHs? So fucking what. All that proves is you're human. We all make mistakes. It's not the end of the world. It doesn't have to define you."

I'd never looked at it like that before. Was running away really an act of strength and defiance? It hadn't felt like it. It had felt like retreating, knowing I was beat. But he didn't see it that way. He still saw something worthwhile and courageous in me. It spurred me on to ask the question I was dreading the answer to.

"Are they going to kill me Greg? Please, tell me the truth."

He smiled. "No. No, that's not on the agenda."

"Then why? Why did they take me?"

"Teresa panicked."

I wasn't expecting that. "What do you mean?"

Greg sighed. "Have you seen it, Rosa? Have you seen how it is for the unchipped?"

I nodded. "Yes. Well, a little. The illegals used to trade with us, food for SIGHs."

"But have you ever been there? Starving, I mean? Unable to find the means to feed your children, scared to even beg in case the man in the street turns you in? Terrified you'll catch an infection from the filthy conditions you live in, knowing you'll die if you do because there's no healthcare?"

"No," I confessed. "No, I can't… I can't imagine what that's like."

Greg nodded. "We do what we can for them. Most of our members are chipped, you know? Working legitimate jobs, putting themselves on the line by stealing medicines from the hospitals they work at, or food from the shelves they stack. They do it to help those who can't get chips."

A penny dropped. "Zachary!" I said.

"Yes, that's right. He was desperate to get off the grid,

get rid of his chip and join the fighters on the ground. But, before that, he used his job to help get lifesaving supplies. But it's not enough. There's too many suffering, there's too much need. We can't carry on this way much longer. Everyone was looking to Teresa for some sort plan, an endgame. They all joined with the intention of stopping the ERP, of helping to build a better society. Many of them took out their chips so they could fight the fight without being tracked. Now they're feeling the pinch too, and with the amnesty Cole's proposing it'll only get worse. So we can't wait much longer. The time to act is now."

"And where do I fit in?"

"Teresa saw an opportunity, a chance to show the recruits some action, to force Cole to move against us, so that we could take advantage."

"I don't understand."

"It's not easy, you know, working for the enemy. She and I need to be seen to be doing our jobs well in order to avoid suspicion. And our job is to promote Cole, keep public opinion on his side. Kidnapping you gives us the chance to do that, once you're found safe and well, that is."

It didn't make any sense. "Why do you want the public on his side? Surely it would be best if he just lost the next election? Get a new PM, maybe a better one?"

Greg smiled slowly. "Meet the new boss, same as the old boss?" he asked. "No. No, he can't be allowed to just slink off into the night, tail between his legs, to go lick his wounds in some disgusting den of opulent decadence. Not after all he's done. And do you know why?"

I shook my head. "Why?" I whispered.

"Because then they've got a licence to do whatever the fuck they want. Free fucking reign, with no accountability at the end of it. No. It can't be. He has to pay. Has to. Because they have to know we're watching. They have to know we know. And we won't stand for it. We can't allow for this to happen again, the cycle needs to stop. We have to tell people the truth, *all* of the truth. And we have to do it right, because we'll only get one shot. They'll make fucking sure of that."

There had to be something I was missing. "What truth?" I asked.

He exhaled and stood up. He was shaking.

"I've said too much," he said, making for the door. "It's not my place. I think I'd better let Teresa handle this from now on."

And just like that, I was alone again.

26
TERESA

"You fucking told her what?"

He was supposed to babysit her, butter her up. Make sure she had the vitamin injections, laced with a little medical grade G to make her more compliant. Flatter her, stroke her fragile ego, but not give the fucking game away. Not yet. Not until I knew she could be trusted.

"I haven't told her everything, I swear. But honestly, Teresa, you need to go see her. She's ready, I'm telling you."

She might have been, but I fucking wasn't.

"I wanted her on a higher dose first," I snapped.

We'd been upping the levels of G-Star in her injections, very slowly. When you're dealing with a junkie, a small amount of what they're craving doesn't even register to them, they just feel 'normal'. Increasing it a little every day would mean she wouldn't notice the high, but she would start to feel a bond, a sense of enlightenment, a feeling of belonging. Well, that's what the experts say.

The truth can be a bitter pill to swallow. I wanted to make sure she had enough sugar in her veins to help it go down.

"She doesn't need it," Greg insisted. "In fact, I think you ought to stop giving it to her. Let her get clean, properly. You owe her that much."

"I don't owe her anything!"

He raised his eyebrow. "Don't worry, I'm not going to let on it was your idea to crucify her family. But honestly, I think she would have joined us already, if she knew the truth. I really do."

"Well, on your head be it," I said. "If she doesn't see things our way, well, I'll be forced to make sure she can't expose us."

"I told her we wouldn't kill her."

"That's not your call to make." I glared at him. He scuttled back to his office, sensing he'd pissed me off enough already and it wouldn't be wise to push me any further. I hate having my hand forced.

When I entered the basement, the change in Rosa was instantly visible. She was sitting straighter, looking brighter. Her eyes met mine instead of shying away.

"Hello, Rosa," I began.

"I'm glad you've come," she said, but without a hint of a smile. "I've got some questions."

She'd found her balls, then.

"I'm sorry I've neglected you." I chose to ignore her statement; I needed to be in control. You can't let the other person steer. "I hope Greg has made sure you have everything you need?"

"What I need is some answers." She wasn't going to give up.

"And that's exactly what I plan to give you." I smiled as sweetly as I could, though she was pissing me off. I sat beside her on the fluffy rug.

"I want to know what's really going on here. What your plans are, and why?"

"Rosa, I'm going to tell you the truth, I promise. But first, let me tell you a story."

"What story?" She was almost scowling now.

"The story of the first time I killed a man."

That got her attention.

"I had a very different upbringing to you, Rosa. And I admit, because of that, I judged you too harshly the first time I met you. I thought you were a spoilt little rich girl. No guts, no spine. But now I'm starting to see I was wrong. In fact, when I was the age you are now, I was in a similar situation to you. Funny how different paths can lead to the same destination, isn't it?"

She didn't look amused. But I continued.

"I was working in a bar. A real shithole. I didn't have a friend in the boss like you did, though, or a free room to live in. It was back when the recession hit, I guess you'd have been about twelve or thirteen then, right?"

She nodded.

"Okay, so you probably don't remember, but back then the whole country was freaking out about Dover. Violence was on the rise. The ERP was gaining the support of all the skinhead nationalist thugs, but they hadn't yet managed to rein them in. Well, it was those types of Neanderthals that used to drink there. I fucking hated everything about them, but I had to smile and serve them anyway. And put up with their disgusting leering. I didn't have choices; I couldn't afford principles. But I did spit in their pints whenever I could…"

She smiled at that.

"So, this one evening, I noticed this guy, sat at the back, all by himself. I noticed him because, when one of the knuckleheads turned around after trying to grab me, I'd hocked up a nice juicy ball of phlegm into his Guinness. When I looked up, this guy was staring at me. Right at me. He'd seen me do it. I panicked for a second. I couldn't lose my job. But he smiled and winked.

"So, the Nazi twat drank his spit pint. But he didn't stop with the groping. Every time I had to walk through the bar to collect glasses, he tried to grab me. You might have noticed I'm not exactly the patient type. Eventually, he pissed me off so much I slapped him round the face. Everyone cheered, even his mates. He was humiliated and stormed out.

"It wasn't until after I finished my shift that I realised he hadn't gone far. As soon as I stepped out of the door, he grabbed me from behind, pulled me into the alley. There was no one around. He started pulling at my skirt, shoving his fucking tattooed knuckles down into my pants. He didn't know that a girl who was brought up the way I was knows to always carry a knife."

"You stabbed him?" Rosa asked.

"Yeah," I said. "Had to. Self-defence."

Except it wasn't. The first slash maybe, the one when I sliced across his arm, causing him to swear and let me go. Maybe even the second. The one that got him in the shoulder and made him stumble backwards and fall to the ground. Maybe that was just to stop him coming after me. Maybe. But the third, the fourth, the fifth? They were pure fucking rage. Pure hatred. When I sliced his Adam's apple, listened to the last breath gurgle from his body, felt his hot, sticky blood all over my hands... I wasn't just attacking him. I was attacking every fucker who'd ever laid a finger on me. From my drunken foster mum to the school bully, and it felt fucking good.

I didn't tell Rosa that, though.

"Anyway, I must have hit an artery in the struggle. So he fell backwards, and I could tell he was dead. I didn't know what to do. I was going to make a run for it, but when I turned around there was the guy from the bar, the one who watched me spit in the bastard's pint. I was trapped."

"But if he saw it, he must have known it was self-defence? What did he say?"

Yeah, he'd seen it alright. *All* of it.

"He held up his hands, must have worried I'd think he was going to attack too. He said he'd heard a commotion, come to see if I needed help. 'I thought I'd come to your rescue,' he said. 'But it seems you know how to take care of business.'

"I didn't know what to do. I was scared. Really fucking scared. I asked him if he'd be a witness, tell the police it was self-defence."

I asked him to lie, basically.

"He said he couldn't. He was known to police himself; he couldn't risk it. But he said he'd help me, if I wanted."

"Who was he?"

"His name was Daniel."

"Daniel *Knight*?"

I nodded. "The same."

"What did he do?"

"He saved me. Not just that night, but for good. He gave me a place to stay, to hide, taught me how to control my temper. Then he gave me a new identity, thanks to his hacking skills, one that wasn't chequered, one that had the education, and the funds, to do whatever I wanted."

"Zara Jinks?"

"Exactly. And he never asked anything of me, Rosa. I don't want you to think I worked for him because I owed him. He's not that kind of man."

"So why did you? Join him, I mean?"

"It wasn't just me he was out to save, it was all of us. He told me the truth, and then gave me a choice. The same choice I'm going to give you. Once you know the truth, what will *you* choose to do with it, I wonder?"

"What truth?"

I studied her. Was she ready? How would she react? I remembered how it felt, when Daniel told me. The disbelief, the white-hot rage… the feeling of impotence. But for me, determination followed. And a purpose. A place to direct the fury that had always burned in my veins. Would she be the same? Or would she wither under the weight? There was only one way to find out.

"Daniel never knew his real father," I continued. "He was a deadbeat, just like mine, ran out on his mother when she was pregnant. But, unlike me, he had a decent mother. And she met a good man, who raised Daniel as his own. He worshipped his step-father. The guy worked hard, loved Daniel's mother desperately, and gave his family everything he had. Thanks to him he had an idyllic childhood, and he was always treated exactly the same as his younger brothers. But the problems started when that little white girl got butchered."

"Lily?" Rosa asked. "I remember her…"

"Uh-huh. Well, then you'll remember the riots, and the hate crimes. People started to sneer and whisper. Daniel and his brothers started getting shit at school."

"Why? Daniel isn't Muslim?"

"What makes you say that? His skin? Muslim isn't always black, you know. But in this case, you're right. Daniel isn't Muslim. Neither was his step-dad, as it goes. At least, not a practising one. He didn't consider himself religious at all, but his parents were, and his surname was. And that was all the bigots of this country cared about.

"So, as I'm sure you know from your experience with your little friend Soheila, things just got worse and worse. Especially for Daniel's mum. A 'true Brit' married to a Muzzie? You can imagine… The ERP was gaining support, nationalist splinter groups were rife. It wasn't a good time.

"Suddenly, out of nowhere, his step-dad announced he wanted them to move to Canada. He had a friend out there who was organising a place for them to stay. He'd already seen to college and school places for Daniel and his brothers, and even arranged a perfect job for his wife. They didn't question it. Plenty of mixed race and Muslim families were jumping ship. But he himself wouldn't be able to join them for a few months. Work commitments, you see, he had to finish his tour of duty, and there was a big event coming up."

"He was in the forces?"

"He was a pilot. A damn good one. He was in the Red Arrows."

The goosebumps rose on her flesh. She had an inkling where this was going, so I put her out of her misery.

"Daniel's stepfather's name was Yousseff Nasir."

Her mouth opened slowly, then shut again. I waited for her to process enough to ask questions.

"He was the Dover bomber?" she asked. "Gridless was started by the son of the Dover bomber?"

"Imagine how Daniel felt, half-way across the world when he heard the news that his beloved step-father had turned terrorist?"

"He couldn't believe it?"

"He didn't believe it. Still doesn't. And neither do I."

"I don't understand."

"Did he fly the Spitfire into the cliff? Yes. That's not in doubt. But was he a terrorist? Was he carrying explosives? Did he, in fact, cause all that devastation? Those are the questions that need answering. And the truth isn't pretty."

"So what is it, this truth you think you know?"

"I told you Daniel didn't believe it, right? Well, lucky for him he'd made friends with a fellow Englishman on campus. Kyle Redwood. Everyone knows Kyle's the best there is when it comes to hacking; it's no exaggeration. I hate to give the fat slob too much praise, but he is a damn genius. So Kyle got on the case. After many all-nighters huddled round a screen in their dorm, they found it."

"What did they find?"

"Testimonials. From young women, girls even. Allegations of sexual abuse against them, by Yousseff."

"So… he killed himself… because he was a paedophile?"

"Don't be stupid. Don't you think if it was true it would have been all over the press? The Muzzie who bombed Dover was also a kiddie fiddler? It'd have been perfect. No, when Kyle investigated the girls, he found they didn't really exist. They had cyber trails, but that's it. They'd been fabricated."

"Why?"

"Blackmail. They blackmailed Nasir into breaking formation, diving into the cliff, killing himself. He had no choice. If he didn't, they'd drag him and his beloved family through the courts and the press. Probably add some charges against the boys too. They'd be disgraced, and their lives ruined. But… a large deposit was made into his account just a few days before he announced the move to Canada."

"How large?"

"Enough to pay for a house, and a first-rate education for the boys."

"That doesn't prove—"

"Kyle did some digging into the background of the 'friend' who arranged the move from the Canadian end. He wasn't a friend at all. He was an ex-British secret service agent, and he was on the ERP payroll. Nowadays, he's employed as a senior exec for DatStats, one of Cole's largest investors."

"You're saying Cole, the ERP, they planned Dover? That's mad! It doesn't make any sense!"

"It makes perfect sense, Rosa, they had the most to gain."

She stood up, tears running down her puffy cheeks.

"You're a bunch of conspiracy theorist whackos! Lunatics!"

"It must seem that way, yes," I said calmly.

"And even if you were right, it still makes Nasir a murderer! To cause all that misery, just to protect himself and his family!"

"Rosa," I took her arm, stared straight into her eyes. "Do you really still believe a single Spitfire crash caused the cliffs to fall?"

"He was carrying explosives, everyone knows that!"

"No. No, he wasn't. And even if he was, a crash on the surface? You've seen those cliffs go down a thousand times. They went from the middle…"

"I've heard the theories," she snapped. "Everyone has, and they've all been debunked a million times over!"

I shook my head. "You've heard the theories you were allowed to hear. The ones that *could* be debunked. The ones constructed by fantastical students, or disgraced academics. Trust me, Rosa. I know. I take down the credible ones for a living. We have to let a certain amount of dissent, of speculation, get out there. You can't win an argument if there's no opposing view. But the real noteworthy objectors? The actual evidence? They get crushed, and destroyed."

"What are you trying to say?"

"That whole area was closed to the public, for conservation work, several weeks before Armistice Day. The story was that there'd been a small cave-in and they wanted to make sure the tunnels, and the cliffs themselves, were all secure before the Remembrance display, right?"

Rosa nodded dubiously. So I continued.

"What you won't know is that the company undertaking the work, Countryside Services, enjoyed massive donations from the ERP as part of their commitment to 'preserving our heritage'."

"That doesn't prove anything."

"Unfortunately, despite those donations, they still didn't have the manpower to undertake the task alone. So, a local company, Greenland Construction, thoughtfully offered the services of several of its workers, including the foreman that ultimately led the work. At first, they all worked together well, but after a few days the foreman, a Mr Harry Savage, declared he was unable to continue working with the men from Countryside, as their public sector methods and training were so inferior to those of his staff... Countryside could never complete the task in time without them, so after ensuring Greenland Construction was fully competent, they graciously bowed out to allow the project to continue."

"So?"

"So, for two weeks the site was entirely in the hands of Mr Savage and his most trusted workers. That's public knowledge, should anyone care to look. But what's not commonly known, because great pains have been taken to hide it, is that Greenland Construction is a subsidiary of the hugely successful Cole Corp. Enterprises, and our Mr Savage is Cole's former aide. In addition to, briefly, running said construction company, he was also the CEO of a major overseas munitions manufacturer.

“Rosa, a single Spitfire did not take down the white cliffs of Dover. A power-hungry billionaire hell bent on turning the country fascist did. Savage and his cronies planted explosives, with the promise they would be well rewarded once Cole came to power, as he inevitably would. Look them up, not one of them is worth less than five million now. They all made ‘smart investments’, apparently…

“I know what you’re thinking. It could all be coincidence, right? But consider this, Rosa: If there’s nothing to hide then why can no record of any of this be found anymore?”

“If there’s no proof, then why should I believe you? Why do you believe it? Have you ever thought this was all just Daniel’s little fantasy?”

“I said there was no record *anymore*.” I pulled a pair of Shades from my pocket and handed them to her. “But you’ll find everything I’ve told you is corroborated by the files on there. I’ll give you some time, it’s not easy to accept, I know.”

I left her in the basement, with the truth laid out before her eyes. And I had to admit, Kyle had been right all along. Keeping that information safe *was* more important than any of our lives.

27
ROSA

I looked through the files. When I was finished, I watched the footage of the cliffs collapsing for the last time, but in many ways the first. I could never stomach it again.

It was all there. Everything she said. And more. The employment records, the faked testimonials, a hacked email between Cole and Savage in which the now PM congratulated his colleague on a job well done, dated November 12th.

All now sacrificed to the god of rewritten history. But Kyle and Daniel had got there first. Before the Public Information Department had been launched, before Cole had the means to truly hide his tracks, from world-class hackers as well as expert ones. Perhaps others had found these files too but they had remained silent. I didn't want to think about why that might be.

The Dover bombing *had* been an attack on the British people. But not an attack on our pride, our heritage, or even our history. It had been an attack on our hearts and minds. The winning battle in a war against our tolerance, our compassion, even our intelligence. And we had surrendered. Given in. Succumbed to the notion of 'them and us', allowed ourselves to be divided. And therefore conquered.

Just as I had been forced to accept that Jimmy's death had

not saved innocent lives, now I had to come to terms with the truth that there never was any great threat against us. Even those of us who did not believe the ERP's end justified their means, we'd still swallowed a lie.

And the perpetrator of that lie was still running the country.

Greg was right. He had to pay. Not just for the past, but to protect the future. I understood it now, the passion and hatred in his voice. I understood why Teresa had squashed my naïve, petulant hissy fit when we first met. This was bigger than us. It was bigger than Jimmy. It was bigger than everything.

I rushed up the steps and banged hard on the door.

"Teresa! Teresa! I believe you!"

But it was Greg that opened it. He held me tight as the waves of fury and pain rocked through me. I sobbed into his chest. He smoothed my hair. Eventually I looked up.

"I want him dead," I whispered fiercely. Greg just nodded.

"We all do Rosa, we all do," he said softly.

"And I want to help."

After that, I was no longer their prisoner. I wouldn't have left if you'd paid me. The world outside was based on lies. I still slept in the basement, but the door was never locked. These were my people. This was where I felt safe. When I'd holed up at Ted's bar and retreated into SIGHs, I thought it was anonymity I craved, but it wasn't. It was purpose.

Even Teresa hugged me the next time she saw me.

"I'm sorry, Rosa," she said. "There really is no easy way, y'know?"

I smiled, hugged her back. "I understand," I said. "And not just about today."

She laughed. "Well, you handled it better than I did, I'll give you that. Took Daniel a good few hours to calm me down. But then, I always was a ball of spit and rage. You're more intelligent than I gave you credit for. You'd have got into the PIDs straight away. Took a whole load of coaching for Daniel to get me through that exam. That's the trouble with fake qualifications, it's all well and good until you have to actually pass a test!"

I felt a level of admiration for her that I had never felt for anyone before. All these years. She'd taken that rage, that hate, and stuffed it deep down inside her. I went to pieces when I was misrepresented; she spent half her life working with the enemy. Sleeping with the enemy even. All for the greater good, all with her eyes on the prize. That's the kind of strength you can't help but be in awe of.

The next few weeks passed too quickly. I'd finally found my place in the world, but we all knew the net was closing in. Thanks to Teresa and Greg, we could be sure they weren't yet able to find us, but everyone knew we couldn't hide forever, not with every police force in the country looking for me. And even if we did, this new amnesty of Cole's was designed to smoke us out. Supplies were getting harder to come by, recruitment dried up.

Christmas came and went, and just after New Year, Greg sat me down on the rug, clutching my hands in his. I could tell by his sombre expression I wasn't going to like what he had to say.

"Rosa," he sighed, squeezed my hand; he couldn't look me in the eye. "We're going to have to let you go."

"What?" I stood up.

"We need to act. You know how bad things are. I don't like it any more than you do, but… there's only three months left until the amnesty is over. Then people are going to start being executed. There's too much suffering already, it has to stop."

"So why can't I stay here? I can help. Whatever the plan is, I can help."

"Rosa… you *are* the plan. Well, stage one anyway. You need to be found, safe and well, give Cole that victory over us. After that, Teresa and I can orchestrate some kind of publicity stunt from the inside. A rally, some kind of celebration, something the public will be watching… we don't know yet.

But he's desperate for some good publicity, so he'll jump at the idea; that's when we'll get him. But we need your help."

I tried to quiet the panic that was running through me. Tried to remember who it was I wanted to be, tried to drown out the selfish voice inside me. I didn't want to go back out there. To that circus. All those liars, all that attention. I was terrified. But this wasn't about me. I had a higher cause now.

I took a deep breath, swallowed my fear.

"What is it you need me to do?"

28
TERESA

She came up fucking trumps, I'll give her that.

"Keep it together, chick," I said, as I led her to the van. "Tears is good, but keep the story straight, right?"

"Right," she said, breathing steady.

"How's that rope burn?"

She pulled up her sleeve to show me the chaffed skin. We'd had some coarse hessian tied around her wrists for a few days. The effect was perfect.

"Okay, honey," I put my hand on her shoulder, "next time I see you it'll be at PID HQ. So just remember to forget Teresa. Remember to— "

"Call you Zara?" She winked, and I couldn't help but smile.

"You got it. Now, when Zachary opens the van he can't hang around. Give him a few minutes, then head for the large tree to the west. You'll see the school once you're there. Kids should be out for break. It'll be nice and dramatic."

She nodded, and ripped her dress a little more.

"I'll be beside you, Rosa, just a couple of hours. Just make sure you really egg up the need for a female, okay? They'll want to give you Greyson. Don't let them. You really are the one in control, remember that. They *need* you to talk. They'll do whatever it takes to make that happen, got it?"

She nodded again. I shut the door and banged the side of the van.

It sped off and my stomach flipped over. Trusting someone else's abilities doesn't come easy.

I made sure I got to PID HQ with plenty of time to spare before the news came in. There was no missing the yell from Mills when he got the call.

"They found the fucking girl," he bellowed. "She's alive!"

The whole office stopped what they were doing. Nothing they were working on was as big as this. Mills could barely contain himself.

"Belinda," he squawked, "you get on to the local police department… They've got her in custody, she has to come here. *Here*! Get it? Pull whatever you have to, she comes to us. Someone get me Heath on the line! *Heath*!"

I thought he might have a coronary. Greyson nudged me.

"Well, this is an exciting turn up for the books, eh?"

"Not for me," I said, turning back to my screen. "I'm not allowed near her, remember? I expect you'll get to be golden boy again."

"Yeah," he grinned. A slow, self-satisfied grin. "Yeah, I expect I will."

Mills got his wish. Thanks to Heath's call to the little country police station where Rosa was being looked after she was sent to us, but Greyson was laughing on the other side of his face when he came up to me a few hours later.

"She won't talk to me," he said.

"Lost your touch?" I said.

"No. No, it's not that. She's been through the mill… She's in a bad way. She wants a female."

"Belinda?"

"No. No, actually… you're not going to believe this, but she's specifically requested a familiar face. She wants you."

I feigned shock. Well, it wasn't entirely feigned. I hadn't been at all sure Rosa would pull it off. One little slip, and my plan would have been scuppered. It was a risk, a huge risk.

But she was the best hope we had, things couldn't go on the way they were much longer. Still, I'd been nervous as hell waiting for news. Not only did she need to convince them of her story, but she also had to be assertive enough to get them to agree to do things her way. It could easily have gone wrong. But, as we'd hoped, it's hard to argue with a crying abductee who's covered in blood and bruises. In the interview room she played the part perfectly, gave them all the false information she'd memorised, agreed to do press statements. And, most importantly, agreed to have personal media coaching from a PID officer… as long as that officer was me.

29
ROSA

The few hours between being dumped in the countryside and coming face to face with Teresa in the interview room were a blur. The screaming faces of the children in the playground, the hustle of their teachers wrapping blankets around me. The police arriving, the journey back to London… all of it seems hazy, I can't picture the details. I was too focused on getting through my part. On doing what I had to do to move us closer to our goal.

But my part didn't end there. Everyone wanted something. The information wasn't enough, the press statement wasn't enough. Morning, noon and night they hounded me for more. Thank God I had Teresa to coach me through it, keep me sane. And thank God I had her to deal with my mother.

It wasn't that I wasn't pleased to see Mum. I hadn't really expected to be, but I was. When she dashed into the interview room all the anger and resentment melted away, just for that moment. I rushed into her arms, and gave into the sobs. The real ones. The tears for all that had truly happened, the things I couldn't speak of… yet.

But I couldn't have gone home with her, even if I'd wanted to. Teresa was very clear on that. Mum was an expert now when it came to public relations. If she was with me, she would take over. Speak for me, on behalf of me, become the face of the Rosa Lincoln Kidnapping, just as she had with the Jimmy Lincoln Death. I had to use this opportunity, while I was the name on everyone's lips, to usurp her media throne.

It's awe-inspiring how quickly and easily the lies fall from Teresa's lips. She doesn't miss a beat. I guess she can't afford to. To have been under their nose for all these years; a lesser liar would have stumbled by now. She had an answer for everything. A watertight comeback for every protest my mother could make.

"I do appreciate how you feel, Mrs Lincoln," she said, when Mum insisted she wanted me with her. "Obviously Rosa staying with you would be the ideal scenario, but I'm afraid your location simply isn't secure enough. Thanks to your valiant media appearances, your whereabouts is very well known. Your daughter is currently the best lead we have in terms of finding these terrorists. Keeping her safe is a matter of national security."

There was little she could argue with. So I was set up in a small flat, in a quiet area of Islington, with round-the-clock police protection stationed outside, and Teresa visiting every day.

I played the perfect little PID puppet. Did every interview and appearance they asked of me. Allowed them to use me, as part of their campaign to whip up fear and frenzy. I was happy to say whatever I was told to say, as untrue as it all was.

Yes, I was raped.

Yes, they are planning an unprecedented attack on our citizens.

Yes, I overheard them praying in Arabic.

No, there should not be mercy. Yes, these animals should be caught and executed.

Yes, I do believe the death penalty is the only way to ensure the safety of our beloved country.

I was happy to spout all those lies, because Gridless needed me to. Lying for the greater good didn't seem as disingenuous as I thought it would. In fact, it felt brave and noble. I began to understand Teresa a lot more.

I asked Teresa every day if we were any closer. What was the plan? How long now? She just smiled, told me to have patience. It was all in hand.

30
TERESA

Cole massaged my shoulders with his fat, greasy fingers. It was two months since we'd released Rosa, and he and I had slipped off for a weekend in the Cotswolds. Serena was attending some charity ball in LA. I couldn't help but think that the cost of her flying over there was probably more than the donation she intended to make. But still, he was happy, and horny, which meant things were going well.

"I've got some very exciting news for you, Zara," he said. "I thought you deserved to know, but keep it on the down low, okay? Look surprised when that boss of yours announces it."

These were the perks of being his mistress: the odd little heads up. I looked coyly over my shoulder at him, fluttered my eyelids and opened my mouth in exaggerated shock.

"Like this?" I teased.

He laughed. "Now, I know you can be more subtle and deceptive than that," he said.

"Ah, but I love to make you laugh," I said, straddling him. He was always more inclined to spill secrets when he was turned on. I ran a fingernail from his belly button to the top of his boxers. "Amongst other things..."

He groaned. "You're the devil sometimes, Zara. Why am I so addicted to you?"

I shrugged. "Because you don't know what's good for you maybe? Anyway, what it is it, this exciting news?"

"We're going to hold a huge memorial service, on the anniversary of that kid's death. 20th August, Hyde Park. Open to the public, everyone can come and pay their respects."

"But, it's been three years… Why now?"

"Well, with all this Gridless stuff going on, and his sister being front page news, Heath thought it would be a good idea to remind people what nearly happened, and get them scared about what these bastards might be planning next. Then, riding high on the back of that, we're going to execute a prominent member of Gridless in September. Show them we are *still* the only party that can deal decisively and swiftly with terrorism!"

"What?" My heart sped up. Jesus Christ. Not Daniel, please not Daniel… "Is that wise? I mean, they were tried and sentenced already… This is a new law… Won't it undermine public confidence if you go resentencing existing convicts?"

"Oh no, not one of the Underground bombers. We have to move with the times. One of the current lot."

I was even more confused.

"But… we haven't caught any? Have we?" Did he know something I didn't?

"No. But we should have by then. Has to be by September you see. Heath has heard some disturbing whispers. There's mutiny afoot. Some damn backbench ingrates. There's talk of a vote of no confidence, a leadership contest. They're watching my every move. Waiting to see how this pans out, hoping I'll mess it up. I have to do something big, get the public on side, otherwise they'll take the opportunity to stick their knives in my back."

"But what if you, I mean we, don't? Catch one, I mean?"

"We can't not. Heath was very clear on that too. If more than six months elapse between that girl getting released and us being seen to have done something decisive… well, the public will lose confidence, it would be disaster. So, if we haven't it'll be a case of pick a criminal, any criminal."

"You can't wait too long," I cautioned. "The country is only sixty per cent in favour of the death penalty. And that's only because you've gone on and on about thorough trials and being completely sure of guilt. I mean, everyone knows these trials take months. If you want to execute in September you have to allow, what, a month for a failed appeal? At least six months for it to come to trial before that… so that would be March. And we're already in February. You need to arrest someone in the next two weeks for it to be feasible."

He sighed. "You're right. You're absolutely right. Damn it. That's not going to happen. Shit. Why didn't Heath think of that? I'll have to call him. Damn fool."

"Wait." The germ of an idea was beginning to form, one that was so perfect, but so heinous all at the same time. I didn't know if I go through with it. But I could at least give myself the option. "Perhaps you don't have to *actually* arrest someone."

"What do you mean?"

"Just announce you've captured a leading member of Gridless. You don't have to name them. You can claim it would harm the ongoing investigation."

"That would certainly buy us more time. I'll speak to Heath, but I'm sure he'll think you've pulled it out of the bag again, Zara!"

Cole climbed on top of me, delighted with my ingenuity. I made all the right noises, but my mind was elsewhere.

I was thinking about Rosa.

She'd changed since she found out the truth. She had a look of purpose, confidence even. She was lightyears away from the post-teen fuck-up injecting poison in her veins we'd kidnapped.

I'd already given her something worth living for. Could I go one step further?

Could I give her something worth *dying* for?

31
ROSA

As soon as she came through the door I could tell something had gone terribly wrong.

I've never seen Teresa look so panicked. She held her finger to her lips. She rushed to the window, to check the officer who had escorted her upstairs to my flat was safely back in his position outside.

"Jesus," she snapped at me. "Why do you look so chipper? Haven't you seen the news?"

I'd not long woken up, and hadn't even switched on my Shades yet. She thrust hers at me, already logged into the BBC site.

Cole Confirms Arrest of Prominent Gridless Member.

If found guilty of terrorism, the suspect, who cannot be named for security reasons, will become the first person executed under the newly revised Anti-terror Act.

"Rosa," she put a hand on my shoulder, "Rosa… I… I don't know how to tell you this, honey."

"What?" My heart was sinking through my stomach. I already knew before she spoke the words.

"Rosa, it's Greg. They got Greg. I'm so sorry."

32
TERESA

She fell apart like a game of Jenga, right before my eyes. I let her. I listened to her scream, watched the snot bubble in her nostrils as she wept. Held her close when the sobs turned to shudders. You have to let the pieces fall before you can put them back together the way you want them.

In reality, of course, Greg was safe and well and totally oblivious to the tale I'd spun Rosa. I knew they'd formed a bond while she was in captivity. Stockholm syndrome, I guess. Her eyes lit up when he walked into the room. It was sweet. It was innocent. And, unfortunately for Rosa, it was useful.

"We won't let it happen," I whispered. "I'll think of something, I promise."

"H-how long have we got?" she asked me at last.

"They want to do the first execution in September," I said. "Cole's spies say he's facing a vote of no confidence, unless he can find a way to reverse the opinion polls by then."

She huffed her disgust. "Then we have to get the truth out before that," she said, her eyes beginning to shine with more than just tears. "It's his only chance."

I nodded. "I agree. I do. And the net is closing; it does have to be sooner rather than later. But it has to be right, Rosa. The right moment. A time when he's riding high. A time when we get it on camera. When the world will be watching, so we can hit them between their ignorant eyes with the truth. I want to save Greg as much as you do but… it's not the goal. You know that. We can't risk everything for just one man. He wouldn't want that."

Gently does it. You can't place the blocks for them, you have to let them do it themselves.

"Jimmy's memorial!" She jumped up out of her seat. "Cole's speaking, right? And it'll be broadcast everywhere!"

I shook my head. "No. No, it's not feasible. We'd never be able to plant a device, the security will be immense. Besides, planted bombs are too risky. Too many innocent people can get hurt. It needs to be a vest, and they won't let the crowd get close enough for anyone wearing one to be effective. We'd never be able to take him out like that."

She was breathing heavily, shaking.

"They've asked me to speak…" she said. "I haven't given them an answer yet. If I agree, I'll be right beside him. I could even shake his hand."

Eyes down.

"Rosa, what are you saying?"

"I'll do it. Let me do it. I'll wear the bomb."

Bingo.

33
ROSA

I'm not doing this for him. Maybe I was. Maybe it was a knee-jerk reaction, born out of emotion, to start with. But the more I thought about it the more I could see the trail of footsteps behind me was only ever leading me here.

She tried to talk me out of it, but I wouldn't listen. Eventually she gave in. I guess she could see the determination in my eyes. The epiphany had hit me like a lightning bolt. It was the perfect solution, the *only* solution. Not just for Greg, not even just for Gridless, but for me too.

I am Rosa and I wish I was dead.

The beat was still there, underneath it all. Saving Greg's life is only part of it, it wasn't him that set me on this course.

"If this is what you truly want, Rosa." Teresa studied me hard. "I won't deny it is the best plan we have. But we could find another way, if you have any doubts, any at all."

"I don't," I said as emphatically as I could. "But I do have a question. How will you do it?"

"I won't. We won't. You would have the button. That's how it has to be. You have control. You can back out at any time. You don't have to press it."

"No." I shuddered a little at the thought of the actual explosion, and hoped she didn't notice. "I don't mean… *that*.

I meant the truth. How will you get the truth out, so everyone can see?"

"Oh, that's not difficult. Kyle can hack into the networks; we can broadcast on every channel. As soon as you, well, as soon as it's done, we can take over the airwaves. Not for long, but long enough. We'll make our statement, show them the evidence. There'll be uproar, Rosa. Revolution. A whole new dawn. And it'll be all thanks to you."

"Then I just have one request," I said.

"Anything, Rosa, you name it. If it's in my power."

"I want to be the one to tell it."

She smiled. "Who else?"

34
TERESA

I'd always planned to use Daniel's statement, but you have to roll with what gets thrown at you. If Rosa was going to give her miserable life for us, letting her record the message was a small price to pay. In fact, the PID in me can see the merit in it. She's a media darling now and Daniel is old news to almost everyone. Except me.

It's only sentiment that makes me cling to the idea of using the original. And sentiment is the enemy of progress. If Daniel were here, he'd use Rosa's too. I'm certain of that.

We recorded it there and then, as soon as her decision was made. The public respond well to passion and emotion, and she was full of it. You can fake a lot, but the genuine article is always better, if you can get it.

We could only be sure of two minutes. After that, if the PIDs had their best on duty – which they would, given the high-profile nature of the event – they would find a way to shut down our broadcast. We had to make every second count.

She had a lot to say. Most of it self-indulgent waffle about how her integrity, and her brother's memory, had been polluted. I agreed she could say whatever she needed to say. She seemed to view this as some kind of last confession, a way to atone for all the shit that had happened since her brother bit the dust. But I made sure she started with the important stuff.

Dover, the chips, the non-existent Underground plot. With my direction, she reeled off the facts one by one like a series of bullets, and we edited in the digital evidence after. The full statement was six minutes long. She went on to address everyone from her mother to that Muslim girl she loves. I doubt it'll ever get that far on air. But it was a catharsis for her, so I let the camera roll until she was done. I owed her that much.

There was another damn good reason for striking while the iron was hot. It's harder to change your mind about a course of action once it's already in motion. An idea is one thing, a thing that is easy to change. But once that idea starts to have a physical presence it begins to take on a life of its own, outside its inventor's head.

When I got back to Gridless, I called everyone together to make the announcement.

They gathered round, all expectant and apprehensive. Things were getting tough, plenty of them were close to breaking point. Some had already left to take advantage of the amnesty. I wasn't ignorant to the whispers flying around.

I had to shut them all up, or I was going to lose control.

"Guys," I stood on a desk, to let them know this was big, "I want to thank you for your loyalty, and your faith."

There were disgruntled murmurs, but I chose to ignore them and carried on.

"I can now reveal the plan, the endgame, the last push over the trenches that will finish Cole, and the ERP, for good!"

That shut them up. There were cheers and applause, and folded arms from the more cynical.

"On the twentieth of August, Cole will take to the stage at Hyde Park for the Lincoln kid's memorial. And we are gonna take him out. Right there, in front of millions of viewers, before hijacking the airwaves to broadcast the truth to every man, woman and child in England… and possibly the world!"

The cheers were louder now, but the questions were coming thick and fast.

"How?"

"Is it a bomb? Or a sniper?"

"It must be a bomb, who's going to wear it? How will they get close enough?"

I signalled to them to hush, and beckoned to Greg.

"Greg, come up here with me," I said. "This is the man, ladies and gents. This is the man we have to thank."

He looked confused, but came forward and stood beside me. I put my arm around him.

"This guy here, he's gone above and beyond for our cause. Thanks to him, we have one hell of an ally. An ally that can get the device where it needs to be. An ally that can give us all the media coverage we need. An ally that just this morning recorded the kickass statement that will wake the sheep and start a revolution! An ally that not only helped come up with the plan, but believes in it so passionately she is going to wear the bomb and give her life for the future of this country. A round of applause please for Miss Rosa Lincoln!"

The room erupted into whoops and claps as the genius of my plan sunk in. Greg looked grey, but he smiled and accepted the pats on the back. No doubt he was wondering why I hadn't warned him, privately. Or perhaps he already knew. It's harder to admit you weren't acting when the audience is congratulating your performance.

I connected my Shades to the large screen on the wall and pressed play on Rosa's message. The room fell silent as they watched.

35
ROSA

Last night I wrote a note. It strikes me now, as the song comes to an end and Cole takes to his feet once again, it was the last thing I will ever write. I pushed it into Teresa's hand this morning, after she attached the vest, before we got in the waiting limo. She had tears in her eyes when she promised she would deliver it.

I picture him. Released from prison, saved from execution. Opening the folded paper, a little crumpled from its journey, reading the last words I ever committed to paper:

Greg,
I hope the truth has set you free.
All my love,
Rosa

There was so much, too much, to say. For once in my life I chose to keep it simple, and trust in brevity.

Cole walks to the microphone now. To make my introduction. *Breathe. Breathe. Breathe.* Not too many of them left. A few more heartbeats.

Just a few more.

36
TERESA

I'm breathing in time with the rise and fall of Rosa's chest. Beside me, Greg fidgets. His eyes dart from the screen, to the door, to the remote detonator right next to my hand.

"Teresa," he says, "give her time. Please."

It seems an odd thing to say. The girl's got three minutes left, tops. Depending on how much of a meal Cole makes of introducing her.

"What are you on about?" I ask.

"Just... don't push the button too quickly. Give her a chance to do it herself, okay? It means everything to her. She should get to be the one."

I smile and say okay but I'm bullshitting. She's not going to press the button. She hasn't got the guts. I know that much about her. She wants to, I bet she's even sure she's going to. But she won't. And we've only got one shot.

She'll never know I was lying. Well, maybe she will for a fraction of a second. But we could never leave this entirely up to her. You can't rely on anyone but yourself.

37
ROSA

"Thank you, Archbishop, for that inspiring speech. And now, it is my very great privilege to introduce an outstanding young citizen."

Oh God. It's happening. I'm going to have to stand. How can I stand when my legs are shaking? How can I do this?

Just one thing at a time. One thing. Just stand.

Now step. One step. Then another. No more than four.

38
TERESA

Rosa starts to rise, but Cole hasn't finished his intro yet. I hope he wraps it up quick, she's looking like she might faint. I turn to voice my concern to Kyle, but he's not looking my way. He's staring at the door.

"What's with you guys?" I ask.

"Shhh," Kyle says. "I heard something, outside."

He barely finishes when the door flies open. Half a dozen uniformed PIDs, with guns, burst in.

How did they find us? How the fuck didn't we know they were on to us?

I reach out my hand quickly, my palm resting on the remote detonator. Glancing at the screen I can see Rosa moving closer to Cole. Close enough.

"Stay back!" I yell. "I have a detonator. Take one more step and I'll blow Cole sky high before you can stop me."

I try to gesture to Greg and Kyle. We can still do this, they just need to start the broadcast. But they're already standing up, hands in the air.

A familiar chuckle hits my ears, just as the scent of Cuban cigars wafts in. "Calm down, Zara," Heath strolls in past the officers, smiling that goddamn superior smile of his. "I'm not here to stop you."

I'm flailing, opening my mouth but I can't find any words to say.

"Your little broadcast can't happen, of course." Heath saunters toward me. "Sorry to disappoint you. I know how it feels to have the scoop of the century and not be able to run with it. And I hear it's a doozy. Pretty damning evidence, so I'm told. Not sure even *I* could spin myself out of that shit storm. So I suppose I should congratulate you, for what it's worth. But you could have at least got someone better for the leading role." He flicks ash at my feet, and taps the screen. Right on Rosa's petrified face. "Not very photogenic, is she?"

My hand trembles on the detonator.

"What's the countdown?" Heath continues, "Any moment now I expect. Oh, don't look so shocked. I told you how difficult it was to work with someone so bloody principled. I should be thanking you for doing me such a favour."

"What do you want?" I ask.

"Right now, much the same as you, *Teresa*, isn't it? After the explosion… well, I think our goals might be different then. But let's just enjoy the show for now, shall we?"

He wants Cole dead? I can't for the life of me work out why. Unless…

"You want to be PM?" I cry.

"Me?" He chuckles again. "Prime Minister? Christ, no. I couldn't think of anything worse. Who'd want to be the dancing marionette, when you could be one who pulls its strings?"

I have no idea what he's getting at. But every instinct tells me if he wants the bomb to go off then I mustn't let it. I keep my hand on the detonator. But not to press it, to protect it. Because I know something he doesn't. I know Rosa. I know she won't push the button. She hasn't got the guts.

For fuck's sake, Rosa, don't press the button.

39
ROSA

"Here she is, the beloved twin sister of our nation's hero. Please show your support for the incredibly brave Miss Rosa Lincoln!"

The applause is white noise. Cole's outstretched hand looms ever closer, waiting for me to shake it. Waiting for me to take it with me, into oblivion.

So these are my last breaths rushing through my lungs. My last moments. My last thoughts. And they're not of Greg, or Soheila, or even myself. They're of Jimmy.

I have one hand in my pocket. The other reaches out to shake Cole's.

And you're all I can see. Not the images around me. Not the baseless perfection we've all been sold. No, Jimmy. It's you. Just you. Your face in the mornings when you were half awake. Your smile when we had a secret. Your frown when I fucked up. I haven't seen you like this for so long. I haven't seen *you*.

So it ends like it began. With you all around me. I never outran you; perhaps I never really wanted to. But fuck you, Jimmy. Fuck you for leaving me. Fuck you for causing all of this.

I forgive you, Jimmy.

I love you, Jimmy.

My finger finds the button.

40
TERESA

The screen fills with fire. The speakers split the air with screams.

She did it. I can't believe she did it.

There's nothing left of Cole, or Rosa, or any of the speakers on the stage. The commentators are going nuts. We should be cutting to the statement now. But only Greg or Kyle can do that, and they're both still standing with their hands in the air.

"Perfect!" Heath puts his hand on my shoulder. "Great job, Zara. And so ends Jeremy's illustrious career. With a bang, not a whimper."

I'm still in shock. Nothing makes sense.

"What?"

"Really? Don't you have anything more insightful to say? You disappoint me. Cole was a great man, but he'd had his day. He was pushing it too far with this death penalty idea."

"That was your idea!"

He smiles. "Was it? Funny, that's not what the records show. Still, his successor will have plenty of support when they pledge to overturn it."

"Successor?"

"Yes. Time for some fresh blood. There are some very promising young talents in the cabinet. People who can be relied upon to do what needs to be done. People who will listen to reason. Jeremy got too big for his boots. You know it started to go wrong when he decided he knew better, and didn't take my advice. It's impossible to have a partnership without trust, don't you think? As to who I'll throw my weight behind now… well, a campaign has to be properly funded."

I can't believe what I'm hearing. Somehow, I'd always believed he really did support Cole's policies. Now I realise he had just been the highest bidder.

"Such contempt on your face," he continues. "Do you still think you have some kind of moral high ground? You've got blood on your hands now, Zara. Innocent blood. And for what? Without your little expose, you've achieved nothing but murder. Shame for that poor girl. But I'm quite impressed with your ingenuity. You actually managed to convince her to kill people. She really trusted you. But we can all be manipulated, you know that."

Greg puts down his hands, walks over to the computer and pulls out the USB with Rosa's statement on it. I can't understand why they're not stopping him.

Heath claps him on the back. "Excellent work, Greyson. Truly excellent. You'll be head of Security by the end of the year, I promise."

Kyle steps forward. "Sir, I…"

Sir? What the fuck?

"No need to kiss my arse, Redwood," Heath says. "I'm a man of my word. You'll get your pardon."

It finally dawns on me: I've been betrayed. Meeting Greg when I did had been too good to be true. Literally. It was never a coincidence. He was a fucking plant. But *Kyle*?

"You motherfucker!" I try to kick at him, but two officers have already grabbed hold of my arms. I'm being marched toward the door.

"I tried to tell you, Terri," Kyle says, "but you didn't listen. You *never* fucking listen. I told you I was done. I told you I couldn't take it anymore. But you don't hear anything but what you want to hear. And then you brought that fucking whore to my safehouse! And I… I…" He starts to sob.

The *whore*? He turned me in after that? No wonder he was so keen to accept Greg. All this fucking time, he's been working for Heath. How did I get it all so wrong? How have I been so blind? I got everyone wrong. Even Rosa.

Rosa.

I wrench one hand free and pull the crumpled note from my jeans. I don't know why I kept it. I throw it towards Greg.

Maybe there was one thing I wasn't wrong about.

"She did it for you, you son of a bitch!" I yell. "She thought it was you they were going to execute. I *told* her it was you! She did this for you!"

He bends down to pick it up, opens it. He scoffs and throws it in the bin, but I can see the colour draining from his face.

"I'm just going to take this USB into the small office, sir," he says to Heath. "Get it erased, and all the back-ups. They're all in there."

Heath nods. "Good man."

As I'm dragged through the warehouse, Greg goes into the cupboard he calls his office. He locks the door.

I'm almost outside now. There's a police van waiting, and no doubt a solitary cell after that. A car door slams and Greyson swaggers towards me from across the parking lot, grinning like the cat that caught the pigeon. I should have known he wouldn't miss an opportunity to gloat.

He looks me up and down, and sneers. "You should learn to treat people better, Jinks. Perhaps, if you spread a little more sugar, your only friend wouldn't have come singing to me like a choirboy. But you're—"

He stops suddenly, stares behind me into the warehouse. Heath's yelling something. I turn my head to see him banging on the door of Greg's office.

"Stop it! For fuck's sake, stop it now!"

I catch sight of the screen. Of all the screens. All the networks. I see Rosa's tear-streaked face.

A gun shot goes off from inside Greg's office. Greyson runs inside. He pushes Heath out of the way and throws himself at the door, trying to break it down.

But it's too late.

Rosa's voice rings out from every speaker, and every pair of Shades.

"My name is Rosa Lincoln, and I want to tell you the truth."

ACKNOWLEDGEMENTS

Writing a book is by no means a solitary endeavour. I first had the idea for *Poster Boy* back in 2014, and since then I have met and worked with so many wonderful people who have all played a significant part in making it what it is today.

Huge thanks go out to Lauren, Lucy and the rest of the wonderful team at Legend Press, for working so hard to make my dream a reality.

My fantastic agent, Emily Sweet, whose belief in my humble little manuscript was inspirational. Thank you for all the support, encouragement and tireless hard work. There really is no one I would rather have at my side.

Then there are those who have been on my team from the very beginning, who invested their time and faith, believing in me even when I didn't believe in myself. Heartfelt thanks to my friends and family who read and commented on the manuscript, and have provided endless support and encouragement: Aisling Mills, Mike Grant, Melanie Sedlmayr, Barbara Evans, Roberta Crosskey and Sharron Swan.

Thanks also to Steve Quinn, for chatting logistics and helping me bounce ideas around when *Poster Boy* was in its early stages, and to Steven Hawley for his insights and entertaining commentary.

I'm for ever grateful to the incredibly talented Rachel Somer, not only for her amazing insights and help with editing the early drafts, but for her constant support, advice and friendship.

There are not enough words to express my gratitude to the incomparable G J Rutherford, who has read, critiqued, and advised on every piece I have written since we first met online in 2014. His unshakable faith in my words kept me going through hard times, and his gentle nagging always helps to keep me on track. His support and friendship have been instrumental in making this book a reality.

And of course, my deepest thanks and all my love go out to my amazing husband, Kev, and my awesome and inspiring children, Mya and Riley. You are my heart, my soul, my everything. I hope I can make you even half as proud as you make me.